M000034253

Worlds Beneath

K.A. Emmons

© 2018 K.A. Emmons. All rights reserved. This book or parts thereof may not be reproduced in any form, stored in any retrieval system, or transmitted in any form by any means—electronic, mechanical, photocopy, recording, or otherwise—without prior written permission of the publisher.

Do not fear the wolves, my child.
For the wolves are but shadows
And shadows are but creatures of your mind.

So guard your thoughts, my child,
Guard your dreams, your fears, your desires;

Beware which wolf you follow,
Beware which wolf you feed.

   - Canis Lupus, chap. 23, verse 16

PROLOGUE

January, 1910

I found it in the washroom. I'd been caught and scolded for having entered staff quarters, but I'd already found what I'd come for and hidden it in the cuff of my sleeve. It came with me down the hallway and up the stairs into the sleeping quarters. It slid out from its hiding place and went beneath my pillowcase. I made my bed up neatly.

The day passed without a flaw—no one found it. I waited for night to fall. When darkness did come, it was the first darkness my eyes had seen since they'd told me she was gone.

I knew about death. But the thing was, I had thought she would come back for me one day. One day when it suited her, when it made sense for both of us. I didn't want to think it was true, what they said about me. That I had no one left. "Given up," they called me—as though it were almost my name.

I wanted so much to believe that it wasn't. To believe that this place was temporary. I would go home one day—wherever home was. She would come back for me. That was what I told myself.

I'd imagined my mother often, using visions of her like a tonic for the sleepless nights. I didn't actually know anything about her, not even her name. So I invented all of it. A mother who was an assemblage of my longings, who was the light at the end of the tunnel.

The worst part of it was, she hadn't just died: she had been taken when I was born—she had left me in this world but escaped its miseries herself. I had thought she was alive, working, living, doing extraordinary things so she could come back for me. But she was dead, and they had just never told me. They waited until I was old enough to bear it, old enough to understand what death was, though I knew from the beginning: this place was a tomb. What they couldn't understand was that it left me with nothing to hold on to, nothing to keep me here.

The light had gone away. There was only emptiness, night.

And so I took the blade from the washroom and hid it under my pillow.

I lay beneath the sheets for a while and waited until the lady had gone through and left. I waited until the beds farther down the row were still and the breathing patterns around me heavy with unconsciousness. I slid out onto the floor, reaching under my pillow for the cold metal blade.

The moonlight was coming through the window, giving me a patch of cool white light like a rug beneath me. I played with the blade and made shapes over my wrist. First lightly but then harder, my heart in my mouth.

Blood slowly rose to the surface of my skin. First in freckles, then in streaks like spilled paint.

There was no noise around me, no warning of her approach, but it was then that I looked up and then that she appeared. I started, so much so that I lost my grip. The knife clattered against the floor.

She was a small apparition. Her eyes were vivid and caught between curtains of dark hair. A small skeletal structure cloaked in a nightgown that ended at her bare, scuffed feet. I didn't breathe a word, and though I shrank back, she drew nearer. She lowered herself to the floor beside me and settled on her folded legs.

Her wide eyes were like holes with hands reaching out. She studied my battered wrist, and her lips parted to ask what I had done. At first I didn't respond at all. I steadied myself.

"My mother is dead," I told her.

And though this wasn't an adequate response, it was all she required.

"I don't have any parents," she said.

I stared at her, not knowing what to say.

She nodded towards the cuts. "Does it hurt?"

I swallowed, glancing down—it did hurt a little when I saw them. "Yes, but…" I clamped my other hand down over the mess. "I don't want to stay. I-I can't stay. I have nothing here. I have—I have nothing to make me stay here. It's dark."

"It's dark now. But the sunrise will come."

I shook my head. "You don't understand. The sun… the sun is dead."

She seized my wrist, peeling my hand away and ignoring my testament. Startled by her reaction, my fingers shrank away from her icy ones.

"Don't talk like that."

She pushed up her sleeves. Black streaks tarnished her thin arms, but I quickly became distracted by her hands and where they went. They folded over my wounds, growing warm—then hot. I made a motion to pull away, but she didn't let go.

I bit my lip, scared to make a sound though pain coursed through my arm like tongues of flame. I searched her eyes, but they were the same as before.

My only focus was on getting away from her—this ghost that had chosen the night I had allotted for my death to visit me. But my efforts dissolved when I looked down. When I noticed that there was no more blood.

The cuts were gone.

"What did you just do?" I asked, my voice quiet and trembling. "What… what just happened?"

Her eyes were void of answers. She didn't say a word.

I leaned closer.

"Who are you?" I asked quietly.

She looked me in the eyes. The moon reached into them.

"I can't say…" She stopped.

Her hands reached to her opposite arms, rolling her sleeves back down again.

"I can't say that I know."

CHAPTER ONE

Fin

The room was swollen with reminiscence. It was like the day I'd met her—except everything was different now. She wasn't who she used to be, and neither was I.

She murmured quietly under her breath as I led her down the hall, cradling her elbows in her opposite palms as I guided her into one of the safe rooms. I saw a faint apparition of my breath as we entered, and I slid the door shut behind us.

"I'm sorry it's so cold in here." I gestured toward the examination table positioned off to the side. "Runner told me he would have everything ready. Apparently that fell through."

The sun was just beginning to reverse its path across the sky beyond the inch of solid glass. I dimmed the panes and went through the various motions of starting a fire, swapping the paperwork I was carrying to the opposite arm.

"It's freezing in here," she mumbled quietly, as if I had provided no explanation.

I turned to look at Mala, still kneeling in front of the small flames, but made no response. She had seated herself on the examination table, still gripping her elbows and staring straight ahead at nothing in particular. When the fire could hold its own, I got up and walked over to a smaller table beside her, where I set the papers down.

"Mala, I'm going to ask you a few questions, alright?"

When she gave no response, I repeated the question. Mala drew

4

in a deeper breath this time, after a few seconds, and I knew she was aware that I was talking to her.

"How do you feel right now?" I tugged a small slip of paper out of the stack. "Can you describe it?"

She continued to study the ghost between us.

"It's cold in here," she repeated softly. "I'm cold."

"I know—I'm sorry. But I need you to talk to me about how you physically feel right now. It's important."

I took the slip of paper and crossed the room again.

"I'm going to make you some tea," I said, opening one of the cabinets and drawing several items out with my focus. "It's going to help you feel a lot better. I know the last couple of weeks haven't been very easy for you."

I noticed slight movements in my peripheral vision as Mala shifted her position.

"Weeks," she repeated. "Has it been weeks?"

"Yes, two weeks now. Since the…" I faltered on the word *execution*. "Since the trial."

Even with the exclusion of the word, she began to shiver with less control. "Since Icarus's death."

I felt her eyes on me for a moment as I filled a small silver bowl with cold water. "Yes."

"And now no one is left," she concluded. "No one from my world."

The fire was blazing now. I moved the bowl into a levitation over the tongues of flame, beginning to add various herbs to the water as it heated. "That's not true. Areos is here, and Runner—they're both from your natural dimension. You went to school with them. Do you remember that?"

"Mm… not really."

"They had different names." I began stirring the liquid as it warmed. "West and… Ruger, I believe. Do those names sound familiar to you?"

There was a long pause while she seemed to think about it, but then she shook her head.

"Here," I said, pausing in front of her to hand over the small bowl of pale golden liquid. "It's hot. Drink it slowly."

She studied it as if I were attempting to poison her, then lifted her head to stare up into my eyes with her hollow brown ones.

"Do you know what this feels like, Fin?" Her words came out quiet, slurred slightly. "To have been so close to someone… and then one day they're not there anymore…"

I felt a chill run its hands down the back of my neck.

"More than you realize," I said.

Her focus darted back and forth between my eyes for a moment before sinking down to the silver half-sphere in her hands. "Because of Hawk?"

"Yes."

Mala was silent for a moment. Then she brought the bowl up to her lips and took a small sip. "What will happen to her?"

Suddenly I was the one who didn't know how to answer.

I had a *job* to do. I couldn't let my mind deviate from the fact. If I was going to survive the process, it would be by not thinking about Hawk. Not thinking, period.

"I don't know, Mala." I placed a hand on the examination table beside her. "I don't know what's going to happen to her."

She took another sip. I could tell it was beginning to require a little more effort for her to keep her eyes open. "What is this? It tastes… strange."

"It's going to help you feel better." I turned back to the table where my papers were laid out and pulled out the protocol to give it one last scan. "You're going to fall asleep for a little while, but you'll feel a lot different when you wake up."

"But I don't understand."

The door opened before I could reply. The sound of footsteps broke the silence around us, distracting Mala from the conversation and saving me from having to fabricate a response.

"You're late, Runner," I told him, still not allowing my gaze to swerve. "Get over here."

"I'm sorry, I was—"

I cut the breathless blue-haired initiate off mid-sentence, lifting a hand for silence. "Tell me about it later—or never, in fact. Here." I handed him the empty bowl, which I took from Mala's hands as they began to go gradually limp. "Take this over to the counter. Put everything else away."

Runner took it from my hand, but made no movement to do as he was told. His gaze flickered from Mala to me.

"Are you going to read her mind?"

I gently eased Mala into a reclining position, trying to ignore her murmured inquiries, and shot Runner a stern glance. "Of *course not*—that would be breaching the code. My job is only to *remove* memories, not read them."

"I'm confused."

"If you didn't retain the information from the council's briefing, I'm afraid you won't be getting filled in. Just do as you're told." I took a deep breath and started to focus on the task at hand, setting the procedure instructions aside.

Gently, I placed my forefinger in the middle of Mala's forehead, letting my thumb rest against her temple.

"Is it always this cold here?" Runner asked from across the room. I heard a cabinet creak as he opened it manually. "The trees look like they're starting to change color."

"It's called autumn," I said, moving my fingertips gently over the span of Mala's forehead in small circular motions.

"I didn't realize there were seasons here."

"Things work a little differently when you exist within a projection of someone else's consciousness," I explained.

"I can't say that I follow."

"Autumn is a dying season," I replied.

Runner hesitated. "Are you saying that Sensei is dying?"

"No," I replied, my voice heavy as I shook my head. "Not him."

It had never rained here before. There were clouds sometimes, but never rain.

The Dimension was a place of spring, with a little summer heat in the afternoons. The dawn came peaceful and warm over the sides of the ravine and awakened the winds, the plant life, and the wild things. It had been something to get used to—I had grown up in the ebb and flow of Ireland's seasonal changes. Spring with its giving way to hues of emerald, summer with its wild scents and overgrowth, autumn and its rivers of gold and blustering winds, and finally winter with its silencing carpets of shimmering white. But here it was different.

It was always spring here—always on the brink of new life. Dawn dissolved to dusk and dusk to another immediate dawn, never night. The stars shone in the crimson color in between. Things were always the same, but in a good way—constant.

Until the day that Icarus fell. The rain came that day and never left. It had started with a soft shower and then turned slowly into rivers.

Each morning I emerged into a world that was stained with the colors of autumn and doused in cold torrents of rainfall. Each day seemed a shade bleaker than the one before.

Today was no exception.

I pulled on my hood as I left the training platform and made my way blindly along the rope bridge. The wood was soft beneath my bare feet, and though the dormitory was barely visible in the veil of fog the humidity had birthed, I singled out the outermost pod. My gait quickened as it finally eased into my view several yards ahead. Shivering, I slowed to a halt as I reached the canvas flap. I knocked gently on the frame. Once, then twice.

The fabric quivered in the bluster for a moment before abruptly parting, presenting a familiar heart-shaped face spattered with freckles and crowned by a frenzy of textured red hair.

"Delta." I nodded an acknowledgment.

She gestured me inside.

"H-how is she?"

"Unchanged."

The canvas slapped shut behind me as my eyes made hasty efforts to adjust. I heard the crackle of a fire before the warmth emanating from it had even registered.

"No improvement?"

"No further decline," she corrected brusquely, her Cornish accent peeking through her every word.

I followed her across the first room, which served as a study lounge. Several female students were seated at various desks, preoccupied and not acknowledging my presence as I passed. I was there every day; this was becoming routine for them.

"Yes, but you said that before." We entered the familiar, dimly lit passageway. "And yesterday she was worse."

"I know you don't trust me because I'm a new initiate, Fin." She heaved a frustrated sigh. "But I will remind you that I *am* from the future—I do know a little about physiology. I worked in a field hospital during the Universal War."

"Humans just can't give up that war complex."

"You know how they are. One thing leads to another."

I dragged my fingers back through my hair. "I just hate feeling helpless, Delta."

"Don't we all."

"But I don't think you understand how different this is."

"I don't know if I would say that," she said. "Mitsue did fill me in on the details of the trial."

I shot her a look. "You consumed *his* biased version?"

"He is my teacher, after all." We came to a halt in front of the familiar wicker door. "And we all have biases, Fin. We all see things differently. The Dimension is in flux right now. No one sees eye to eye on the topic of the prophecy—or Hawk's claims. It's open to interpretation."

"And has it occurred to you that perhaps therein lies the problem?" I felt my jaw tighten slightly. "The fact that none of us seem to see anything through Sensei's eyes, only our own? He's only staying out of all this because *we're pushing* him away, you know. Hawk is pushing him away and she doesn't even realize it."

Delta looked at me for a moment without saying anything, and when she did make a motion to speak, I cut her off.

"Please." I finally gestured toward the door. "Can I just go in?"

She hesitated but a moment before opening the door.

"Just an hour today," she said, stepping aside. "She's very weak."

I nodded, passing the threshold. The door closed behind me.

The room was glowing with a mixture of dawn and lamplight. An empty chair was placed against the wall to my right. I focused it across the room and took a seat beside her.

For a long time I said nothing. I sat there and watched the sheets rise and fall as she breathed. When she exhaled, I could see the outline of her rib cage pressing up against her chest.

The dawn gradually thickened, diminishing the light from the various flickering flames until their illumination was of almost no effect.

"Well, it's done," I said, sighing. "I'll admit I almost wish I had kept my mouth shut."

Hawk made no movement. I wasn't sure if she could hear me, but I couldn't help but feel like somehow she understood. I was too used to seeking her advice to stop, even if she couldn't answer.

"It's just that the past fortnight was such an uphill battle with Mala," I went on. "She pleaded with the council for permission to attend Icarus's execution, but was denied. After that it was like she just...snapped. It wasn't until later that I found out that she had begun to secretly utilize her powers to injure herself—to the point of making an attempt on her own life, I was told. Her roommate reported this, and naturally the council gathered to assess the situation."

I watched Hawk as I thought through the past several days, a feeling of regret unsettling my stomach.

"It was a last resort. I wouldn't have wished the outcome on an enemy, but I know her, and I am more acquainted with the fallout of the situation than anyone. I made a strong case for the resetting of her long-term memory, and in the end I won." I bit my lip. "But even as I sat there with her in the safe room, preparing her for the procedure, I searched hard for an alternative—of any kind. Any fragment I could use to break through to her, but in the end, we were still at square one and there was nothing I could do."

I watched the sheets rise. Fall.

"I suppose it's not always a tragedy to forget—in some ways it may work for the greater good," I went on. "Mala had nothing left... her family, Raiden, Icarus—any attachment she had was stripped from her, and God knows I can understand how hard it is to go through losing so much. If it helps her in some way that I took away the burden of that reminder, then so be it."

My words, though perhaps true, were no consolation for my restless conscience.

"But not every problem can be so easily erased." I pushed my voice out, though it began to succumb to the gravel of sleep deprivation. "No one understands why the trees are dying. Or why it's so cold—or why this *bleeding* rain won't stop. Everyone thinks Icarus is dead, Hawk. They can't see the canary in the coal mine. Because they didn't believe a word you said."

I paused again, watching her. Watching for faint, flickering movements behind her closed eyelids.

"I once told you that things grow at the bottom of the ravine even if we can't see it—even though we don't know if it even exists all." I lowered my voice. "He couldn't survive an endless free fall for this long. He would already have died from the various stressors—his body wouldn't be able to take it. There has to be something down there. Because *he's* down there."

My mind was weary with the thoughts that had haunted me since the day of the execution. My gaze traced her features, catching on a hand that was like hewn marble. I wanted to take it in my own, but I stopped myself.

"But if there's something at the bottom... I don't understand how he could have survived the impact." My attention flickered away from my words.

Hawk breathed in.

"But he did survive it," I continued slowly, "because you're still alive."

CHAPTER TWO

Fin

The dull rusty gray of a sunset was making its way in through the window of the dormitory pod as I stood at my dresser and splashed water over my face. With the rain having yet to cease, it was almost impossible to distinguish sunrise from sunset; each was but a dull illumination behind a thick blanket of clouds.

Though the cold water against my skin roused my senses, I couldn't remember the last time I had actually slept. I lay awake in my bunk and thought about what was to become of us—what was to become of her. I thought of that day in Howth. And why I'd decided to stay.

I remembered having noticed that her hair was longer. She usually kept it short, around her shoulders, but in the turmoil of the unfolding events with Icarus, her thoughts had been in a thousand other places. I'd sat there on the blanket we'd spread out over the soft grass, watching her as she rose and went to the edge of the cliff, gazing out over the thundering sea below. The breeze was stronger there, and it ran its coarse fingers through the length of her hair.

That day in Howth was a memento mori of my past life. I felt almost guilty—Hawk and I had discussed the Dimension and the possibility that the ancient "key" to slider selection lay in the fact that every living breathing human was potentially a slider—a protector below the skin, unrealized. Yet somehow it wasn't that urgent conversation that stood out to me most, but her hair and her voice and the way the sunlight reflected in her eyes; the echoes of my sisters' laughter. I remembered best the ghosts, not the fragments of the puzzle I knew I would soon be forced to analyze.

Moments after Icarus had vanished over the ledge, Hawk had collapsed and I had caught her in my arms. She had been on the platform throughout the execution ceremony, watching as the inevitable unfolded in front of her—her own execution, though no one but she, I, Sensei, and perhaps Icarus knew or believed it. The looks other students had given her had not escaped my notice. It was clear that the claims she had made at the trial would not come without consequences—indeed, her announcement, like all truth, had already created division among us. It was almost a blessing in disguise that unconsciousness had taken her for the time being. She couldn't be taken into custody or tried until she woke up, buying me some time to build a case for her. Though there had been some discussion over what should be done with her, I did as I saw fit, as if no other suggestion had been given.

I believed in Hawk. I was privileged to some knowledge of the future that the rest of the student body went on in ignorance of: Hawk and Icarus were one and the same. If Icarus survived—and so far, he apparently had—then so would she. Though her situation was bleak, I reminded myself that it was only a matter of time until her awakening. We just had to keep her alive until then.

Two group dormitory pods had been constructed for the new students who had been initiated before we sealed the portal. Delta Flynn, one of the new students, was versed in futuristic methods of healing, so I entrusted Hawk to her care for the time being. I was breaking student-body rules by entering the girls' dorm each day to visit Hawk and update myself as to her condition, but with the chaos that had erupted around the execution, my actions went practically unnoticed.

The rain pattered against the glass windowpanes, lighter now. I buried my face into the towel I'd taken off the dresser. Pulling off my shirt, I went about focusing open drawers in search of a fresh change of clothes. I kept my movements as quiet as possible. The initiation of new students, though good, had forced us to consolidate within the dormitories, giving me two new roommates, both of whom were asleep.

I found a shirt just as I heard the canvas flap behind me swallow someone inside. Identifying the footsteps, I didn't bother looking up.

"You're finally back. Does this mean you actually slept?"

I slid the drawer closed. "On the contrary, Mitsue, I only came back to wash and change."

"For what occasion?"

"It does not concern you."

There was a pause; then I heard him walk across the room to his desk.

"If any lesson came from Icarus's execution, I would have hoped that it was that everyone's actions indeed concern everyone, Fin," he said. "One's sins do not necessarily taint only them."

I nodded solemnly. "A fact you would be wise to remember."

He said nothing, and I started for the door, pulling the shirt over my head as I crossed the room. I parted the canvas flap to reveal the rain.

"Fin." I heard Mitsue turn to speak over his shoulder. "Convey my condolences to Sensei."

I held the canvas open in midair for a moment with my focus, turning to look at him quizzically.

"About Hawk," he added.

I stood there but a moment before stepping out.

"Convey them yourself."

———✦———

"Something warm to drink, Fin?"

I put up a hand, shaking my head. "The fire is more than enough. I'm soaked through—this rain just won't let up."

The glass wall at the end of the room had been dimmed, submerging the room in darkness fought back only by the firelight. The furnishings were sparse and the table was bare, but something sweetly scented brewed over the fire. Sensei gestured for me to take a seat.

"It's gotten worse," I said. "It comes in waves—heavier then lighter, it seems. And the trees…"

"The trees are changing, yes," he finished for me. "I have eyes."

His tone wasn't cutting as much as it was injured, weary. I could understand.

"I assume you've had an account from Runner," I began, resetting the conversation. "Mala's procedure?"

Sensei slowly nodded. "He said it was 'successful.'"

"Regrettably, as successful as it had to be," I replied. "It was the last thing I wanted to do, but I just couldn't see a way around it."

"Have you seen her since?"

I shook my head. "I plan to as soon as dawn comes. She's resting now, and Runner is with her. There will be a lot to review... but if I taught her once, I should hope I could repeat the process."

"Was she very shaken?"

"She had a very... strange attachment to Raiden, Sensei," I said. "And I believe she had an affectionate relationship with Icarus at one time. It was just too much for her to face losing her family as well as the two of them."

A pause.

"But she hasn't lost both of them." Sensei looked up from the fire before which he was still standing. "Has she?"

I considered his words. "No, Sensei. She hasn't. But you know full well that you and I are the only ones who believe Icarus is still alive. No one believed Hawk at the trial—"

"Except you."

"Except me." I pressed my fingertips to my eyelids, reliving the night for an instant. "Sensei, why weren't you there? She needed you."

"She doesn't need me, Fin," he said. "Not anymore. She needs time to find herself... space—"

"Sensei, she doesn't need *space*, she needs *you*." I cut him off, looking back up. "She's... I've been to see her every day. I've sat beside her. I've watched her. Her strength is fading."

Sensei was silent for a moment, though he didn't seem caught off guard. He came to the table and settled into the seat across from me. "Did you not just declare that you believed her to be who she said she was?"

"With all my heart, Sensei."

"Then external evidence is irrelevant," he concluded. "You doubt yourself, Fin. If you believe in her, be strong in that belief. Do you actually believe that she will die?"

I looked into his eyes from across the table and shook my head.

"Why?"

"Because she *is* the Sunrise the prophecy speaks of," I said. "Her withdrawal into darkness brings about this autumn, this rain—this season of mourning. But Icarus *is* alive and thus she remains, and thus Icarus will remain because I will make her fight this out. I don't know if she hears me, but I speak to her every day and..." I stopped and swallowed. "I believe she *will* awaken. Though sometimes even I have to fight back the doubts that seem to be poisoning us all," I said. "My true fear, Sensei, is that now, even in her comatose state, she may be safer now than she will be if... *once* she awakens."

"To what do you refer?"

"I refer to her announcement of her own identity, Sensei," I replied. "I reference the fact that rather than believing, everyone has doubted. She's not a savior, but a blasphemer in their eyes—at risk of a trial of her own, in fact. I would not be surprised if the council is already plotting to that effect."

He fell contemplatively silent.

"Would you not intervene in the event of a trial?" I pressed him.

"I could not, Fin."

I stared at him. "*You could not?* Why on earth wouldn't you? Sensei, you chose her!"

"It is not that I *wouldn't*, Fin, it's that I'm not able to," he cut in, pushing back his chair to rise. "I do not carry the authority. Things are not as they seem."

"I don't understand you."

"I've given you the authority—*her*. Icarus, the student body, all of you." He walked to the fire again. "Can't you see? You are no longer beneath anyone's charge—you are no longer children. This is your time of culmination. You have been given all the authority you need."

I watched the flames, considering the implications.

"Well, Sensei," I said, "I'm afraid we're only killing ourselves with it."

"Then be the exception."

"I am trying, Sensei, believe me," I said. "But how on *earth* can we have reached the culmination of which the prophecy speaks when we're in such turmoil—when things are worse than they have ever been?"

"You are mistaken, Fin, if you believe the culmination to be the end," he said, still focused on the flames lapping in the hearth. "If it is to be called anything, it should be the beginning."

"But how are we to face this without them?" I asked. "Our reemergence into darkness—we don't even know what it is. We don't even know what we're up against! We *need* her…" I trailed off, stopped.

"*Them*," I corrected myself quietly. "We need both of them, *here*, with us. Yet Icarus is gone and Hawk is…" It ached to speak of it— to think of it. And I could tell it had the same effect on Sensei, though he seemed to draw strength from a deeper reservoir. "I don't know how to bring her back, Sensei."

He made no response for a moment, seeming to consider what I had said.

"Perhaps you will not need to, Fin."

His response startled my gaze up from the surface of the table. "What are you talking about? Sensei, I can't—"

"It's not your responsibility, Fin."

"But it is, Sensei," I said firmly. "You don't understand, I…" I didn't allow myself to finish.

"I understand more than you realize," he said calmly. "But the time has come for you to trust her—trust that her identity will be her salvation."

I felt the corners of my lips twitch into a rueful smile. "If only my belief in her *was* of some effect."

"You believe that it isn't?" he asked. "Do you truly believe that your love for her is fruitless, Fin? That it holds no power and makes no impact?"

I didn't know how to answer. I wanted to leave—I didn't want to hear these words. They burned like hot iron against my skin.

"Icarus has kept her alive for this long," I said, finally. "I only pray that his power continues to renew what little she has left." Lifting myself from my seat, I looked Sensei in the eyes. They were full of things I couldn't understand, not even in the warm illumination.

"And I hope to God that they don't bring charges against her, though you know as well as I that when she awakens, they almost certainly will."

I felt immediately guilty for the tone I had taken, but I left without apologizing. Something inside my chest was reaching a boiling point, and I wasn't sure how much longer I could cope.

My words to Delta resounded in my thoughts.

I hate feeling helpless.

It was something I had felt when I'd embraced my mother and sisters for the last time, and it was something I felt yet stronger now.

I pulled my coat up around my neck and stepped out from beneath the shelter of the platform. The rain was coming down in torrents, fighting against me as I made my way back in the direction of the dormitories. I barely noticed that I was shivering—soaked. My mind was brimming with someone else.

I wasn't halfway across the bridge when a familiar voice broke the barrier of my thoughts. A familiar Cornish accent called my name.

"Fin, wait!"

I turned abruptly.

Though her face was hidden beneath a draping cloak, I noticed wisps of red hair venturing out into the wind from beneath her hood. Her footsteps were almost frantic as they came across the bridge to meet the place where mine had stopped altogether.

"Delta, what's wrong?"

She shook her head, catching her breath. "Nothing, nothing is wrong—"

"Then what—"

Delta didn't let me finish.

"Fin, she's awake!"

CHAPTER THREE

Icarus

There was a weight against my eyelids. Neither cold nor warm, but denser than air, thicker. There was no sound, no sight, no feeling in my limbs except for the awareness of this presence shifting from my eyelids to the rest of my body, washing over my skin. I moved my fingertips first. I felt something like sand, and the sensation seemed to startle my mind awake.

I flexed my fingers again, and the same feeling rolled through them. All of a sudden there was sound—but then again there wasn't. Everything around me was muffled white noise.

Awareness trickled slowly in.

Where am I?

Gradually, I opened one eyelid, then the other. At first I saw nothing. Nothing and then a blur, and after the blur, a color.

Blue. Then green.

Light filtered down through what seemed like miles of void space overhead. I moved my hands and then my arms. I began to feel my legs, and then all at once I felt the urge to breathe.

Water poured into my lungs.

Instantly my body convulsed. I made efforts to reject the water I had inhaled, but only more flooded in as a result. I crumpled, and the roaring sensation of submersion filled my ears. I swam my arms frantically in front of me and tore myself toward what I assumed was the surface. The density of the water around me was still at first, like that of a tranquil pond, but the closer to the surface I dragged myself, the more acutely aware I became of the fact that movement was slowly and then rapidly entering the water around me. At first it was a gentle pull; then it was a swift current.

My lungs burned. I felt the vague warmth of light on my face.

I broke the surface, gasping. My vision cleared and my eyes grabbed hold of a blurry snapshot of a landscape as I was sucked under again and thrown by the current against something—hard. I felt the oxygen I'd managed to take in rapidly abandon my lungs. I felt myself go upside down and then right side up again; then I was struck with something, and finally I surfaced. Coughing violently—submerging again before my lungs were ready.

Chaos swirled overhead. My arms fought frantically with the angry matter around them, searching for anything to grab hold of in the tumult. But the water was cold—freezing, in fact, making movement more difficult as the seconds ticked past.

I pulled myself to the surface again, gagging. This time I was able to see more clearly, though only for a split second. I comprehended white water swirling around me, and then I was thrown against a rock. Flecks of gold danced over my vision.

Struggling to keep my head up, I fought to swim in the direction of the embankment. When I surfaced, I caught unfocused glimpses of dark green—what I believed was shore.

The river had other plans. She pulled me down into her mouth and clenched her jaws tight, sweeping me farther downstream and past boulders I managed, by chance, to avoid. I was coughing furiously with each sporadic rendezvous with the water's surface.

Next time I came up for air, I managed to fight the undertow long enough to keep myself above the surface for a moment. I saw more clearly what lay ahead. My heart jarred against my teeth.

The rocks abruptly vanished, giving way to a stretch of rolling, clear water, then nothing. A place where the river ended—a waterfall.

With what little energy I had left, I fought like hell. My arms were afire as I dug frantically at the water around me, willing myself in the direction of the embankment. In a heartbeat, I was swept over the brink. I saw the empty expanse below for a fraction of a second before I felt the riverbed drop out from under me.

A voice that didn't sound like my own ran scared out of my throat as I fell. In the onslaught of adrenaline, time seemed to slow.

The impact was as hard as lead. For an instant I felt the tension fade from my limbs, and I began to think I'd drifted into unconsciousness. But then I breathed in and there was the stinging of water in my lungs again.

I was still submerged, and if I was going to drown, it would not be in quiet unconsciousness. Persuading myself against my body's instinct, I swam harder than I thought myself capable of. By the grace of God I broke the surface close to shore.

Finally.

Coughing up water uncontrollably, I pulled myself closer to the embankment before me with one arm. When I could finally stand, I did so. As I stumbled onto the sand, my strength abandoned me entirely and I collapsed onto my face.

I could still make out the resounding roar of the falls from somewhere behind me; then slowly it faded.

My eyes closed.

———✦———

How long I slept, I couldn't say. When I awoke, my strength was renewed enough to slowly press myself up to my knees and then, gradually, to my feet. I ventured sluggishly from the sand, stumbling and dizzy, into the wild grass.

Behind me, like a vein of white marble splitting the cliff side, was the waterfall. The river branched out from there to part the thick forest and vanish into the darkness below the canopy, rolling onward.

I stopped there, frozen in my stance for a moment.

Forest surrounded me—moss-coated trees reaching their long fingers skyward. The only tiny patch of sky I could see through the canopy above spoke of rain.

I took a few steps into the shade of the trees. My eyes scanned the wilderness around me as I finally swallowed back my heart.

Before the river—what had happened *before* the river?

I had no idea where I was.

With the sun enshrouded in clouds, it was impossible for me to grasp what time of day it was. I ventured deeper into the undergrowth, parting it with my hands. I became aware of a sweet, earthy smell rising from the places where my feet fell, and then of the fact that I was missing my shirt, clothed only in faded, soaked jeans. I glanced down just as a snake slithered over my feet.

Startled, I tripped. My hand went to the moist bark on one of the tree trunks and I caught myself. My eyes darted frantically to check the rest of the ground around me. The throaty call of a bird echoed distantly.

I was soaked to the skin, and although it was warm, the exposure left me with chills tracing my spine. I ventured away from the clearing until I lost any sense of a return route; the pounding of heavy tons of water had faded from earshot.

Vibrant green moss surrounded me. It coated the forest floor, blazing the trunks of trees and seeming to invite my gaze up to the almost opaque sea of foliage overhead. In every direction there was nothing beyond green, unsuppressed life. Trees grew thickly together among an almost translucent fog that veiled the agglomerations of tangled red roots.

At first I walked at a steady pace, but then in spite of the exhaustion in my legs, I broke into a full run. The trees distorted into a chaos of green hues around me. I tripped and fell; I rose; I continued until I thought my lungs would burst.

I came upon a particularly massive tree. I found footholds easily among the gnarled mess of tree skin. My arms moved as if they were carrying the weight of several bodies and not just my own. I could barely maintain a steady focus as I reached for higher branches and swung myself up. My fingertips stung with the sensations of fresh scrapes, and the only sound beyond the silence was my own frantic breathing.

I climbed for what must have been a good twenty minutes. The highest branches were a long way up, but I knew my efforts would be worthwhile. I would get a good vantage point, and maybe from there I could determine where on earth I was—or at least where the forest ended.

Pulling myself up into the U-shaped crook of the treetop where two adjoined branches split, I balanced myself there, catching my breath. Slowly I stood, my hands taking clusters of leaves in their anxious grasp. I was hundreds of feet up—one glance below made my head spin.

I broke through the layer of mossy foliage. To my left, to my right, ahead of me and behind me, as far as the eye could see, was forest. Endless, thick green forest. And a bird sang in the distance.

CHAPTER FOUR

Hawk

My eyelids met with resistance as they slowly ventured open. There was a weight against them—against my entire body—pinning me down against something that was soft and firm all at once. When my vision cleared, I comprehended blue, that was all: large beams of light cutting down through wavering shades of emerald and turquoise.

There was no sound, no feeling in my fingertips, or the rest of my body for that matter. I was aware only of this presence that was like invisible iron, holding me down below the colors, which now rolled with movement.

It was reminiscent of the sky, or of a storm, freckled with scattered fractions of sunlight. I pressed my eyes closed again. My lips parted. I breathed in.

It wasn't air. It was water.

It poured down into my lungs like an icy waterfall. I writhed violently, fighting to pull myself to the surface, though I had no clear sense of direction.

My motions were frantic as my arms tore at the substance around me. Thick, dead-calm water, which gradually gave way to something else. As the violence of my efforts increased, everything around me almost instantaneously melted away.

A hand seized my wrist.

"Hawk, it's okay."

I tried to pull away, but the grip was firm.

"Let me go!"

"Hawk, be still." The voice was muffled. "I promise it's all right."

I squinted, searching frantically through the distortion for the body to which the voice belonged. Fuzzy orbs of orange light were scattered about me. A hand still held mine in a vise.

"Let me go," I insisted, breathless. "Just let me go, and... and I'll be calm."

It released and I twisted away from it, rolling onto my side though it dizzied me to do so. The faint sounds of movement reached my ears. The tinkling of glass, and then water being poured—the last sound I wanted to hear.

"Here," said the voice. I could now identify that it was female. "Try to drink a little of this. It will help."

"No," I said. "I don't need... I don't need anything to drink."

"How do you feel?"

I hadn't even thought about how I felt until then. I was light-headed and feeling somewhat sick to my stomach from my sudden movement, but beyond that I felt only numb. There was no real pain. I began to feel the warmth of my sweat against the sheets spread over me.

"Where is he?" I heard my voice ask, though it was but a slurred whisper.

No immediate answer came. I heard footsteps.

"Fin?"

I tried to respond, but this time my voice sank back into my throat.

"I can get him for you," she said, and I felt a hand at my wrist again as she checked my pulse. It stayed there for a moment, and then, seeming satisfied, her footsteps carried her farther away. "Try not to move."

The door opened and closed, sounding a million miles away.

I brushed back the blankets as soon as I knew she was gone and willed myself to sit up. The world spun violently around me.

"Ow." I pressed the heel of my hand to my forehead, squeezing my eyelids closed for a moment as I steadied myself. "Where on earth am I?"

Internally I searched my body again for signs of distress, but, finding none, continued to slip my legs over the edge of the mattress.

I sat there as still as I could manage, attempting to swallow back the lump that had formed in my throat.

I'm in a dormitory pod. No doubt about that.

I could feel the swaying of the wind rolling beneath the floor like ocean waves, rocking the room gently. I detected a repetitive patter against the roof. Something that was like a distant memory from my life on Earth.

"Rain?"

How was that possible? It never rained in the Dimension.

My brain didn't want to analyze, and my body begged to lie back down, but I ignored both. I had too many questions that needed to be answered.

The voice, though I still had no idea to whom it belonged, had said she was going to find Fin—and I was glad because the questions I had were ones that probably only he could answer.

I let my hand melt away from my face and opened my eyes to prove myself right. I was indeed in the dormitory, and it was raining outside—pouring, in fact. Melancholic gray clouds were visible beyond the small porthole window, and the wind was howling through the spaces in the woven walls. Dusk lay over the ravine like a blanket.

What on earth is happening?

Before my mind could ask another question, the door behind me opened, this time with more force. Fin was before me faster than I could turn to check.

"Hawk." He took one of my hands in his, kneeling beside my bed. "Thank God you're awake. How do you feel?"

His voice was breathless, panting, and I couldn't remember ever having been so relieved to hear it.

"I'm alright." I made an effort to answer clearly. "How long have I been asleep?"

"You've been more than asleep, I'm afraid," he said, exhaling the words. "You've been in a coma for two weeks."

My heart froze.

"*Two weeks?*"

He nodded.

I stared at him, and in his green eyes I saw things I wasn't sure I was ready to take on.

"Fin," I said slowly as my memory began to come back to me like a high tide to its shore. "Where's Icarus?"

He studied my face for a moment, and his expression faded from one of relief to deadweight.

"Fin?"

His eyes came back to mine and he lowered his voice. "At the bottom of the ravine."

My heart fell through my stomach. He put a hand up before I could say anything.

"Wait until dawn comes—until we're alone," he said softly, shooting a pointed glance past me to where the other presence still lingered. "We'll talk about it then."

April 1911

I lay awake for what felt like hours, listening to the patter of the rain on the window. The wind howled down the abandoned streets and whistled through the cracks. A steady drip, drip, drip in the pan at the end of my bed kept me wide awake.

My eyes burned as I stared up at the cracks in the ceiling, only visible because of the lamplight leaking in.

For days it had rained. For days I hadn't seen her.

I pushed back the covers, slipped out of bed, and crossed the room, making as little sound as I could. The door to the girl's room creaked as I opened it, and for a moment I held my breath.

Then I saw her at the far end of the room: a lump under the dull gray quilt, a swath of long brown hair.

I began to breathe again; my feet padded over the cold, damp floors. A rat scurried beneath the bed as I approached. Glancing around me, I placed a hand on her shoulder.

"Charlotte," I whispered. "Charlotte, wake up!"

CHAPTER FIVE

Fin

I pulled Delta aside as I was leaving that night.

"Don't say anything to her." I lowered my voice once she had closed the door to Hawk's room. "About the possibility of a trial. Nothing is definite yet."

She looked up at me, one eyebrow raised. "Are you certain about that?"

"I don't think anyone is certain about anything right now," I replied, returning her gaze. "So we can't speak of things we don't know for sure. I want to have a chance to speak to her first."

Delta's quizzical expression remained an instant longer and then dissolved. "I see."

"Give her whatever she wants," I continued, pulling my coat on. "I'll be back as soon as dawn breaks."

Leaving Hawk was the last thing I wanted to do, but I was also very aware of the war zone she'd just emerged from, and the fact that she would need rest to survive the new one she had just emerged into.

And so I took my leave, wondering silently about my own words. Whether the council was as undecided as I thought—*hoped*.

While she rested, I had one other obligation to follow up on. I wrestled with insomnia until dawn and then went to hunt down Runner. I found my blue-haired student hunched lifelessly at a desk in the safe room I'd left him in.

Crossing the room, I paused behind his chair before clearing my throat pointedly. He started to attention, sitting up.

"Er—whassup?"

"Where is she?"

Runner started raking his fingers back through his hair. "Who— oh, Mala?"

"Who *else* would I be referring to?" I asked, trying to keep my irritation at bay. "Runner, I left you with *one* job—"

"Hey, hey, hey, it's all good!" he said, stumbling to his feet. "She woke up and I, uh, talked to her and stuff."

"Did you follow the protocol?"

"Yeah, I did all that—I read all the paperwork." He bobbed his head in an unconvincing nod. "Then Mitsue came by like you told him to and took her out for orientation. After that I didn't have anything to do, and I was up half the night, so—"

"Mitsue?" I repeated, cutting him off. "What do you mean Mitsue took her out for orientation? I didn't tell him to do that."

Runner looked at me for a second and then shrugged. "Well, he told me you did, man. What was I supposed to do?"

"I don't know—maybe check with me before you let my student wander off with someone?" I sighed, frustrated. "Anyway, it's too late now. How long ago was that?"

"Uh, let's see, um..."

"Never mind." I put up a hand. "I'll check with Gaia. She keeps pretty well on top of that kind of thing—Mala's probably already safely in her dorm."

"Yeah, I'm sure."

"No, you're not." I shot him a look, starting back across the room. "You just want to shut me up. Get this place cleaned up before you leave, understand?"

"Dude, I've been up all night!"

"And I haven't?"

I heard him mutter something derogatory about the Irish under his breath in response as I focused the pocket door open and stepped out into the hallway.

Sessions were in full swing when I arrived on the platform—and when I say full swing, I overstate. With so many students preoccupied in frantic meetings and studies to analyze our sudden plunge into autumn, session attendance had dwindled; some classes had even been postponed. We were heading slowly but surely into a state of emergency, and everyone was beginning to feel it.

And still no one seems to have connected the dots—the reason why all this is happening.

I found Gaia in a small circle off to one side of the training platform, leading a group of bundled-up students in a practice centered on focus locks. I noticed several objects in mid-levitation as I sidled up alongside her.

"Gaia, you haven't happened to see Mala this morning, have you?" I asked, keeping my voice at a respectfully low volume. "Runner mentioned Mitsue came to collect her and give her an orientation tour—is that true?"

Gaia hesitated for a moment as she watched one of her students practice. It was impressive to see someone so young taking such a tone of authority with students who were several years her senior.

"I spoke with him briefly, yes," she said. "I thought that was per your arrangement?"

"It was not."

Her dark eyebrows pressed in toward each other beneath her crown of brunette dreadlocks. "Did you not discuss her transfer?"

"Transfer?" I repeated, at a loss.

"Mitsue said that with you having just returned from a teaching hiatus, you wouldn't want the additional responsibility," she clarified. "That you had entrusted Mala to his tutelage?"

My lips parted slightly, but I closed my mouth before I had a chance to say something that would break the code of conduct.

"Did he indeed?"

She studied me for a moment as I fell silent.

"I'm sorry, Fin." She sounded confused. "Should I have said something?"

I shook my head. "It's no concern of yours. Don't apologize." And then under my breath added, "I should have been there when she woke up."

I knew there was nothing else I could do. Gaia confirmed that Mala had returned to her assigned dorm pod to rest, freeing me to return to Hawk. I tried in vain to clear my thoughts as I left the platform and walked briskly back out to the dormitories.

The autumn air was crisp around me, fragranced with moist wood and decaying leaves. My hands tingled from the cold and retreated into my pockets. The ravine had transformed from steep walls of lush growth to a blanket of fiery technicolor, which, in any other circumstances, would have been nothing short of breathtaking.

"Shouldn't you be in bed?" I asked, entering Hawk's room, forcing lightheartedness into my voice.

Hawk didn't look up when I spoke, and she didn't reply. She was at the end of the room, gazing out the small glass window.

I closed the door softly behind me. "How do you feel?"

There was a long pause; then I saw her shrug.

I walked farther into the room and around to the side of the bed. "Are we going to talk, or are you going to ignore me?"

"I'm not ignoring you."

I sat down on the edge of the mattress and folded my hands. "Alright, then what do you call this?"

"What does it look like?"

I no longer needed an answer to my question. I could tell by the familiar roughness of her tone that she was feeling better.

"It looks like you're noticing the rain has stopped," I said, still casual. "Do you want to know when that happened?"

"Before dawn?"

I nodded. "After you awoke. It lightened gradually and then stopped altogether."

Having been awake all night, and for lack of anything else to do, I'd listened to the rain as it slowly diminished. I'd gotten up to check the window and caught a dim glimpse of the Chief Star peering out from behind considerably less cloud cover.

"It will rain again." Hawk drew in a deeper breath. "It's only stopped temporarily."

I looked at her for a long moment, saying nothing.

Hawk hadn't turned to look at me since I'd come in. She was still in an oversized black shirt and shorts, the clothes Delta had provided for her. Her hair was a tangled mess reaching down over her shoulders, and her feet were bare.

"Why aren't you dressed?" I asked, ignoring her last statement. "It's freezing in here. You must be cold."

"I'm not cold," she said to the window. "And even if I was, I deserve to be."

"And why might that be?"

Hawk finally glanced over her shoulder at me. Her eyes were dark, tainting the skin below them an insomniac's purple. Her lips were like faded roses.

"Why do you think?" she asked.

"Why do you answer my every question with another question?" I asked, not about to give her the consolation of a real answer. "If you want me to feel sorry for you, I'm afraid that's not what I came here for."

Provoked, she turned to face me fully. "Don't feel sorry for me—feel sorry for yourself. You're the one who will fall victim to what I've brought down on our heads. This is *my* fault."

"This is your fault?"

"The rain, the autumn, all of it," she said, turning again. "This season of death."

A pause. Wind.

"I'm dying, Fin," she continued neutrally. "I'm dying because he is most certainly dead already."

"If he were dead, you would be too."

"You don't know that." Hawk shook her head. "No one knows how entanglement on this level works… how long it may take for me to feel the effect."

I pretended to consider the heavy implications. I rose slowly and walked back around the bed.

"Then explain why the rain has stopped. Or tell me why you awoke out of your coma," I began. "Why you obviously have enough strength to be up, around, and arguing about this—"

"I am not *arguing* about this," she insisted. "I am stating *facts*, Fin. You know nothing of which you speak—*nothing*."

I shot her a look. "You're afraid to believe he's alive because you don't know how to fix this. You'd rather accept that it's all meant to fall apart."

There was fire in her eyes when she finally lifted them from the window to look at me. "I cannot believe you dare to speak to me that way."

"Why? Because you've been ill?" I asked roughly. "And your nurse isn't here to shoo me away?"

She stepped forward, her lips pressed together, whiter. "Do you not know who I am, Fin?"

"Full well," I replied, abandoning my aimless course to intersect with hers. "I think *you're* the one who doesn't—"

"I'm the one—?"

"—and if you do, you most certainly don't act like it!" I cut her off before she could finish. "I never would have guessed you were the type to let yourself be defeated."

This caught her off guard.

"Fin, look around you!" She flung a hand in the direction of the window. "The trees are dying—the Dimension is in chaos! *I'm* the one who initiated Icarus. *I'm* the reason he was executed! What do you expect me to do—rejoice?"

"No." I stopped abruptly before her. "I expect you to get dressed, get out of this room, and do something about it."

Her eyes stared at me, wide—wild. Hurricanes confined to a skull.

"You disgust me," she said.

"You infuriate me," I replied.

"Leave my room."

"No."

"Fin—"

"You act as if only *your* future hinges on the outcome of this situation, Hawk," I said, lowering my voice, though my words seemed louder than if I had shouted them. "It doesn't affect just you—we are all suffering, questioning… doubting. Even if no one else knows, you and I both know that this is up to *you*."

"But I can't!" Hawk's voice cracked, faded. "Icarus is…"

I stepped slightly closer. "Dead?"

She didn't reply, but she didn't back away.

"I think we both know you're what's keeping him alive."

For a moment I just stood there, looking down into that ghost of such a familiar face. Then I pulled in a breath.

"I'll 'leave your room' now," I said, reiterating her words with no sympathy. "But just know that if you give up on him now, you're giving up on *all of us*."

Hawk watched silently as I took my leave. Delta was waiting for me just beyond the door, but I ignored her inquisition as I strode down the hallway and threw open the canvas to let myself outside. I wasn't in the mood for questions, and I didn't imagine I ever would be.

"The time has come for you to trust her—trust that her identity will be her salvation."

Sensei's words haunted me for the rest of that day. And I would be lying if I said I didn't resent them to some degree.

Perhaps her identity will be her salvation, but what on earth would be mine?

"She is the most stubborn, pigheaded..." I reached my dorm and tore open the canvas flap. "Arrogant, difficult..."

I pulled off my coat and tossed it to the floor. There was a mess awaiting me at my desk. A sea of tests, notations, stacks of books— molted feathers I'd saved in a glass vial with my ink pens.

"I don't understand how Sensei deals with her sometimes," I grumbled inaudibly, dropping into my seat. "Unbelievable."

"What was that?"

I'd barely noticed Mitsue at his desk situated at the opposite end of the room. His face was void of the glasses he no longer wore, having mended his own vision. His long black hair was pulled back into a bun. I heard his pen scribbling against the paper he was hunched over.

"Nothing I wish to speak of," I responded irritably. "But perhaps you can clue me in on why you felt the need to steal Mala out from under my supervision under a false pretext?"

"Steal her?" he reiterated, as if it were a joke. "I *aided* Mala while your own student lazed at a desk—"

"That's not what he told me—"

"I assumed you would thank me," he continued, ignoring my interruption, "for being gracious enough to lighten your workload by taking her under my wing. It's clear you've been rather preoccupied—"

"I had urgent *business*," I corrected firmly. "You had *no right* to interfere—"

"Urgent business being Hawk?"

I immediately faltered, which seemed to satisfy him.

"So it's true, then," he said smoothly. Without waiting for an answer, he continued. "She's awakened. I presume you've been to see her?"

I began sifting through the disheveled stack of paperwork in front of me. "Feigned ignorance does you no credit, Mitsue."

"How is she, then?" he asked. "I inquired about her when I was in audience with Sensei this morning, but found that he hasn't been to see her yet."

I glanced around to see if any of my other roommates were in. They weren't—it was just the two of us.

"Not that we can blame him for that," Mitsue continued, the charcoal pencil in his fingers flying fluently over the page. "Sensei has a greater standard than even we do, and after everything that happened, I can't imagine that he would—"

"Taint himself by affiliation?" I finished for him, my voice dripping with sarcasm. "Of *course not*. Did you go to warn him of the scarlet *B* you've marked her with?"

"I wouldn't do him the dishonor, no," he replied, as if my question were valid. "But our meeting wasn't unrelated, as I'm sure you can guess."

"I'm sure."

"I wasn't about to wait to gather my information on her condition from you," he went on. "How could I possibly count on Hawk's lover to give me an unbiased report of the situation?"

My jaw tensed, and though my body begged to do other things, I forced myself to turn around to face my desk again. "We aren't lovers."

"Then what else could possibly explain your partiality?"

I scanned the page in front of me, though I comprehended nothing. "Try truth."

"Truth?" He tried on the word. "Is that really what you're after, Fin?"

I turned and shot him a glance. "What are we all after, Mitsue, if not that?"

He set down his pencil. "In that case, you'll be pleased by the proposition I have for you."

I said nothing, waiting for him to go on.

"If you must know, I went to see Sensei for a myriad of reasons, but chiefly on behalf of the council," he said, turning to meet my gaze, "after I'd heard of Hawk's awakening from her comatose state."

"From whom did you hear of it?" I asked, attempting to eradicate the telltale tension from my voice. "It happened only just last sunset—almost no one knew."

An expression of contempt twitched at the corners of his mouth. "You aren't the only one with reliable sources, Fin."

I felt my fingers contract slightly around the page still in my grasp.

"Anyway." Mitsue drew a pointed breath. "I met with Sensei to discuss how we will handle Hawk's case."

I calmly placed the paper down in the opposing stack. "Is it that she has what you've always wanted, Mitsue? Is that why you despise her?"

"On the contrary," he replied, pushing back his chair. "I think she despises me for sending her ridiculous excuse for a pupil over the cliff."

"Ridiculous? I see." I lifted the next page. "But not quite as much of a black mark to the Dimension as your own student was, correct?"

"I didn't select Raiden."

"No, but you initiated him once you discovered he'd breached our walls," I said, keeping my voice neutral as I heard his footsteps approaching. "You could have wiped his memory and sent him back—but you chose to test him and admit him into our ranks. A dangerous slider who would face the eventual conviction of murder."

"He was not convicted at the time," Mitsue continued before I could protest. "He was, in fact, valuable until he was murdered himself—by Hawk's own initiate."

"Who, by his irresponsible behavior, pulled you from your world and family," I interjected as I rifled through the pages, "and severed you from any 'value' you could possibly have utilized in Raiden."

The footsteps slowed to a halt. I looked up at him and found affirmation in the bitterness behind his expression.

"It was all Icarus's fault," I finished bluntly. "And his blood alone won't quench your thirst."

Mitsue stood there for a moment, though seeming more contemplative than caught off guard. "You miss the point."

"But I am not inaccurate," I replied, maintaining my tone. "You blame her."

"And the blame would not be incorrectly placed," he said coldly. "However, we abide by a certain code of conduct, you and I, and according to that ancient standard, she is deserving of punishment." Mitsue paused, continuing around my desk as if to evade my sight line. "She made herself the 'Sunrise,'" he concluded in a formal tone. "Now she will face the consequences of her claims."

My heartbeat rattled against my rib cage like a prisoner with a will to escape. My gaze had yet to move from the place he had just been standing.

"If she is indeed the Sunrise of whom the prophecy speaks?" He grunted, pausing. "Then by all means, let her save herself."

Something inside me reached a boiling point. I pushed my chair back so violently it clattered to the floor. Before Mitsue could react, I grabbed him by the collar of his shirt and drove him forcefully back against the wall.

"If you so much as go near her—" I leaned into him, lowering my voice "—I promise you I will break every bone in your body."

Mitsue stared at me, an expression of subtle amusement on his face. "You stoop to threatening me like a child, Fin?" he asked quietly. "Really?"

A moment passed, then I withdrew my grip, jarring him again. My heart was beating in my head.

"An unfortunate stance," he continued. "Considering we are to work together now, you and I."

I opened my mouth to speak, but found nothing to say. Instead I took a step back.

"Which brings me back to the proposition from the assembling council, Fin." He straightened his shirt. "Though in the end, it is not so much a proposition as it is an order that must be obeyed."

He paused, watching my expression closely.

"I've been selected for the council that is to take on Hawk's trial, Fin." He stepped away from the wall. "And so have you."

CHAPTER SIX

Icarus

The sparks lifted from the flames, drifting up to contrast against the somber shades of twilight. I lay stretched out in the dew-licked grass with my fingers interlocked behind my head, gazing up.

The sky had let loose its burden to deluge the earth below. It had rained steadily until nightfall, then cleared by slow degrees. Fortunately, the forest was thick, and the canopy of leaves sheltered everything below, making finding dry wood a possibility.

I'd found some refuge beneath a large willow. Its branches and leaves flowed down to the forest floor. Beneath this curtain I'd found enough dry ground to attempt a fire.

It took hours to persuade a flame to spark from the friction of two sticks as I rubbed them together. I'd stripped off my clothes and hung them from a low branch, close to the flames. Though I'd settled as close to the fire as I could without burning myself, I still shivered uncontrollably as I watched the tiny patches of sky reaching through the murmuring canopy above me.

"Why can't I remember?" I asked the one distant star I could see. "This all has to mean something, but I can't remember how I got here."

Did I come here by choice? Or by force?

If by choice, then... why? What was my objective in coming here? Where did I come from? Did I come alone, or with others and then we were separated?

Why did I awaken in the riverbed, and why didn't I drown there?
"How is any of this remotely possible?"

It was easier to list the things I knew than the things I didn't. I knew that I was alive, freezing, and lost on a number of levels. The rest I couldn't explain. My head felt about as turbulent as the rapids had been. My thoughts were throwing me against the rocks, and no matter how hard I fought with them, I couldn't seem to break the surface.

What is even my name?

So basic, yet I couldn't answer even that.

The fire seemed to laugh, tossing bits of glistening gold up into the air as if to mock me.

Shivering, I folded my arms over my chest. I forced myself to think about something else—how the fractured sky stuck in the branches like debris.

The gathering darkness felt strange—as if night was somehow foreign. Like I hadn't experienced one in some time.

"Which makes *so much* sense," I muttered to myself sarcastically.

For a moment there was a gentle breeze. I closed my eyes and became suddenly aware of the sounds around me: the lulling symphony rising from the damp ground like dew—cricket songs punctuated by the gurgles of tree frogs, and the occasional lament of a mourning dove from somewhere close by. They were separate sounds at first as my hungry brain tried to identify each one, but gradually they blended themselves into one seamless song. Then the noise faded and my senses slowly numbed.

When I opened my eyes again, it was at the insistence of a voice.

"It isn't how I thought it would end." The words were quieter than the breeze had been. "But this is how it will end. This is what we trained for."

The voice was heavy, serious—like a dam holding back a raging river. Somehow the voice was more familiar to me than my own.

"This is where we jump, Icarus."

"Icarus?" my voice repeated.

"This is where we jump."

"But I don't understand."

My eyes flew open as a searing pain prickled up my right arm.

"*Ow*," I hissed, rolling immediately onto my opposing side. "What the—?"

Startled, I clapped my hand over the source of the sting. I couldn't really see in the lack of light, but I could guess from the sensation that I'd dozed off and rolled too close to the fire. I winced as I peeled back my fingers to glance down at my upper arm.

"Man, it's freezing."

I had only a few pieces of wood left from the pathetic amount I'd been able to gather. I placed them into the huddle of hot coals and settled into a seated position. I watched as the flames slowly rose from the dead and caught on to the shreds of bark.

"Icarus." The word came out over my lips again. "*Icarus*. That's so… familiar."

Before I could question it further, a sudden noise snatched my attention.

My eyes scanned the perimeter of the willow tree, where its leaves almost met the earth, darting back and forth. I felt the muscles in my back stiffen.

I waited, holding my breath. I listened for something above the insects, which by now had faded like white noise. The wood hissed.

Then a low rustling among the brush. Close.

I squinted, trying to detect what direction it was coming from. The left… but then the right. It was a confusion—spiriting from one side to the other. Each time I tried to pinpoint the source, it would emit from the opposite direction.

"What the…?"

I struggled to my feet, and as soon as I did, the movement became consistent. A darker patch materialized against the inky blackness beyond the boundaries of the willow's shelter, a barely distinguishable shadow. I couldn't make out the shape exactly, but there was no mistaking the sound: a long, low howl.

I stood there, frozen in every sense of the word, and listened. Why I wasn't terrified, I couldn't say, but I wasn't.

I strained to keep my eyes focused in the darkness on the place where I'd detected the shadow's presence. The fire crackled and I heard a soft swishing as leaves were pushed gently aside by a form. At first it was a gray smudge against a darker backdrop, but as it neared and the growing flames illuminated my surroundings once again, I found myself staring at something as white as snow.

A white wolf stood at the edge of the clearing.

I watched it, my heart in my mouth. It stepped up to the flame that separated us, halting there and staring at me through intelligent eyes in shades of icy blue.

I stared at it for a long moment. It licked its lips and then moved its eyes to the flame.

I started backward slightly as it threw back its head and let out another long, mournful cry. My heartbeat shook my rib cage. The wolf took a step back, refocusing on me in a way that seemed fiercer than before.

My brain was sending me signals that I should respond somehow—as if the creature expected a response. As if it wanted me to take some kind of action.

All at once, it retreated; bursting past the curtain of branches, it was gone.

I stepped cautiously away from the aura of heat radiating from the flame, having forgotten about the cold and the burn across my arm. I pulled my clothes down from the tree branch. Reaching the edge of my circle of protection, I slowly parted the branches and stepped out, pausing—listening.

A hundred yards ahead I caught a glimpse of the wolf on a mossy embankment. The starlight stained its coat a faded shade of lavender. Its fierce eyes locked with mine.

It gave another faded howl, then turned and darted away into the forest.

Taking a narrow breath, I followed.

CHAPTER SEVEN

Hawk

I'd never seen fire as bright as those trees. Pure gold couldn't hold its own against the colors that washed the ravine. I watched the wind make attempts to sabotage everything in my line of sight from where I stood at the platform's edge.

I'd forced Delta to let me out. I was tired of her constant supervision and weary of consuming strange liquids.

How was it possible? How could someone survive such a fall?

I turned over these questions in my mind as I stood there, hunched at the rail overlooking the drop. Fin's heated words played on repeat in my tired head.

"Are you afraid to believe he's alive because you don't know how to fix this? You'd rather accept that it's all meant to fall apart?"

"He is the most stubborn... pigheaded..." I sighed under my breath, pressing my eyelids shut for a moment. "Arrogant..."

All were true—but was he right? When it came down to it, opinions aside, was I actually just... afraid because I had no idea where to go from here? I could resent his correction as much as I wanted, but I couldn't hide from the fact that something inside me *knew* he was speaking the truth.

The season change, the chaos—yes, I did believe that it was because of what had happened to me and Icarus, but *was it* irreversible? Was I really dying, when I seemed to be improving with each passing day? Was Icarus actually dead, when everything inside me couldn't seem to come to terms with the idea that he was gone?

Though my words had been spoken in the heat of anger, I'd been sincere in what I had told Fin about entanglement. No one really understood how, or *why*, it even worked. Sensei had taught me the theory, and it aligned with our prophecy perfectly. It was the reason Icarus had been able to shift; cutting our hands and allowing our blood to mingle had temporarily bestowed on him a portion of my identity—the same phenomenon had happened between Raiden and me the day he'd made an attempt on my life. Any two students could do it. But only the Sunrise and the Sunset *intrinsically* shared blood, without having to beckon it to the surface with the blade of a knife. It explained why I could feel Icarus's pain and why he shared the nightmares of the attack on me a hundred years earlier.

Sensei had used hurricanes as examples to explain it to me. The spin and trajectory of one commanded the motion of the other. The distance that separated the two storms, the turbulence in between— it was all irrelevant. As soon as one had decided its course, the other had to follow suit, countering with an opposing spin, balancing out the other to create harmony.

It authenticated Fin's insistence that I would already be dead if Icarus had in fact met his end at the bottom of the ravine. It seemed to stack evidence in favor of his survival... and my own.

But if this were true, if I myself was what was actually fueling Icarus's survival, how was I going to find him? How was I going to bring him back? *How am I going to fix this?*

That was where my knowledge ended—I had no idea.

Everything inside me longed for Sensei's voice and the balm of his wisdom. But there was a rift between us, a river of black water, and I didn't know how to mend it.

"When I needed you most, you abandoned me," I said, gazing absently downward into the blazing colors. "I needed you at Icarus's trial and you didn't defend me... You let everyone believe I was a liar instead."

I hadn't mentioned it to Fin yet, but I was beginning to wonder what consequences I would face because of my declaration the night of Icarus's trial. It hadn't escaped my notice that I was already being treated differently than before. No one had come to see me aside from Fin, and I had a feeling Delta knew more about the attitude of the student body than she was letting on.

Everything inside me wanted to walk that familiar hallway and let myself into Sensei's room. I wanted to tell him that I was sorry, though I didn't know exactly what for. I just needed him. I was confused, and I didn't know where to turn—I needed guidance. I didn't know whether to trust Fin or trust myself: to trust that Icarus was alive and that I would live, or to give way to my headful of screaming doubt.

But I couldn't bring myself to do it. Even looking in the direction of the hallway that would lead me to him wrenched my insides and infected my thoughts.

Why wasn't he there? Why wasn't he there? Why wasn't he there?

If he really cared, and if I was really his chosen, wouldn't he have been there? Did he save me from one death only to deliver me to one of a different kind?

Instead, I stepped off the platform and started down the pathway. My footsteps were silenced by the thick blanket of golden pine needles. I pulled the cloak Delta had begrudgingly allowed me to borrow closer around my throat.

Students scurried along the walkways and rope bridges above me. The pods were alive with activity, as was the gathering platform below. It was no wonder that the training platform was so empty— everyone was either in the dorms or on the crowded platform where Icarus had been executed only a couple of weeks earlier.

Reaching back, I pulled the hood up over my head. The sun had begun to lower somewhat, and the late afternoon shadows lay heavy across the landscape, aiding in my camouflage.

As I drew nearer, it became obvious that a meeting was taking shape on the platform. I strained to see from where I had halted behind a group of trees.

I was able to identify only one figure as she separated herself from the rest and started for the path. Though I hadn't wished for any confrontations, I didn't shy away as she came up toward me.

"Mala," I greeted her when she was close enough. "A word?"

She didn't start when she saw me. Instead, she smiled. Delta had filled me in on the procedure Mala had undergone, and I could tell that she didn't recognize me.

"Yes?"

I feigned a shy, polite expression. "I'm sorry—you don't know me. I'm new here."

Her face brightened a little. "Ah. One of the new initiates?"

I nodded slightly.

"I am too," she said. "Or… in a way, that is. Mitsue said I was found and brought here."

My interest was piqued. "Mitsue?"

"My teacher."

"But I thought Fin was your teacher—he's the one who initiated you," I said, confused. "Delta said that Fin—"

"Then I'm afraid you're mistaken," she interrupted with a shrug. "That would be Mitsue."

I nodded slowly, processing this.

"Well, anyway." I cleared my throat. "I don't mean to hold you up. I just was curious as to what's going on down there." I jerked my head in the direction of the gathering platform. "Is there some sort of meeting taking place?"

She hesitated. "Well, sort of. They're assembling the council for the trial—I don't know much. I was only there to watch. Mitsue said it would be educational for me."

"Who's being tried?"

Her perfect white teeth found her bottom lip. "Mitsue told me not to say—not yet."

I had to hand it to my colleague. He had mastered the art of wrapping a student around his little finger.

"You don't need to name names, then." I shot a quick glance around us as I stepped closer. "I wouldn't want to get you into trouble. But perhaps you could just tell me what *sort* of case it is? Surely that's not too revealing."

She studied me for a moment, uncertainty in her brown eyes. "Alright," she said finally. "Like I said, I don't know much… They don't really talk about the details until the actual thing."

"But?"

"But they said something about blasphemy," she admitted. "Someone has made some false claims about being the 'Sunrise' that the prophecy speaks of. I haven't even read it myself, so I don't have an opinion, really."

"Then read it," I said bluntly, ignoring the sinking feeling that was settling into the pit of my stomach. "Don't make the same mistake I made with…" I stopped before I gave myself away. His name haunted my thoughts. I changed tack. "So they didn't say who this blasphemer was?" I asked, though I hardly needed confirmation. "Or when it's to be held?"

"They did say," she replied uncomfortably. "She's a well-known teacher among us. As to the date…" She trailed off, gesturing down in the direction of the small gathering. "I believe that's what they're deciding now."

I said nothing in response. My mind was reeling.

Mala shivered, rubbing her hands over the length of her arms. "It's freezing out here. Is it always this cold?"

It took a moment for her question to penetrate the mire of my thoughts. "No," I said. "Not always."

She cleared her throat uncomfortably. "I should really be getting back."

"One more thing." I stopped her before she could resume her brisk walk. "Do you know who's been appointed yet? For the council that will be reviewing the case?"

"I do, but I'm afraid I'm not the best with names." She let out a nervous laugh, stroking her forehead. "But you mentioned one of them a moment ago—"

"Mitsue?"

"No," she replied, vaguely irritated. "He's on the council, yes, but his name I would obviously recall."

I was quiet for a moment as she thought.

"Fin," she pronounced finally. "He was the one I was thinking of. You mentioned him, yes?"

Words escaped me. After an uncomfortably long pause, I forced myself to reply. "He is one of the chosen?" I felt a knot tighten in my chest as I turned to glance down again at the platform, at the indistinguishable agglomeration of bodies. "Are you certain you heard correctly?" I asked, though the words didn't sound like my own.

"From what I gathered, yes."

I pressed my eyes closed.

Fin?

Mala cleared her throat. "Forgive me, but do you know him?"

The voices swelling from below mixed with the wind and vanished momentarily from earshot. I turned back to face Mala and found her waiting for my response with skeptical curiosity.

"No," I said, forcing my feet forward, back up the walkway. "Not at all."

I barely comprehended the walk back to the dormitories. I spoke to no one when I entered the group dorm, and I didn't acknowledge anyone who spoke to me.

Mala's smooth, neutral voice rang in my ears like a siren.

Fin? Fin is on the council that will conduct my trial? And he didn't even tell me?

"Delta," I said, unbuttoning the borrowed cloak as I entered my cell, "have you seen Fin lately?"

She was standing off to the side of the room, in front of the small apothecary table, where she was crushing herbs. Her red hair was a wild tangle as her gaze bolted up.

"No. Why?" she asked, her voice carrying that irritating tone of command masked by feigned concern. "Do you not feel well?"

Tugging off the cloak, I laid it over the back of a nearby chair. The one Fin usually used.

"I'm fine," I said. "I didn't know if he'd come while I was out."

"And if he had, it'd serve you right." The grinding of stone against stone resumed. "You shouldn't be going out yet. You should be in bed."

I ignored her tone, pausing beside my bed. "Can I ask you something?"

"By all means."

"How long have you known of my impending trial, and who told you?"

Abruptly her motions stopped. "I see he's broken it to you, at last."

She hadn't turned to face me. I stared at the chaos of red.

"No, he has not. But he told *you*?" I tried to push the incredulity out of my voice. "Fin told *you* about *my* trial—and he didn't tell me?"

"Fin didn't want to worry you," she said, turning finally. "It's been rumored for a good while now, and Fin didn't want to burden you with it when you were sick, and nothing was certain anyway."

"Yet he felt the need to burden *you* with it." I still hadn't broken my stare. "It was obviously solid enough information for *your* ears."

"Hawk, would you calm yourself? I only wanted to help him—he knows that."

"Does he?" The words came in a feigned burst of laughter. "Does he really?"

She sensed my bitterness, and her expression hardened. "Who do you think has been caring for you all this time, Hawk?" she asked. "When no one has wanted to touch you with a ten-foot pole?"

She gave me no chance to reply.

"*Fin and I.*" She stepped away from the table. "Fin has taken a great risk in doing what he has done for you, and as his friend, I have tried to support him—I've been the only one here to do so, in fact. So I'm sorry if it comes as a shock to you that he would inform me of the possibility of a trial."

I looked at her, then shook my head. "No. It doesn't shock me."

A pause slipped in. The fire crackled in the hearth, beginning to set the room aglow as the sun lowered.

"Did he…" I hesitated on the words. "Did he tell you that he was selected for the council?"

Delta didn't respond at first, but then gave a slow nod. "He did."

"How long has he known?"

"As to that, I really couldn't say."

My gaze didn't move from hers for a moment. I tried to decipher the look in her cold green eyes but found it next to impossible.

"Why didn't you tell me?" I asked, swallowing past the tightness in my throat. "I've been well enough these past few days. It's *my* trial—why on earth didn't you say something?"

"He asked me not to," Delta replied. "I thought it best for him to tell you in his own time."

"I see," I said. "So this was something you both discussed and conspired about."

Delta's expression stiffened, but before her lips could part in retort, a new voice cut in.

A voice with a familiar Irish accent.

"Who's conspiring?"

I'd forgotten to shut the door completely on my way in. It hung there, half open on its hinges—but leaving a gap wide enough to frame the familiar, rigid figure tucked snugly into a wool overcoat. I wanted to turn away as soon as he stepped inside, but I forced myself to stay where I was.

"No one's conspiring," Delta firmly replied. "I was merely discussing with Hawk the fact that—"

"We were discussing my trial, Fin." I cut her off, smiling tersely. "But of course, you know all about that."

A dead silence fell across the small room. No one spoke.

Fin's mouth opened slightly, but he said nothing. His green eyes locked with mine as he stood there, still on the threshold.

"Fin." Delta finally broke the silence. "I tried to explain—"

"Would you give us a moment, please, Delta?" he broke in before she could finish. He stepped in all the way.

For a moment Delta seemed slightly taken aback; then reluctantly she slipped past him. Fin reached back and closed the door after her. His eyes stayed locked with mine.

"I have nothing to say to you, Fin," I said bluntly when the sound of her footsteps had faded.

"Hawk, please, hear me out—"

"No, *you* hear me out!" I exploded, stepping closer. "I'm about to face trial on the charge of making false claims, and you didn't even tell me? When you've known all this time?"

"Nothing was certain—"

"Really?" It was hardly a question. "Yet you've been chosen for the council? I saw the assembly on the gathering platform."

"I didn't know until today! How was I to tell you about something I didn't even know myself?"

"Then how did *she* know?"

"I told Delta *nothing* of my involvement," he said with emphasis. "She knew only that there were rumors. I've said nothing to anyone."

The tightness in my chest increased as I searched for honesty in his eyes.

"How could you?" My voice came out quiet, small. "How on earth could you, of all people, get involved when you know that everything I said at Icarus's trial was true?"

Fin pulled in a breath as if the words pained him. "Do you think I want to?"

"You didn't refuse, did you?"

His gaze snapped back to mine. "If you think I didn't refuse the task—if you think I didn't try, in every way imaginable, to convince the council to drop the case—then you don't know me at all."

I felt completely void of words. I was empty.

Fin's jaw contracted as he swallowed and stepped closer. "I would sooner face death than sit on this council, Hawk, and I intend to refuse it, come what may."

"Don't say that," I said, shaking my head as I attempted to clear my thoughts. "Don't joke about something this serious."

A pained laugh escaped him. "Joke? Is that what I am to you, Hawk?"

The heaviness of his tone drew my gaze up to meet his.

"You take everything I say so lightly." His voice was a whisper when he spoke again, hurt lingering in his eyes. "Like you don't even realize how much it kills me to even talk about this—to see you doubt me at every turn in ways that I would never dream of doubting you."

"I didn't say I doubted you."

He studied my face silently for a moment, standing closer than I realized.

"No," he agreed quietly, nodding. "Perhaps not with words."

The fire had all but died, leaving us in almost complete quiet for a moment that passed in an eternity.

"I cannot sit in a place of judgment over you, Hawk." Fin finally broke the tension between us, taking a step back. "Not when I know who you really are—when I believe in you like I do."

"It was unfair of me to suggest that you should do anything but accept the position," I said. "Of course you have to. You have no choice—"

"I have every choice." His tone was firm. "Do you think I care about the code at a time like this? Have I ever held that in higher esteem than I hold you?"

"Don't say that."

"Why?" he asked bluntly, giving a slight shrug. "Because you love Icarus?"

I shook my head. *If only it were that simple.*

"Because I love no one," I replied. "Not even myself."

There was a silence; then Fin stepped closer.

"Hawk, I swear to you I told no one," he said softly. "I asked Delta not to tell you only because it was hearsay at the time—I wanted to wait until I had facts to bring it up with you."

"I know," I said. "I believe you. But you still realize you have no choice but to do as the council says, Fin. We're already in enough turmoil as it is, and if you refuse, they'll—"

"They'll what?" he interjected tersely. "Send me off the cliff too? I don't *care*, Hawk."

"Yes, but I do!"

Fin opened his mouth to retort, but I stepped closer before he could.

"If the worst comes, Fin," I said, quieting my voice, "and it may—"

"Don't say that."

"I need you," I said. "*They'll* need you."

His brow was weighted with my words, the creases etched with shadows the dusk had cast.

"If you get yourself killed, I'll never forgive you," I said, giving him a weak smile. "You have to do this."

For a long moment we stood there; then he drew a deeper breath. "On one condition."

I raised an eyebrow, refocusing.

"If you actually want to bring him back alive, you can't go into this without a plan." He glanced past my shoulder to the small dorm window overlooking the ravine. "I won't let you."

I followed his gaze to the glass. The sun had set now. The golden light had faded from the windows and given way to the dull purples and blues that invaded the room in its stead.

I looked back to his eyes. "What do you have in mind?"

February 1912

On the cold nights, I'd sit on the floor by the stove in the kitchen and watch Charlotte churn the butter or peel the potatoes. I couldn't help her; they'd only double her workload if I did. They wanted her fingers to look the way they did—with broken nails and worn to the bone. So instead I watched her.

I studied her face, her cheekbones, her fingertips, her eyes as they flashed with something she never let anyone else see. I watched the way she looked at things; I noticed the way she breathed, when and how she would brush her hair aside, how she would stand on occasion to stretch. I studied her with an open book on my knees. And I drew what I saw.

The fire would snap, and my pen would scratch across the yellowed pages of the old black sketchbook I had found. Usually she would ignore me. Usually she wouldn't speak, because, despite what everyone thought, Charlotte didn't live here. Charlotte lived in her mind, a place where no one else could go—not even me. I stood outside with the others, peering through the windows. I drew what I imagined the inside to look like.

She'd look up sometimes and ask if she could see what I was drawing. I'd shake my head. When it's finished, I would say. Then, under my breath, When we're finished.

CHAPTER EIGHT

Icarus

I followed the white wolf until I saw only vague glimpses of it among the trees in the distance. At first it was only a few yards ahead, and then, without seeming to have picked up its pace, it was hundreds.

Did I slow down? I couldn't tell.

I was exhausted, but I'd tried my best to follow it. My arms and legs felt more and more like lead as I climbed slick, mossy embankments, ducked under low tree limbs and crossed narrow, gurgling streams.

The night had worn away to dawn, and dawn to morning. Warm yellow rays descended through the cracks in the leafy canopy above, speckling the ground below with patches of light. The temperature gradually rose, and the humidity in the air hung like a translucent veil among the trees.

Every now and then I stopped, listening carefully for the sound of movement in the brush or the lonely echo of a howl far ahead. Eventually even these noises faded and vanished.

Where the hell did it go?

I was still trying to get my head around why it hadn't attacked me and instead had acted as if I should follow. Things like this didn't just happen—but then how could I know for sure? I had almost no recollection of what was normal.

I don't even know where I am or how I got here—or who I am.

I was coming to the conclusion that there was no way for me to find answers to my questions. I was alone and relying only on a hope that I would eventually remember and that I was suffering from some kind of temporary memory loss—but how did I *know* I was suffering from memory loss? If I couldn't remember anything, I wouldn't be able to recall whether something had happened to me to cause me to lose my memory. What if it wasn't memory loss? What if I wasn't forgetting anything at all, and this was just how things were? What if this seemingly delusional state I was in was actually reality?

But wouldn't it all seem more familiar? Why was it that this world felt foreign—and the echoes in my head so familiar? Which led me to an even more unnerving question: *Which one is real?* Which was to be trusted? And if one was real and the other an illusion, how would I be able to make the distinction?

And beyond that—how could I trust *myself* to make a distinction when I had no basis of what *was* real to begin with?

I was lost in every sense of the word—that was all I knew for sure. My only company was this ravaging cycle of thought. It rewound and replayed in my head until I started to feel sick to my stomach.

The more I thought, the more everything around me seemed to decay.

But then there was that voice. It was so familiar. The words she had spoken were like ones I'd heard a thousand times before in my head, but I didn't know where.

Who is she?

A rustling from the brush to my left yanked me from my thoughts, stopping me in my tracks. For the first time in what felt like a while, I took in my surroundings. Up until then, I'd been trekking, preoccupied, through lush forest. Now I'd reached a clearing, and I found myself standing in the middle of what looked like an ashy caldron.

All around me were walking palms burned to mere skeletal frameworks, like a community of teepees that had been abandoned by their dwellers. Larger trees had been stripped of their foliage and bark, and the soft carpet of moss beneath me had been replaced by a layer of flocculent ash that sprang into the air like dust with each of my footfalls.

Startled, I did a double take, unsure of how the landscape could have changed so rapidly without my noticing. I coughed into my elbow as the thick scent of dead fire pushed its way into my lungs. Glancing back in the direction I'd come, I tried to determine where the living forest had ended, but couldn't find the place. In every direction, the burnt forest seemed to stretch on.

Confused, I bent down to touch the ground. The ashes weren't warm.

I studied my fingertips for a moment, lost in a confusion of my own thoughts. I made slow, circular patterns over the pads of my fingers, watching as the particles sifted softly back to the earth.

The sound of heavy breathing caught my attention. When I lifted my eyes, they were met by another pair.

Startled, I fell backward.

A wolf again stood before me, only several feet away. This one was black with eyes like two flames captured in a skull, staring out at me with the same, unsettling resolve that the white wolf had.

Its coat was thick, but it hardly made up for the thin, almost starved-looking frame hidden beneath this façade.

My heart rose into my mouth as I squirmed backward, stirring up the ash beneath me. There was about seven feet between us, and my instincts told me to run, but my muscles instantly seized.

One heartbeat, then a second.

A low growl escaped its throat, its eyes remaining on mine. Out of the corner of my eye, I saw a black blur among the trees and then to my right another. And then another, until suddenly I could identify that there were at least four wolves present in the wasteland around me. Distant howls rang through the air.

I was still shimmying backward instinctually as the first one continued its approach, and then I scrambled to my feet and made a dash for it—or tried to.

I felt its teeth graze across my ankle, tearing my voice away from me as I began to fall again. My vision was an ashy blur; then suddenly there was a chaos of feathers and a long, shrill cry.

I gasped involuntarily, shielding my face.

Suddenly I felt moss against my skin. The scent of smoke was gone. I opened my eyes, letting my hands fall away. The wolves and the feathers had vanished.

Above me was a familiar willow canopy doused in yellow morning sunlight, and beside me was a dying fire.

I was back at camp.

I pushed myself up into a seated position, frantically scanning my surroundings for any signs of the wolves, but there was none.

Had I even left to follow the white wolf? Had it just… been a dream? Was all of it a dream?

I glanced down at my arm and saw that the burn mark was still there.

Right—I rolled too close to the fire in my sleep, I remembered. But suddenly that wasn't the only thing I remembered.

My heart was still racing as my brain retrieved the vision, whether real or just a dream, of ash and terror—then feathers.

Hawk.

CHAPTER NINE

Fin

No one had ever been executed, not until the incident with Icarus. But that had been a special case: he'd killed someone. Hawk had only attested to being someone whom no one believed she actually was. Even if she was found guilty, there was no way she would face execution.

Our code of conduct was very straightforward when it came to correcting misbehavior within our ranks. Students had been exiled in the past—"fallen sliders" who had neglected the code to the point of having to be sent back to their natural worlds with cleansed minds—but things had changed since the portal had been indefinitely sealed. Exile was no longer a possibility.

I knew this left the council with only one alternative to resort to.

Several days passed, and the day of Hawk's trial finally dawned. The gathering platform was alive with activity. The council was beginning to assemble at a long rectangular table.

A bluish flame flourished out from the center of the platform, and a conduit of fire skirted its edge, nearly translucent in the sun's harsh illumination. A large blue circle had been drawn, and students clad in warm woolen clothes were slowly beginning to take their seats. A blanket of thick frost had risen from the ground overnight to coat every blade of grass and fallen leaf.

I stood at a distance, waiting until I knew I had to make my entrance. It was the last thing I wanted to do, but I forced myself to remember the plan Hawk and I had made several days before.

Just relax, I coached myself. *Don't doubt.*

But as I traversed the short stretch in front of me and mounted the steps to the platform, my heart was pounding.

This was *really happening.* By the expressions on the faces of my fellow council members, I could tell I had my work cut out for me.

Mitsue was seated at the farthest end of the table, poring over a stack of notes he'd apparently compiled. His hair was in a long braid. The one other male student and three female students who made up the rest of the council were either already seated or standing close to the table, locked in quiet conversations. The theme continued in the hushed murmur that arose from the audience of sliders around us.

I swallowed back the tension in my throat as I attempted to ignore the general feeling of condescension in the atmosphere. My eyes caught those of Delta, who was seated close to the front row. Her lips were pressed into a small encouraging smile that couldn't hide the depth of her concern. I returned it, lifting a hand in a halfhearted wave before making my way to the table.

Mala had approached Mitsue in the meantime, leaning in to whisper something into his ear. She straightened up as soon as my presence was noted, her long coffee-colored hair draping over one shoulder.

Mitsue glanced up. "Ah, Fin. Have a seat."

I took the one directly next to him, though my attention didn't deviate from his new student.

"Mala, how are you?" I asked, though it was obvious she didn't recognize me. "I haven't seen you in a while."

She was dressed in a black skin suit layered with a thick wool coat, and tall boots of matching color. Her soft brown eyes gave me a quick once-over.

"I-I'm sorry," she stuttered, though she sounded more skeptical than apologetic. "Have we met?"

"No, you haven't exactly." Mitsue decided for her before I could answer. "Mala, this is Fin. Remember I mentioned there were other session leaders? He's one of them."

Mala nodded thoughtfully. "I see. Well, hello, Fin."

"I see Mitsue has been filling you in," I commented. The sharpness in my words was aimed at my colleague. "Are you settling back into sessions?"

"Not yet." Mala's face went pink. "Mitsue doesn't think I'm ready yet. But I said—"

"Soon," he interjected, clearing his throat. "You must have patience. Now why don't you go find a seat—we'll be starting shortly."

I watched Mala's expression falter for a moment, but then she obediently did as she was told, leaving us to take a seat among the rest of the crowd.

Mitsue smoothly returned to his paperwork.

"So…" I said after a moment. "You've been keeping Mala from sessions."

"As I said," he replied, not looking up, "she's not ready."

"Everyone knows she's a fully capable slider, Mitsue," I said. "She's proven her abilities."

"Proven her abilities in a completely different state of mind, you mean," Mitsue corrected me. "She's at a very delicate stage right now. I think it's for the best."

"And did you consult anyone on this decision?"

He turned to the next page. "Do I need to? I'm her teacher."

"Teacher or dictator?"

He looked up now. "Are we going to be professional about this or not?"

I didn't answer. I straightened in my seat as Gaia approached to begin placing metal cups of lavender water at each of our places. We acknowledged each other politely.

"I would advise you to watch your step, Fin," he said when she had passed. "Mala should be a gentle reminder, in fact."

"A reminder of what?"

"Of what could…" He seemed to turn the thought in his mind. "Potentially happen."

I looked at him, pretending to be caught off guard. "To Hawk?"

"The verdict is inevitable."

I studied him for a moment before turning to face forward. "I don't know that *inevitable* is a very good word at a time like this."

"I disagree," Mitsue corrected me. "It's a perfect word."

The sun was considerably higher in the cloudless sky now, washing the Dimension in shades of warm yellow. A large contrast from the darkness that had overpowered the sky only several days before.

One of the female students made a motion for everyone to sit, and the audience settled onto the platform.

The student beside me, a girl named Azalea, with a strawberry blond pixie haircut and freckles, picked up one of the papers in front of her, clearing her throat.

"Everyone—silence, please," she said. "Hawk, you may come forward."

Those were the words I'd been waiting for—dreading.

Hawk was still dressed in all black, though this time wearing a long-sleeved shirt that covered the markings on her arms; the ringlet around her finger was the only one that was visible. She had tamed her wild torrents of hair back into a tight bun.

She was expressionless. Her dark, familiar eyes were unreadable.

"Do we have your word that, according to the dictates of the code, any and all information you provide us with will be strictly factual?" Azalea recited the formality.

Hawk gave a single nod. "You have my word."

Azalea looked past me to Mitsue, who pushed back his chair to rise.

"Hawk, you've been accused of attesting to a false identity—blasphemy, according to our code of conduct," he explained formally. "At Icarus's trial you were quoted confirming the fact that you are the 'Sunrise' anomaly our prophecy has foretold—in fact, that you and Icarus are both the patriarchs of our Dimension."

I took the first opportunity to interject. "May I request that you read the actual statements?"

Mitsue looked irritated by the question, but proceeded to snatch the appropriate page from his notations anyway. He turned back to Hawk.

"You were quoted saying, 'I have no illness other than the sickness my half-soul has had to endure in its chains for the past century. No, my judgment has not been clouded,'" Mitsue read aloud. "You alluded to, and then later confirmed, the fact that you believed Icarus to be the other half of your soul—making him the 'Sunset' anomaly of which the prophecy speaks."

Though my asking him to go over Hawk's statements was part of the plan to remind everyone of her 'guilt,' it still took me back to that night. Listening to her voice speak those same words; watching her go up in flames.

"You stated that Raiden had 'baited you with Icarus in order to see if he was accurate in his assumptions of your identity,'" Mitsue continued quoting. "When he realized that they were, you said, based on your resulting course of action that gravitated toward Icarus, he then used you to lure Icarus back to the gathering platform in order to fulfill what the prophecy required."

Whispers rose around us.

"I went on to ask what you were implying by that," Mitsue continued. "To which you merely replied, 'I think you know.'"

I turned to Hawk, but she said nothing.

"Do you deny any of these statements, Hawk?" Mitsue asked, gesturing toward the pages stacked neatly in front of him. "Or do you wish to clarify what you meant by them?"

"I do not," Hawk replied bluntly.

A brief silence fell; then Mitsue gestured in the direction of Azalea.

"Since you've chosen not to dispute these statements," she began, "we feel it isn't necessary to bring forth a myriad of witnesses to testify against you."

Hawk looked at her for a moment. "Good. Because I take full responsibility for everything I said that night."

A slight murmur arose from the students seated around us. I sighed, loud enough to be heard, stroking my forehead with my fingertips. Mitsue took note.

"All that remains, then, is to determine whether your statements are true or false, Hawk," Azalea continued. "As we have already reviewed, during your questioning at Icarus's trial, you first alluded to and then confirmed that you believe and declare yourself to be the manifestation of our ancient prophecy. The Sunrise."

Hawk gave one affirmative nod.

"However," she went on, "Icarus is now dead, making this statement an untruth. We all know that whoever the patriarchs are, they are inseparably entangled. And if you and Icarus were the upholders of our Dimension, you would have died also, Hawk, when Icarus was put to death."

"Correct."

"And so you've been caught in a sort of..." Mitsue interjected, then paused, seeming to consider how to phrase it. "Disillusioned lie?"

I saw Hawk's jaw tense.

"It was neither disillusioned nor a lie," she replied, her voice steel. "I spoke only what I know to be true. I was the first slider; I know and believe the prophecy in its entirety, and I can come to no other conclusion."

"We don't bring your rank into question, Hawk," the female student seated beside Azalea commented. "But if what you are saying was true, would Sensei not be here to defend your case? Would he not have defended it at Icarus's trial?"

Hawk made no response to either question. She stood there, head bowed slightly and her gaze on the floor.

"Hawk." Azalea spoke up after a pause. "I would like to make it clear that we are not unsympathetic to your cause. Icarus's and Raiden's deaths brought much darkness into the Dimension, and you were, in many ways, at the heart of that darkness. You've endured much over these past weeks, and I think I speak on behalf of the council when I say that I feel for you."

Hawk said nothing.

"Our goal is not to bring more destruction," she continued, "but justice and peace. Our wish is not to condemn you, but to present you with an opportunity."

Hawk's eyes shifted back up, meeting mine for the first time.

"An opportunity?" Hawk asked, feigning ignorance. "An opportunity for what?"

Azalea hesitated for a split second. "To recant."

"Recant?" Hawk repeated, as if the word were bitter across her tongue. "Which statement?"

"All," Mitsue interjected firmly. "Your statements about yourself, your identity, and Icarus's. Do you regret any of it?"

"None."

"You take nothing back?"

Hawk shook her head firmly.

Azalea cleared her throat uncomfortably. "Then... I can't imagine there's need for further questioning if you're already pleading guilty."

"I'm not pleading guilty," Hawk said icily. "I'm guilty of nothing—I will recant *nothing*."

"Yet you have no logical explanation to back up anything you've told us." Mitsue leaned forward, folding his hands on the table. "You have no proof whatsoever."

"I have only my word."

"If your word was true, wouldn't Sensei be here to affirm it?" Mitsue interjected irritably, reiterating what Azalea had asked earlier. "I think it's clear that the prophecy states the split souls will be here to lead us, and that neither of them may die—that they are so connected, in fact, that if one is killed, the other will instantaneously die," he went on. "And as we've already explored, if this was the case, you would be dead."

I saw Hawk's gaze harden. I decided to cut in. "I suggest the council take a brief adjournment to discuss," I said. "It is impossible for us to proceed without further analysis."

"I disagree," Mitsue replied before anyone else could. "I don't see why there's need for further discussion when Hawk has already condemned herself—though it seems she already did so at Icarus's trial."

"I believe Icarus's trial is another subject entirely, Mitsue," I corrected him. "This is a very separate event."

Mitsue's gaze, until then, had been locked into Hawk's. Now he turned and looked at me. "Is it, though? When we know how involved Icarus and Hawk—and Raiden, for that matter—were with each other."

I raised an eyebrow slightly at the mention of his late student, but Mitsue hurriedly continued before I could inquire.

"In any case," he said, "I refer to Hawk's statements."

I nodded slowly, studying him.

"We understand, Mitsue. Thank you." Azalea spoke up. "But I think Fin is right. We should at least take a short break and talk, just us, before we come to any final decision."

I was surprised that she had sided with me, and apparently Mitsue was too. The expression he wore was anything but pleased.

The student at the opposite end of the table announced the adjournment, and we filed off the platform as the uproar of chatter from the audience quickly resumed.

I glanced over my shoulder just in time to meet Hawk's gaze as she was escorted away for the time being. I tried to ignore the sensations that bit into my heart.

Azalea sidled up beside me as we descended the steps. "You can't win this one, Fin," she said out of the side of her mouth. "Believe me."

I wasn't sure how to respond, so I didn't.

"I know it's difficult for you, but there's too much evidence against her."

Mitsue was just in front of us, his long black braid trailing down his spine. I could sense his awareness of our every word.

"You don't understand," I told her. "As you said, we've endured so much death already—I just can't... I can't let her go through that. Not after everything that's happened."

We reached the pathway leading up to the training platform, where we slowed to a halt, now far enough away from the gathering platform so as not to be overheard.

"Are you suggesting that we would put her to death, Fin?" Azalea asked, sounding surprised. "I don't think that's in the cards, do you?"

I shook my head slowly, observing Mitsue's whereabouts out of the corner of my eye.

"If only that were the case," I said, lowering my voice. "I just hope she gets a lighter sentence—like Mala."

"Mala?"

I nodded. "The council's ruling was to reset her memory. Mitsue alluded earlier that this may be the case with Hawk as well, and I hope to God he wasn't saying that in jest."

"Why would he joke about such a thing?"

I shrugged. "I just hope it's a viable option... though there's always a chance that her subconscious is too strong for every memory to be wiped away."

Azalea seemed unconvinced, but I could tell she was thinking about it.

"I hadn't even considered that," she admitted after a moment. "Blasphemy *is* a pretty big offense. I think it's... it's something that can't be taken too lightly."

I looked around us. The rest of the council was clustered in various small groups, obviously in deep discussion. Mitsue, being closest to Azalea and me, took the opportunity to step into our conversation.

"What shouldn't be taken too lightly?" he asked, though I could tell he had overheard the conversation in its entirety.

I shot a glance in his direction, as if caught off guard. Then I stepped back.

"Nothing," I said, bowing out of the conversation. "Nothing at all."

I let him think I was nervous. I acted on edge and left my colleague to undoubtedly spill everything I'd just told her to my rival.

I could tell, even from a distance, that my plan was working. I stood several yards away, tuning in to no particular conversation but picking up on the general theme of them all. Mitsue had already worked on them. Bitterness was on everyone's tongue.

If Hawk maintained her rebellious stance, the rest of the trial would go without a hitch. All the right ingredients were there: Mitsue was breathing revenge, and he was poisoning everyone else with it. My feigned desire for Hawk's sentence to be lightened and her own relentless attitude were creating a perfect storm. It would only entice Mitsue to do just the opposite. He wanted to see me suffer.

Instead of joining any of the discussions, I climbed the rest of the pathway to the training platform. I still had a little time to kill, and I was eager to get away from everyone.

Despite the frost, the sunlight was warm as it filtered down through the bare tree arms. I breathed deep, letting the crisp air sting my lungs as I attempted to clear my aching head.

I had no doubt that Mitsue resented Hawk for dividing him from his family and his student. Something in my gut told me that Mitsue had expected to gain something from Raiden, though what I had no idea.

My thoughts drifted to my conversation with Hawk only a few days earlier as I trekked up the steep incline.

"So you think Mitsue would snap if I just push it a little further?" she had asked me. "What about the rest of the council?"

"They look up to him, especially after all of this," I had replied. "He's been a strong figure lately, and I think everyone admires him for his losses and how well he's handled it."

"You've lost just as much—if not more."

"But this isn't about me," I'd interjected, not wanting to talk about it. "If you stay strong, if you intimidate them and continue to give them reason to search for a way to punish you, they'll find a harsher way to do so. If I continue to beg for a lighter sentence for you, they'll do just the opposite."

She raised a thin, dark eyebrow. "Which means the drop?"

I nodded. "Which means you'll still have your mind intact. You'll still remember who you are—which is what we need most right now. That's our only hope of ever finding Icarus—we need your memory intact."

When I stepped up on the sheltered training platform, a wave of nostalgia came over me.

This was where Hawk had trained me—had taught me how to hone and control my powers back when I was still afraid and running from myself. And now, from that same vantage point, I could see my teacher's trial unfolding, her life and freedom hanging in the balance.

How far we have come.

I watched my colleagues below, fragments of a council focused more on what others would think of them than that justice would prevail. To my right, I could catch a glimpse of Sensei's apartment window beyond the training platform, and the faint lights emanating from within.

Why isn't he down there? Why isn't he defending her?

Questions plagued my mind until it hurt, but I couldn't allow myself the time to dwell. I leaned on the railing and gathered my thoughts until it was apparent that the council was ready to resume. Then I forced myself back down the pathway.

My heart was racing against my will by the time I reached the gathering again. I was the last one to be seated, just as Hawk was being ushered into the circle once more.

Azalea rose from her seat with a small piece of paper. "Hawk, come forward."

Hawk didn't resist as she stepped up to the white line that had been drawn across the floorboards.

"After having considered your case carefully," she began hesitantly, "I regret to inform you that you've been found guilty— by your own confession and by an overwhelming amount of evidence against you."

There was an instantaneous uproar. What Azalea said next was almost inaudible, but seated next to her, I heard every word.

"After discussing the matter in depth," she went on, raising her voice above the low roar, "it's been brought to our attention that, for something of this magnitude, we cannot risk a memory reset not taking full effect."

I kept a steady gaze on Hawk, watching her expression closely. My palms were beginning to sweat.

"With exile unfortunately being an unviable option—" she paused, paper still in her hands "—we come to no other conclusion than that the only way we can protect ourselves is to weed out anything that stands against our mission or tries to misguide it, especially in these uncertain times."

I could feel Mitsue's intent eyes to my left.

"Hawk, by your word and by the evidence that has been brought against you, you have been found guilty of blasphemy." Azalea spoke in a tone of finality, setting down the paper. "With the arrival of the coming dawn, you will be executed."

A stunned silence fell.

Hawk bowed her head respectfully, and I felt a tidal wave of relief crash down over me. Though the rush of noise around me only increased, it seemed to fade out of my plane of thought, leaving only the heaviness of my breathing.

The chairs were pushed back; bodies rose. The audience, though angrily divided, slowly began to dissipate. Hawk's eyes met mine for a solitary moment before she was seized by the wrists and led away.

I lingered a moment longer before I slowly rose and slid my chair neatly back into its place.

For everyone else, this was the end.

For us, it was only just the beginning.

CHAPTER TEN

Hawk

The day faded away beyond the window, but the voices in my head didn't.

They thought I was a liar. They thought I was a blasphemer—worthy of the same kind of "death" my other half had been condemned to, though they had no idea this was actually to my advantage—and theirs. Because my fall wouldn't bring death, but life. At least that was what Fin and I were placing our hope in, when we'd sat in my room days before and discussed how we would "hijack" the trial—manipulating the council into giving me a harsher sentence and giving me permission, in a sense, to go find Icarus.

It had worked—in fact, it had all gone without a hitch, though it had been more difficult than I had anticipated: playing into their hands, knowing what would unfold if I did. I didn't truly believe I would die, though a doubtful voice still gnawed at the back of my mind.

Throughout the trial, I could see it was just as hard for Fin. And somehow that gave me the strength I needed to keep going.

After my sentence was passed, I was led by a guard back to the dormitory pod where Icarus had been kept the night before his execution. The sentry, a young male student, asked if I had any requests.

I had.

Sensei. More than anything, he was what I wanted—what I

needed in that moment, which felt like my darkest hour.

But when I began to think about Icarus's trial, and how Sensei hadn't been there, and how he had been absent from my own trial, I could only reply, "No."

I sat on my bed and watched the sun set in seclusion, dosing the ravine in bright shades of orange. The temperatures were rising as my strength and determination grew.

What will happen to the Dimension if I die? What will happen to all of them—my people?

What will happen to Icarus?

I pressed my eyelids closed and locked the thoughts out of my head.

"I've made my decision," I coached myself under my breath. "Now's not the time to question it."

But waiting was getting to me. I kept thinking about Icarus's execution and how ceremonious and drawn out it had been. Could I bear to undergo that all over again?

No. I'd already fulfilled my loyalty to my people by allowing them to try, condemn, and humiliate me. I'd endured all of their punishment. I might have submitted to the code, but I would not submit to more torment than I knew I could endure.

I got up and crept quietly to the small window, carefully removing the glass. A soft, cool breeze pressed into the room. It was far too small for a human to fit through, even someone my size. But I finally felt strong enough to shift—and in my alternate form it was like an open door.

Still overwhelmed by the heat that had overtaken me from my core to melt my skin away into feathers, I freed myself into the soft evening air and lifted into the updraft.

Suddenly I was far above the dormitories, gazing down into a bed of soft, hazy precipitation freckled with woven pods that softly swayed with the gentle movements of the breeze. Everything was put into perspective from up here. All of our rules and frantic pursuits of justice—they all seemed so small from this height.

I didn't want to wait for the ceremony; I just wanted to jump. But there was someone I needed to talk to first. Someone I couldn't possibly leave without seeing—just once more. And with his sleeping habits, I knew exactly where I would find him.

As I focused on the training platform, I noticed pale blue bursts of light shooting cairns out from under the shelter of the thatched roof. Despite everything, I smiled inwardly.

I landed on the railing just as Fin channeled an orb of energy across the platform to take out the brick beside me. He started.

"You'll get yourself killed if you're not careful," he chided, lowering his hands. "Who let you out?"

I melted back into human form and hopped down from the railing. "I was sick of waiting. The window was big enough to escape through."

The corners of Fin's lips moved toward a smile. "How did it feel to finally shift again?"

"Wonderful," I confessed. "My strength has increased considerably these past few days. Thanks to Delta's wonderful bedside manner."

Fin noted my sarcastic tone and rolled his eyes. "She was only trying to do what was best for you."

I wasn't convinced, but I let it go. "Right."

"Surely you didn't come here just to argue," he said.

"You're right, I didn't," I answered, stepping closer to him. "I just came to say goodbye."

Fin's attention snapped from beyond the rail to my eyes. "You're leaving?"

I tried to grin, but it felt forced. "You were there. Come on—you know this."

"I know *that*, but I mean..." He faltered. "Right now?"

"No time like the present." I sighed neutrally, folding my arms over my chest. "We didn't work so hard only for me to back out of the whole thing now."

Fin thought about it for a moment and then nodded. "But you do realize that..." He trailed off, stopped.

I waited for him to continue.

"If you jump yourself," Fin went on slowly, "they'll consider it suicide."

I shrugged. "It's not like I have some tremendous reputation to maintain at this point."

He sighed a little. "True."

"So let them think what they like." I paused. "This is the only hope we have of getting him back, Fin... and I hope you realize that it's because of you that I believe that," I confessed. "For a while I thought I was… well, I thought I would die and that we would lose everything. But you've shown me that that isn't true."

Fin looked at me for a moment, an expression I couldn't quite read settling across his face.

"I only said those things because I believe in you, Hawk," he said. "I wouldn't have done everything I did for someone I didn't believe in."

"And I certainly didn't make it very easy for you," I added sheepishly. "I'm sorry."

Fin shook his head a little. "Don't be. We all doubt sometimes— it's just the way we deal with the doubt that matters."

"Mm." I followed his gaze to the outer limits of the platform's shelter. "Sensei said something similar once. That both doubt and faith are commendable. That both are the way of the student."

He started toward the platform railing. "Did you talk to him?"

"I couldn't…" I began to follow. "I wouldn't even know where to begin."

He came to a halt at the platform's edge, resting his hands on the railing. "Because you're angry with him?"

My lips parted towards a reply then faltered as I considered it.

"Honestly, Fin?" I rested my elbows on the railing. "I don't know what I feel towards Sensei. Anger, hurt… confusion? I don't even know how to put it into words. I just…" I sighed the rest out, feeling empty. "I don't understand him anymore," I said quietly after a minute. "I sometimes question whether I ever did."

Fin was silent for a moment. The winds were beginning to awaken, but now they were a little warmer than before.

"Even so…" He turned to face me. "Are you sure you don't wish to speak with him before you go?"

"I—there's no time. Everyone's going to be waking up soon. I need to get down there."

Fin seemed unconvinced as he studied me, but he let it go. "I understand," he said. "You should go."

I pressed my lips together slightly, into a smile that wasn't one, then straddled the railing. I eased my legs over the opposite side to face the ravine.

"I just can't get something Mitsue said out of my mind," he

murmured. "At your trial, he made the connection between Icarus's case and yours because of 'how involved you, Icarus, and Raiden were with each other.'"

"Well, we were, in a way."

"Yes, but somehow I don't think he just meant because Raiden was stalking you both. There was just something about the way he said it."

"Why?" I asked. "What did you make of it?"

Fin's green eyes swept across the ravine as he thought. "I can't say that I rightly know yet," he replied absentmindedly. "It's just a hunch. I have nothing to go on—in fact, I don't even know why it bothers me, exactly."

"You have good instincts, Fin," I told him. "Listen to them."

"Even when they make no sense?"

"Especially then."

He sighed, straightening up. "How am I supposed to figure things out while you're gone?"

"You'll find ways," I said, gazing steadily downward. "And I'll be back."

"Of course you will."

I nodded. My voice came out slightly quieter now as I looked into his eyes. "Of course I will."

"So this is goodbye?" he asked, not moving.

I thought about it and then shook my head. "No," I said. "Just… see you soon."

As I sat there in the predawn light, locking eyes with him from several feet away, it began to creep into my consciousness that this could be the last time I saw him. He searched my eyes, seeming to dig deep in himself for some word of encouragement he could give. I felt a strange twinge in the pit of my stomach.

When I finally did speak, it was almost involuntarily as I leaned slightly toward the edge. "Fin?"

Though his eyes were still focused on my own, he didn't reply.

"Thank you," I said softly.

"For what?" he asked. "For doing so much less than I wish I could have done?"

I shook my head. "No," I said. "For believing."

"Hawk, just…" He trailed off, then stopped. "Just… be careful."

I said nothing. I swallowed, turning back to face the fall.

"I will," I whispered, barely loud enough for him to hear. "I promise."

My heart hesitated in my chest and I closed my eyes.

Then I pushed off.

The Dimension blurred past in a roar of wind screaming in my ears as I tumbled. The colors of the sunlight were a chaotic sea around me. The air was like cotton beneath me as I plummeted, pressing tangibly against my skin but giving way at the same time. It was almost as if I wasn't falling but being pulled down by some otherworldly force that deemed me too great a temptation to resist. I was in a race to meet it.

All my instincts told me to shift, but I didn't allow myself until I reached the mist. I let my skin melt away as it billowed up around me, allowing the flame-like energy to rinse over me. The sound of wind passing through feathers filled my ears.

When I opened my eyes, all I saw was white. Pure, thick, milk white. The mist only grew denser with my rapid descent.

I spread my wings wide in an attempt to slow myself, but it made no difference. If anything, the force only grew stronger.

I quickly retracted my wings, bracing myself as I bulleted downward through what seemed like an endless sea of nothing.

Tongues of flame suddenly erupted around me, almost as if the oxygen itself had caught fire. Startled, I threw myself to the side, though this didn't offer me any escape. In fact, my attempt to evade the heat seemed only to provoke it to greater strengths.

I was tossed from side to side as the fire engulfed me, though, strangely, it left no marks. The roar of the wind still hadn't left my ears. It filled my senses until my vision began to falter.

My eyelids were beginning to grow heavy. I saw Fin in my mind's eye, the way he had looked leaning on the railing as we spoke our final words.

Be careful.

I fought to keep my eyes open, to spread my wings gradually against the screaming wind, but my muscles felt like lead. The heat around me had dissipated, though I couldn't see what was happening around me. I was too dizzy.

A split second passed in an eternity. The roar seemed to suddenly cease to a dead silence. I landed, and everything flickered out.

I became conscious of my breathing first. My slow inhales and exhales.

And then I began to realize how cold it was—how cold *I* was.

My feathers were gone, leaving my flesh exposed to the frigid atmosphere around me.

Why is it so cold?

My brain ached with questions. I slowly coaxed my eyelids open, though at first I was met only with tangled blurs my mind couldn't make sense of. I lay still, feeling a twinge of nausea in my stomach as my mind attempted to sort out the disorientation.

White. That was all I comprehended at first. Solid white with a splash of evergreen; deep, lush green pines frosted in…

"Snow?" I sat up so abruptly that the world pitched around me like a ship in a swelling sea. "Where on earth…"

I'd landed on a thick blanket of packed white powder. It coated the ground and frosted the trees—the dense army of massive pines surrounding me. Their trunks were thick and gnarled with age, allowing them to extend up against the milky, overcast sky like towering giants reaching for the source from which the white flakes were cascading.

Everything was silent. There was no wind, no fire, no noise whatsoever except the pounding of my own heart.

I had impacted an embankment, where thankfully the snow was thick enough to absorb my fall, keeping me in one piece.

My sleeve had caught on some exposed brush and torn at the shoulder seam, creating a match for the tear in my black jeans at the knee, where my skin was scraped and bloody.

I sat catching my breath for a moment longer before struggling to my feet. The snow drifted up to my knees, making it difficult to catch my balance at first.

I steadied myself, reaching down to touch the wound on my knee. I closed my eyes for a moment, attempting to calm my heart. I felt the blood slowly reverse its trickle, creeping back up to the wound before it resealed itself, returning to normal-looking flesh.

I tried to process what had just happened.

One thing was obvious: the ravine did, indeed, have a bottom.

And I had arrived there, and I had survived. Which could only mean Icarus was somewhere down here too.

I just had to *find* him.

Straightening up, I trudged forward. Moving through the snow was like moving through knee-deep water, but denser.

I tripped and fell several times, but picked myself back up again, shivering as the cold seemed to sink deeper into my bones.

Spatterings of snow fell gently from the trees as the branches became too heavy to support themselves. The muted sounds as they thudded against the thick white carpet below were the only disruptions in the dead silence as I progressed down the embankment.

My balance had finally caught up to me. The thickness of the snow lessened slightly, allowing me to walk a little more freely as I made my way through the trees.

I glanced around and tried to get my bearings, peering up at the sky overhead.

Somewhere above me was the Dimension. The dormitories strung between the two sides of the ravine, the platforms where I'd trained. Somewhere above me was *everything*—and everyone—that I had done this to protect. They were why I was down here.

I breathed into my cupped hands. "They just don't realize it yet."

That didn't matter. It didn't matter if they or anyone else believed me. I knew why I was here.

I paused for a moment to study my surroundings, wondering at the strangeness of it all. I couldn't remember the last time I'd seen snow, or felt this cold.

But then again, I *could* remember.

My hands slowly eased up over the markings around my arms as I swallowed back the tension that immediately began to form in my throat.

It was so long ago.

Yet somehow it seemed like just yesterday.

I felt the memory of the night as it began to clamp down on my brain, sinking its teeth into all the places I tried so desperately to lock away.

I felt the skin beneath my hands begin to warm up slightly, though I knew full well it wasn't from my own touch, but the ghost of another's.

A twig snapped, ringing louder than a gunshot in the silent air. I whirled to my left.

At first I saw nothing. Nothing beyond the trees and the silent layer of white. The quiet, looming army of giants guised in bark and evergreen foliage.

Then came another snap—this time louder, clearer. It came again and again until finally the source of the disruption appeared—stepping out from the cover of one of the massive pines. A paw—then a leg and a head. A muscular body swathed in wild fur.

A wolf. A black wolf.

I couldn't breathe. I stood there as still as stone, staring at it. And it stared back at me just as intently, its eyes as yellow as melted gold.

Time seemed somehow siphoned away as a channel formed between our eyes. My heart crept up into my throat.

At last I quickly snatched a glance over my shoulder to assess my escape options. The moment our eyes disconnected, I heard the same snapping sound that had caught my attention.

Bracing instinctively, I whipped back around, stumbling back against the tree.

But this time it was gone. The forest around me was empty and silent.

December 1913

"Charlotte," I whispered. "Charlotte, wake up!"

She swatted my hand off her shoulder, barely conscious. I persisted: "Charlotte, open your eyes."

My eyes were fixed on the window, though the light of dawn had barely even begun to reach its fingers over the horizon. Charlotte would have to be up in a few hours to take out the ashes from the stoves. She would see me at lunch and give me her same crooked smile and ask how I was. She would give me some of her portion of bread. She would brush the sweat and soot off her face with the back of her thin hand.

She was always up before the rest of us. She was always given less food. I would not know, until years later, that it was because of the markings.

I hated to wake her. But I knew how she loved the first snow.

"Ed," she murmured, rolling over, rubbing her eyes. "What is it?"

"Look!" I hissed, and scurried to the window on tiptoe. Bewildered, Charlotte followed, casting glances over her shoulders to make sure I'd not called unwanted attention to us.

Below us the streets were coated in a thin blanket of white, stained yellow by the dwindling lamps. She stared for a long time before she said even a word.

"I shouldn't have woken you, I know," I said.

She shook her head. "It's alright, Ed."

We watched the snow as it fell. I shivered in my thin shirt.

"Are you cold?" she asked.

I nodded, stealing a glance at her; the features of her face were softly illuminated, barely visible in the predawn light. "Are you?"

"Yes," she replied softly. "Yes, I am." Not moving her eyes from the window, she laid a hand over her heart. "But only in here."

CHAPTER ELEVEN

Icarus

Had it all been a dream? The white wolf, the ashy remains of a forest fire, being attacked by the black wolves, the familiar trilling call—had it all just been an illusion?

How could it all have seemed so real, yet been a dream?

When I'd startled awake at the white wolf's arrival, I'd rolled too near the flames and singed my arm—and I still had the mark.

So what was reality? What was an illusion?

The two seemed to blend together. Nothing made sense, but I remembered one thing—the only thing I needed to.

Hawk.

Suddenly the portal had swung wide open. In remembering her, I seemed to remember everything else, as far as I could tell. Everything that was important.

I was an anomaly. I was someone who had run from myself for as long as I could remember. Until I had found her—no, until she'd found *me*.

I couldn't remember all the details as clearly as I could remember her face, her eyes, her hands, her touch. The black markings that wrapped her arms like war paint.

She was the reason I had stopped running. From life, from myself, from what I was capable of. She was the reason I had even made it this far. I'd survived because of her... or maybe she had survived because of me. Or maybe we had survived because there was something bigger than us—something beyond us—declaring that we were *meant to*.

The Dimension came rushing back more vividly than if it had materialized before my eyes. The colors of the sky as the sun swayed from one horizon to the next. The scent of burning incense wafting from Sensei's office. The faint calls of raptors as they took to the sky each dawn, and the orchestral sighs of the wind in the trees each sunset.

I left camp as soon as the sun had risen high enough to filter down in golden shafts through the canopy of trees.

I walked through the forest in torn jeans and bare feet, feeling intoxicated somehow, like a man possessed. My mind drifted and danced with the gentle wind as it brushed through the leaves.

Hawk... Hawk... Hawk.

She consumed my thoughts.

I was lost in an endless forest—I had no idea where I was. Yet I smiled as I continued to lose myself.

The glowing blue words that had appeared on the gathering platform stuck in my mind. *The prophecy.*

It was somehow more than words. I could *feel* it deep within me.

Suddenly I heard the sound of another set of muted footsteps alongside my own. This time I wasn't afraid when I looked over my shoulder and saw the white wolf falling into step alongside me, several yards away.

It vanished and reappeared in almost ghostlike blurs as it wove between the trees.

I watched it, slowing up. It hesitated as I did.

Straightening, it raised its head slightly. I took a step closer, curious. It tossed its head in the direction that led us forward, immediately picking up its pace again.

Instinctively, I chased after it. Somehow, I felt like I wasn't following the wolf this time: I was allowing it to lead. We were running alongside each other like brothers would.

I could scarcely feel the ground as it passed beneath my feet, streaming by like a raging river, as if the forest was moving, not us. Trees darted past me in indistinct blurs. My only focus was the wolf as it sprinted on a path parallel to my own.

Its muscles rippled beneath its thick coat as its paws pounded against the earth.

Brush tore across the legs of my jeans, and low branches licked at my bare chest as I darted past.

We ran for what felt like an eternity. Far away from where I'd awoken at camp.

Had my memory returned because the wolf had appeared? Or... had it appeared because I had finally remembered?

Each time I attempted to cut through the line of trees to draw nearer to it, it countered to recreate the distance, as if taunting me. I stumbled and fell to my knees.

"Stop," I panted, laughing. "I... I can't breathe."

It pranced to a halt, its eyes shining in the sunlight.

It threw back its head and a howl rolled up into the air in a puff of steam.

Sweat began to trickle down my forehead as I turned and followed. I noticed that we were almost at the forest's edge. I blew out a sigh, reaching a hand back through my hair. "I've been searching for the forest's end for days... I've traveled miles."

The wolf stared at me impassively.

We emerged from the forest into the clearing, a wide circle where the trees were sparse and wild irises filled the space between them as if strategically planted.

The soil was richer here, showered in petals that clung to the soles of my bare feet. Something in the center caught my attention: a large flat stone that appeared to be covered in markings. I couldn't quite make them out, so I stepped shin-deep into the irises for a closer look. That was when I realized that they weren't markings, but tiny white flecks.

From out of nowhere, a cool breeze grazed my skin, raising the hair on my arms. When I looked up, I noticed that the white wolf had ventured into the circle to join me. Its pure white paws wove gently through the tender green stems.

When it reached the perimeter of the stone circle, it halted, looking up into my eyes.

I felt the cool breeze caress my skin again, though none of the flowers or trees stirred around us. Nothing moved... except the white flecks spattered across the stone in front of me.

I narrowed my eyes, leaning slightly closer.

The flecks lifted from the surface of the stone and spun like a squall of snow in the bluster of winter, though when they reached the stone's edge, they vanished.

"How the..."

I stepped closer. And closer. Until my toes were nearly touching the stone's surface and I could almost feel the flecks against my face as they danced wildly in the wind that seemed to generate from this strange, circular space.

"Snow?" I whispered as I stared, my fingers tingling with desire to reach out and touch it. "But how...?"

The white wolf circled around to the opposite side of the stone surface, looking across at me again as if daring me to cross.

The longer I stood there, the more impatient the wolf seemed to become. Once again, it threw back its head and let loose a howl that seemed to rattle through my body. Startled, I jerked away—but in doing so lost my balance.

I stumbled forward and fell into the stone circle, landing on my forearms and palms. The air rushed out of my lungs. But I scarcely comprehended the pain. I felt every muscle in my body tighten as I slowly lifted my gaze.

The cold white flecks battered me in the gusts of wind. All around me, in every direction, there was snow. Snow and towering pines as far as my vision could reach. I felt my breath rush out in an astonished exhale, instantly condensing in the freezing air around me.

I glanced frantically down at the ground beneath me. The stone was still there—but around me now there were pillars, ancient stone structures, cracked and crumbling, surrounding the circle.

My heart was pounding in my chest as I slowly stood, taking in my surroundings, stepping backward, tilting my face toward the gray sky. Snowflakes landed and melted against my cheeks.

The forest was thick around the circle where the pillars rose up, just as thick as the forest had been at the base of the waterfall.

"Impossible."

I stepped forward and began walking across the span of the circle to the column that rose up opposite. As I reached it, I traced my fingers over its surface. The snow came down and the towering pines swayed in the wind—giant's arms blanketed in pristine white.

I started to take a step forward, off the stone platform—but as suddenly as this had all appeared, it was gone. The world around me flashed away.

I was left standing at the edge of the circle, on the opposite side now, face-to-face with the white wolf.

Breathless, I glanced down and my eyes went wide. I was surrounded by irises.

CHAPTER TWELVE

Fin

I couldn't say I'd let her go. Hawk wouldn't be controlled by anyone. She was like the wind in that regard—like fire. But watching her go was the hardest thing I had ever done.

I was left to hold my breath all day, to wonder and worry, and to act as if I knew nothing when they found her dorm empty. The guard who had been posted outside was punished with laborious tasks, though he swore he'd done his job, and the rest of the Dimension fell into a more complicated state of unrest. Reports of what had happened were taken to Sensei by other members of the council before I had a chance to deliver the news myself. He was in meetings for the duration of the day, giving me no opportunity to so much as speak with him.

As I'd suspected, the rumor quickly spread that Hawk had jumped of her own volition. Mitsue took it the hardest. Hawk's disappearance seemed to have a deflating effect on him.

I threw myself into my work, attempting to focus on the needs of my students instead of the anxiety taking over in the pit of my stomach.

Did she make it? How would I know if she made it? How would I know if she was okay?

The questions repeated in a vicious cycle in my head until I could think of nothing else. I did the only thing I could do: I watched the weather. I watched for changes to the point of inwardly flinching almost every time the sun went behind a cloud. If her health had affected the Dimension around us to the degree that it had, I had no doubt that if something worse had happened to her, I would be able to determine that through the same means.

The frost had melted, but the wind still blew fiercely down the belly of the ravine, unchanged. I made note of it before I bunked in for the night, trying in vain to sleep.

How can I possibly rest when she is down there and I'm not?

I believed that she would survive it, more than anything. But the fears that lived in the back of my mind still bared their teeth during these quiet hours.

Unable to sleep, I brushed aside the sheets and let my feet to the floor. I hadn't bothered changing before bed, which saved me some time now as I pulled on my coat and focused the canvas flap open, escaping into the cold.

The majority of the Dimension was asleep save those who were still tidying up from the execution that had never occurred. As I stood there, watching for a moment from the rope bridge, I couldn't help but wonder at the lack of belief among us. At times I felt like I was the only one who saw straight through the façade to just how divided we really were.

I decided to take my troubles to Sensei, but when I knocked on his door there was no answer.

Feeling no more at ease, I turned and walked slowly back down the length of the hall, heading in the direction of the training platform. I would force myself to get some practice in, even though I was in no mood to channel. My plans changed slightly when I stepped back out into the open space.

Across the platform was a familiar, cloaked figure. Though this time her hood was pulled back, allowing her wild mane of red hair to crest her shoulders as she leaned on the railing and gazed out over the expanse below.

I watched her for a moment in silence, wondering how I could escape without her noticing. I hoped she would slip away after a minute or two, but she didn't.

"Are you going to just stand there in the shadows?" Her dry accent finally countered the silence. "Or don't you want to speak to me?"

I felt my ears redden. "It's not that."

"What, then?"

I walked over to the rail, though the action filled me brimming with déjà vu. I had been in this very place, standing beside Hawk, only hours earlier.

"I just can't sleep," I said, placing my fingertips on the rail. "I can't... make my brain stop."

Delta turned to look at me, her emerald eyes piercing in the low light. "Thinking about her, you mean?"

I hesitated for a moment, but it was impossible to deviate from the question under the intensity of her gaze. I nodded.

"It wasn't your fault, you know," Delta replied quietly. "You did everything you could to help her, Fin. She made her own choice."

"As did you." I shifted the conversation. "I'm indebted to you for everything you did to try to help her."

"It's my job, Fin," she said almost curtly. "It was only a few months ago that I had no idea this place even existed." Her eyes scanned our surroundings as she pressed her lips into a firm smile. "I'd do anything I can to help get us through this," she finished. "That's why I'm here."

I nodded again. A silence passed between us.

Delta drew a deeper breath, still leaning on her elbows. "That's not what's eating you, is it? Hawk's disappearance."

I thought for a moment about how I should respond, a little surprised at the sharpness of her intuition.

"No, Delta, it's not."

"Because you know something that the rest of us don't know about her."

I immediately froze.

"Don't you?" She pressed the question, though the tone of her voice was anything but prying.

"I know she didn't commit suicide, if that's what you're asking," I responded carefully. "I know that she jumped, I know that she's gone, but I know that she didn't kill herself."

"How can you know that for sure, Fin?"

"Because I just do, alright?" My voice cracked slightly as my gaze snapped back to meet hers. "I *know* Hawk. I was..."

I'd said too much already, but Delta's intent eyes didn't miss a thing.

"You were there... weren't you?" She checked over her shoulder to see if we were being observed. "This morning... when she jumped."

I wasn't about to lie by denying it, but I had no intention of elaborating any further.

"There was something Mitsue said at her trial that just got under my skin," I said finally. "That's all."

Delta grunted. "I doubt that's all... but what comment do you refer to?"

"He seemed to allude to Hawk, Icarus, and Raiden having some sort of connection with one another," I said. "Do you remember that?"

Delta was thoughtful for a moment. "I think I know what you're talking about. Wasn't he only referring to the attack Raiden had made on Icarus and Hawk, though? I wasn't initiated yet, obviously, but I've heard about it plenty."

"But there seemed to be something more to it than that. It's just a gut feeling."

Delta grinned a little. "You're one of those gut-feeling types, then?"

"I guess you could say that, yeah."

But it was more than a feeling. It was something I had no idea how to explain—not even to myself. Mitsue's words had been hanging heavy on my mind since the moment he'd spoken them.

Raiden had been Mitsue's student; Mitsue had been the first to encounter Hawk after the accident that had occurred when Raiden and Icarus had channeled against each other; and Mitsue had been the one to work with Hawk to erase Raiden's memory—or at least attempt it. It seemed that every situation involving Raiden somehow involved Mitsue as well.

I'd had ample opportunity to further question Mitsue, but I was too filled with rage to face him. I was too daunted by the idea of completely losing it.

"Mitsue made strange comments regarding Raiden at Icarus's trial, too," I continued contemplatively. "When he mentioned that it wouldn't be unusual for Raiden to have attacked Hawk."

Delta's brow furrowed. "But I thought he attacked Icarus as well? Believing them to be the patriarchs."

"That was the case, yes."

"Then why should he leave that bit out?" Her confused expression remained. "Why would he make it about Hawk if it was about both of them?"

I looked at Delta for a long moment, thinking about her question before coming up with one of my own.

"Icarus initiated his classmate right around the same time you initiated," I began slowly. "Areos. I believe you've trained with him on occasion?"

Delta's eyes narrowed slightly. "I may have. I may not have."

"Well, I've heard he's a wizard." I gazed past the railing. "He went to school with Raiden too—he and Runner both. If there's anyone among us who could possibly help me figure this out... he may be just the right person."

Delta seemed to consider it silently for a moment. "I could mention that you want a word with him if you'd like."

I glanced over at her. "Is that an offer to help?"

Delta's lips moved gradually towards a crafty grin. "Take it however you like."

———

"I may have gone to school with Riley—Raiden, I mean. But to be honest, no one really knew that much about him. No one knew he was an anomaly, and no one ever really questioned his cover story about where he came from."

"Where did he say he was from?"

Areos shrugged, reaching up to adjust his round wire-rimmed glasses. "Some suburb near LA. I can't recall the exact location."

"Who was closest to him?"

Areos leaned back in the plastic, classroom-style chair and gave me a dubious glance through his spectacles.

"Not to sound rude, Fin," he said, sounding just a little suspicious. "But why exactly are you so interested in Raiden? He's dead. What good is it to learn all these details about him now?"

True to her word, Delta had followed through with our plan the next morning. She'd invited Areos to meet me in one of the safe rooms after sessions ended.

There were many ways in which Areos had changed since he'd been initiated. And then there were many ways that he hadn't. He still narrowed his eyes and crossed his arms and asked far more questions than I wanted to answer. I tried my best to roll with the punches.

"Areos, listen." I sighed, resting my elbows on the table we were seated at. "I think you and I both know that Icarus isn't dead."

He stared at me blankly. "He fell off the cliff."

"He's the Sunset."

"I don't care what he is," Areos retorted. "He jumped off a friggin' cliff, Fin. He's gone. He's—"

I cut him off. "He and Hawk are the *backbone* behind this entire movement, Areos. Hawk jumped because she *had* to. She has to find him; otherwise none of this will matter. We'll be like a ship without a mast."

"Even if this *was* the case, what would it have to do with Raiden? How is he relevant?"

It was a solid question, I had to admit.

The truth was, my mind was full of questions, and each seemed to somehow trace back to Raiden.

Raiden had suspected Icarus of being a slider, but Icarus wasn't the one he'd been looking for. He'd used Icarus to lead him to something more—Hawk. Of course, it was true that he needed them both in order to obtain the blood of the Sunrise and the Sunset. But why hadn't it been the other way around: why had he envied *Icarus* so deeply?

Mitsue seemed to know something about Raiden—something beyond what the rest of us knew. And somehow I couldn't help but feel that if I figured out what that was, I could help Hawk.

"There is a bottom to the ravine, Areos, and Hawk is down there," I said finally. "Whether you believe it or not. And Raiden… wanted her. I don't know why, particularly, but I know that there was something about her that allured him."

"And you think Mitsue knows why because he was the one to erase Raiden's cognitive?" Areos crossed his arms over his chest.

"He tried and failed to," I responded. "He was unable to get beyond the surface of Raiden's mind, considering that he's a physical embodiment of the myriad of students he's killed."

Areos stared at me for a second. "And this was from Mitsue's lips?"

"He reported as much to the council."

"What if he was just lying?" Areos leaned back slightly, keeping eye contact. "What if he *could* see past the surface into Raiden's deeper thoughts?"

"But what would be the point of keeping that information to himself?"

"I wouldn't be the person to ask," Areos replied. "People do strange things for strange reasons."

I ran my thumb over my lower lip, my head bobbing in a slow nod. "True."

"But to be honest, Fin—" he leveled his gaze, looking across the table "—I think you may be overlooking something more important than whatever it is Mitsue's hiding."

I raised an eyebrow. "Which would be?"

"Look, I don't pretend to understand this place or how any of this works—because I don't. At all." He let out a frustrated laugh. "But if you believe Hawk and Icarus survived the fall and that they're down there…" He trailed off. "Wouldn't Raiden have also survived?"

My stomach sank. How could I have missed something so important?

"Yes," I pronounced slowly. "There's… there's no reason why he wouldn't have. I can't believe I didn't consider that sooner."

God, why did I let her go?

I hadn't. She had chosen.

"I know they survived, Areos," I said, feeling numb. "And there's… there's no reason why Raiden wouldn't have survived the fall either. And I…"

The light streamed in through the wall of glass at the end of the room. Beyond the glass was the ravine. The light. The dawn. And below all of that—far below… was Hawk. Somewhere. With him.

I shoved back my chair, rising.

Areos glanced up at me. "And what?"

I didn't want to speak the words, yet I could no longer retain them. I slowly shook my head. "I've never felt more helpless."

His hazel eyes were equal parts of sympathy and confusion. I turned towards the sliding pocket door, focusing it open.

"Where are you going?"

My jaw tightened. "To put the feeling to death, Areos."

CHAPTER THIRTEEN

Hawk

The wolf hadn't attacked. And I couldn't stop asking myself why.

Why hadn't it?

Instead, it had stood among the thick clusters of pine trees, as still as if it had been made of stone, staring at me through eyes of glistening gold. Eyes that would haunt me long after it had vanished and I had trekked deeper into the forest to search for shelter as the sun lowered in the overcast sky.

I'd scanned the snow for tracks as I'd cautiously woven my way through the clusters of massive trees. My footprints were the only markings to taint the unadulterated blanket of white.

I could see my breath with each nervous exhale, puffs of soft white against the darkening woods around me. The gentle wind had died down to nothing, bathing the landscape in a silence that rang in my ears.

The snow moaned softly as it parted with the pressure of my every step.

I tried to focus, though the uneasiness that had settled into my stomach made it almost impossible.

Fear is a human emotion, I told myself silently. *You're not human anymore. Get over it.*

I forced myself to stop thinking about the wolf and instead focused on finding shelter for the night. The task was easier said than done.

Thankful that I'd finally grown strong enough to shift at will, I threw myself backward and let my skin give way to feathers.

I rose into the thick evergreen branches. The giants that had loomed so proudly above me were swiftly reduced to dwarves.

My vision was sharper in this form, and the texture of the forest below seemed to roll beneath me like an ocean wave, swelling and dying only to rise steadily again.

I tipped my wing slightly and listed to the left. The landscape rose around me as I lost a little altitude.

The forest stretched out for miles, completely flat; then it began gradually to slope. I followed it, tracing the small rolling hills as I soared over them, staring down as if searching for prey.

Finally, I found what I had been looking for.

My wings were heavy with fatigue as I tucked myself into a tighter shape and bulleted down to the tree line again, fanning out to land softly at the edge of a wide clearing. It was exactly what I had been scanning the landscape for—a break in the trees. When I landed, I immediately began to realize it was more than that.

From above I'd seen nothing beyond snow-covered trees and a cotton-like surface beneath to match. But as I landed softly, barely making an impression on the surface of the snow in this form, my surroundings took on a new dimension.

Rising from the ground at the clearing's center were what looked like chiseled stone pillars. They stood approximately ten feet high and were capped by a thick layer of snow, explaining to me why I had not seen the structures from the parallel angle I'd been flying at a moment ago.

I cocked my head to one side, studying them.

What is something that looks so… human made doing down here?

I shifted back into my natural form and took a step forward. Immediately I sank knee-deep into the snow. I carved a steady trail to the closest pillar, squinting to see past the thick curtain of dusk.

I leaned closer, brushing away flakes of snow that had been plastered to the surface by the force of a prevailing wind. I could see what looked like scratch marks of some kind—an etching of sorts.

I narrowed my eyes until finally I could make out the faint shape of what looked like a flower.

"That's so strange." My breath painted the air in front of me as I spoke. "Who on earth made this?"

I didn't expect a reply, but I got one. In the form of a long, low howl from not too far away.

I realized I was in the worst possible place at the worst possible time. Wide open on every side with no viable defenses.

Quickly, I leapt back into raptor form and took to the trees again.

If I'd been thinking, I might have at least attempted to make a mental note of where the structure was, so that I could at least try to retrace my steps. But my mind was fairly one-track at the moment.

I was in flight mode.

I tore blindly through the forest, diving out of the way of trees. Even in this form I could hardly tell where I was going; I could hear the howls still, distantly.

I hadn't slept in what felt like days; wolf or no wolf, I had to land sooner or later or else lose my shape.

Don't even think about it. I forced myself back into concentration. *You're solid. You're fine. You've got to keep him alive.*

When I finally landed, it was among a thick patch of trees. I shifted back into human form, exhausted.

I was able to quickly dig away the snow at the base of one of the larger pines, shielded by its low branches.

I listened intently for the throaty sounds of the wolves' cries as I tried to efficiently assess my surroundings, scanning the ground for fallen limbs that could possibly be dry enough to start a fire with.

I was starting to become aware of the fact that the wolves were not my only threat. There was something far more pressing.

Shelter, I coached myself. Though all my brain could think about was how much I wanted to sit down and rest, just for a moment.

I found a large branch and dragged it over to the clearing I'd made. I propped it against the gnarled trunk of the pine and scouted the ground around me for a few smaller ones.

Placing the branches at forty-five-degree angles, I buried the base of each in the snow and took the rest for a fire. There was no foliage or uncovered brush to thatch the hovel with. The swaths of pine boughs would have to be enough.

I slipped inside what little cover I had created for myself and knelt to start constructing a fire with the remainder of the wood.

If only I had been strong enough to stay in hawk form, I could have slept in the trees.

I probably still would have frozen to death.

I wondered if the wolves would see the flames from the fire or smell the smoke. But I pushed the thoughts away.

You have to survive, Hawk. That's all.

As it was, I was having a hard time moving my fingers. Shivering, I cupped my hands and breathed into them. White puffs slipped past the spaces between my fingers.

The wood was too damp to start a fire with. So I called upon my deeper powers to aid me.

I tried to relax enough to focus all my energy into channeling an orb between my hands. It manifested in medium size and blue light—as cold as my hands were.

No... Stop thinking about the cold.

Clenching my jaw, I began to think about heat and warmth—fire. Raiden's infuriating ability to channel it.

I remembered the way it had looked in his hands as he rolled it around between them like something as innocent as a dodge ball, how the bright shades of orange and iridescent yellow had lapped at his skin without burning it.

Yes, he'd murdered many others to acquire this skill even I had yet to hone. But I was the Sunrise.

I squeezed my eyes shut and slowly began to force all of my remaining energy into my hands. I didn't allow myself to check, but I could feel the warmth increasing—turning red, gradually.

I took a deep breath, trying to envision it more clearly in my mind's eye.

I saw Raiden there. I saw the burning tree in the safe room, the look in Raiden's eyes as he'd observed his own handiwork. I remembered our conversation after... how he'd seemed almost pleased when the realization had hit me.

"You're not one student... You are many."

My own words haunted me.

I wondered how many he had killed and if that information was even recoverable. These thoughts led me to another set of inevitable questions.

If Icarus survived the fall, if I did... What if Raiden did, too? I wasn't unaware of the fact that it was possible. Yes, Icarus and I were the patriarchs... but a fall was a fall, wasn't it? Wasn't Raiden just as capable of survival as I was?

The sudden crackle of a flame drew me out of my thoughts.

My eyes quickly opened, and a tight ball of flame instantly caught my attention.

I breathed a sigh of relief, too exhausted to smile even inwardly as I lowered it gently into the array of sticks and twigs I'd gathered. After a moment the flame took, and soon the fire was crackling.

I warmed myself and then slipped out to find more sticks. It was pitch black, but now I had a torch—or at least one to practice with.

I added the wood I'd gathered to the fire and nestled as close to it as I could without singeing myself. The warmth soaked into my skin. The gentle snapping of the oxygen escaping the logs was the only sound to disturb the forest around me.

My brain wanted to think about the wolf—the black coat and the golden eyes. But I wouldn't let it. No, I would think about the pillars I'd found in the forest, rising toward the sky, and the etching of the flower.

Was any of that even real? I'd been so frantic in my escape I couldn't even seem to remember whether I'd really landed there, whether I'd only imagined the pillars standing like silent statues in the snow.

I should have made myself stay… I should have taken a closer look. But I was so tired…

The flames crackled in the silent woods around me. My eyelids weakened.

———

I awoke to cold.

The fire was dead, a black mark on the ground in front of me.

I squeezed my eyelids shut again and listened, coaxing fresh blood into my cold fingers as I flexed them.

A gentle breeze stirred above me in the treetops. I felt a few flakes find my face through the spaces between the foliage.

Evergreen fingers feathered out above me, shrouded in icy white capes.

So this hasn't just been a long, terrifying nightmare…

I was still shivering, but not uncontrollably. I'd made it through the night, and the fire had sustained me—or perhaps I had sustained it. I couldn't help but be a little proud of myself for having finally succeeded in channeling flame. I knew I would need it again.

I forced myself up into a seated position and crawled out of the shelter on my hands and knees. When I straightened up, I immediately began to assess my surroundings.

All around the shelter were tracks. They wove between the pines, scattering off in different directions and circling the small huddle of pine branches I'd constructed.

I bent down for a closer examination, swallowing back a tightness in my throat.

Fin had taught me how to track, and these prints I could identify immediately: the paw prints of a wolf.

"How did it find me all the way out here? I flew for miles."

Of course, there could have been more than one. There could have been an entire *pack*. I had no idea. This realization did nothing to ease the tension in my gut.

I wasn't one to be ruled by fear. Even if that fear killed me or at least brought me close to death—I wouldn't let it control me.

Leaving camp behind, I followed the freshest set of tracks. They led me between and past the trees—hundreds of them.

I followed the trail over embankments and through small clearings littered with rabbit tracks—the only other sign of life I'd seen thus far, aside from the wolf. They seemed to go on forever, becoming fresher and fresher, as I seemed to be gaining on this invisible force, until finally they stopped.

At the edge of a lake.

I let out the breath I hadn't realized I'd been holding, gazing out over the vast, open expanse stretched out before me.

Strangely void of the ivory blanket that enshrouded everything else, the ice was as clear as mirror glass, reflecting the overcast sky above like the stillest water would. I'd never seen any surface so smooth.

The sunlight filtered down through the cotton-thick cloud cover, giving a soft glow to the iced-over lake below. I took a few steps, testing the thickness and listening to how it handled my weight. The ice made no complaints. When I looked down again, I could see my reflection as clearly as if I had been standing on the surface of a looking glass.

I reached up slowly and touched a strand of hair aside, noticing the tears in my clothes; the black marking on my left forearm peeked through slightly. I shivered into my collar and stepped farther out onto the lake, scanning my surroundings for any sign of the wolf.

After a moment it became clear that I was alone. It was as though I'd fallen from my home into a hell all my own. One that was snow white and dazzlingly beautiful... but deadly.

"Oh, Icarus." I heard my voice escape me softly, felt my eyes pressing closed. "Where are you?"

The truth was, I couldn't feel him. Not here. I couldn't shake the feeling that something about this place was terribly... off.

I'd flown and trekked through miles of forest, yet seen no sign of human life. Only wolf tracks.

Icarus had jumped—he'd fallen just as I had. But if he was down here, then *where is he?*

When I looked down again, I found another pair of eyes staring back at me—a pair I didn't recognize.

My heart leapt into my throat as I started backward. The reflection followed, its horrified expression matching my own. I struggled to keep my balance as I reeled.

The face that stared up at me from the ice was not my own—at least, I didn't think so at first. It was sunken and bruised—bloodied. The body was frail and restrained in a black dress tattered and torn open in places.

"No." The word was a whisper—a terrified puff of steam in the frozen air. "It can't be."

I reached up to clasp my opposite forearms. I felt the fabric of my jacket against the palms of my hands. I was still wearing the same clothes, yet my reflection seemed to be declaring that this was only an illusion. It reflected something deeper.

I shook my head slowly, staggering frantically backwards, still clutching my arms.

"No." The strange voice slipped past my lips with more force this time. "No! Stop."

Losing my footing, I went down hands-first, slamming into the ice. Suddenly the apparition was right in my face, staring up at me through the crystal-clear surface.

The eyes were piercing and dark, but somehow faded at the same time. Filled with something I could never mistake, a fear that had haunted me for the past century.

Charlotte. My former name echoed in my head, though not in my own voice.

I scrambled to my feet, staggering backwards. My heart only quickened as my past self followed me, seeming to mock my every effort to escape it.

I lifted my gaze abruptly from the image in the ice as a long, low howl penetrated the air around me. Suddenly I realized how far out I was.

My heart leapt to my throat as I scanned my surroundings.

The howl came again, this time rattling through my center, sounding as though it were just in front of me, though there was nothing there. When I looked down at my reflection, there it was. A dark, hunching outline of a wolf just behind me in a battle-ready stance.

I spun around, braced for an attack that never came.

There was nothing there.

What...?

Breathing heavily, I glanced down at my own blurred reflection. The wolf was once again just behind me.

I turned instinctively, this time watching the reflection below as it countered my movements. I felt a chill rush down my spine.

I took only a few cautious steps before I broke into a run.

With every growl, I shot a glance down at the surface of the ice, and every time it was closer—there were more wolves. First two and then three. Four.

I was in the middle of the lake now. The wolves chortled in unison from just behind me—to my left, my right. Circling.

My reflection was panicked and my eyes were darkened.

"Stop!" I was gasping for air as I staggered away. "Please! I—"

The wind rushed out of me as I impacted the surface of the ice, the back of my head going down hard enough to show me some constellations.

Though I couldn't see what I was battling against, my gut reaction was to leap back up into a defensive stance.

A distinct cracking noise rose around me as the ice beneath me shifted slightly.

My heart hesitated in my chest.

The ice groaned beneath my body weight. Then there was a pause.

I pressed into the palms of my hands, attempting to sit up. The ice cracked a little more.

One heartbeat.

In one swift motion I jumped to my feet. My eyes latched onto my reflection for a split second that seemed to lag, dragging by in slow motion as the apparitions of wolves circled her... *me*.

Then they pounced. The ice gave way.

The howls muted as my body instantly tensed, my muscles locking up though everything inside me screamed for them to move. Ice-cold water swallowed me whole, pouring into my mouth and lungs.

I wasn't sure which way was up or down. I tried to thrash my arms up overhead, but they were like lead weights saddling my torso.

When I finally managed to lift my head in the direction of my last air source, my heart sank in my chest.

It was but a patch of light far above me—yards away and listing farther and farther to my left as I drifted.

I needed air. And there was solid ice over my head. I instantly panicked.

Forcing my heavy body to move, I thrashed forward with as much force as I could summon, tearing my arms through the icy water and pushing myself upwards, back in the direction of where I'd plunged through.

My lungs burned for lack of oxygen and begged to dispel the water that had invaded them. I couldn't open my mouth: I knew I would only take in more than I had already.

Eventually I felt my back brush against something—hard. The ice's surface.

Where is the opening?

I struggled to turn myself around so that I was looking up through the ice, though my vision was weakening.

I'm so tired...

Then I saw something beyond the ghostly lights that were beginning to flicker across my vision. And it wasn't the opening.

A dark shadow stood over me, looking down: a black wolf,

separated by a layer of solid ice. But I still heard the sound as it howled.

Sensei... The thought was slow in coming, almost not there at all. *Please save me...*

Please...

My eyes drifted shut. I breathed in and water poured into my lungs.

I awoke. Sputtering, coughing. Gasping for air.

I started to become aware of the cold, hard ground below me. I was curled in the fetal position and sheathed in my own icy sweat.

I am... back at camp? It was a nightmare...

"Thank you." My voice was a broken whisper as I tried to catch my breath. *"Thank you."*

I pushed up into a seated position, pressing the heel of my hand to my forehead, where I could feel my heart hammering like a bird aching for its freedom.

I breathed the sweet air in deep, attempting to steady myself. Which took some time.

When I finally ventured outside the shelter, the sense of déjà vu was strong as I emerged on my hands and knees.

The forest was still around me, not moved by even the gentlest breeze. Everything was washed in a dead silence.

Tracks were everywhere: the paw prints of a wolf that had raced around through the trees, evidently circled my camp—and now stood before me, several yards away.

I caught my breath. My muscles tensed as it locked eyes with me from across the space between us.

In its golden eyes I now saw remnants of my own icy ones. In them was everything I couldn't seem to escape from, no matter where I went or how hard I tried.

There it stood. Staring at me through the trees. Bone thin.

And then it was gone.

It took off at a run, and I found myself once again alone in the silence. But I wasn't one to be ruled by fear—even if it killed me.

So this time I turned my focus to the set of tracks before me, and I followed.

January 1914

It was cold that winter. The kind of cold that stings the lungs and burns the feet. And our feet were bare, always, even in the dead of winter. We were never given shoes; our skin grew callused. I can only ever remember having two gray shirts and one pair of overalls.

We were like uniformed prisoners, with hungry bellies and dirty faces. We all wore gray.

Well, everyone except Charlotte. Charlotte wore black.

CHAPTER FOURTEEN

Icarus

I felt sunlight on my face. Warm, streaming sunlight.
A bird song echoed distantly. Then a voice.
"Icarus…"
I wanted to answer, but I couldn't right away. I waited until I heard it a second time, then a third. Then slowly I managed to open my eyelids.

I found myself standing at the edge of the training platform, leaning against the railing with the sun on my face.

"Mmm." I took a deep breath and straightened, stretching my arms over my head as though I'd just awoken. "What is it?"

A pair of familiar arms locked gently around my waist, drawing me back closer against a warm body. I relaxed instinctively in her grasp.

"Daydreamer," she renamed me quietly, and I felt the warmth of her words between my shoulder blades. "Don't you have anything better to do?"

I felt a smile melt over my lips as I turned around in her arms.

"Nothing," I said, looking down into her face. Her dark brown eyes. "Nothing better…"

Hawk tried to hide the half-smile, but it was too late.

Suddenly I felt weightless as the connection between our eyes seemed to pull us closer. I leaned in and let my forehead make gentle contact with hers.

"Icarus," Hawk said again, "I miss you."

"I miss you too," I whispered, leaning closer, letting my lips softly brush hers. "So much."

Hawk didn't kiss me yet. I could tell there was something on her mind.

"Where are you?" she whispered. "I've searched everywhere, and I can't..."

I reached one hand up, letting my fingers brush back through her hair. "What?" I prompted quietly. "You can't what?"

She slipped her palms up around my face. She kissed me.

At first it was soft, gentle—like silk against my lips. But then it became something more. Something like fire.

She pulled back for a moment and said my name. Our foreheads remained connected.

"I can't find you, Icarus," she whispered.

I awoke.

I was stretched out in the irises, my face toward the blue sky. Clouds passed in wisps. The scent of the blossoms around me rose from the ground like dew, so thick it was almost a flavor instead of an aroma. It tasted like the kiss. Her lips.

I tried to remember them. The way they had felt on the eve of my execution, when she had visited me in my cell, when we had kissed. It had been different from any other kiss I'd ever experienced, but then I'd never been kissed by a hurricane.

Was she looking for me? Was that why she had said she couldn't find me?

"Of course she is," I told myself. "Of course she's looking for you. She knows you're alive."

Because she was alive. Because I hadn't been killed by the fall.

I tensed slightly, a sudden thought taking hold. A revelation that sent a cold feeling over my body and into my bones.

"What if the fall didn't kill him?"

My thoughts surged back to that day on the gathering platform. Fighting Raiden in the cotton-thick fog until, at last, I had pushed him.

I had thought I was saving Hawk and myself. I had thought I was finally tasting sweet revenge on the tip of my tongue. But what if it wasn't true?

If Raiden had survived the fall as I had, and if Hawk had actually come after me... I'd done nothing more than place her in a more dangerous situation than ever.

Why did he want her so badly?

Raiden's goal was to eliminate us both. To take our blood and our identities and guide the future with his own hands. That was his motivation. He knew Hawk and I made up the split soul, but he had been jealous of *me*, not her.

The thought of being down here with an enemy I had tried to kill was not what frightened me the most. It was the idea of Hawk taking the fall to come find me.

The gentle sound of paws wading through the growth pulled me out of the storm of my own thoughts. I pressed up onto an elbow.

A few feet away, the white wolf circled then settled contentedly into the bed of purple springing up around us. It stared at me through the green stems.

I narrowed my eyes. "I feel like you know something about this place that I don't. That's why you led me here... isn't it?"

The liquid trill of a bird sounded distantly in the forest. A gentle breeze swayed the trees.

The wolf and I continued to stare each other down until finally I pushed myself up completely. I leaned forward on my knees and gazed across the empty space in front of me to the place where the stone spread out across the ground.

From time to time I could hear the wind or see flakes of snow as they danced in its turbulence. Traces of snow rising and dipping back below the line of purple heads.

I glanced over my shoulder after a moment and found that the wolf was still staring at me with its sharp blue eyes.

"What?" I asked again. "You want me to do it again?"

The white wolf raised its head slightly. A pink tongue flashed across its lips.

"Alright." I sighed, getting to my feet. "I'll do it again."

I made my way through the flowers, treading lightly until I reached the place where the irises came to an end and the large round stone lay before me.

I drew a deep breath and stepped forward. The landscape transformed instantaneously around me.

The flowers, the forest, the bright blue sky, the wolf—in a flash, it all dissolved. Suddenly snow-blanketed woods surrounded me.

Even though I'd seen this place a hundred times, I still had to catch my breath every time I saw it. I'd spent every ounce of energy I had trying to figure this place out.

Was I looking into another world of some kind? Or was I hallucinating? Was it something static—something that I couldn't access. Or could I?

"What good is being able to see into a world if I can't even get in," I complained, stepping off the stone on the opposite side now, back into the forest and the irises. "I don't understand."

I sighed in frustration and glanced over at the wolf; it was still relaxing in the circle of flowers, keeping a curious eye on me.

"Why bring me here?" I asked, though I was talking more to myself. "If this place doesn't mean *something*—" I stepped back into the circle, back into the snow and the darkening woods that spread out vividly around me "—then what is the point of any of this?"

For a moment there was silence, and then the sound of nails ticking against the stone surface. I turned to glance over my shoulder.

"So you've joined me in my misery," I muttered in the wolf's direction. "If you had any purpose in bringing me here, I wish you would just… just show me. Don't keep me guessing."

The white wolf did nothing for a moment, and then it stepped around me, crossing over to the opposite side of the circle. Scanning the surroundings beyond the stone platform, I saw nothing at first. Then I noticed something I hadn't before.

"Tracks?" The word rolled out quietly. "Human tracks?"

Had they been there before? They couldn't have been. I'd studied every inch of this place—as far as my vision could reach from the platform to which I was confined.

Instinctively I made my way around the wolf and began to step off the stone. But half my leg vanished in thin air the moment I did.

I pulled myself back, withholding curses.

"I don't know what to do from here." I turned around to face the wolf again. "They're the right size, and they match her boot print."

I raked my fingers anxiously back through my hair, edging as close as I could to the circumference of the circle.

The boot prints led gradually up to the pillar nearest to me, then stopped abruptly, turning to trail off in the opposite direction—blurred slightly as though she had picked up her pace to a run.

I knelt at the edge to try to examine the prints more closely. My vantage point wasn't the best, but I gathered enough to authenticate my hunch.

Icarus, where are you? I can't find you.

I pressed my eyelids closed, pinching the bridge of my nose as I thought back to the dream.

"You were *so close*, Hawk." I sighed. "*We* were so close."

I felt a head of thick white fur nudge against my shoulder. I drew a deep breath and opened my eyes again.

The wolf brushed past me and stepped easily off the stone in one fluid motion. To my surprise, it didn't disappear back into my world. I sat back on my heels as I watched it trot curiously through the snow, reaching its large head down to inhale whatever scent it could detect off the prints. Then it glanced up at me.

I straightened back up, my heart beating faster now as I took a step forward to follow. I cautiously slid one foot over the edge—

And it vanished from my view.

I cursed silently, back-stepping a couple of paces.

"So you can get to her, but I can't?" I questioned, raising my voice so that it looked up at me again. "How is that fair?"

It stared across the snow at me for a moment, then gave its coat a shake.

"So she's down here," I pondered aloud, puzzling it out in my head as I spoke. "But she's... over there."

Wherever "there" is.

The bottom of the ravine, though it existed, was definitely still a mystery.

"I don't understand." I rubbed my fingertips across my forehead as the wolf finally approached again, stepping back onto the stone with the lightness of a feather. "Is it a whole separate world? Are our landing points really *that* far apart?"

A world apart?

I stood there and watched the wolf as it circled me.

"If I can't enter this place to find her—" I glanced around at the snow-blanketed landscape "—I have to find a way to bring her here.

She was so close… It's almost like something drew her farther away."

Doubts ran their teeth across my thoughts. Fear.

How can I be sure they're Hawk's footprints? How can I be sure she even came after me? How can I trust a dream? How can I even trust myself? I only just remembered my own name, for crying out loud!

But if they weren't hers, and she didn't come, and the dream was just a fabrication of my greatest desire… well, then I had no hope. And I refused to accept that.

Taking a determined breath, I walked again to the edge of the circle and paused in front of one of the crumbling pillars. My eyes scanned it rapidly, searching for a place where the ancient-looking marble jutted out.

I slid my fingertips down the surface gently until I found a rough patch.

Bracing myself just slightly, I quickly flicked the palm of my hand over the sharp edge. I felt a tingling sensation surge through my nervous system.

When I pulled my hand back, there was a thread of blood stretching across my palm. I immediately felt a wave of déjà vu.

I caught my breath, turning to glance at the wolf, which was now across the circle from me.

I took a few steps towards the center, and it met me there. Its ears perked slightly, and its eyes sparkled a shade of turquoise.

I knelt in front of it, bringing us to eye level, and extended my hand slightly.

It looked at me curiously for a moment before it gradually bent its neck down to examine my hand. I felt its cold nose as its rapid inhales and exhales brushed over my palm. After a good moment or two, it finally seemed satisfied.

It sat back on its haunches and stared me squarely in the eyes, as if communicating that it was my move.

I took another deep breath, trying to relax as I glanced down at my hand again.

"I can't get to her, but you can," I said quietly, glancing back up. "So go find her."

It watched me.

"Go find her," I repeated, this time more firmly.

It shadowed my motions as I rose to my feet.

It took a few steps forward and then halted at the circle's edge, glancing from me to the set of footprints and then back to me again.

"Go!" I shouted finally, unable to contain my frustration any longer. "Go find Hawk!"

Then finally—finally it was like it had found what it was looking for. It leapt from the circle and sprinted into the snow, vanishing among the trees.

I stood there and watched it go. A moment later a long, shrill howl rolled up through the treetops.

I glanced down at my hand again. A pool of crimson blood had formed. I let go of a sigh and whispered, "Find her."

CHAPTER FIFTEEN

Fin

"Where are you going?"

I could hear Areos's brisk footsteps catching up to mine. The safe room door rolled shut.

Striding across the platform, I headed for Sensei's office, hoping he was actually in this time. I couldn't help but notice that he'd been frequently absent since Icarus's execution. He was never around during sessions, and it was becoming a rarity to find him in his apartment.

"To find answers, as I said." I glanced briefly over my shoulder at him. "If Raiden is still alive—if he's down there—I have to at least try to help her."

"Even if he is alive—even if they're *all* alive down there, Fin," Areos reasoned behind me, "how are you going to help her from up here? There's nothing you can do."

"There is *always* something you can do," I corrected him firmly. "Knowledge is power, Areos. If you have an enemy, you learn everything you possibly can about him. An object is only as strong as its weakest point."

"Okay, true," he agreed, catching up. "But what good will knowledge do if he's completely out of your reach?"

I thought about the question as we made our way down the hall toward Sensei's apartment.

"To be honest with you, I don't know," I confessed as we came to a halt in front of Sensei's door. "Maybe it won't matter. I just have…"

"A gut feeling?"

"Exactly."

Areos didn't look satisfied, but he knew better than to question further.

I took a breath and lifted my knuckles to the ornate wood to deliver a few rapid knocks.

I waited for an answer. His voice from within. Anything.

But nothing came.

I knocked again. "Sensei?"

After a long pause, Areos adjusted his glasses. "Is it locked?"

I shook my head. "He never locks it. No."

"Then why don't we just go in?"

"Are you serious?" I turned and looked at him. "Break into Sensei's apartment while he's absent? That would be breaching—"

"It's not breaking in if it's not locked," Areos cut in, as if he were citing a law. "Besides, wouldn't he want you to access whatever you needed in order to help Hawk?"

I considered what he was saying. I couldn't help but remember what Sensei had said only a fortnight before—about how he no longer carried the authority to command our initiative.

We did. *I* did.

Swallowing, I reached out for the knob and turned it quietly. The door creaked open on the room's darkened interior. I hesitated for a moment before stepping inside, Areos just behind me.

It was getting close to sunset. The clouds had covered the sun, and a gentle drizzle had begun to fall. The fire crackled listlessly in the hearth, and the faded scent of incense lingered in the air.

The room was void of life. Void of Sensei.

I heard Areos close the door carefully behind us. "What is it we're looking for, exactly?"

I scanned the room. "When Hawk initiated Icarus, she told me that Sensei kept an updated portfolio about him, knowing that she would one day want it."

"So?"

I crossed the room to Sensei's desk. It was littered with quills, made out of Hawk's molted primaries, and crumpled, ink-splattered pages, as if he had been working on a complicated letter.

I tugged open one of the desk drawers. "So perhaps he kept files on Hawk and Raiden both."

"Hawk?" Areos questioned, stepping farther into the room now. "Why would you need to learn anything else about her? I mean, she's your..." He trailed off abruptly as I shot him a firm stare. He cleared his throat. "She initiated you, right?"

"Trained me," I corrected him. "Sensei initiated me."

"Still," he said. "You guys are so close—what could you possibly not understand about her?"

I held back a sigh. "If only you knew," I muttered, continuing through the drawer.

The contents of the desk yielded nothing. I continued to the bookshelf.

"It's raining," I commented after a while, running my fingertips gently over the bindings as I read through the titles. "I wonder how she's doing."

Areos glanced over at me from where he was standing in front of the waning fire. "You really think she's still alive, don't you?"

I nodded.

"Fin, I don't understand how you can believe so strongly in something when there's no way for you to know if it's true," he said. "I mean... this place itself is fantastical, yes—but I've seen it and I've experienced it with my own senses, and... I can sort of get my head around that now."

I pulled out a book entitled *Canis Lupus*. "Yet?"

"Yet I cannot believe that Ion—Icarus—and Hawk..." He fumbled for the right words. "I cannot believe that they are anything more than... what they are."

"And that would be?"

"*Students*." He sighed. "As normal and ordinary as us."

I blew the dust off the front cover of the book. "Speak for yourself, Areos."

"I *am* speaking for myself, Fin," he retorted. "I'm as normal as they come—I have no idea why I was even chosen for this."

"Is it necessary that you know, Areos ?"

He shot me a glance. "Didn't you yourself say that knowledge is power? What's the point of it all if we can't know why?"

I flipped open the front cover of the book as I considered how to reply.

Before I could even comprehend the rune-like writing on the first page, the floor-to-ceiling bookshelf before me slid slowly open, penetrating the silence with the grinding sound of stone on stone. I started backwards.

As it rolled slowly aside, it began to reveal a second set of shelves underneath. Shelves lined with rows and rows of manila files. Finally, the grinding stopped and the shelf settled up against the wall.

I stared, wide-eyed, for a moment before glancing down at the book in my hand.

"What the..." Areos didn't finish.

"We don't always need to know why things happen, Areos," I answered finally. "Sometimes you just have to accept that life would be boring if we understood it all."

I set the open book face-up on Sensei's desk and curiously approached the new set of shelves that had appeared before us.

The files were all individually labeled, but didn't seem to be arranged alphabetically. I took a guess that perhaps they were organized from earliest to latest initiates, and pulled out the first file, which I was expecting to be Hawk's.

I was wrong.

"Lost sliders," Areos read aloud, peering over my shoulder. "What does that mean?"

The folder was thin between my forefingers and thumbs, not containing many pages. Still, something in me was almost afraid to open it.

"Icarus was not the first slider to be tried and punished for his alleged errors, Areos," I explained quietly. "There were others, long before I was ever initiated. Anomalies who were brought into our Dimension but refused to conform to the code of conduct or used their powers to act violently."

"So they were executed, then?"

I shook my head, finally easing the file open. "They faced the same procedure Mala underwent."

"Meaning their memories were erased and they were banished?"

I nodded. "No one really knows what happened to them, exactly. Except Sensei, it seems."

There were several pages in the folder, each bearing a name, a photograph, and a list of rudimentary biographical information. My eyes scanned the dates of their initiations as I flipped through the pages, and I quickly noted that each of them had entered and left the Dimension long before I had been brought here.

Nothing seemed amiss until Areos tapped a finger on the page we were looking at. "Whoa—what's up with that?"

"What?"

"All of these birth dates are from the past," he said. "So a lot of these sliders are no longer living—or are labeled 'deceased.' But this one's labeled 'murdered.'"

I looked more closely at the carefully scrawled line of text Areos was addressing and read it over quietly. "But it says nothing about who the perpetrator was... That seems strange."

"Maybe it wasn't known," Areos offered.

I looked more closely at the image, studying the features of a young man's face.

He was of Native American descent, with broad shoulders, long dark hair, and piercing eyes. According to the profile, he had lived to around the age of nineteen.

I turned the page to the next profile, and to my surprise I found the same line of text on that page: *murdered*. The young man in the photograph looked barely my age.

"Two in a row," Areos muttered, sounding just as shocked as I was.

"Three," I corrected, turning to the next page. "And only several years apart—look." I tapped my index finger on the row of numbers.

"That seems weird," he responded thoughtfully. "What are the chances of that?"

I turned to the next page. "What are the chances that none of us have ever heard about it?"

"Maybe someone found out they were anomalies—even after they'd been banished."

"Maybe." I found similar stories on the next few pages. "But if their memories had been erased, someone would have really had to know how to draw the truth out of their subconscious, because it would have been nearly impossible for them to recall what they learned here."

"Maybe it was someone who knew what they were doing," he said, stepping around me to the bookshelf. "Who knew how to detect that they were different somehow."

I grunted. "If that were the case, then this person would have had to stay alive for a pretty long time, Areos." I showed him the date on the last profile labeled "murdered."

He adjusted his glasses and squinted at it for a moment. "That was only several years back."

I turned the folder back to face me and examined the profile photograph more closely. There was something strange about it, though I couldn't place it at first.

He looked around my age with a medium, Hispanic complexion. His hair was messy and fell down over his eyes, obscuring his face a little. The photograph was grainy, and the subject had obviously been in motion as the photo had been taken.

"Okay... so I'm not finding a folder for Raiden." Areos's voice pulled me out of my thoughts. "But it looks like this is Hawk's right here."

He slid the appropriate folder off the shelf and handed it over.

"Where do you think Sensei is, all this time?" he asked. "What if he walks in any second now?"

I considered the idea. "I guess we would have some explaining to do," I answered. I walked over to Sensei's desk with the folder to take a seat. "But like you said—I think he expects us to take this into our own hands. Maybe he already knows we're here."

"You talk about him like he's some kind of all-seeing eye."

I grinned. "Something like that."

No sooner had I spoken the words than the door to Sensei's office swung open—so hard that the doorknob pounded into the wall behind it. Areos and I both started.

"What are you guys doing in here?"

I relaxed as soon as I saw the swath of blue hair.

"What are *you* doing in here?" Areos groaned before I could respond. "I thought you were studying or something."

Runner closed the door behind him with a little more grace. "Already done," he announced. "I thought I'd come see where you guys vanished to when sessions concluded. I saw you sneak off."

"I didn't sneak off," Areos responded irritably. "Fin had some questions regarding..." He trailed off, giving me a glance over the rims of his spectacles.

"It's okay," I said, carefully clearing a patch on the desk. "It's not a secret. I had a few questions in regards to Raiden, Runner. I thought maybe Areos would know."

"I went to school with him too, you know," Runner commented, sounding mildly annoyed as he began exploring the room listlessly. "Why didn't you ask me?"

"Because I'm just slightly more resourceful," Areos replied. "No offense."

I withheld a sigh, setting the folder down.

"I may not have run in the same circles as Raiden," Runner retorted, stopping in the middle of the room. "But I know people who did."

I glanced up, my interest piqued. "Such as?"

Runner shrugged, reaching up to massage the back of his neck. "Mel—or whatever her name is here. They were tight. Like, she was his girl."

"Right," I said, remembering. "They were dating."

Runner shook his head. "They were beyond dating. They were like—"

"We get it, Runner," Areos cut in, rolling his eyes. But I wanted to hear more.

"He had her face painted on his car, for God's sake," Runner finished anyway. "Like, the dude was head over heels for her... in his own strange kind of way."

"So he confided in her, you mean?"

"I think they confided in each other." He paused and laughed slightly. "Not that it matters anymore, since we wiped her memory."

"Because I was ordered to, Runner—we were *both* ordered to," I reminded him, a little frustrated.

He nodded solemnly. "I know, and I respect that, but..."

"But what?" I asked, leaning forward to rest my elbows on the desk.

Runner seemed lost in thought for a moment as his eyes fixed on something that wasn't there. "You weren't there when she woke up," he said at last.

I studied him for a second, trying to understand where he was going with this.

"Remember how you told me she would have a lot of questions?"

I said nothing, waiting for him to come to a point.

Runner took a few steps forward, pausing in front of the desk, looking at me with a dawning seriousness in his eyes.

"Well, she did."

I took Hawk's folder out of my shirt when I got to my dorm and stuffed it into one of my desk drawers under a mess of papers. I hadn't opened it yet.

In the end we'd had to close the book—and the shelf—unsuccessful in our mission to find Raiden's file, or anything else that might have been of use to our cause. Nothing except the information Runner had finally decided to let me in on. I couldn't believe I hadn't thought to ask him about it before—he *was* the one who had assisted me through the entire procedure with Mala.

I was beginning to see that I couldn't necessarily trust my own judgment.

Is it because Hawk is gone? Or is it because I know, deep down, that I lost her in a way that my heart can't bear to accept?

I needed someone else's opinion—someone who was more stable. Someone whose brain wasn't caught in a whirlwind like mine was.

Was I even right in suspecting Mitsue of something underhanded? What if my suspicions were wrong? What if I was *completely* off track?

I left the dorm before my roommates returned and headed across one of the narrow rope bridges in the direction of the group dormitory. The wind blew down the ravine in cold torrents.

I knocked on the door frame once, then twice. The door opened, revealing a familiar mane of untamed red hair and a heart-shaped face.

"Fin," Delta said, sounding a little surprised as she gripped her shawl more closely around her shoulders, "what are you doing here? Has something—"

"Nothing has happened," I replied before she could finish the question. "I just… I came to talk to you. I was hoping to, anyway."

She looked at me for a moment and then stepped to the side, waving me in as she shot a glance beyond my shoulder. "Does anyone know you're here?" she asked, focusing the flap shut behind us.

"Of course not," I said. "Is anyone else in?"

Delta shook her head. "The girls are at evening sessions, so it's safe right now. But you do realize—"

"I know," I said, sinking into one of the chairs. "I'm not supposed to be in the females' dorms, and we could both get in trouble for this—but I didn't know who else to turn to."

She said nothing for a moment, staring at me like I was a puzzle she was trying to solve. I avoided her gaze.

"I've just…" The rest of the sentence faded. "I've lost everyone I can trust, Delta."

Delta pulled up a chair and sat down across from me. "Everyone as in Hawk," she said slowly.

I closed my eyes at the mention of her name. "Don't make fun of me."

"I'm not, Fin," she said quietly. "I just know that it's true. I know that you still love her."

I tried to ignore the words, but they cut deeper than even I could comprehend.

"I didn't come here to talk about me," I said, my voice cracking. "I came here to talk about Raiden. And Mala."

"Mala?" Delta reiterated, sounding surprised. "What does she have to do with all this?"

"More than I imagined," I replied, sighing. "Apparently there was much I overlooked. Areos came to me today, and we spoke at length, but he offered me no new information beyond the realization that Raiden is still alive—that he must be if Hawk and Icarus are."

I stopped, looking up from my hands at last to meet her eyes. "But I know you don't believe that," I added quietly. "I know even you believe they're all dead—"

Delta cut me off, shaking her head. "No."

I looked at her questioningly. "What do you mean?"

She looked at me for a long moment before saying anything, seeming to choose her words carefully. "I mean that…" She paused for a breath, not breaking eye contact. "I didn't believe at first. But I've made up my mind to be honest with you, Fin. Mitsue is my teacher, and I trusted his flowery words when he told me he would help me 'move up in the ranks,' so to speak. I believed him when he promised me power, and I was... I was foolish to feel that my allegiance should be to him. I was wrong."

I shook my head. "You owe me no apology. I knew you were under his influence—I knew there were things he knew only because you had told him, and vice versa. You knew about Hawk's trial before she did, and you acted as though I had confided in you."

She stared at me. "You see that I betrayed you, yet you don't hate me for it." It was more a soft-spoken statement than a question. "How is that so?"

"I have no right to hate anyone," I said quietly. "If losing my home... and my family..." I trailed off, my voice breaking. "If it's taught me anything, Delta," I began again, "it's that we cannot afford to hate. It defeats the very reason we were created."

She said nothing.

"Runner told me that Mala asked him a question when she awoke from her coma," I continued, rerouting to the original topic. "It was after the procedure—after I'd already wiped her conscious memory. I wasn't there when she awoke, but she asked Runner why she remembered being attacked."

"Attacked?"

"She couldn't remember who he was, obviously. But the memory obviously ran deeper than just her conscious mind—it was in her subconscious. Runner had no answer for her, of course, but..." I broke off as I considered it myself. "I think we both know who it was."

Delta's eyes narrowed thoughtfully. "Which would align with what Mitsue said at the trial," she concluded. "About how it wouldn't be unusual for Raiden to attack Hawk—because he had attacked others. Others like Mala."

My thoughts leapt back to the folder I'd held in my hands only an hour earlier. The folder labeled *Lost Sliders*. Suddenly it clicked.

I shook my head. "More than just Mala."

I felt Delta's eyes on me, burning with questions.

"Delta, Mitsue knows something," I said, my voice more urgent now. "I don't know how much... but there has to be a reason why he wants to keep Mala close to him."

"You think Mitsue knows that Raiden attacked Mala?" she asked cautiously. "You really think he would keep that back?"

"He's hungry, Delta," I said. "He's hungry like I am—he's starving for something he can't have. Something he knows he'll never be able to have again. It's like a hole inside him that he keeps trying to fill—to fill with revenge, with power, with—with anything that makes him feel less empty, be it for only a moment..." I sighed, trailing off.

"I found a file in Sensei's office containing Hawk's background information," I explained. "I felt like if I could learn everything I could about her and Raiden, then maybe I could finally understand what this all means. I didn't find one for Raiden, but I... I found Hawk's."

"And?"

I swallowed, my throat feeling suddenly tight. "I couldn't open it."

She took a quiet breath. "Fin... why?"

I wanted to tell her why. I wanted to tell someone because I felt like if I didn't soon, the unspoken words would destroy me from the inside out. I wanted to just say it—I had waited forever to just say it.

I was afraid. I was afraid, and I didn't even know why.

I was afraid to know how all of this was connected, if it even was. I was afraid I had misjudged the entire situation and only helped Hawk plunge headlong to her own death. I was afraid I had lost her.

But I didn't say that. I only shook my head and forced myself to straighten up.

"I have to talk to Mitsue first," I said. "I have to confront him about this. I know too much now to stay silent. I have to at least try to get him to open up."

Delta looked at me like someone who saw past masks, and for a moment I was afraid she would see me underneath it all.

"That's not the reason," she began quietly, though her voice held back a storm in the undertones. "Is it?"

She did see me. And now I was about to lie further—I couldn't.

"No, Delta," I said. "It's not the reason."

As if perceiving how close to the edge I was, she didn't push me further. She took a step back.

"I would wait until dawn if I were you," she suggested, pulling her shawl back over her shoulders. "And I would be careful."

"I will be."

"And I would open Hawk's file first."

Something inside me faltered.

"You've been there for her this far, Fin," she said, leaning forward. "Don't let go because you're afraid of what could happen if you hold on."

I thought about what she was saying. What it all meant.

I had set out to understand the situation, to understand whatever it was Mitsue was holding back: Raiden, Hawk, Icarus—all of it, for one purpose only. To be there for her should the need arise.

And now I held in my hands perhaps the final piece of the puzzle I'd been searching for... and I was a scared, selfish child looking for somewhere to hide. For someone to tell me everything would be alright.

But nothing was alright—nothing could be.

"I will," I said. "I'll open it."

Delta nodded once. Then she slowly rose. "They'll be getting back soon," she told me in a low voice, though there was no one around to overhear. "I just wouldn't want..."

She didn't need to finish. "I'll leave you now," I said, standing.

A fragment of a smile passed over Delta's lips. She led me to the door and focused open the canvas, allowing me out without another word.

Afterward I felt as though I should have thanked her. Yet parting in silence had almost felt more natural for us, in some strange way.

I returned to my dorm, quiet on my feet.

Mitsue was already asleep, and I was reminded once again of the irony of it all. "Sleeping with the enemy" had a fresh meaning now.

Silently I took a seat at my desk and struck a match. The quiet sizzle of the flame seemed to fill the air around me, and then it was overcome by the softness of an orange glow.

I opened the appropriate drawer and took out the manila file with Hawk's name scrawled neatly across the label. It felt warm between my fingertips.

I checked over my shoulder to ensure that I wasn't being observed. When I was satisfied that I was as alone as I could be, I placed the file down on the desk in front of me and, taking a deep breath, I opened it.

CHAPTER SIXTEEN

Hawk

I tracked the wolf for what felt like hours. The sunlight filtered down through the trees as I ventured deeper into the desolate wilderness around me.

I caught glimpses of the black wolf every now and again, fifty yards ahead or so. A black smudge among the pines that began to give way to lanky birches instead. Everything around me was a blend of charcoal gray and parchment white. The sunlight rained down to play tricks on my eyes, dancing among the rigid branches and seeming to multiply the number of wolves I was following; they flashed in and out of the trees.

I felt as though every time I blinked, every time I closed my eyelids, I saw a pair of eyes that were darker than the night sky. I saw a face that was like a ghost of my own.

Charlotte.

It wasn't a name; it was a curse that echoed in my head in a voice that was still somehow familiar, though I hadn't heard it in a century. A voice that I'd heard as a child, grown up with, whose octaves I had listened to as they evolved to deeper tones. A voice that was an empty echo.

A voice I had one night saved from its own destruction.

Oh, how many times have I regretted healing you. How often do I wish I had just let you bleed...

The breathing of the wolves around me seemed to grow more

audible the more I thought of my past. Of the nightmares that had haunted me since the night it happened. *The nightmares that Icarus and I had shared.*

As I stole a glance around me, I found myself part of a pack—a pack of howling, darting blurs among the trees.

I ran with the black wolves, increasing the pace of my footfalls as the snow cover grew thinner. I darted through the trees and slipped on the embankments that rose and fell like waves on the sea. Everything was whirling around me, seeming to shake beneath my feet as if it all would burst at any given moment. The trees swayed, and the wind began to blow harder than before; then suddenly it all stopped.

The wolves skidded to a messy stop in the snow. I halted with even less grace, slipping on a slick patch of packed snow. My knees betrayed me, and I sprawled to the ground. The air rushed forcefully out of my lungs as I landed.

Ouch.

Pain surged up from the frozen earth to sink its teeth into the palms of my hands.

Sucking in a breath, I pressed myself up into a seated position. The other wolves had vanished. Only the one remained.

Its eyes shimmered gold from where it stood at the top of an embankment, staring down at me.

I squinted in disbelief, stealing a quick glance around me, amazed that the rest of the pack had dissipated so quickly.

As I climbed to my feet, I noticed I was bleeding. A messy streak ran the length of my right palm, and a spattering stained the ground below.

Clamping my free hand over the wound, I watched as the wolf clambered down the side of the embankment.

It stalked purposefully towards a hollow place beneath a large skeletal tree that had fallen to rest over the embankment. Crouching down, it vanished inside.

I glanced around hesitantly before taking a few steps closer to examine the space.

It was a dark cave of medium size, a tunnel burrowing deep into the embankment. I ducked cautiously beneath the remains of the tree.

Out of habit, I shot a glance over my shoulder, still not convinced that the other wolves were gone. But there was nothing behind me except the lonely forest.

I lowered to my hands and knees and carefully made my way inside.

The scent of fresh earth swelled around me as I felt my way through on my hands and knees. I winced as the dirt stung in my wound. I didn't stop long enough to heal it.

I could hear a scratching sound not far ahead.

At first the earth was just a cold ache under my hands, biting at the skin on my palms, but then gradually it was less and less abrasive—in fact it was...

"Warm?" My chapped lips parted in a whisper. "How is that possible?"

As soon as I glanced up from the darkness just in front of me, I glimpsed a faint stream of yellow light ahead. A short, wolfish bark emanated from that direction.

I gulped back my hesitations and pushed myself onward. The space seemed to grow tighter and tighter until at last the tunnel let out—opening to a meadow.

I felt my eyes widen as I scrambled to my feet. I could scarcely believe what I was seeing...

Everything was green. Everything around me was warm and vivid and veiled in almost disorienting shafts of sunlight. Cicadas hissed distantly, and a robin warbled from the treetops. I stood at the edge of an overgrown thicket.

Every trace of snow or ice had dissolved. It was almost as if that had all been a dream—a nightmare I'd been living until the moment I'd emerged from the tunnel.

Behind me was a lush, overgrown forest, and before me was a wide stretch of wind-whipped alpine grasses and a tumultuous sea of wildflowers. Hues of burnt sienna, deep violet, and sunset orange rolled out in every direction, creating a wide circle—a valley surrounded by blue-tinted peaks that rose like warriors to guard it. The fragrance of sage and pine was like incense in the air.

The wolf stood several yards ahead—an almost eerie contrast against the soft background colors. Its golden eyes watched mine as if waiting for me to stop admiring the view and proceed.

I stepped forward, and in tandem with me, the black wolf leapt back into motion, leading me onward. Butterflies circled overhead, and the quiet rhythm of the wolf's pace added soft percussions to what was like a concert rising from the ground. I reached down and felt the softness of flower petals pass across my fingertips like silk as I followed.

Where on earth am I? How has everything changed so suddenly?

My observations offered me no explanations. We walked, and I kept a careful eye on the mass of black fur in front of me.

We were nearly across the meadow now and approaching the rugged tree line that seemed to be pulling us back into the forest. That was when something caught my attention in the distance, an ashy contrast against the bright blue.

Smoke.

My footsteps slowed as I studied the thin wisps of gray. The wolf glanced over its shoulder almost as if to check that I was still following. Its eyes locked with mine, and I shook out of my thoughts, picking up my pace again. I noticed vaguely that the butterflies were gone.

My curiosity hushed my instincts as I entered the shadows of the trees; dark evergreens rocketed up around me once again.

The forest floor was carpeted in golden pine needles, and cedars swayed gently in the breeze around us. For the first time in what felt like a long time, I could feel my fingers again. My lungs didn't sting with my every breath. Finally calm enough, I healed the wound on my hand as I treaded forward quietly.

I scanned the forest, and after a moment caught sight of an ashy gray puff moving among the trees. It was about a hundred yards ahead. I squinted, trying to see past the trees as we wove in among them. The wolf moved with the stealthy agility of an expert.

As we got closer, I could just make out the outline of a roughly constructed shelter. Large branches were lashed together with rope made of wild grass, and covered with moss and pine needles. It stood in the middle of a large clearing, with a tattered curtain of woven grass dividing the interior from the dwindling fire just outside.

There was no flame. Just blackened logs sending up smoke like a eulogy to what they had been before the spark came.

I froze in my tracks, my spine tensing.

The wolf continued into the campsite.

Someone is living here.

I stole a hasty glance around me, checking for any sign of life hidden among the trees. Then my attention shot to the black wolf as it tossed back its head to let out a long, low howl. I started as another wolf immediately emerged from the shelter, as if beckoned.

I glanced back in the direction of the meadow. When I looked back, there were three wolves.

My heartbeat quickened.

The wolf I'd been following since dawn locked eyes with me once more. Brush scratched my legs as I reluctantly moved forward into the clearing. The soil was soft under my feet.

I cautiously approached the fire, moving slowly.

Hours old, for sure, I thought, studying the smoldering remains.

My gaze shifted back up to the wolves around me and then slowly to the shelter. I took a step closer.

They made no reaction.

My fingers shook as I cautiously reached out to brush the curtain of the shelter aside.

Abruptly, one of the wolves exploded into a howl. I whirled around.

One wolf had stepped to the perimeter of the circle, its eyes focused on the woods around us. The others watched it, their ears bent forward alertly.

My own eyes rapidly scanned our surroundings. I saw nothing; then I realized it wasn't something the wolf had *seen*. It was something it had evidently *heard*.

A distant howl echoed through the air—a response to the black wolf's cry.

But there was something different about it. There was something in the tone that ached and bent and caught me by surprise. There was something about it that caused sweat to prickle across the back of my neck as I stood there in front of the shelter, swallowing back my racing heart.

It wasn't a wolf. It was a human.

February 1916

We sat on the ledge overlooking the city below. Her feet were bare, and I could see the vague hues of her veins under her pale skin. I looked at her like someone stares at a painting in a museum: in awe but understanding little.

She sipped smoke off the end of the cigarette, exhaling gray blurs past the tangled hair that hung in her face.

"Charlotte, how did you do it?" I asked eventually.

"Do what?"

The words were stuck in my throat. I tapped away the ash from my cigarette. "That night," I said. "When we were younger. When you first found me."

"What about it?" she asked.

"I tried to kill myself, remember?"

She hesitated. "Did you?"

"Don't you remember it?" I asked, stunned. "You... you're the one who..."

"Who what?"

"You healed me that night. I would have died if you hadn't."

A weary smile pushed at her lips as she blew out more smoke. "Whatever you say, Ed." She slipped back into the room, brushing past the curtains.

"Do you not believe me?"

"Healing you? No." Her eyes were knife sharp. "I'm nothing special."

She walked away before I could respond, so she never heard what I said to the sky.

I said, "You're wrong, Charlotte."

CHAPTER SEVENTEEN

Fin

It was almost dawn when I pounded on Sensei's office door. My heart was thundering nearly as hard.

"Sensei, I *know* you're in there. I *need* to speak with you."

When no answer came, I pounded harder.

"Sensei, let me in." It was practically an order. Had I been in my right mind, I might have realized just how disrespectful it sounded.

But regardless, the door opened on its own, sending me stumbling into the room's dark interior. The firelight was the first thing my mind comprehended, and then the door slammed shut behind me. When I straightened, I found Sensei at his desk, quill in hand, eyes fixed on the page in front of him. The dawn seemed to deepen the shadows across his face as it crept in.

"Sensei," I repeated, catching my breath, "didn't you hear me banging on the door?"

"Yes." He continued to push the quill across the page. "I heard you."

"Why didn't you let me in sooner?" I asked.

"I was waiting for you to let yourself in," he replied.

I felt my jaw tighten.

I strode across the dimly illuminated room, halted at Sensei's desk, and planted my fists down firmly on the surface. I waited until the quill finally faltered in his fingertips and he looked up. I looked into his eyes and swallowed back my heart.

"How long have you known?" The words came out as heavy as lead. "Sensei, please tell me you didn't know…" I trailed off, shaking my head. "What am I saying? Of course you knew!" I nearly shouted. "How could you?"

"How could I what, Fin?" he asked quietly. Calmly. As he always did—as he always *was*.

Completely unaffected, detached and removed. Standing outside it all—above it all.

"How could you keep it from me?" I asked, my voice cracking. "How could you have not told me? After all this time, after—after you knew that I…"

I stopped, my eyelids clamping shut. What I had seen in Hawk's folder was there in front of me every time I closed my eyes. The words I had read silently to myself by candlelight rang through my thoughts like sirens.

Charlotte… Charlotte… Charlotte…

I heard Sensei set the quill down. There was a creak from his chair as he leaned forward, bringing his voice closer to me.

"Do you believe me to be her keeper, Fin?" he asked. "Do I govern her or preside over her as a guardian? Do you believe me to have any more authority over her than you do?"

I felt as though my insides were collapsing. I felt like the air had been sucked from my chest. I had no idea how to reply. I couldn't.

"Fin, if you believe me to be in some position of authority over her, then you are greatly mistaken." His words were firm. "It was not my place to tell you; it was hers."

I wanted to shout the words—I wanted to scream them. I wanted to vent all the rage I felt boiling over inside me *somewhere*. I was angry… I was so angry. I was angry because I knew he was right.

But instead the words slipped out in the shredded remains of a whisper. "Well, she didn't…" I said. "She didn't tell me."

Sensei said nothing. He waited patiently.

"I would have done anything for her," I said finally. "I would have done anything if she had just said the word."

"What would you have done?" Sensei asked, though he didn't pause for me to answer. "There was nothing you could have done, Fin. Do you believe Hawk to be incapable of taking care of herself?"

I shook my head. "Not in the least."

Sensei looked at me for a moment and then back down to the page. "It was very long ago, Fin. It is something she strives to forget."

"I could have helped her."

"We will never know what we could have done."

I opened my mouth to speak, but no words came. I stepped away from the desk and walked to the fire.

"I wish I could have been there to kill him," I said. "I would have made him feel the pain he caused her."

"Vengeance is the road to death, Fin."

I shook my head slowly, staring down into the flame. "How can you speak so calmly about it—when you *know* what happened to her? When you were the one who intervened? You know better than anyone!"

"Because it is something I redeemed her from," he replied. "But she has to discover that redemption for herself. There is a reason I keep the files out of reach, Fin."

I turned to face him, steadying myself against the mantel. "How did you know I took the files?" I asked. "You weren't—"

"You think because you did not see me that I was not here, Fin?" he asked, pushing back his chair to rise. "You are mistaken. That is when I am most present."

He began gathering up the papers he had been working on, shuffling them into a tidy stack. He glanced up briefly. "Do you really think you could have opened the case if I hadn't wished it?"

"So you wanted me to see what I did?"

"It was not that I wanted you to, Fin," he replied. "There are some yearnings of the soul that cannot be denied."

I stared at him, searching his eyes for an explanation. "Sensei, the lost sliders…" I trailed off, my voice vanishing in my throat. "You know who the killer is." I didn't ask it like it was a question, but it was. His eyes hadn't left mine.

"Should I not be the one asking you this question, Fin?" he asked calmly, seeming to make a study of me.

I stared at him for a moment, swallowing hard. The dots in my head began to slowly make connections. I suddenly remembered something—someone.

Crossing the room, I stopped in front of the bookshelf. My eyes scanned the appropriate shelf, and my finger trailed slowly after it, hesitating on the binding of *Canis Lupus*. I gently tugged the book out from the shelf and separated the covers.

When the shelf had retracted, I reached for the first folder. I carried it to his desk and dropped it open before him. It opened to the exact page I was looking for. The face that had stayed with me since I first saw it—so familiar, yet unrecognizable.

A grainy, blurry photograph. An obscured face. A head of messy dark hair. Medium-toned skin.

The last on the kill list.

My fingers were clammy as I separated the photograph from the paperclip that held it to the page. I examined it more closely—what I could see of the face. The eyes, the mouth, the color of the hair…

"He reminds me of someone." I brought the photograph farther into the candlelight. I glanced at Sensei. "With shorter hair and different clothes." I began to reconfigure the photograph in my mind. "He looks so much like…"

My eyes darted back to the profile page, shifting up to the name. Though I could hardly believe it when I saw it.

"Riley." I exhaled the word, stunned. "That's the name Raiden used when he first came to us."

Sensei said nothing. He listened and he watched my hands as they feverishly sifted back through the pages of lost sliders.

"But the date of the first murdered slider predates Riley's birth." I glanced up at Sensei, still holding the photograph in my hands. "Which would mean…"

It was starting to come together in my head.

I felt my brow furrow as Sensei lifted the folder and shifted expertly through the pages.

"The first date," he said simply, tapping the appropriate page. "It was very long ago."

My gaze shifted from the page to his eyes and then back to the page.

It was the first slider Areos and I had encountered when we'd searched the files the day before. The broad-shouldered young man with long jet-black hair, a dark complexion, and eyes as depthless as the night sky.

"He was Raiden's first victim?" I questioned, confused. "But how is that possible? That was a century ago."

"Were you able to even identify who Raiden really is?" Sensei asked. "Or when he was born?"

"Areos and I weren't able to find any evidence of his even *being* a slider," I confessed. "It makes no sense—he killed all of these students, yet it's as if..."

"Raiden is but a shell, Fin," he said gravely, looking down at the file. "One of many."

Something inside me balked at the implications. I thought back to the previous sunset. To sitting down at my desk with Hawk's folder and finally, finally forcing myself to open it. I remembered the words and the sinking feeling that had settled into my gut with each sentence.

Charlotte... born 1901... possessor of deep powers and an uncanny ability to shift... was attacked and raped in the summer of 1918.

The last line had been like a knife in my chest. A blade digging deep—finding every sensitive area in my soul and drawing a well of blood as it sank in.

"So the real question is, if Raiden is but a shell"—I looked at him—"then who is living in Raiden's body?" I stepped back a little, looking Sensei directly in the eyes. "Because regardless of who he really is, he's the one who killed all of those lost sliders. He's the one who had a thirst for *her* blood—someone who couldn't give up the idea that Hawk had... slipped through his fingers."

I set the photograph back down on the desk. The unreadable eyes stared up at me more vividly than they had before.

"He's the one who's at the bottom of the ravine with Hawk right now," I continued quietly. "You rescued her from someone who has been racing time to find her again. Someone who has been using *our blood*—killing sliders—to make himself immortal and undetectable—unstoppable."

Sensei lifted the profile of the young man with the long dark hair and studied the picture for a moment. I watched his eyes flick subtly back and forth in the candlelight.

"Did you know from the beginning that Raiden was really Hawk's past attacker, Sensei?" I asked, urgency rising in my voice.

"I have told Hawk since the day I brought her here that she is a warrior just below the skin," he said quietly. "And as such, she chooses her own battles, whether she believes it or not, and this is her battle. I cannot fight it for her, nor can you."

My eyes shifted down to the photograph of Riley. "You can think what you like, Sensei," I replied coldly. "But if I had known while he was still here, I would have killed him—and I couldn't care less about the consequences of revenge."

"Not even when you have seen what it has done to Mitsue?"

"He seems relatively unaffected, I can assure you."

"If you believe Mitsue to be inherently evil, Fin, you are wrong." He pinned the photograph back onto the appropriate page. "He faces the same temptations as you, only he has fallen for them. The consequences are eating him alive."

I wasn't sure how to respond to that. It was hard for me to think of anything beyond Hawk, let alone feel even the smallest shred of sympathy for Mitsue.

All the loose ends—the many, many loose ends—were finally tying slowly together. We had all known Raiden was a killer... but now I knew who he had killed and who he had tried to kill. His attempt to take Hawk that day on the gathering platform had not been his first attempt. The very thought was enough to make my blood boil.

"Why didn't you stop him?" I demanded. "Or was that his battle—to destroy the rest of what Hawk had left?"

Sensei closed the folder. "You speak as if you are angry with me, Fin."

"And would it not be justifiable if I was?" I said, exasperated. "You have been so absent from us lately, Sensei. Hawk is gone. Runner has reported to me that Mala was previously attacked by Raiden. I now know that Raiden is Hawk's rapist from her past, and I believe beyond the shadow of a doubt that they are *all* still alive at the bottom of the ravine—and I have had to deal with *all* of that *myself*, Sensei. Did you not consider that I may have *needed you*, Sensei?" I asked, my voice breaking. "That I would have given anything for even a *shard* of your guidance?"

"Fin," he said quietly as he turned to gaze into my eyes, "why did you not just come to me?"

My teacher's words rang in my ears louder than if he had shouted them. The look that lingered in his eyes haunted me long after I had silently taken my leave, focusing the door softly closed behind me.

I felt just as I had the morning Hawk had said her final goodbye at the edge of the training platform and disappeared into the mist. I felt as I did every night when I lay awake, pining endlessly for her, for my parents, for my sisters, for my home in Ireland. I felt like everything that had once been inside of me was gone. I was empty, hollow.

I had never felt more torn apart in all my life.

I forced myself to focus on the one thing I knew I had to do. I felt I had unearthed enough evidence to piece the puzzle together, but I still needed to confront Mitsue. I knew I would not be able to rest until I did. Even then, I doubted my mind would ever be at ease again.

Dawn had broken by the time I reached my dorm, but when I stepped inside, I found Mitsue still in bed. I walked over to my desk to check the drawer, ensuring that the folder was still safely hidden exactly where I had left it. Then I tore the blankets off his bed.

He immediately started awake, sputtering curses.

"Get up," I ordered. "We need to talk."

He was a disheveled mess, shirtless and wearing sweatpants. His hair was plastered over his face. He muttered inaudibly as he straightened himself up into a seated position. He shot me an irritated look.

"What's wrong with you?"

I felt my jaw set. "What's wrong with *you*?"

His eyes narrowed slightly, though I could tell he had no idea what I was talking about.

"You lied," I clarified, not breaking our eye contact. "About Raiden—when you and Hawk were supposed to erase his memory. You told the council that you had not been able to see past the surface of Raiden's cognitive—and that was a lie."

"It was not a lie!" Mitsue sputtered, fighting with his hair. "Have you ever tried to eradicate the memory of someone who holds the brain capacity of a dozen or more other sliders, Fin? It's nearly impossible—it *is* impossible. It's like a spider's web. It's *completely* unreadable."

I looked at him for a second, considering my words before I spoke them. "Seven," I corrected, recalling the number of profiles in the lost slider folder. "Not a dozen. And I could also remind you that it's not your place to read the subject's memory. Your objective was only to erase it," I said firmly. "You know anything less would be a breach in our code of conduct."

"Of course—"

"Yet you saw more than you reported to the council." I cut him off to continue. "You reported, in fact, that you saw nothing beyond just his recent memories—"

"Which is true!"

"Which is *false*." I emphasized the last word through gritted teeth. "You saw much more than that. You *knew* that he had attacked Mala."

I saw a flicker of something pass through his eyes. Then he shook his head ardently. "I have no idea what you're talking about."

"Then why was it so important for you to take her under your tutelage?"

"I've already given you my reasons for that."

"No," I said. "Runner told me that Mala had vague, subconscious memories of it upon her awakening. I know that's why you took her."

Mitsue stood up now, his lips pressed into a thin, angry line. "You think you understand everyone's motives so well, don't you?" he asked scornfully. "You think you can just step in and take her place as Sensei's favored one by demonstrating your valor and consideration. I know you have about as much respect for our code as Icarus did—none at all."

"You're deviating," I pointed out.

"Am I?" He took a step forward, looking me squarely in the eyes. "Fine. I'll tell you why I took her—and I'll tell you why I lied to the council. But if I tell you that, I'll tell you something else I saw in Raiden's mind, something that would frighten even you, Fin, something to do with Hawk."

I already knew what he was alluding to, and already I could feel sweat prickling at the back of my neck. As far as I knew, Sensei and I were the only ones who had knowledge of Hawk's past, and because of that, I knew her secret would be safeguarded. If Mitsue knew, everyone soon would.

I was afraid of what he was about to say. As much as if it had been my own secret.

"Raiden attacked other sliders—killed other sliders. We know this," he continued. "He attacked Mala—yes, that much is true. I saw it in his mind like a thousand vivid snapshots. He did abuse her, though she still loved him and so tolerated his aggressive nature—"

"And you told no one of this?" I asked, disgusted. "You learned that one of our students had been abused, and you did nothing?"

"On the contrary, I knew better than anyone how to care for her," he replied icily. "So aside from your underwhelming performance of late, yes—I did have other motives for taking her on as a student."

I studied his face long and hard, and then I slowly shook my head, stepping around him.

"No," I said, thinking it through. "No, helping her was not your main motivation, Mitsue—I know you. You assumed she would eventually open up to you. Perhaps on some subconscious level, she would give you some insight into who Raiden really was."

I slowly walked to the porthole window. Light was leaking in.

"We all know that no one was closer to him than she was," I finished. "You knew that she loved him at one time—and that love reaches far beyond the boundaries of the thinking mind."

"What good would learning about a dead student do me?"

I felt an unsatisfied smile pull at the corners of my mouth for a moment. "Oh, I think you and I both know he's not dead," I responded. "*They're* not dead. And I think you want to figure this out just as much as I do—but for different reasons."

I could feel his gaze burning holes in my back. For a moment the room went completely quiet.

"You know *nothing* of what I deal with, Fin," he said, seething. "*Nothing*—so don't you *dare* pretend to."

I gazed at the view beyond the window. The shriveled autumn leaves as they blew past in the gusts of wind. The mist far below. Then, in my mind's eye, I saw what I knew was beyond the mist.

I thought about her. And suddenly I could no longer bear it.

I whirled around to face Mitsue.

"I know nothing?" I hissed. "I know *nothing* of how it feels to have lost everything?"

He looked at me, stunned. I took a step closer.

"Mitsue, I know much of loss, believe me." My words came out in tatters. "I am not a stranger to what you have felt these past weeks. I am an embodiment of it—I am *broken* because of it!"

I stopped as my voice cracked. I forcefully blinked back the sting of tears.

"So don't you dare tell me that I don't know what you're dealing with." I lowered my voice now. "I understand far more than you realize."

A silence inserted itself into the conversation. For a moment there was conflict in his eyes, bitterness and hurt.

"Fin, in Raiden I saw a deep longing for Hawk," he said numbly. "You're right—I should have reported these things to the council. I did not. You can give an account of my failure to the council if you wish to. There's nothing I can do to stop you. But know this…"

He took a step forward and lowered his voice. I felt my pulse rising.

"I don't know much. It is true that the majority of his memory was completely hidden from my view. But I know that Raiden wanted her. He wanted her more than anything else—more than Icarus, even." His gaze shifted past my shoulder to the window behind me. "And if he is alive down there," he continued quietly, "you would have reason to be worried about her."

It was nothing I hadn't already considered. Yet the words still cut deep.

I forced myself to breathe, to swallow back everything I felt. I took a few steps forward and placed a hand briefly on Mitsue's shoulder as I passed him.

"I *am* worried about her," I told him quietly. "More than you could possibly imagine."

I heard him turn behind me as I parted the canvas in front of me.

"Fin, wait."

I hesitated in the doorway, standing for a moment between the breeze and the calm.

"Are you going to report my…"

His actions, his failures, his shortcomings. He didn't finish because we both already knew.

I wanted to. I had every reason to. He'd condemned Hawk to death. As much as Hawk and I knew it had to happen, it didn't change the fact that I had watched him happily go about planning her trial and execution—watching every trace of pain as it crossed my face.

I pulled in a deep breath, realizing suddenly that my hands were in fists.

Turning to look over my shoulder, I locked my eyes with his. "Return Mala to my care by sunset and I won't say a word."

He stared at me for a moment and then bowed his head submissively.

I turned to step outside. The canvas shut behind me, and the cold wind brushed my skin, though I scarcely felt it.

My hands were still in fists.

CHAPTER EIGHTEEN

Hawk

I watched as the wolves paced in anticipation. The one occasionally howled and was then answered by a far less animalistic-sounding cry from somewhere deeper in the forest. A human voice.

The air was dead around me, without so much as even a gentle breeze to disrupt the silence, amplifying his agile footsteps all the more when they finally came into earshot. I held my breath as I watched the source of the sound enter the circle.

It was a man—a young man. The wolves rose immediately to swarm around him.

"Easy, easy," he said, hushing them. "I heard you call."

He had a rugged mountain voice that was somehow far older than his young face and body appeared to be.

He crossed the clearing and disappeared into the shelter. I could catch glimpses of him through the voids in the moss-covered roof. I wondered if he had noticed the hawk perched in the treetop above his camp.

He emerged a moment later with handfuls of wood, which he dropped alongside the remains of the fire. I watched him closely, studying him as he knelt beside it, presumably to begin rebuilding it.

He was tall, with long raven-black hair that flowed over his shoulders. His skin was an almond tone, and his eyes were as black as the ash staining his fingertips. The wolves were at ease around

138

him, and he seemed just as familiar with their presence. He wore black pants, threadbare at the knees, and was bare-chested with his shirt tied around his waist.

He glanced around occasionally, as if expecting to see someone emerge from the forest at any moment. He spoke to the wolves, though he concealed his words in soft, indistinguishable tones, almost as though he knew I was straining to listen. Almost as if he knew there were ten thousand questions ravaging my mind.

Patiently, painstakingly, he rebuilt the fire, humming softly as he worked. The wolf that had led me there kept glancing occasionally in my direction. There was an almost knowing look in his golden eyes as he watched me from the ground below. After a moment, he slowly approached the base of the tree I'd evacuated up into. My heart immediately began to race, though I knew I had no reason to be nervous in this form.

The wolf placed a paw on the tree's rough trunk and gave a sharp bark. The young man immediately straightened to attention, glancing at the wolf.

"What is it?"

He followed the wolf's gaze up the tree to the branch where I had perched. His dark eyes fixed on me, curious and inquiring.

"Leave her be," he told the wolf. "She'll come down when she's ready."

I froze inside.

She? How does he know?

He smiled a little and then went back to stacking wood. I began to realize that he had been speaking generally—simply using "she" rather than "it." I relaxed a little. I was too on edge, and I needed to keep my cool.

The fact was, I had found someone. Not Icarus, but *someone*— and that was worth something. The wolves had led me here for a reason.

I needed to know who he was, and where he had come from, and how he had come to be here—and if he had seen Icarus. I needed to know why this place was so different from the landscape I'd fallen into. Nothing made sense, and now I finally had an opportunity to get some answers, or at least try to. But what I needed to learn from him, I couldn't up here.

I would be lying if I said I wasn't scared. The very things that were potential beacons of hope were also bright red warning flags. There was no way for me to know what I was walking into.

I waited until nightfall. Until the sky was dark and the stars were like sparkling pinpricks in satin overhead. I watched him light a fresh fire after failing to rekindle the last, using two rocks. It reminded me of my own newly acquired ability to channel fire. When I thought about it, I could practically feel the heat tingling in the tips of my wings.

He sat down, cross-legged, by the fire, and the black wolves dispersed into the woods, seeming on edge as the starlight flickered down through the trees. I heard distant howls on occasion.

The young man's features were illuminated by the crackling fire. He seemed to have all but forgotten I was there. He held a small journal in his hand and seemed to be writing or making a sketch with charcoal.

Finally, he rose again and went inside the shelter, and the opportunity for me to make my entrance presented itself.

I left the branch and flew several yards into the forest. I landed softly on the ground below and transformed back into my human form. I didn't want him to know I could shift; that had to remain a secret.

I straightened my clothes and took a shaky breath.

I slowed to a halt at the very edge of the clearing, waiting to see if and when he would emerge from the shelter. When he didn't, I finally stepped forward into the clearing.

I walked farther in towards the flickering shades of yellow and orange. The snap of a twig under my foot disrupted the chorus of crickets and the distant, occasional howls. It was enough to cause an audible stir from within the shelter. A moment later the curtain parted.

The dark eyes met mine from across the flames. He stared at me like someone who hadn't seen another living soul in a hundred years.

He stepped out completely. The connection between our eyes didn't falter.

"Who are you?" he asked, in a curious voice edged with an accent. "Where did you come from?"

I pulled in a deep breath, debating what kind of cover story to give.

"The wolves," I replied slowly. "I followed one of the black wolves, and it led me here."

I swallowed, watching his expression closely.

"Where exactly is this place?" I asked.

He stared at me for a moment longer, seeming puzzled by the question, and then he looked around us. "Must everything have a name?" He seemed to be musing more than asking. "It is reality. I know nothing beyond it."

"Nothing?" I questioned. "You've always lived here?"

He nodded. "It certainly feels like it."

"Are you alone here?"

He nodded again.

"How is that possible?"

He shrugged, turning his attention back to me. "Could I not ask the same of you?"

He could indeed.

I struggled to come up with something to say.

"I awoke in a place like this, but covered in snow." I thought back to the tunnel in the embankment. "And then the wolf led me here. The wolves you talk to."

He studied me a moment longer and then smiled. "I talk to them because they are mine."

"Yours?"

He knelt beside the fire, picking up the journal and closing it. "It is hard for you to understand, but if you stay, you will learn that no one knows where exactly this place is."

He paused to pick up a stick with which he began prodding the fire. "And no one knows how to leave," he said, seeming to muse once more to himself. "Or should I say, escape."

I watched him for a moment. "I don't want to stay."

"You wish to find your way home, then?"

I nodded, then looked away from him. Because it wasn't the whole truth. I already knew there was no way I could trust someone I didn't know. But I also knew I needed to get to know him enough to find out why he was here and whether he could help me find Icarus.

He gestured for me to take a seat at the fire across from him and I did so, checking over my shoulders for wolves at the same time.

"I guess that would depend on how you define home," I said. "What is your name?"

He moved one of the logs, sending up sparks. "Maicoh."

"Hawk."

He seemed to consider it for a moment. I decided to ask another question before he could begin to consider the implications of my name.

"What did you mean when you said that the wolves were yours?" I asked. "How could you possibly have tamed them when they seem so wild?"

He smiled. "I have not tamed them. In fact, it would be closer to the truth to say that I am theirs."

I furrowed my brow. "I don't understand."

"I know," he said. "But you will soon. You learn to use your mind down here, believe me, Hawk."

He hesitated, letting his gaze venture up to the sky above for a moment.

"In other worlds, your mind has power even though you cannot see it," he went on. "But here in this world our desires, our hatred, our passions—they grow teeth and claws, and we see with our own eyes how much power they have. A power so strong that it is very, very hard to control."

I watched him as he lost himself in the stars overhead, strangely comfortable with my presence for someone he'd only just met. There was something almost eerily familiar about him—about this whole situation.

"So… the wolves control you?" I asked, still trying to get my head around it. "You made them, but they control you?"

"Yes," he replied, going contemplatively silent for a moment. "They led you here, didn't they?" he asked finally.

I nodded. "They've been following me since I first came here. I haven't been able to shake them, no matter where I go."

"You have been following *them*," Maicoh corrected me. "But perhaps it is a good thing. Perhaps they will lead you to whatever it is that you are seeking."

A distant howl rose above the cricket songs around us. I shuddered inwardly, recalling blurry visions of my face reflected in the ice.

"They've led me to nothing but you, thus far," I confessed after a moment. "But perhaps that's because you can help me."

"I cannot help you unless I know what it is you're looking for." Maicoh squinted at me. "But I have a feeling it is not merely a way out."

"You presume correctly," I replied. "I'm searching for someone. Someone very important to me."

Maicoh didn't reply, but he didn't stop studying me either. His eyes were reflections of the flames as they wavered in the gentle breeze. I couldn't help but wonder what he was thinking.

"I know he's down here somewhere, and I need to find him," I went on cautiously. "Have you seen anyone besides me since you've been here?"

He shook his head. "I have seen no one but you, Hawk."

I knitted my brows together, puzzled. "How long have you been here, exactly? How did you get here?"

He opened his mouth to reply, but then stopped. He glanced back down at the journal in his hands. "You have much to learn, Hawk."

I wanted to press the question, but we were alone in the forest, in the dark, and I still had no idea who I was dealing with. I had forced myself to approach Maicoh only because I knew I had to. He was the only human I had encountered thus far—and he wasn't Raiden or Icarus. I had to find out who he was. If he really had been down here for as long as he was leading me to believe, then maybe he could help me find them.

I watched as he rose to his feet and offered me a hand. I didn't take it, but I copied his motions anyway and then took a subtle step backwards.

"You have nowhere to spend the night, do you?"

I shook my head hesitantly.

Maicoh swept a hand in the direction of the shelter behind him, stepping aside simultaneously.

I shook my head again. "I really couldn't. I—"

"I have no desire to sleep tonight, believe me," he interrupted gently. "Please, be my guest. You may have my shelter to yourself, and I will stay outside. We may talk more in the morning, perhaps?"

I studied his face for a moment and then nodded slowly.

"Yes," I replied. "We will talk more—and you'll explain more."

143

It came out sounding like an order, but strangely he didn't seem offended in the least. He bowed his head respectfully.

"I will explain everything that I can," he replied solemnly. "I promise."

August 1918

"Charlotte, what's wrong?"

The curtain had fallen. We were backstage. The hum of the crowd filled the air, which was thick with the scent of cigar smoke. She was staring out the window like she usually did, watching as the people returned to their cars and left the theater. But her eyes were different somehow.

"Nothing," she said. "It's just..." She shrugged. "A hollow feeling."

"Hollow?"

"Like I'm searching for something," she replied. "Something more."

"How do you mean?"

She shook her head and looked back at me. "I'm not sure."

For a while I believed I could melt the shield she'd built for herself over the years we'd spent growing up in hell. The fortress she'd constructed almost as if to hide the markings, the markings no one could explain.

"How did your parents die?" I had asked her once.

She had told me that she didn't know.

She never wanted to talk about it; she never could. That was because there was no evidence proving that she even had parents. I had almost begun to believe that she wasn't human at all, but a spirit—always slipping just out of my grasp.

One night it overwhelmed me; it reached inside me and wouldn't let go. I stood there watching her smoky exhales touch the glass window and listened to her talk about her future in the sun, in the warm, bright places. The places where I would not be. The places I could not follow her to.

Perhaps I couldn't. But while I still could, I did follow her. Into the darkness, into a rage. Into a rage I would regret only once before I put it to death permanently. My hands found her and held her down until suddenly there was nothing there.

Charlotte. She was mine for a moment and then gone. Gone, gone.

I left the theater, I left the city, I fled. I wandered in the darkest places and mixed myself in the darkest things I could find. The places where the worn-out, faceless, nameless people went. The people my mother would have lived among. I found myself in the desert, in conversation with a poet—a gypsy who claimed to read the stars.

There is an ancient prophecy about a soul who will piece it all back together, my son, she told me, with ragged hands lifting themselves toward the sky. And not death, not hell, not all the evil in this world can stop its steady approach. They're stars, my son... the stars that split and brought us to Earth. The beginning.

Who are you talking about? I had asked her.

The heavens and the Earth were born unto us, a supernova, said she. A soul split in two. Thus we poured forth: one. Stars in need of no darkness to shine, trees in need of no light to grow; the sun and her stars find voice between a sunrise and a sunset. For the universe exists between two halves of the same spirit: a Sunrise marred by the fruits of this world, a Sunset marked by all that it could become...

Poetry, lost, she said. She knew only those verses, handed down to her through the generations. But I didn't need to hear anything further. Something inside my chest clicked.

Charlotte. My own star... marred by the fruits of this world. The "Sunrise," the soul who was "there from the beginning." The one who had healed me.

The one I would scour Earth to find. To become.

CHAPTER NINETEEN

Fin

"So Raiden is the unidentified killer." Areos blew out a sigh, pushing his glasses back up the bridge of his nose. "I can't believe I didn't connect those dots immediately—we already knew he had killed other sliders; it would make sense."

"Raiden isn't even Raiden," I replied, keeping my voice low as I turned to look out over the edge of the platform. "Raiden—Riley—is but another skin suit our unidentified predator stole off someone else."

"So..." Areos looked over at me, one eyebrow raised. "What's his real identity, then?"

I grunted, squinting into the evening sunlight. "That's the real question, isn't it?"

Sessions had just concluded for the evening—my first with Mala back under my tutelage. I'd requested to speak with her afterwards and so waited for her to finish catching up with some of her classmates. Areos had snagged me in the meantime to resume our discussion.

"How did you find out Riley was one of the victims?" Areos asked. "How did you match the identities?"

"Something seemed familiar about Riley's photo," I said. "I hadn't even noticed the name at first. I just couldn't put my finger on what it was exactly—not until I had talked it through with Sensei."

He thought about it. "So the killer is wearing Riley's identity. But he's really someone from the past—someone who's been using other sliders as lifeblood."

"Correct."

"Kind of makes you wonder."

"About?" I glanced over at him.

He shrugged. "If he can shift into the identity of one slider he murdered, could he do it with others? It would make it almost impossible to track him down, and it would explain why he's been able to evade human detection for such a long time."

I considered it. "So you're saying maybe he can shift shape?" I asked. "Like Hawk can? Except into different human forms instead?"

"Precisely."

I was silent for a moment. "Leave it to you to examine something from every possible angle."

"I wasn't a straight-A student for nothing."

"No, it appears not. Though if your hypothesis is accurate, it only makes the situation more dangerous for her."

"If the killer is—"

"In another form, yes," I finished for him. "She may never have even seen the file for the lost sliders, and she may never have worked with those students personally. They may only have been in the Dimension for very short periods of time—I know I don't remember seeing them. There's no guarantee that she would recognize them if she laid eyes on them."

"Because she would be looking for someone who looks like Raiden."

"Exactly."

I shuddered inwardly, considering what this implied. "There's no way to know she'll encounter Raiden."

"There's no way to know whether she'll encounter Icarus, either," Areos added, cynicism creeping into his voice. "There's no way to know whether they're even still—"

I lifted a hand to stop him. "Don't say it. I don't want to hear it."

He studied me like I was a cipher. "Fin, what if it's just something you'll have to accept in the end?"

"I would sooner accept that the world will end tomorrow," I said firmly. "If we don't have at least some level of belief, Areos, we have nothing. That's something you might consider."

He cocked his head to the side uncertainly. "I sometimes wish I had your faith, Fin," he said. "Really. I do."

I shot him a look. "Well, I can tell you one thing for certain about faith, Areos. It doesn't just fall into your lap."

His lips pressed into a small grin and he nodded. I could tell he wasn't satisfied.

"Just think," I went on sarcastically. "You'll have plenty of opportunities to cultivate it once we emerge back into our own worlds. When the cavern is unsealed."

"How are we to proceed without Hawk and Icarus, though?" he asked. "If they are indeed the patriarchs, as you say? Shouldn't they be with us?"

"Yes, they should."

"If they *are* alive… do you have any idea how we're going to get them back?" Areos pressed the question. "Do you even know how you're going to use what you've learned to help Hawk?"

I pulled in a breath, beginning to feel a prickle of irritation. "You know, when you ask questions like this, Areos, you remind me that you're human."

He rolled his eyes, but before he could ask another question, I felt a hand on my shoulder. I turned and found Mala standing behind me, her face as tense as if she were approaching her executioner.

"You, uh…" She cleared her throat. "You wanted to see me, Fin?"

"I did, indeed," I replied, bowing out of my conversation with Areos. "How did you like sessions today? Does it feel good to be back?"

"I guess so," she replied, sounding uncertain. "Is it supposed to?"

I gestured for her to follow me across the platform. I wanted to talk to her somewhere more private. Away from the many prying eyes—and ears.

"You used to really enjoy sessions," I told her. "You're a natural when it comes to channeling."

"But I suck at it."

"Because you keep telling yourself that," I said as we rounded the corner and continued down the long hallway. "You'll never succeed if you expect to fail."

149

"It's not that I expect it, necessarily." She stumbled over her words, trailing behind me. "It's just that... I don't know. It all feels so new."

"You're afraid."

"You could say that."

I focused open one of the pocket doors and gestured for her to enter. Instead, she hesitated cautiously at the threshold.

"Fear is a shadow, Mala," I told her gently. "It's all in your head. You're the one who decides whether it gets out or not. It's your choice."

Mala stared at me for a moment, wide-eyed.

"Come on," I said, finally stepping into the room when she didn't. "Sit down."

She hesitated a moment longer before following me inside. She started when the door rolled shut behind her.

"It's okay," I assured her quietly. "Everything is fine. Relax."

I focused two tatami chairs to the far end of the room, and we sat down at the chabudai table. Mala picked her fingernails nervously as she settled across from me, having yet to make eye contact.

"I want you to know something heading back into all of this, Mala," I told her calmly. "You are an accomplished, intelligent, and capable student. You've done things that humans could only dream of doing, and you've done them well. You have a lot to be confident in."

She swallowed. "Mitsue didn't think so. He said I was inexperienced."

"Then he was not being truthful."

"He said that I was partially to blame for everything that has been going wrong," Mala went on. "That I was one of the instigators of the fight that brought about the evacuation. But I don't remember any of that—I don't even know what he's talking about."

She finally shifted her large brown eyes up to mine for the first time. I could see faint ghosts of terror in their dark centers.

"Is it true that this is my fault?" she asked. "That I caused this?"

Feeling the muscles in my jaw tighten, I leaned forward on the chabudai. "None of this is your fault, Mala, absolutely none of it. Don't let anyone tell you otherwise."

"But what if it is?" she countered gravely. "I can't remember it, so how would I know?"

"You may not remember, Mala, but *I do*, and you can trust me when I tell you that you did everything within your ability to help Icarus."

"Who's Icarus?"

"No one we need to talk about now," I replied. "What else did Mitsue tell you?"

She considered it for a moment before saying anything. I could see the gears turning behind her eyes.

"He told me I couldn't join sessions until I proved myself," she said. "He told me he knew things about me that I couldn't remember—but then I did. I did remember, vaguely."

"What did you remember?"

She shrugged, swallowing. "Him."

"Who?" I asked.

"That's the thing." She sighed, frustrated. "I don't... I can't..." She stopped, closing her eyes to steady herself. "I don't remember his face or his name—I don't remember anything beyond how it felt," she began. "I remember how it felt to be afraid. It's so strange... I really can't remember anything beyond that."

"And Mitsue wanted you to remember?"

She nodded a little. "He told me my subconscious would help me remember. That it was 'all in there' somewhere. I guess when you care about someone, it never really goes away. He said it was important—that people's lives were at stake."

"And probably that you could rejoin sessions once you gave him that information, I'm guessing?"

Mala looked at me and I knew the answer was yes. She didn't even need to say it.

I leaned back in my chair, turning to look out the glass wall to the ravine just beyond.

Hawk was gone, Icarus was gone, Sensei was practically a hermit these days, winter was breathing down the back of our necks, and the Dimension was in chaos. If ever I believed in some form of the apocalypse, this certainly had all the earmarks of its beginning.

In the midst of the storm, it was so easy to forget that we were all still living, breathing souls. That we had emotions. That we weren't immune to hurt and manipulation and heartache. That, beneath our armor, we were all bleeding in one way or another. That we had wounds and desires and longings. I was sitting directly across from the evidence of it.

"Mala, I won't lie to you," I began finally. "I know who this person you remember is."

Her eyes widened.

"And I want you to believe me when I tell you that it is better for you to forget."

"What? I don't understand—"

"Mala, he's dangerous," I stated gravely. "You have to let go."

When I turned to look back at her fully, she was still staring, her lips parted slightly. Confusion mingled with the fear in her eyes now.

"He attacked you, Mala." I pressed the fact. "He meant you harm—he used you to get to someone else, and I don't want you to allow anyone to do that ever again."

"But he's the only one I can remember, Fin!" Her voice cracked. "I don't know much, but I *know* that he meant something to me."

"But he doesn't really exist, Mala," I told her. "I know you can't see that now, but I promise you, one day you will."

She looked at me for a moment, her brown eyes still just as wide, and then she fiercely shook her head no. "I can't."

"Mala—"

"I can't, Fin!" She stood up abruptly, sending the tatami clattering to the floor. "You don't understand what it's like! I can't remember *anything*—I must have come from *somewhere*, I must belong to *someone*!"

"You belong *here*," I said, with emphasis. "You belong with us. This place is your home, Mala."

She shook her head again, her tousled dark brown hair falling into her face. "It's not," she said firmly. "There's more—I know that now. Mitsue made me see it—*you* made me see it. I can't just let go of what little I have left."

"Mala, please, just listen to me—"

She took a step closer, staring down into my eyes. "I can't let go, Fin," she said softly, but with an iron resolve. "I don't know how."

There was something about the way she said it. Something about the tone of finality in her voice.

I wanted to say something. I wanted to help her. I wanted to tell her that I was sorry for what she couldn't remember, and for what she could. I was sorry I hadn't been there for her like I should have been.

But I couldn't find the words. My voice died in my throat.

Mala stood there a moment longer, her gaze still locked with my own, even as tears began welling up in her eyes. Then she turned and strode across the room, pushing aside the door and leaving me to listen to her footsteps echo and fade down the hallway.

Leaving me to wonder how everything had gone so wrong. Why I had *let it* go so wrong?

Why didn't I fight for her? For Hawk, for Icarus, for us? When there was so much more I could have done. Why?

Mala was humble enough to absorb the blame for the current state of the Dimension in its entirety, when in fact she hadn't even lifted a finger towards its destruction. Was I so proud that I couldn't see that my hands weren't clean in this?

At Icarus's trial I had been silent. And I had done only what I thought was best at Hawk's.

Was I right? Had I been right in throwing her into the hands of her worst enemy—someone who desired nothing more than her blood in his veins? Or had I been so caught up in doing what was right that I had actually helped bring about the exact opposite?

If I had done the right thing, why wasn't Hawk back? Why hadn't she returned with Icarus? Why was it still winter? Why were things still the way they were?

Why are we still so lost?

The look in Mala's eyes had scattered any shards of confidence I'd had left in myself.

I let out the breath I hadn't even realized I'd been holding, pressing my fingertips to my forehead.

"Oh, God." My words came out almost without my permission. "What have I done?"

"Fin?"

The familiar voice startled me out of my thoughts. I dropped my hands to turn and glance towards the safe room door, which was still rolled open. I saw a shock of red hair woven into a loose braid.

I quickly stood.

"What happened?" Delta asked. "I passed Mala as I was coming from the platform."

I focused the tatamis back into place. "I failed, that's what happened."

I could hear the faded sounds of students' voices down the hall. When I looked up at Delta, she was staring at me, puzzled, with her arms folded over her chest.

"Are you feeling sorry for yourself, Fin?"

I didn't answer her. I finished putting the room back in order and then headed for the door. I was about to brush past her when she grabbed me by the arm.

"Fin, for God's sake," she said. "What is it—what's happened?"

I wanted to answer, but I wasn't sure that I could. My throat felt tight. I shook my head.

Delta didn't release my arm.

When I finally turned and looked at her, I found a sharpness in her eyes I had not seen before.

She looked at me like she could see me.

"Delta." Her name came heavily off my lips as I looked back at her. "I have failed."

"Who?" She lowered her voice, maintaining her grip on my arm. "Who have you failed? Fin, you've failed no one."

"That's where you're wrong," I said, pulling my arm from her grasp. My skin instantly felt cold where her hand had been. "I have failed everyone."

Delta straightened, her jaw set. "You know what I don't understand about you, Fin? You never explain yourself. You're too afraid to say what you actually think, yet you expect others to know how you feel."

"I don't expect anything from anyone," I corrected her, my voice rising despite myself. "I expect something of *myself*, Delta, that is all."

"So now you're just angry because things didn't work out exactly as you planned?" She raised one eyebrow. "Do you imagine yourself in such a high place of authority that you have control over these things, Fin? Does that responsibility not lie with someone much greater?"

"Not in Sensei's eyes, no," I replied. "He's given us that responsibility, Delta. He's told me this over and over again, and I haven't been listening. All this time I wanted to think that whether we pulled through this or not didn't hinge on us, but it does."

"If that's the case, what good will condemning yourself do, Fin?" She spoke firmly. "What good will that do any of us? If you've tried your best, that is all you can do."

"You should ask Mala if she thinks I've done my best," I retorted. "Or Hawk, or Icarus—"

"Or you could ask me," Delta cut in, raising her voice to match my own. "And I would tell you that you've been our lifeblood since Hawk and Icarus left us—you've spread yourself as thin as paper trying to protect us! But sometimes you just can't, Fin."

My eyes remained connected with Delta's for a moment before I shook my head and stepped over the threshold, pushing past her and emerging into the hallway. "You don't understand."

"Fin, wait!"

But I didn't. I strode the length of the hall and crossed the platform, avoiding anyone who attempted to talk to me. I entered the next hall, identifying the dark mahogany door immediately.

I halted when I came to it, lifting my clenched fist to knock. But I stopped. My hand hesitated in midair for a moment as I remembered Sensei's words.

"I was waiting for you to let yourself in..."

I took a breath and lowered my hand to let my fingers wrap around the doorknob instead. I gave a firm push, and the door slowly creaked open.

The room was completely dark—not even a fire was lit this time. The scent of incense was gone.

"Sensei?"

I stepped farther into the seemingly vacant room, leaving the door open. The light from the hallway parted the darkness enough for me to navigate my way to the desk, where I lit a candle.

The room seemed completely void of life, though I questioned even that now.

"Sensei," I repeated quietly, scanning the room, "are you here?"

There was no response. The room was empty.

I could barely make out the vague illumination of the sunset beyond the heavy drapes that now hung over the windows.

I squinted, lifting the candle to take a closer look at my surroundings. Nothing seemed amiss. All the dusty old books, papers, and various artifacts were squared away in their proper places. Nothing was missing except for Sensei. It was when I replaced the candle on the desk that I finally noticed the folded square of paper placed in the center of the desk. With my name scrawled across the front.

My heartbeat picked up slightly when I saw it.

I shot a glance around me before quietly pulling up the desk chair and taking a seat. I listened intently for voices and footsteps in the hallway beyond. When I was confident that no one was approaching, I unfolded the pages and read silently.

Fin,

The time is coming for you and the rest of the student body to prepare to leave the Dimension, this place of training I have built for you, and reemerge into your natural worlds. I have trained and equipped you with all that you will need. You believe in the prophecy—you know it by heart. Allow it to lead and guide you, and no darkness will be great enough to overpower you.

Before this Dimension ever was, there was only my word. My word, which came into existence like energy splitting—one soul into two. Those two halves of one spirit: the patriarchs, sent scattering through time and space to land where they did. Hawk and Icarus. A Sunrise marred by the fruits of this world, a Sunset marked by all that it could become if only it would turn away from a darkness of its own making.

The Dimension, a place of protection for you all. A projection of my own consciousness—a manifestation of my word; you must by now know that you came from this power. That you have it within you to create even greater things.

The time has come to spread your wings. You all are no longer fledglings; you are no longer children. Perhaps in my absence you will find the space and motivation to move into your true roles of leadership. Do not be discouraged, Fin. Trust your heart, for it is pure and inclining towards that which is right.

Yes, originally there was nothing at the bottom of the ravine— until they created their own dimensions as they fell. Projecting their own subconscious worlds into existence. Creating their own realities. Breathing their own small universes into existence; living parallel to one another without even realizing it themselves. Trapped inside dimensions of their own making. Opening not the darkness, but their own eyes to create that reality which lies within. In the ravine, those who have fallen will create with their own consciousness that which is real to them. And for Hawk, Icarus, and Raiden, those realities will each be vastly different. The worlds they create with their minds exist in layers—on top of and alongside each other, touching only if their own subconscious builds a bridge, connecting the one to the other. They are the only ones who can free themselves from their own chains.

Icarus has forgotten who he is. He has spent his life running from an identity he cannot comprehend. He has lost himself. And finding himself will not come without cost. Just as valuable as the blood that flows through his veins, his redemption will be bought only with blood of equal value.

As you know, Hawk is originally from what is now considered the past of planet Earth. She was found in a basket left on the back doorstep of the orphanage in which she grew up. Her markings made her undesirable to all around her, causing them to fear and abuse her. All but one—a motherless boy whom she would save from taking his own life at a very young age. This boy was called Edwin Wraith. He saw that she was different and loved her for it, until one day he envied and despised her for the same reason.

Yes. Yes, Fin, it was from him that I saved her. But his desire for her did not fade in her absence.

Edwin dedicated his life to finding Hawk, then known as Charlotte. He wandered in the darkest places and mixed with the darkest things he could find. Searching for clues, he heard a mere verse of the prophecy from an old woman who wrote it off as lost poetry of the ancients. For Edwin these words would resonate more deeply than he could have expected.

I christened Charlotte Hawk and brought her up as I would a daughter, safe within the walls of the Dimension. Meanwhile, Edwin grew. He stumbled about in the darkness, learning the ways of the mystics and mediums—searching for identity in all of the wrong places. But eventually he met like-minded journeyers—sliders who, in those early days, had come and gone from the Dimension, unable to adhere to the code of conduct. Edwin slowly pieced together the prophecy, gaining new verses from each of his victims before putting them to death and assuming their identities, which he used to gain power and keep himself from succumbing to age.

Through space and time, he tracked Hawk, always but a step behind her. He knew she still walked the Earth, and nothing would deter him from his search for her. He forged identities and moved constantly. He was resolute in his belief that the blood that coursed through Hawk's veins would, at last, be his redemption. He believed that by finding Hawk, he would find the other half of her soul along with her.

Eventually, Edwin found himself living in the identity of his latest kill, Riley, in Los Angeles, where he began school again. There, he met Mala, and although he abused her and treated her harshly at times, she made him feel what he had longed to feel with Charlotte.

When Mala went to Icarus instead, it hardened his heart. He believed it was an omen. There was something about Icarus— something he couldn't identify. When Icarus hurt Mala, she went running back to Riley, and he took full advantage of the situation, convincing her to tell him everything she knew. And what she knew was where he could find another world—Charlotte's. Hawk's. And thus, he entered our Dimension.

I tell you Edwin's story—Hawk's past—not to alarm you, Fin, but because I know that you wish to help Hawk. And you can by leading the world she has left behind. But as to the battle she faces in her world beneath the ravine, that you must leave her to fight on her own.

In attempting to take another's life, Icarus has fallen. And though he has survived, his reentrance into the Dimension will not come without a great sacrifice. Do not despise him, Fin. For it must happen this way in order that all things may be restored. Work with him—help each other. For the Earth you will find upon your reemergence will not be one of blatant evil and despair, but one of hidden destruction. A kind that disguises itself as good. Do not be afraid. Do not lose faith, even when it seems that all has been lost— for all is never lost.

I have been with you all since the beginning. I have loved you, and I have shown you all that I am, and all that you are. The time has come for you to believe that all I have said of you is true. This is the culmination for which you have trained. I have every faith in you,

Fin. You are ready, my son.

Though I will not be with you in physical form as you emerge from the Dimension back into your natural worlds, know that I am there. Indeed, that it is the times when you do not see me that I am there the most. I am with you always. And one day, you will learn to see me again; one day there will be no place where you will look and not find me.

Wait for Icarus.

Your loving teacher,

Sensei

CHAPTER TWENTY

Hawk

Slowly, I opened my eyes. Shafts of golden sunlight reached down through the gaps in the shelter's roof like long fingers to caress my face. Everything was blurry shades of caramel and white. The frayed edges of the birch bark trembled in the gentle breeze as it sighed in through the cracks.

For a moment I remembered nothing; then all at once, everything.

I sat up straight, giving my surroundings a quick examination. In the light of day, I could finally see what was inside the shelter. Tucked into a corner was a dull-looking knife chiseled from stone, a quiver's worth of arrows, a bow, a woven basket, and a small stack of what looked like handmade parchment paper tied together with long strands of wild grass.

Easing onto my hands and knees, I crept closer to the grass curtain separating me from the outside and cautiously peered out. I could see the remains of the fire gently flickering, but there was no sign of Maicoh or any of the black wolves. I sat back on my heels.

Feeling slightly more at ease, I took a closer look at Maicoh's personal belongings. Lifting the stack of paper, I carefully undid the knot and began thumbing through what were evidently charcoal sketches.

Each was remarkable, to say the least, and most were drawings of the wolves: violent, detailed images of teeth and claws as they tore apart some innocent form of prey. There were sketches of tall, swaying pines, towering mountains, cascading waterfalls, and open meadows. Landscapes so realistic that, were it not for the absence of color, it seemed as though I could reach in and feel the textures beneath my fingertips.

I flipped through the rest of the pages and then tidied them back into an orderly stack. I ran my fingertips over the smoothly carved arrows and lifted the stone knife to study it. When I heard footsteps, I quickly brushed aside the curtain and emerged outside.

Maicoh had just stepped into the clearing, a black wolf at his heels and a bundle of wood in his toned arms. He raised his eyebrows when he saw me.

"Hawk," he said, greeting me plainly, "I trust you slept well?"

"I slept adequately," I replied. "Thank you."

"Dreams?"

I watched him as he stopped beside the fire, dropping the branches and twigs into a pile.

"Dreams?" I repeated. "What do you mean?"

Maicoh straightened up, rigorously dusting off his hands. "This place can do strange things to the mind. Sometimes I hardly sleep at all."

"Maicoh, if you've seen no one down here," I quoted him from the night before, "then why do you seem so... unsurprised by my coming here?"

Before he could respond, a low howl erupted from somewhere close by.

Maicoh paused, listening. I watched his expression, his eyes as they darted back and forth, studying seemingly nothing. Then he relaxed again.

"The wolves have brought you this far, haven't they?" he asked, though he didn't wait for an answer. "They appeared, you followed, and now we find ourselves together. Surely that must mean something."

"How do you mean?"

"They've taught me everything I know," he said, turning to look at me again. "And they will teach you if you let them guide you."

A moment later one of the black wolves emerged from the tree line and came to a stop beside the fire in front of Maicoh. He bent down to place a hand on its head, looking into its eyes.

"He's hungry," he said after a moment, almost more to himself than to me. "Didn't you tell me you were looking for someone, Hawk?"

I nodded.

Maicoh slapped the wolf playfully on the side and then got back up. "I know this place like the back of my hand. I know every tree, every embankment, every lake and waterfall. If who you seek is lost in this world, I promise you we can find them."

Something about the way he said it brought my guard up.

I couldn't help but feel that there was a lifetime of secrets hiding just below his confident skin. Where did he come from? Who was he really? I had so many questions, but I brushed them to the back of my mind for the time being.

"Very well," I said. "Lead the way."

"It was like I had awoken from a dream—a long, strange dream that even now I cannot fully understand. When I awoke, I was in a wide-open meadow. There were flowers around me and mountains rising up to touch the sky. There was no one around me—not a single form of life beyond the butterflies and the birds that sang in the brush."

"No one was with you?"

"Not a soul."

The light came down strong and hot through the trees as we walked. Maicoh took off his shirt as he told me his story. A wolf ran ahead of us, and another two flanked us on either side. I found myself checking over my shoulder occasionally in search of more.

"And that is how you came to find yourself here?" I asked.

He nodded.

We started up another embankment. Moss coated the roots of trees as they protruded from the ground like veins in a human hand.

"This person I'm looking for, Maicoh," I began cautiously.

"Ah, yes," he said as we wove our way through a stand of large pines. "Tell me about them. Maybe then I can be of some help to you."

"You already have, believe me," I assured him. "But it's true when you say that perhaps I am here for a reason. Finding... Icarus is my reason."

I had fallen to find Icarus, and now I finally had my chance. Regardless of whether I could trust Maicoh or not, I couldn't ignore the hunch that I had found him for a reason.

Maicoh glanced over at me. "What is he like?"

"He's on the taller side, with hair the color of the earth after a storm. Eyes as blue as ice." I listed off his features, recalling his face in my mind's eye. "He's very..."

My words broke off. I didn't know how to finish that sentence.

Icarus. What is *he like?*

Such a simple question, yet the answer was so complicated. Yes, I knew him as part of me. I knew him as the other half of my soul... but did I really know *him*? Icarus, who had stared at me from next door. Icarus, the healer. Icarus, whom I had trained and pushed to the very limit. Icarus, my student—the one who had betrayed us, who had broken the code and handed us all the consequences.

Icarus, who had kissed me.

How could I put him into words? There was so much to him, so many layers. So many things I still didn't know—things I wanted to find out.

"He's very different," I concluded at last. "Like me."

"Different." He tried the word on his tongue. "If he is like you, then it is in a good way that he is different."

I felt a smile pass over my lips. I focused on the ground in front of me.

"But he could be anywhere," I said. "The place where I landed was so much different from this place, Maicoh—a different world, almost."

"You must start somewhere."

"I can't argue there," I agreed.

After that we both fell silent for some time. We climbed over logs and ducked beneath the low limbs of trees. A pileated woodpecker drilled in the distance.

At last, a thought occurred to me. I tried at first to silence it, but before long it was a wrestling match.

"Maicoh." I spoke up after a little while. "There's something else you should know."

"About Icarus?"

I shook my head. "Not him. Someone else—someone very dangerous."

"In this world?" He shot me an inquiring side glance. "It can't be. As I've said, I've seen no one here but you."

"And you're *sure* about that?"

He nodded, his long black hair brushing across his muscular shoulders. "Yes, very sure. But you say this person is dangerous?"

"Yes," I said, attempting to swallow back the anxiety. "I wasn't the only one who fell."

"Fell?"

"Yes. It's hard to explain, but there were three of us," I replied. "There's no way for me to know if... this person survived—maybe Icarus and I only did because we're different. I'm not sure. But I'd be lying if I said it hasn't been hanging on my mind since I found myself here."

"How do you know that he is not like you?" Maicoh asked as we continued through another grove of trees. "If you survived, would he not have at least tried to do the same so that he might find you?"

"I think not. I know him and he's no ally of mine," I answered bluntly. "If he did survive, then it will be a misfortune. That's why I'm warning you—be on your guard."

He said nothing. We trekked through the forest in silence until we had retraced my initial steps all the way back across the meadow to the tunnel I'd discovered.

"This is what I was telling you about, Maicoh," I told him, kneeling down to peer inside. "This is how I entered."

Maicoh squatted down beside me to look into the tunnel's black opening. "So you found no one in the world where you awoke?"

"No one," I replied. "No one beyond apparitions, that is. Ghosts of who I used to be."

Maicoh rolled forward onto his knees, leaning farther forward to examine the tunnel. "Ghosts?"

"You spoke of dreams," I said, sitting back on my heels. "Well, I had them there—violent ones. Your wolves attacked me in my dreams, Maicoh. How do you explain that?"

I was half joking. I knew they weren't *his* wolves. But when he pulled back from the dimness of the tunnel, I could see in his eyes that he was taking me seriously.

"My wolves?" He repeated my accusation, seeming surprised. "You think that they were my wolves?"

"Didn't you say the black wolves were yours?"

"Yes, I have my own," he replied sternly. "But so do you, Hawk. You would be wise to learn how to tame them."

I looked at him, puzzled, as he crawled back into the tunnel, waist deep.

"I thought you said they could not be tamed," I reminded him, "that they controlled you."

"It is true," he replied bluntly. "But that is my choice."

"But why?" I asked, watching him as he shimmied in deeper. "Why not control them when you have the ability to? Why do you let them control you?"

"I trust them because they are mine," he said, his voice muffled now. "Because they are born out of a desire much deeper than my life can contain."

There was a streak of dirt across his tanned face when he crawled back out of the tunnel. "You are not the only one who is looking for someone."

I raised an eyebrow, my lips parting towards a question, but before the words could come, another sound erupted. It came from the tunnel. A soft scratching noise, barely noticeable over the yelps of the wolves and the gentle hum of insects.

Maicoh noticed immediately: he stiffened, listening.

The noise paused a moment and then came again, louder—followed by a soft, throaty growl. This caught the attention of the other wolves. Their ears slanted attentively.

Maicoh swiftly rose, gesturing with his hand that I should do the same. "Up—up now," he hissed.

"What is it?" I jumped to my feet. "What's wrong?"

He shook his head briskly, his long black hair lapping over his shoulders. "Ask nothing, Hawk—run!"

"But why?"

Exasperated, he shoved me hard in the direction of the meadow. I stumbled forward, catching myself before I could fall. The black wolves around me, suddenly greater in number, leapt to attention like obedient soldiers, awaiting the command of their leader.

I ran only a few yards before I jerked to a stop and spun around to see what was happening. There was a loud burst like the sound of a sudden explosion and then a blur of teeth and fur and claws emerging quick as lightening from the mouth of the tunnel. White fur clashing with dark-tanned skin. Maicoh and a white wolf locked together in battle.

For a moment I did nothing—I watched, frozen, in a state of shock. And then all the words that had delayed in my head, bumping into one another, rushed out all at once.

"Stop!" I surged forward just as the other black wolves did. "Maicoh!"

I didn't know what to do—I had no weapon and even less of an idea of what I was dealing with. I lunged forward into the blur and grabbed hold of the white wolf. With a quick jerk of its body, it tossed me aside as if I weighed no more than a rag doll, and then turned back to Maicoh. With one fierce swipe, it tore his shoulder open. I heard him cry out.

I scrambled to get to my feet, my heart pounding in my chest just as the wolf took Maicoh down to the ground and crouched on top of him as though he would tear him to pieces. And then, to my astonishment, in a split second, Maicoh's flesh, both torn and untorn, began to give way to fur—mangy, tattered fur as black as his own eyes. I began to feel a familiar tingling sensation in my own body.

One moment there was a massive, rock-solid white wolf on top of a bleeding, shouting Maicoh, and the next the white wolf crouched atop another wolf. One of the same size, but black.

There was a pause, and then it was as if a spark had ignited. The two wolves exploded into battle, a writhing, snarling blur of black on white. Maicoh's clan of black wolves seemed to chant as they rapidly circled the fight.

I was too shocked to breathe, let alone move. I'd barely gotten to my feet. *Maicoh can shift? Is this possible?*

A throaty howl rose from the white wolf as Maicoh landed a blow to its face—claws out. It stumbled out of its lock with Maicoh, whimpering.

Maicoh jumped to all four paws, recovering immediately. He bared his teeth and lunged, open-mouthed, for the white wolf's jugular. He missed.

In one fell swoop, the massive, snow-white creature turned to instead seize Maicoh by the throat. Maicoh let out a pitiful scream, his paws scrabbling at his assailant.

This jolted me from my daze.

Hawk, don't just stand there! Do something!

I lunged forward into the fight, arms wide. "Get back!" I shouted at Maicoh's wolves, as though they could understand. I quickly raised my hands over my head, palms facing each other, and focused on the tingling sensation that had yet to leave my body—channeling that energy as best I could.

Don't shift, don't shift, don't shift...

I forbade the thought of feathers—of wings, of taking flight— though every fiber of my being shouted for me to take wing, to fly up and up, away from the savagery, away to safety. Instead I thought of the color red. Of the lapping movement of flame, of heat—

Fire broke out between my palms, an orb of dancing bright orange flame. The black wolves around me immediately started backwards. But the white wolf didn't falter. It shook Maicoh in its jaws, dropping him only to strike again and again. It dove forward, baring its teeth.

I took aim. I threw—hard.

There was a sound like the rushing of wind as the fire fed frantically on the oxygen, and then a burst as it impacted the white wolf's back, catching its coat in a frenzy of violent flame.

There was an instant of startled reactions, the sound of stumbling—and then there was a howl more shrill and frantic than any I had heard before. I felt my stomach wrench, my throat tightening.

The white wolf rolled frantically across the grass, its muscular body becoming merely a writhing smudge.

I was breathing hard as I lit the fire between my hands again, preparing for a second strike. But it wasn't needed.

The white wolf struggled to its feet and limped frantically away, darting back into the tunnel that led back into the snow-covered forest. It vanished inside, leaving an ashy trail.

I stayed tense for a moment, waiting—watching for any signs that it might return. The sun hid its face in the clouds, leaving the forest overcast.

The black wolves fell back slightly, still staring up at the flame between my hands. A gentle wind began to rustle through the flowers. Suddenly it felt cooler than it had only moments ago, as if the wolf had brought something from the other side of the tunnel with it into this world of spring.

Finally, I released my breath, vanquishing the flame as I dropped my hands to my sides. My skin still tingled.

My attention drifted to Maicoh, who had morphed back into his human form. He lay as still as stone. The black wolf nearest to him crept closer to cautiously sniff his open wounds.

"Maicoh." I dropped to my knees beside him. "Maicoh, can you hear me?"

I gently placed a finger to the veins in his wrist, looking for the faintest sign of a pulse.

"Maicoh."

He was bleeding at the throat, at the back of the neck, and at the chest, where large gashes let go of streams of blood. His eyes were closed.

I frantically repositioned my fingers on his wrist. I felt no pulse. No heartbeat.

"Come on, come on," I murmured silently, feeling the wolf's breath at my back. "You can't die, Maicoh... not now."

July 1927

"Please—please, just let me go." He trembled behind the point of the knife, his dark eyes wide. *"I don't have what you're looking for!"*

I felt a smile twitch at the corners of my mouth. *"On the contrary. You are what I'm looking for."*

The blade glinted against his throat. We were alone in the forest; the wind stirred softly in the trees.

"I don't understand."

He was of Native American ethnicity, his skin deeply tanned. His eyes darted back and forth as though he had something to hide.

"The universe exists between two halves of the same spirit," I pronounced slowly. *"A Sunrise marred by the fruits of this world, a Sunset marked by all that it could become…"*

I stared deep into his eyes. *"Does that mean anything to you?"*

He shook his head fiercely. I flicked the knife.

"Alright!" The veins in his neck pulsed as he yelled. *"I'll tell you!"*

I withdrew the blade only a little, waiting.

"A beginning, and an end," he stuttered. *"An eternity birthed in a state of possibility. Unobserved, hidden from our vision…"*

His words were accented. He stared into my eyes with a confidence I despised.

"A universe that is a question, that is both alive and dead until we make the decision." He gulped, breathless. *"And open not the darkness, but our eyes to create that reality."*

A wave of revelation washed over me. It was as though the veil had finally, finally been pulled away. I saw more of the image. And what I saw changed everything.

"Now tell me something, Maicoh." I leveled my voice. *"How do you know those verses?"*

"H-h-how did you know my name?"

"Because I've been watching you," I answered quietly. *"For quite some time, in fact. Now answer the question."*

"I don't know!" His voice was frantic. *"They're just… they're just there in my memory. I don't know how they got there… It's like something from a dream. I don't understand it myself. It means nothing to me! You have to believe me!"*

I shook my head slowly. *"I'm afraid I don't—and I'm afraid I won't be able to keep this blade outside your body for much longer unless you tell me how you knew that verse." I hushed my voice. "And how you can create fire with your hands."*

He tensed, his expression morphing to one of terror. "What? No! I can't!"

"Yes, you can. You do it every day, in fact, when no one's looking. When your family's not around to see. That's why you spend so much time by yourself, isn't it?" I shook my head slowly, my lips twitched. "You can't play the game with me, Maicoh."

"I'm telling you the truth, I swear!" he shouted in my face. "I... I don't know how I can do it. I was just... I was just born that way. It..." He tapered off. "It scares me."

I studied him for a long moment; then I drew a breath. "Well, in that case, I'm here to help you, Maicoh," I told him, seizing him by the hands. Too fast for him to react, I whipped the blade of the knife down across his palms.

"No! No, stop—what are you doing?"

I shoved him backwards, hard, against the trunk of the tree. Slitting my own palms, I grabbed him by the hands, allowing our wounds to spill into each other. I held the knife between my teeth for an instant.

He screamed as searing pain ripped through my arms and presumably his too.

I felt dizzy for an instant, but I bit it back, pulling away after a moment to take hold of the knife again with my free hand.

"Don't worry, Maicoh," I said, breathing heavily, looking directly into his face. "You don't have to be afraid anymore."

He began a reply, but never finished.

I silenced him.

CHAPTER TWENTY-ONE

Icarus

In front of me, behind me, to my left, to my right—everywhere. No matter where I looked, there was a pure blanket of white covering the ground. It laced the trees and descended from the sky in perfect flakes.

The world around me was frozen, yet somehow I didn't feel the cold.

I stepped forward, forward, forward, and then paused at an embankment. Everything was more vivid than I remembered. Everything was scented more strongly than I had ever experienced before. It was almost a stronger sense than sight. It was as if everything, even the snow, had a smell. It was like my senses had been enhanced times ten.

I didn't know what it was I was looking for, but I kept my gaze on the ground just the same. My eyes scanned the snow for tracks and found scatterings of hundreds. Rabbits, squirrels, tiny footprints from tiny feet. Finally, I found a set that were larger and familiarly shaped.

I chased them like prey, inhaling a familiar scent, something so recognizable, yet I couldn't place it intellectually. My heart just kept giving me cues to run.

I skidded to a stop at an embankment where a massive dead pine had fallen.

Catching my breath, I scanned the terrain ahead. Patches of frozen dirt undusted by skid marks and paw prints. That was when I noticed a set of tracks trailing behind me, too.

I stepped to the side. They followed like a shadow.

When I looked down, I realized why. I had a set of my own—massive pure white paws.

I'm a... I'm a wolf?

My senses took over: a new scent, mixed with the familiar one the tracks had been deluged in. My eyes connected with the source. Splotches of blood painted the snow.

I followed the scent of the trail to a tunnel that was tucked beneath the fallen tree. A gaping black hole I had scarcely detected among the array of branches.

I charged in blindly, relying solely on my sense of smell to guide me. The ground, stinging cold beneath my paw pads, gradually grew warmer—softer.

Suddenly there was a new smell—the aroma of fresh earth.

Steps, steps, steps, then something like a pinprick of light staring me down from the tunnel's end. The scent of wildflowers drifted in to meet me, followed by a voice. I felt a surge of adrenaline as I picked up my pace.

The tunnel's end seemed to pull itself just out of my grasp with each step I took. Finally, I beat its pace and emerged into the outside world: a meadow at the forest's edge.

Where snow and ice had been, there were now daisies. Where shivering pines had arisen, there were now cedars and birches filled with bright green leaves. The sky was teal, cloudless.

I comprehended all of this in an instant. Then my focus lowered to the wolves—and the two people accompanying them. One I didn't recognize, and the other I knew better than I knew myself.

Hawk.

Suddenly it was like I had lost all control. One moment I was standing at the mouth of the tunnel; the next I was locked with the male like I wanted to tear out his heart.

A chaos of sound whirled around me. Howls and a familiar voice, the one I'd heard so many thousands of times in my own head the past few weeks. The sound of it alone was enough to throw me off balance, but the claws across my face certainly helped too.

My eyes watered as I shrank back, stumbling over my own paws.

The young man who had stood in front of me only moments earlier was gone. A mangy black wolf took his place. My brain tried frantically to process all of this, but everything around me was a blur.

I wasn't sure who jumped first, but in an instant we were clawing each other again. I felt blood rising to the surface of my skin. I snatched him by the throat and bit down until he whimpered. Then, all of a sudden, there was a burst of fire—followed by searing pain.

I wasn't sure where it came from, but then as I fell away, I saw the smoke rising from the surface of Hawk's palms.

She can channel fire?

The thought was there, and then it was gone, and so was he. So was the light, the sky, the trees and Hawk. The tunnel swallowed me whole.

My eyes flew open.

My first instinct was to glance down at my body. My very human body.

Sweat poured down my skin as I eased myself up into a seated position. For a moment I hunched there, breathing heavily.

"What is it with these dreams?" I grumbled. "I'm losing it, I swear."

It had all seemed so real; it was hard to believe it had been just another nightmare. Something inside me seemed to whisper that it wasn't.

My eyes drifted to the circle in the center of the bed of irises. The place where the snow still danced and swirled. I sat there and stared like an idiot, watching as the wind from the other world moved the snow across the stone.

What was I even doing at this point? What was I doing beyond waiting—and for what? For her to do something—for her to make a move? For her to figure this place out and swoop in to save me like she always did?

How many times had Hawk yelled into my face that I was capable—that I could do anything if I just applied myself? If I just trusted who I was, closed my eyes, and took the leap?

How many times had she told me to quit doubting? Her words still rang in my ears.

I collapsed back into the irises, running a hand over my unshaven face.

"The heavens and the Earth were born unto us, a supernova, a soul split in two," I murmured. "Thus we poured forth: one. Stars in need of no darkness to shine, trees in need of no light to grow; the sun and her stars find voice between a sunrise and a sunset…"

A sunrise… and a sunset. The words throbbed in my head like a migraine, forcing me to press my eyelids closed.

"For the universe exists between two halves of the same spirit: a Sunrise marred by the fruits of this world, a Sunset marked by all that it could become. A beginning, and an end, an eternity birthed in a state of possibility; unobserved, hidden from our vision, a universe that is a question…a question that is both alive, and dead until we make the decision, and open not the darkness," my voice lowered to a whisper, "but our eyes to create that reality."

A universe. A question.

A sunrise, a sunset—a question. Both were questions.

Hawk was a question—there was nothing even remotely definite about her, and that fact had always scared the life out of me. She was volatile; she was a live volcano everyone thought was dead. She was apocalyptic—but in the best way.

I was done with dreaming about her. I was finished with the ghost of her beside me—I wanted flesh and blood and bone. I wanted to reach back through space and time and reverse all my stupid mistakes. I wanted to be the Sunset—her other half. A person who was actually worthy of his name.

Because I wasn't. No, I was lying in the irises with spiders in my hair, wishing everything was different.

I clenched my teeth together, getting to my feet this time. Once again, I entered the circle. My blood ran cold the instant my feet touched the stone. The forest around me dissolved.

Flakes fell gracefully from the sky.

I walked around the edge.

I reached past one of the pillars, the skin on my arm gliding across the cool stone. My arm straightened, and my fingertips disappeared. I felt warmth on the other side, though I couldn't see it.

I pulled my arm back again. I looked up at the sky and my breath rolled up like a cloud.

"How can I find you when I can't get to you?" I asked the emptiness. "How do I even really know you're there?"

I hated myself. I *knew* she was there; how could I even ask? I could feel her. Yet still I doubted myself. Still, I yelled at the sky like the lost, angry, confused human boy that I was.

"I don't know where you are, Hawk! I need a sign. I need something—I need *you!*"

I fell back against the pillar, knocking the rest of the air out of my lungs as I slid to the ground.

"Why did you let me love her, Sensei?" I whispered. "Why did you make me her equal when I am clearly not?"

It was Sensei who had brought us together, made us for each other. And I almost resented him for it.

"I am not her equal, Sensei. You were wrong," I said quietly. "She is above me in every way—and I have failed her. You could have chosen anyone—you could have created Fin to be her other half. He's so much better than I am—he knows her so much better. He loves her, even..." I trailed off, pausing for a breath.

"I love her too," I finished. "But then, doesn't darkness always fall for the light?"

I felt the sting of tears rising as I pinched my eyes shut.

There was a silence as thick as cotton. Then there was a sound, a noise like paws moving across snow, frantic panting. When I turned to look, I caught a glimpse of a white coat singed with charcoal gray.

My eyes widened as I jumped to my feet. I stepped as close as I could to the edge without vanishing back into my own reality, waiting for it to emerge into the clearing. When it did, I saw that it was limping. Large ashy blotches marred its coat.

"My God." I knelt down as it stepped into the circle. "What happened?"

I reached out to touch it, but it shrank away, giving a small warning growl.

"Hey, it's okay." I backed off only slightly. "I can... I can heal you."

Another thing I could finally remember about myself. It was like water slowly dripping through the cracks.

"I promise I won't hurt you." I spoke to it gently. "Just stay still, okay?"

After a moment it seemed to comply, settling carefully back on its haunches. I placed my hand softly at the base of its burned neck and slowly began to move it across the length of its back. I could see the pink, singed skin underneath.

"What happened to you?"

I ran my hand across its coat and watched as the fur and skin where my hand had been returned to its natural state. I continued to gently stroke its back, feeling the power pulsating at my core rush the length of my arms and into my fingertips.

"So you didn't find her." I moved my fingertips over its face. "I don't know why I thought you could. I just..." I trailed off, my mind flashing back to the dream. The nightmare. The paws that had replaced my hands and feet. The vivid filter through which I'd viewed the world. The scents, the sounds, the faces—

The fire in her hands...

I pulled back. The wolf opened its eyes again.

I swallowed, feeling dizzy from the power I'd lost.

"You did find her, didn't you?"

CHAPTER TWENTY-TWO

Hawk

I checked Maicoh's pulse again. Out of the corner of my eye I could see his wolf pacing. The others were nowhere to be seen.

"Come on," I whispered, leaning over his body to look into his face. "This can't be happening."

I needed Maicoh. Without him, I was alone in this unfamiliar world. He had done nothing but fight to protect me thus far—now it was time for me to do the same for him.

"Back off." I shooed the wolf away as I moved closer to Maicoh's body. I tugged free the knife he'd been carrying at his waist and took his hand in my own.

Carefully, I pressed the blade to his palm, coaxing a thin ribbon of blood to the surface of his skin. The wolf, still staring me down, gave a soft growl.

After finishing with Maicoh's hand, I carefully made an identical cut on my own. I could feel my heart beating in my throat as I tossed the knife to the ground and slowly inverted my hand. My blood trickled down into Maicoh's wound as our hands joined.

I took a deep breath and closed my eyes.

Please let this work...

The last time I had entangled with someone, it had been with Icarus the day we had shifted together.

I focused intently on the sensation of warmth between our hands. My thoughts ebbed and flowed listlessly, and in an instant the heat between our palms became painful, searing.

I bit back a moan as my body tingled with a sensation that felt like death. Golden freckles danced behind my closed eyelids as the sounds around me died away.

Then, in a heartbeat, it was all over. I opened my eyes.

Maicoh was still sprawled in the grass beside me, still bloodied with claw marks. His body remained motionless.

For a split second I doubted myself as I sat there, still holding his hand, searching for some hint of life in his face.

Come on…

I listened for the sound of his breath, but heard only the hushed tones of the wind as it caressed the forest.

Finally, Maicoh's chest rose and fell as he gasped for air. Relief washed over me as he coughed a few times and then slowly opened his eyes to squint up at me.

"Hawk?"

"Right here," I said.

His eyes fell shut again. "How did you…" The wolf leaned in to lap his face gently. Maicoh moaned and swatted it away. "The fire… How did you…?"

"Shh," I said, ignoring his question. "Now's not the time."

"Did it come back?"

"Did what come back?"

"The wolf," he said, struggling up into a seated position. That was when I noticed our hands were still joined; he clasped mine tightly. "The white wolf."

I shook my head. "It's gone, Maicoh."

"Are you sure?"

"Yes," I said. "I'm sure—don't move around too much. You're hurt."

His sharp eyes scanned our surroundings. I stood to release my hand from his while extending the other to help him up.

"Let's get out of here while we still can," I said. "Do you think you can walk?"

Maicoh was unresponsive for a moment; then he nodded slowly and took my hand. "I think so."

"We should really get you to someplace you can wash off," I commented, scanning the extent of his injuries as he struggled to his

178

feet. "Your wounds are pretty bad."

He winced, but gave a quick nod. "There is a river not far away."

"Just direct me," I said, looping an arm around his torso for support. "And I'll get you there."

The going was tough, and I couldn't help but feel somewhat guilty. I could have healed him right then and there and saved him the pain. It would have been the humane thing to do. But then there was the flip side of the coin: Maicoh was a skin suit full of secrets. There was something very, very strange about him, and it wasn't just that he could shift shape. It was something else—something I couldn't identify. And until I could, I wasn't about to reveal my own powers. I'd brought him back from death; that would have to be enough help for now.

The river was only a short trek away, tucked into the forest and lined with budding birch trees. The water ran deep and crystal clear. I turned around while Maicoh stripped off his tattered, bloodstained clothes and waded in. I heard him swallow back a pained groan as the cold water touched his wounds.

I turned back around and walked to the riverbank again, settling on a rock.

"Why did the white wolf attack you?" I asked. "I thought the wolves were on your side."

"Not the white wolf," he said, and dunked his head below the surface. He came back up a moment later and shook his hair out of his face. "The white wolf is different from the black wolves, Hawk," he finished, taking a breath. "It's dangerous."

I thought about what he was saying, making no reply at first.

Maicoh ran a hand over his face, then gazed at me. Water shimmered over his skin as he stared at me curiously.

"While we're on the topic of wolves," I began, "do you want to tell me how you could shift into a wolf yourself?"

Maicoh sank into the water up to his chin and smiled. "Do you want to tell me how you can shift into a hawk?"

I opened my mouth, then closed it again. My heartbeat picked up its pace.

"I know it was you," he continued gently. "Last night, up in the tree. Your name... Did you think I would not make the connection?"

The truth was, I had no idea how he could have made that

connection. He hadn't seen me shift—I'd gone to great pains to keep myself concealed.

"And during the attack," he went on, "you had *fire* in your hands. I saw it. Where did you learn to do that?"

"Did you hit your head when you fell?" I asked, trying to sound self-assured. "I'm a *human*, Maicoh. Don't be ridiculous."

"But if that is true, how do I have these visions of you bringing me back to this world when I had begun to leave it?" he asked, almost pleading. "Hawk, after the attack… I heard you… I *felt* you—"

"I stayed with you until you became conscious again," I explained briskly, leaving out the part about him dying. "I thought you were gone for a moment there."

"I believe I was, Hawk," he said, coming a little closer to the riverbank. "I believe that you are a human girl, yes. But I believe that there is something else—a world beneath that quiet skin. One you will not let me see."

I forced myself to swallow back the uneasy feeling in my chest.

"I could say the same of you," I told him matter-of-factly. "I don't think your arrival in this world is quite as simple as you make it sound."

"Perhaps it is, perhaps it isn't." Maicoh shrugged his shoulders. "Whether you believe me or not is your choice, Hawk. But believe me when I tell you this…" He trailed off, seeming to wait to make sure he had my full attention. He did.

"This world can be a very dark, dangerous place, Hawk," he continued, staring up to where I was seated on the rock. "If you wish to find Icarus, you must trust me enough to let me help you—and if you wish to stay alive here, you must tread very, very carefully."

His words did nothing to calm the unsettling feeling that was beginning to grip me from the inside.

"Alright," I said, deciding it would be wise to feign compliance. "I trust that you have been here longer than I have, and that you must have a better understanding of this place. Is that enough for now?"

He nodded.

"And you will help me find Icarus?"

"Of course," he said, wading over to the rock. The water receded to his waist. "But you must promise me one thing—can you do that?"

I cocked my head to the side. I wanted to shy away from his

sudden closeness, but I stayed where I was.

"I can't answer that until you tell me what it is," I came back firmly.

"You must never go near the white wolf." He lowered his voice. "As long as you are with me, I will do all that I can to protect you from it, but if you are alone, do whatever it takes to escape it, Hawk. Never follow it."

"But aren't you at all curious about—"

"No," he cut in, seizing my hand suddenly in his own. The same one I had cut, though it looked completely normal now. "And you have to promise me that you won't follow it."

Why would I follow a creature that had almost torn him to shreds?

"I promise," I replied finally, though it was a lie.

Maicoh slowly released his grip on my hand, as if only just becoming aware that his fingers were still clasped firmly around my wrist. I stood up to put some space between us.

"Now you tell me something," I said, my voice commanding. "How is it that you can shift?"

Maicoh gestured for me to turn around while he emerged from the water and re-dressed. I studied the forest around us, ever aware of his movements behind me.

"I learned."

"From whom?"

"Experience," he said carefully. "Acquiring teachers."

"So you've known other humans?" I asked.

"Many," he said. "But not here. And none quite like you."

"Where *exactly* did you come from?"

I heard the rustling of fabric behind me. "You ask many questions, Hawk."

I hesitated, wondering whether I was pushing too hard. "It's in my nature." I decided to go a little further. "There are some things I need to know."

"There are some things you *can't* know, Hawk," he said. "Some things you are not ready to know."

When I turned around, he was right in front of me. I took a small step back.

"You think I do not understand you, Hawk," he began quietly.

"But I do, because we are alike, you and I—we are different from others. We are both searching for something."

It was the second time he had said it: that he was searching for something.

"You saved me," Maicoh said quietly. "I know you are denying it because you do not trust me—yet, but..."

His eyes scanned my face. There was something almost unsettling about the way he looked at me, though I couldn't understand why.

"Thank you," he finished. "Thank you, Hawk."

I studied him back warily. "You really want to thank me?"

Maicoh hesitated, then lowered his head in a solemn nod. "Of course I do, Hawk."

I stepped around him, starting for the edge of the forest. "Then help me find Icarus."

April 2015

He started backwards when he finally looked up and saw me standing there. We were the only ones in the high school lab. It was spring break; no one was there.

"Holy sh—" He stumbled over his words, along with the leg of the table. He fell to the floor, the glass beaker slipping from his hand to shatter against the faded tiles. "Who the hell are you? How did you get in here?"

I hadn't moved from where I was standing. I slipped a hand into the pocket of my overcoat, pulling out the small black sketchbook I'd carried with me for the past century.

"Just passing the time," I said casually, flipping it open to a particular page, a particular drawing of the young man in front of me. "Drawing a picture of you."

He gaped at me from the floor, an intensely disturbed expression on his face. I sized him up in a glance. Hispanic ethnicity, dark, intelligent eyes, fingers stained with chemicals, and wearing a lab coat with a hoodie underneath.

"And I could be asking you the very same question, Riley." The heel of my shoe clicked softly as I took a step closer. "How did you get in here? It's spring break, isn't it?"

He didn't answer the question. The color had begun to drain from his face. I wondered if it was the scar across my face, a memento from my last kill.

"H-how... how do you—"

"How do I know your name?" I finished the question for him. "That's such a boring question, don't you think? They all ask that one. All you need to know, Riley, is that you are the next piece in the game." I was standing over him now, looking down. "You're going to help me find what I've been searching a hundred years for." I reached behind my back for the knife while extending the other hand to help him up. He didn't take my hand.

"I don't understand," he said quietly. "W-what are you talking about?"

I sighed. "Why don't I ask you a question instead, hmm?"

"What's..." He swallowed. "What's that?"

"Why do you only come here when you know no one's around?"

I kept my hand extended. "Is it because you like to be alone? Or because that way no one will figure out who you really are?" I hesitated. "Or should I say... what you really are."

"I don't understand—"

"Sending objects into levitation by accident? Blowing out lightbulbs, computers, and Wi-Fi routers with your very thoughts?" I quickly breezed through the list, shaking my head. "I think you understand exactly what I'm talking about."

I seized him by the wrist and dragged him to his feet.

"And I think you're nothing more than a sign, Riley," I said softly, my fingers wrapping around the handle of the knife. "A sign that I'm getting warmer... closer."

"Closer to what?"

"Her," I whispered. "Now give me your hands."

No one heard him scream. No one saw his body fall and fade away as mine transformed seamlessly into the exact image of the slider I'd just killed. I leaned back against the lab table, dizzy, the knife still in my hand.

Something in the pocket of the lab coat vibrated. I tucked the knife into my belt and took out what I would soon understand to be my guide to all things Riley.

1 new text message

I unlocked the screen with my thumbprint. Riley's thumbprint.

From: Mel <3

Really stoked to finally meet you in person this coming semester, Rie! See you on campus?

I read the message over once, twice. The press of a button took me back to the home screen, where a photograph of a girl with dark brown hair and eyes and golden skin had been selected as the wallpaper. I studied it for a moment before tapping back to the message.

I typed a reply.

From: Riley

Looking forward to it

CHAPTER TWENTY-THREE

Fin

The letter was clenched in my hand and limp with moisture by the time I had crossed the bridge to Delta's dorm. Icy drops of rain pelted my skin with each of my steps. I was breathless as I pounded on the door frame. The canvas quivered in the wind.

"Just a moment," I heard a familiar muffled voice reply from within. A split second later the canvas parted to reveal a puzzled Delta. "Fin? What in the world—"

"I know it's late," I interjected before she could go on. "But it's urgent."

"It better be." She jerked her head, gesturing me in. "Quiet on your feet. The girls are sleeping."

I followed her wordlessly to the sitting area at the far end of the room. Delta focused two chairs up to the fire and gestured for me to sit.

"In truth, I'm surprised to see you," she said. "Given our conversation earlier today."

I bowed my head slightly. "Yes. I..." I hesitated. "For that I apologize. I was short with you when you were only trying to help."

Delta waved this off. "Don't apologize. You were angry—not with me but with yourself. That much I gathered."

"You gathered right."

"It's just *why* you are that I don't understand," she continued. "You act as though all of this lies on your shoulders and no one else's. You can't do it all, Fin. Even Sensei does not expect that of you."

"On the contrary, Delta." I unfolded the letter in my hand, smoothing the wrinkled pages. "He expects more of us."

"What makes you think such a thing?"

"His letter says as much." I held up the pages briefly. "No, he doesn't require our efforts and our ceremonies and our sweat. Yes, he wants us to have more faith, more trust."

She leaned forward slightly, her brow creased. "Sensei wrote you a letter?"

I nodded slowly, my mouth dry.

"Why would he not just speak to you in person?"

"Because he's not here to do so," I told her flatly. "He's left us, Delta. He's left the Dimension."

The words were as heavy as iron weights. Her eyes widened in the firelight.

"What?"

I extended the letter towards her. "Read it for yourself."

Delta's eyes remained on mine for a moment before she took the crinkled pages from my hand. She read in silence. A crimson strand of hair slipped down in her face.

I planted my elbows on my knees and ran my fingertips back through my hair. Sensei's words played on repeat in my mind in the quiet that followed.

How could he leave us? How could he believe us to be prepared for such a thing? I wasn't. I needed him—now more than ever.

At length, Delta folded the letter back up. I straightened in my chair.

For a long moment she looked at what seemed to be nothing in particular. Then finally her troubled eyes focused on me.

"So it's true, then," she commented. "It's true, and for so long I have been in doubt."

I waited for her to go on.

She swallowed. "Hawk and Icarus are the Sunrise and Sunset sliders. Our patriarchs."

I nodded.

"And we executed her," Delta mused quietly. "We took her life and his... my God."

"No one took her life," I corrected her. "Mitsue, the student body—none of them has that authority. They may think so. But Hawk laid down her life of her own free will. Why do you think she jumped?"

Delta made no response. She bowed her head slightly, seeming to understand.

"Raiden, a killer with unidentified victims," she mused quietly. "The lost sliders… victims with an unidentified killer." She shook her head slowly. "You were right, Fin. How did you ever piece that together?"

"I merely kept my eyes open," I replied flatly. "And as someone once accused me, I listen to my gut."

Delta's lips pressed into a small smile.

"I never suspected Raiden was from Hawk's past," I clarified. "When I was looking through the lost sliders' profiles, I recognized one of the faces. I couldn't place it for the longest time, but during my last conversation with Sensei, it clicked."

"Did he tell you why he had to save her from Edwin?" Her eyes flicked to the page again, briefly. "It doesn't say here… What happened?"

My throat felt suddenly tight. I reached out to take the letter back. "No," I lied. "He didn't."

"Perhaps there was a fight."

"Perhaps."

She handed the folded pages back to me. "Regardless, now we know something for sure."

I looked at her questioningly. "What do we know?"

"Hawk is alive down there with a killer," she stated. "And so is Icarus."

I nodded despondently. "I don't know what to do, Delta," I muttered, pressing the heel of my hand to my forehead. "I just… I know Sensei said this is her battle, but something inside me can't accept that. There must be something I can do."

"There is, clearly." Delta gestured toward the letter still in my grasp. "He says so—lead. Wait for Icarus."

"And that in and of itself is troubling."

"How so?"

"'Wait for Icarus…'" I repeated my teacher's neatly scrawled words. "'Help Icarus, lead with Icarus.'"

"And?"

I stared at her. "What about Hawk? Why does he mention nothing of her? Why only Icarus?"

"Perhaps because he believes her to be more capable than Icarus, having trained in the Dimension for far longer than he has."

I was silent for a moment.

The explanation was a viable one. But something still bothered me.

"Maybe so," I concurred finally. "For now, we must concentrate on the bigger picture. That being what on *earth* we're going to do now that Sensei has taken his leave."

"Call a gathering, Fin," she said. "Read them the letter—these are his final words to us."

I shook my head. "I'm not sure that would be the right thing to do."

"But in it he himself supports Hawk and Icarus as our patriarchs," she objected. "It's the only way they can be made to believe, Fin— to hear it from Sensei himself."

"If only it were that simple."

"Fin—"

"No one can be made to believe anything, Delta. Not even by Sensei." I paused. "If they even believe he wrote it. I have no actual proof."

"You think they would accuse you of forgery?"

"They accused their own Sunrise of blasphemy, didn't they?"

Delta bit her lip, glancing past me to the window beyond.

"Areos fears the killer may be able to shift shape between the various identities he has acquired," I said, changing the subject. "If he's right, and he very well may be, that would leave Hawk exposed. He may no longer look like Raiden. She wouldn't even recognize him."

"What makes you think he's capable of shifting shape? Perhaps he can't switch back to his old identities. Maybe he must remain in the body of his latest kill."

I tilted my head slightly, thinking. "But the fact remains that he has had a taste of Hawk's blood, that day... on the gathering platform before Icarus pushed him over the edge of the ravine. He's no fool—he experienced a shifter's blood. That knowledge will not easily be erased."

"She's escaped him thus far, Fin." Delta rose to stoke the dwindling flames. "Take heart from that."

"Believe me, I'm trying."

"Besides," she went on, "Icarus is down there. Her other half."

I glanced away.

"Do you not believe that he will do everything in his power to find her?" She pressed the question. "Though their worlds may separate them? Is not love a greater force than that?"

Love.

How could a word so filled with light tear through my chest like a bullet? Would he do everything in his power to find her? Did he love her? Of course he did. For who could not love her?

If I was honest with myself, I would admit that this wasn't the question that bothered me. No—did *she* love him? That was the ache in my chest. The one I swallowed back constantly. The one that never saw the light of day.

Yet Delta saw it. I could tell by the look in her eyes.

"Of course he will," I said finally, my voice cracking. "We're relying upon it."

I rose slowly and walked to the window.

The Chief Star was scarcely visible in the slate-gray sky as dawn crept in. The rain had lightened, leaving a thick fog to billow up from the belly of the ravine.

If only you were here. If only...

"You're right, Delta." I forced myself to refocus. "We must call a gathering. I have to at least make it known that Sensei has left. As to the rest of his letter, I leave it to them to decide their own beliefs regarding Hawk and Icarus." I paused, still looking out over the mist below. "Do you think you could help me organize a gathering before the sun sets?"

I heard her footsteps quietly cross the floor. She stopped beside me at the window.

"Of course," she said softly. "I will attend this morning's sessions and tell everyone there."

The two of us stood in silence for a long moment.

"Fin." Her words came quietly when she finally did speak. "I hope you know that I wish to help you. With whatever you need."

I hesitated, then turned to look at her.

"I'm here for you," she went on quietly. "No matter what. Remember that."

I glanced down at the floor. "I know that, Delta. But what I need, you could never give me."

I felt the intensity of her gaze brush my face.

"And what would that be?"

I opened my mouth to speak, then closed it again. I shut my eyes. For so long I had swallowed the words back. For so long... How much longer could I keep them inside?

"Delta, I just..." I began, then trailed off.

I felt the warmth of her hand on my arm.

"I'm just so..." My voice broke off, a lump forming in my throat. "I'm so afraid."

It was like those three words had been the only thing holding the hurricane at bay. Though I blinked fiercely, a tear slipped past my eyelashes and streaked down my skin. I sucked in a sharp breath.

"I'm so afraid, Delta." My voice could barely support a whisper. "I'm so afraid I'll lose her. Just like I lost them."

Without a word Delta pulled me into her arms. I felt her sigh against my skin.

"Fin."

Hot tears pressed past my eyelids now, and my arms went around her as the room blurred and my eyes closed.

"Like you lost them?" Her voice was a whisper. "Your family?"

The words tore into me, ripping away what little strength I had left. I broke.

"I just... miss them so much," I sobbed. "Why couldn't I... why *didn't* I do something? Why didn't I save them?"

"Fin, you tried—"

"Did I?" I pulled back and stared at her. Her face was a blur past the tears. "Did I really?"

"Fin."

Just my name. She said nothing else, but her eyes, an emerald blur through my tears, spoke a thousand words. Morning light began to reach in through the window.

"I wish I'd been the one who was left behind," I whispered, my gaze dropping back to the floor. "Why couldn't it have been me?" My voice sank. "Why do I destroy everyone I love?"

Her hands slipped down to my chest now. I felt the tension in her fingertips. I heard her take a sharp breath.

"Fin," she said softly, "how can you think that?"

My lips parted slightly for words, but I had nothing to say. I was hollow.

I felt Delta lift my chin gently. Her eyes gazed up and into my own, soft, searching.

"If only you could see yourself the way I see you, Fin," she whispered. Her fingertips caressed my face.

I said nothing for a moment. Then slowly I shook my head. "Delta, you can't say these things—not to me."

Her expression didn't change. Her eyes remained captivated by my own.

Her hand trailed softly, slowly from my jawline to my cheek, brushing away the tears with her thumb. "Would you rather I lied?"

I faltered, unsure of what to say. I tried to glance away, but the intensity of her gaze seemed only to draw me in closer. I grasped at the floodwaters as they poured past, trying desperately to bridle the storm that was raging under my rib cage. It refused to be silenced— I was too far gone.

I shook my head slowly. Our foreheads made gentle contact. "Delta, I—"

Softly she placed a finger against my lips. "Everybody needs someone, Fin… even you."

I wanted to pull away. I wanted to step back—but when I did, my back merely found the wall. My heart rate picked up, beating over the ache in my chest. The tears still burned my eyes. The ten thousand other emotions warred inside me, smoldering like rocket fuel.

My hands slipped around to the small of her back, and I pulled her closer. My other hand closed around a fistful of her hair, and I pressed my lips against hers. I kissed her.

CHAPTER TWENTY-FOUR

Hawk

It was strange to be part of a wolf pack. And it was even stranger to keep company with someone who could shift into their fierce, four-legged counterpart. There was something about him— something that was so familiar yet foreign at the same time.

I watched him carefully as we scoured the forest for signs of Icarus, making our way through the seemingly endless cascades of pines.

We ventured into the valley and searched the woodland glades for signs of life.

We stopped at a stream for a drink, and I took a cautious seat on the edge of one of the large rocks along the bank.

"Let's go back to the edge of the meadow," I suggested. "To the tunnel that led to the world where I awoke."

Maicoh's shirt was tied around his waist. His marred skin glistened with sweat in the sunlight as he knelt beside the water, cupping it in his hands. "Why?"

"Gut feeling," I replied. "I feel like there's something to that place—something I'm missing."

"Hawk, it was only this morning that I nearly lost my life there," he retorted sharply. "Do you so easily forget?"

I leveled my gaze on the gurgling, ice-blue water. "Of course not—I just can't help but feel like I need to go back. I don't even know why."

He ran a handful of water back through his sweat-soaked mane. "You cannot always listen to your feelings, Hawk. They misguide you."

I hesitated. "Aren't you at all curious about where the white wolf comes from?"

"Not in the least."

"Not even when there seemed to be something so—" I searched for the right word, "—otherworldly about it?"

Maicoh straightened from his squat. "It tried to *kill* me, Hawk. It's *dangerous*."

"You speak of it as though this were not your first encounter."

His mouth opened, but no words came out. I leaned forward on the rock.

"Are you lying to me, Maicoh?" I asked slowly. "I should remind you that I saved your life this morning. I think you at least owe me your honesty. Don't you agree?"

For a moment he said nothing. Then he rose to his feet. "The white wolf is a killer of the black wolves. As long as I have been here, I have not known the two to coexist. It is always one or the other."

I raised an eyebrow, unsure what he meant.

He walked over to the place where two of the wolves had huddled to bask in the sunlight. As soon as Maicoh was close, one scrambled to attention.

"One or the other?" I repeated questioningly. "So what decides which wolf survives, then?"

I watched as he reached out a hand to stroke the black wolf's head with the backs of his knuckles.

"The one you feed," he replied.

We both had bundles of firewood in our arms as we trekked across the glade and back into camp. The sun had lowered in the sky, washing the woods around us in rust. The wolves trotted playfully around us.

"Are you hungry?" he asked as he rebuilt the fire.

I was seated cross-legged on the soft ground, my back up against the thick trunk of a pine. I shook my head.

"You haven't eaten all day," he pointed out. "Yet you are not wearied."

I watched him as he placed the logs. "I have been distracted," I replied neutrally. "With more important things than hunger."

"With finding your friend?"

"With finding Icarus, yes."

At this he fell silent for a while. Soon the air was filled with the sounds of crickets and the crackle of the fire. The forest grew cool with the coming of twilight, and bats flitted through the treetops.

Maicoh seemed distracted. Eventually he settled down in front of the fire with his sketchbook. The wolves had taken off into the forest—all but the one that could almost constantly be found by his side. Seeming frightened of the flame, the thin, ravenous-looking creature nestled up against Maicoh.

Cautiously, I took a seat opposite.

"You're quite the artist," I commented lightly. "Where did you learn to sketch like that?"

He glanced up a little. "You have seen my drawings?"

I gave a halfhearted smile. "I couldn't help but notice the sketches inside your shelter. They're very interesting."

Seeming satisfied with the response, he resumed his work.

"How do you draw so lifelike?" I asked, thinking. "I haven't seen work like yours in a very long time."

"I sketch what I see," Maicoh replied simply. "It is lonely here at times. When I draw, I forget for a while how alone I sometimes feel."

I observed him quietly for a moment. The flames hit an air pocket and sparks flew.

"But you have your wolves," I pointed out, only half serious.

"And now," he added, "I have you."

Something inside me faltered at this. I straightened slightly and searched for a way to change the subject. He beat me to it.

"I am sorry that we could not find him," Maicoh said after a long moment. His voice was low. "I can see that he means much to you."

I studied him. "Yes. Yes, he does."

"Mm."

"But tomorrow is a new day," I commented flatly, glancing up at the patch of sky above us, where the sparks were making their ascension. "The sun will rise."

He didn't respond. The charcoal scratched against the page.

"I should like to meet him."

I started to attention once again. "Icarus?"

Maicoh didn't look up from the page. "As I have said, Hawk—you are different. I should like to meet this one of whom you think so highly."

My brow furrowed. *Of whom I think so highly?* I'd given him only rudimentary details about Icarus, leaving out all traces of personal feelings I had towards him.

Where is all of this coming from?

"As I said," I replied firmly, "we should set out at dawn."

"Yes," he replied. "Dawn, and no sooner."

My gaze went to his over the flame, inquiring.

"This world is not the same at night, Hawk." His tone was grave. "It belongs to the wolves—and they are not tame."

My interest piqued at his words. The copper eyes of the wolf peering out from behind Maicoh remained fixed on my own.

"The wolves," I repeated almost inaudibly. "Of course."

After that, the two of us fell silent.

For a long time, Maicoh stayed awake by the fire. The charcoal in his fingers moved expertly across the pages of his sketchbook. I stayed awake with him. I pretended to watch the flame, but in those embers all I saw was his face. In the wind all I heard were urgent whispers and the occasional howl of a wolf in the distance.

I waited up with Maicoh until finally he closed his book to announce that he would go hunting.

"Didn't you say it was dangerous?" I asked carefully. "The wolves?"

He stood and stretched his arms overhead. "You cannot fear that which you are."

I cast him a doubtful glance. "Is that not what we fear most?"

I could tell my response wasn't welcome. He frowned.

"If you wish to find Icarus when dawn comes, you should rest," he stated firmly, almost as if it were an order. "And if you know what's good for you, you won't leave camp."

"Is that a threat?" I asked.

"It's a word of advice." He stepped back from the fire. "From someone who knows these woods far better than you do."

The wolf at his side leapt to its paws as Maicoh shifted, as his tan skin and rigid frame gave way to jet-black fur and fierce golden eyes.

He paused only for a moment at the edge of camp to glance over his shoulder at me, then turned and let the darkness swallow him. The black wolf followed like his shadow.

I heard a howl rip through the air.

I held my breath and waited until the thunder of paws had died away. Until I knew I was alone.

If I am going to go, this is my chance.

I was light on my feet as I slipped away from camp, into the shadows. I glanced over my shoulder. The fire flickered a silent farewell.

Picking up my pace, I wove my way through the trees. I had little sense of direction in the darkness in this form, but I knew exactly what I was looking for.

My footsteps rang in my ears, muted thuds against the thick carpet of pine needles, as I trekked farther into the woods. Strands of spiders' silk attached to my hair and clothes, and bats whistled overhead. A half-moon began to rise above the distant mountain peaks.

Which way was the meadow? Where did the woods end, giving way to the glade that Maicoh and I had crossed to find the tunnel? The entrance to my world...

I have to find the entrance to my world.

I sucked in a breath, faltering as my eyes caught on a dark blur darting through the brush up ahead. I folded myself back behind a tree trunk and waited silently for it to pass. I heard its paws pass softly across the ground and then fade into the distance.

I exhaled a sigh of relief.

Crouching, I darted away from my cover and continued at a run. In the crescent moonlight I could just make out the clearing at the edge of the tree line.

The woods were a maze. I skipped over tangled roots and avoided rocks as best I could in the low light. I longed to shift, but I was hesitant to do so. I regretted this decision immediately when I tripped and fell on my face.

I gulped back a yelp of pain as I felt the warmth of blood rising slowly to the surface of my cheek. I blinked furiously as I raised my head. I was about to force myself back up onto my feet when something stopped me cold. Something standing directly in my path.

My throat tightened. I felt a droplet of blood roll slowly down my face.

Poised before me, washed in moonlight, was the white wolf.

Part of me was in awe. Part of me was hoping it wouldn't tear me limb from limb. But it remained as still as a statue as I cautiously pressed myself up into a crouch.

"You came back," I whispered.

Getting to my feet, I took a careful step forward. It watched me closely.

"I promise I won't hurt you," I told it, and then cringed a little. "What happened before—I… I didn't mean to hurt you."

My mind reeled back to that morning: the fight and the fire I'd held in my hands.

"I mean… I did, at the time, but…"

Another step brought me close enough to see its finer details. The shape of its eyes, the dirt on its paws, the texture of its perfect coat.

I felt my brow furrow as I studied it. Still it made no motion to back off.

"The burn marks," I mused softly. "Your wounds—where are they?"

My mind began searching for the answer I knew it wouldn't give. I couldn't take my eyes off its flawless, snow-white coat.

How could it have healed so quickly? There was no way.

"Impossible," I whispered, almost close enough now to feel its breath as I extended my hand. "How did you heal so quickly?"

It lifted its massive head slightly, its sharp eyes seeming to telegraph that I was in no danger.

I knelt beside it, my hand still extended as I came down to its eye level. Giving in to its primal instincts, it gathered the scent off the palm of my hand.

"Did you…" I trailed off, still trying to piece it together myself. "Did you heal yourself?"

It continued its ticklish in-and-out breathing up my forearm. I looked down at my hand as it brushed against the wolf's soft coat. As I did, my attention caught on my fingertips. My fingertips that so easily transformed into feathers when I gave the word.

Wings...

As if pulled by the current of a raging river, my mind raced back to the day that the wind had swept into Sensei's yard, breaking the branch that would send me crashing to the ground. To the moment Icarus's hands had erased the blood that had stained my feathers, healing my wound.

Icarus...

My eyes slowly widened, lifting to meet the wolf's. It stared back at me, almost as if to affirm my thoughts.

"Icarus." My voice was hardly a whisper. "Did..."

I couldn't finish. I stared into its eyes, searching.

"Did Icarus heal you?"

Without hesitation it pushed its head forward into my chest, taking me aback slightly with the force. It seemed to urge me to my feet. Slowly I stood.

It leapt back now, seeming only more eager for me to follow. It tossed its head in the direction of the clearing just beyond and danced closer to the trees.

"Can you lead me to him?" I asked, taking a step in its direction. "Can you lead me to Icarus?"

It gave no response. It turned and took off at a run.

I snapped into action, giving myself no time to doubt. I chased after the wolf—the dangerous wolf I'd been told to stay away from. To never follow.

We sprinted through the blur of trees and then into the open space, the meadow where the sky burst open above us and the stars seemed to rain down like flecks of silver. The wild grass around us transformed into waves of sterling, swayed by the bellows of the mountains.

We were exposed now, stripped of any cover we might have had from the piercing golden eyes of the black wolves. Yet somehow I didn't seem to care. Somehow the threat had left my thoughts completely. My focus remained on the flashes of white in front of me.

All I could comprehend were my footsteps, each seeming to whisper *Icarus, Icarus, Icarus.*

We crossed the meadow to the other side of the forest, darting in amongst the trees until we found the place where the tunnel yawned open before us. The white wolf darted into the dark hole, and I dropped to my knees to start crawling. The earth swallowed us underground.

The dirt was soft under my palms. A pinprick of light beckoned in the darkness. There was a sharp bark.

We emerged into a world of snow, basked in the light of a new dawn. It was exactly as it had been when I'd left. Nothing had changed. Except now there were no black wolves to be seen.

I scrambled to my feet, catching my breath. Puffs of vapor lifted from my lips and into the freezing air.

"He's here?" I panted. "But I searched everywhere."

The wolf gave another short bark in reply as it turned and resumed its sprint, tossing its massive head in a way that seemed to taunt me to keep up.

I took off after it—running hard. Bolting past hundreds of mighty trees and leaping over any obstacle that came between me and my target.

We were blurs among the quiet woods around us.

All at once, the snow deepened past my knees and I fell. The air whooshed out of my lungs in a surprised yelp as I crashed into the thick blanket of powder.

Get up, get up, get up!

Frantically, I tried to leap back to my feet. Like hungry quicksand, the snow sucked me down into its clutches again.

Growling angrily, I grappled with the white matter until I was standing again. The white wolf was but a smudge in the distance now.

Déjà vu.

"I lost you once, Icarus," I murmured softly, dusting myself off. "I'm not losing you a second time."

I closed my eyes, shutting out the world before me. I felt my skin begin to heat up as I locked my focus.

Taking a deep breath, I threw myself backwards into the air. A burst of flame and then feathers.

The trees seemed to bow respectfully as I lifted past them, my eyes scanning the white ground below for my target. The fray of white on white. Were it not for its movement, I scarcely would have been able to detect it.

Tucking my wings, I bulleted down into the forest again, swooping low over the wolf. Its paws only became more of a blur in response. I pumped my wings as though my life depended on it. It was only when they began to feel as though they would tear away from my body with the strain that we came at once upon a clearing. The wolf came to a halt. I hovered in midair, stunned.

In front of us was the stone platform surrounded by crumbling marble pillars.

I dropped into human form, landing in the soft snow. The wolf seemed unalarmed by the transition.

"Impossible," I breathed, taking a tentative step forward.

It was like a memory of a dream. A place I had feared I would never find again.

I dusted the snow off the place where I had found the etching on the pillar. My fingertips burned against the cold marble.

"The iris," I whispered as the familiar shape came into view. "How did you know to bring me here?" I asked quietly. "What is this place?"

It replied only by staring a moment longer and then, licking its lips, stepping around me. It stalked through the snow to the edge of the circle where the stone began. It turned to look at me, as if checking to see that it had my full attention. It barked sharply.

"What is it?"

Its ears flicked to attention and it pawed the earth anxiously.

I stepped closer, curious.

In response, it lurched forward, leaping into the circle—and vanishing altogether.

I froze, stunned.

What on earth?

I darted to the stone's edge, looking down at the place where the paw prints abruptly ended. My gaze continued onto the marble surface.

For the first time, I noticed that this was the only place that snow wasn't. The stone was the purest white, camouflaging itself in the snow yet not overcome by it.

The closer I looked, the more I saw. Flecks of what looked like soil were trapped in the cracks here and there, and bits of what looked almost like flower petals danced in the wind, disappearing as they passed over the edge. A breeze blew gently, neither bitter nor cold, but warm.

"How the..."

I stepped closer and then closer. I slowly reached out a hand.

My fingertips disappeared.

My heart leapt to my throat as I stood there, feeling as much made of stone as the pillars around me.

The farther I reached, the more my hand disappeared, the more I felt the warmth emanating from the other side. The brush of flower petals, the rush of the sweet wind, and then—

Another hand. Fingers that filled the spaces between my own. Soft, warm, familiar skin—beckoning goose bumps to the surface of my own.

I had no time to think—it pulled, and I let my instincts take over. I fell.

Into the circle. Into sunlight—bright and sweet like summer. Into an atmosphere filled with the sounds of birds' songs and the scent of wildflowers. Into a pair of familiar arms.

With a force that felt like we were burning through the Earth's atmosphere, we tumbled to the ground. Into the soft grass where the white wolf lay.

Into the irises. Into a tangle of Icarus.

October, 2015

The first time I met him was at a club. Mel was by my side, and we were off in some corner when we bumped into one of his roommates. Mel had been surprised to see him; apparently he wasn't the partying type.

"West, what are you doing here?" she asked, suppressing a laugh. "Don't you have, like—"

"Homework?" He paused to adjust his glasses. "Piles. But someone has to drive these idiots home."

"Idiots?"

He gestured beyond the people crowding around us to a couple of guys. One was conversing with two attractive girls; the other was standing nearby, merely spectating. Not saying a word.

His clothes were dark, as was his hair. But his eyes... There was something about his eyes that bothered me. He stared ahead at nothing, but he looked as though he saw something there—someone. In the midst of the party, the noise, the chaos, he was quiet... detached. Like I was. He was there, but he wasn't.

Mel and West, the young man with glasses, were still talking, but I had tuned out of the conversation entirely.

"Introduce us," I said to West, indicating the silent guy and clearly catching Mel a little off guard. She gave me a puzzled glance and then took me by the hand.

West led us over to the small group of college guys. Everyone was drinking and laughing and acting unintelligent. All except this one guy; my eyes hadn't left him. And he hadn't stopped staring.

West cleared his throat. "This is Ruger." He gestured to someone else. I didn't bother to check who. Then he gestured at the staring guy. "And this is, uh, Ion..."

"Ion, hey," Mel said. Obviously, she already knew him. "How's it going?"

Ion didn't say a word; his eyes narrowed a little, but he continued to stare at something the rest of us couldn't see. When Mel said his name again, he finally snapped out of it.

"What?" He blinked and turned to look at us. All he noticed was Mel. "Oh, hey."

"Hey," she said back. She didn't just know him—she liked him.

I, however, instantly despised him. But then I remembered that I hadn't come here for nothing—I was here for a reason. I was here to look for her... for another anomaly that would lead me to her.

And how would I identify this anomaly? Not by looking, but by discernment. People who merely look miss everything; it's the ones who peer deeper and see not merely the quietness, but the haunted look behind the quietness—they're the ones who find what they're looking for.

When I saw Ion, I knew immediately. He was one of them.

So I swallowed back the urge to kill him then and there and stuck out my hand for him to shake.

"Ion," I said, forcing a smile, "I'm Riley."

CHAPTER TWENTY-FIVE

Icarus

Would she recognize me from how quickly my wounds had healed? Would she know me, or would she run from me? If I asked her with my eyes, would she follow me? Would she trust me enough?

A droplet of blood traced her cheek. Her lips parted in pursuit of words that came in whispers. Her eyes made me fall in love again.

"You came back."

You came back.

I wanted to answer—to speak. To tell her that it was she who had come back, who had followed me down to the mouth of the hell I deserved.

She came closer, moonlight spilling over her shoulders. Her scent as she knelt in front of me—saffron. Spices. Her fingertips were like ice.

"Did you heal yourself?"

Words ached in my throat, but everything began to fade, dimming. Her eyes were the last to go.

"Did..." Her voice tapered off, muffling as the rest of the world dimmed. "Did Icarus heal you?"

Icarus. That word.

My name.

"Icarus."

I wanted so badly to respond, to speak, but I could not. I felt as though I were underwater. The world around me turned to black.

"Icarus…"

Hawk…

"Icarus!"

At once it was as if I pulled out of my stupor. My eyelids flew open as I instinctively bolted up into a seated position. It took a moment for my mind to come back into focus. A sharp bark helped speed up the process.

The white wolf stood in the center of the stone circle, crouched slightly and wagging its bushy tail furiously. When this didn't get a coherent response, it lunged forward and nailed me back into the irises with its oversized paws. I sputtered, the air rushing out of my lungs.

"What is it?" I moaned, exasperated. "Get off."

The wolf only seized the cuff of my pant leg in its large jaws.

"Hey!" I fought to push it off, but the effort was useless. "Cut it out—"

It let go and retreated to the circle. That was when I noticed something—what it must have been trying to alert me to.

A disruption in the air at the circle's edge. A distortion against the otherwise undisturbed forest around me. Sunlight and rustling leaves—everything around me was crystal clear except for the almost undetectable distortion that seemed to emanate from its source like ripples on a glassy pond.

I slowly rose to my feet.

Hesitating at the stone circle's edge, I peered across at the place where the atmosphere seemed to churn. Then I stepped into the ring and the world transformed around me.

And I saw her. Her perfect fingers as she cautiously extended a hand, testing the porthole's integrity.

Hawk stood at the opposite side of the circle. And for a moment I was too stunned—too in awe, too wonderstruck to move. To think or breathe.

My strength fled me. My fingertips began to tingle as I moved forward steadily, unsure why I could see her although she clearly couldn't see me, but I didn't care. I couldn't take my eyes off hers.

I stopped in front of her, observing her covertly for a moment before, grinning, I reached out and took her by the hand.

A stunned expression passed over her face. She was exactly as I remembered her, yet there was something different. Something in her greenish-brown eyes. Something in the way her unruly mane caressed her face. Something in the way the blood stained her cheek, just as it had in the dream I'd only just awoken from. Something was so different, but perfect.

As my fingers filled the spaces between hers, something that felt like fire ripped through my arm. I went weak at the knees.

Stumbling backward slightly, I pulled her into my world. She came in like a comet, a burst of fire and ice that hit me point-blank and sent us both tumbling to the ground. The irises caught us like a safety net.

"Icarus!" My name burst off her lips.

I shook my head in disbelief, too overwhelmed to breathe, let alone communicate coherently. For a moment we both lay there, gasping for air as though neither of us had breathed since we saw each other last.

Hawk rolled off my chest to scramble up into a seated position. I did likewise.

"Icarus," she repeated, breathless, as she stared into my eyes with her wide wild ones. "I can't believe it."

She threw her arms around my neck, falling into me again. Still void of strength, I melted back to the ground again. My fingertips tangled in her hair.

"You're alive," she whispered. "I can't believe I found you."

I pulled her in closer, my face resting in the curve of her neck. I breathed in.

Saffron.

"With you, Hawk," I whispered back, "I can believe anything."

———◆———

"Did you speak with the council yourself, or did Sensei decide to open their eyes?"

"Not... exactly."

I stooped to pick up another branch. "Wasn't it he who sent you?"

Hawk was quiet as we continued gathering dead branches from the forest floor. The sun was beginning to set.

"Or did the council simply regret their decision to send me to my grave?" I added, only half joking. "I mean… your coming here must have at least in part been their call, right?"

Hawk shifted her bundle of branches and twigs to the opposite arm. I could practically hear her thoughts in the silence that followed.

"Surely, if the Dimension was plunged into winter, they must have made the connection," I continued. "They had to have seen that it was because of… because I fell. Because you did too, in a way."

She turned to face me, a tempest in her eyes. "The council, Icarus?" She grunted and bent down to snatch another branch. "The council sees nothing except what they wish to see."

My eyes followed her. "How do you mean?"

"I mean that they didn't send me. Nor did they regret condemning you to death," she stated flatly. "At least, they didn't seem very remorseful at my own execution."

I almost dropped the firewood in my arms. *"What?"*

Hawk shrugged a shoulder. "Did you expect them to treat me with any more grace than they treated you, Icarus?"

"Of course!" I almost choked. "I mean, come on, you're—they have to understand that you—"

"That I'm the Sunrise?" She gave a short, mirthless laugh. "That you are the Sunset?"

She spilled the wood into my arms, doubling my load. "Icarus, if only they all had your faith."

She turned and started back in the direction of camp. I followed her.

"What was your crime?" I asked, still incredulous.

"Blasphemy," she answered. "At least that's what I was told when I finally awoke from my coma."

I could hardly believe what she was saying. I couldn't help but ache inside when I thought of the Dimension as it had been to me when I'd initiated: perfection. A place of refuge. How had we screwed ourselves up to such a degree? I knew my hands weren't clean in this.

"So they sentenced you to death?"

Hawk shook her head. "It would have been a much lighter sentence had Fin and I not played the system for all it was worth."

"Meaning?"

"Meaning I was a nasty little rebel," she clarified. "And they decided erasing my memory just wouldn't cut it. What if it didn't work? Then they would have to put up with me forever."

I couldn't help but smile a little.

"We both knew it would be a disaster if I couldn't remember who I was," Hawk continued. "How would I be able to find you? No, a harsher punishment only worked to the good. I knew I needed to get down here anyway."

She turned and looked at me as we made our way through the trees. "I needed to get to you."

I was trying hard to keep a level head; this was a serious conversation. But all I wanted to do was kiss her.

"So I watched the weather change as I recovered. The rain finally stopped and the sun came out," Hawk continued. "And I watched from my cell as they prepared the gathering platform for my execution ceremony." She paused, her lips pressing into a thin line. "I jumped before they even finished."

The white wolf trotted playfully up alongside me as we entered the clearing where I'd set up camp the past several days.

"What about Sensei?" I asked her. "Did he know about any of this? Did you speak to him before you left?"

Hawk hesitated for a moment. "As he knows all, I am sure he was aware of our plans. No doubt Fin consulted him throughout."

I dropped the wood into a pile and knelt in front of it. "And not you?"

Her lips parted slightly, but she only shook her head. "It's complicated, Icarus."

The white wolf seated itself at her feet as she struggled with the words. I began to construct the fire.

"How is anything between you and Sensei ever complicated? He's always been—"

"My father?" she offered. "My refuge? My savior? My everything?" Hawk rubbed her eyes, shaking her head as if trying to escape the thoughts. "I feel so far from him now, Icarus." Her words had a rough edge. "I don't even know how it happened."

"What you feel and what is actually true can be vastly different, Hawk," I said, stacking the branches. "You might have lost sight of him, but I think it's impossible for him to ever lose sight of you."

"I just can't stop wondering why he wasn't there," she said after a moment. "Why he was absent at my trial and yours. Where was he when we most needed his defense?"

Her voice was scarred with vulnerability, and I could understand exactly how she felt.

I sat back, the fire lit now. I felt the wolf as it brushed up against my back.

"Hawk, I wish I could answer you," I responded quietly. "It would take less time for me to tell you the things I do know than the things I don't." I got up to take a seat beside her. "But someone once taught me that trust—" I locked eyes with her in the low light "—trust is far superior to knowledge."

Hawk didn't speak. Her eyes sparkled in the glow of the flames.

"Maybe he wasn't there…" I tapered off. "Maybe he isn't here now… because he doesn't need to be." I lifted my gaze slightly. The stars were making their first appearances overhead. "God knows I've often felt as though I'm living in hell down here. That there are so many questions I've yet to find answers for. That I'm confused and sore and… aching for home. But…" I shook my head. "None of it matters in the end, does it?" I whispered. "Because in the end, isn't this what we trained for? Isn't this where we jump?"

For a moment I couldn't read her expression. I waited silently, but she never spoke.

She reached out a hand, and her fingertips gently found my cheek. *Fire.*

My thoughts fled me, along with the feeling in my hands. Chills raced down my spine as Hawk's gaze drifted over my face.

For an instant there was nothing around us, above us. No sky, no stars. The cries of the wolves in the distance, the chirping of the crickets—it was like the volume of the atmosphere crashed to a sudden mute. There was my pulse. There was Hawk's gentle inhales and exhales as her lips brushed softly against mine.

A strange, warm, yet aching sensation rushed over me as though I'd stepped beneath a waterfall. I lost myself in the feeling of her skin, of her hair as it caressed my face—as she drew closer. I couldn't breathe, but I felt almost as though I didn't need to.

In my mind's eye I saw her as I had the day we'd met. A hundred years of everything I had never known I needed, wrapped in skin, stained with the markings of the Sunrise.

Hawk pulled back just slightly, just enough for our eyes to meet, and then her forehead was against mine, and we were both sighing as though we'd swum from the bottom of the ocean to come up for air.

"Oh, Icarus," she said softly, her lips only slightly disconnected from my own, "I missed you."

The silence was still there, but now I could hear the wolves as the fire grew.

I began to realize that there was more than one. Out of the corner of my eye, I could see them making their way through the trees and into the clearing, encircling the flame; white coats of fur seemed to be everywhere.

We were surrounded by white wolves.

In other circumstances I might have been taken aback. I might have wondered where they had all come from. But now I was just a wildfire, trying to find enough words to contain how much I had missed her too.

But wildfires can't speak.

Trembling, my fingertips wandered back into her hair, and my lips melted against hers again, first like the quiet of the flame, and then again like the howling wolves around us.

Finally, our faces separated. Hawk's head came to rest against my chest. For a moment her left ear pressed to what must have sounded like thunder. Then she straightened to look me in the eyes.

"We're going to make it out of here, Hawk," I told her quietly, though I felt as though I needed the assurance more than she did. "Now that we're together, nothing can stop us."

She smiled a little, for my sake. "You know, there were days when I felt as though I would never find you," she said, her eyes flicking up to the sky momentarily. "The ravine is a very strange place, Icarus. It's like we were living in different worlds—parallel without realizing it. As though the ravine's bottom exists in layers, and if by chance you find each other, then you're the lucky ones."

"Perhaps it's not by chance."

"Mmm." She hummed an agreement. "But then nothing seems to happen by chance down here." Her voice dropped to a whisper. "The wolf led me here for a reason."

Hawk paused and looked away, seeming to have remembered something. Her smile faded from her lips. "At least that's what he told me."

When she looked back at me, I could see the wheels turning.

"*He?*" I asked. "Who are you talking about?"

CHAPTER TWENTY-SIX

Fin

Dawn crept in slowly. It illuminated the pages spread out on the desk in front of me, where I sat resting my forehead against my fist. I'd had Hawk's file open all night. Her photograph stared up at me; her eyes were the color of the night sky and just as filled with the realms of the unknown.

Mitsue had long since risen and left for dawn sessions, which I had decided to skip. Time seemed to merely slip listlessly past me.

I sat at my desk and I read the pages of Hawk's biography. I read Sensei's hand-scrawled letter; I studied it until my eyes ached. My body yearned for sleep, but the storm in my soul wouldn't allow it. Each page seemed to burn in my fingers as I turned it.

Each time my gaze met with hers, frozen in the black-and-white photograph, I felt as though my life flashed in a succession of visions before my eyes—my life with her.

The morning she had jumped, disappearing into the mouth of the ravine in a burst of fire and feathers. The day we had spent on a cliff side overlooking the sea in Howth before I had left my family behind for the sake of the Dimension and its purpose.

The day I'd told her that I loved her. The day she had wept and returned my embrace, but not my words—never my words. Perhaps I was just sorry for myself; I wasn't sure at this point. Did I simply hate myself for having fallen so hard for someone I knew could never love me in return?

No... If only it were that simple.

The fact was, in all my blundering and searching, I had still never once betrayed her. Never once taken my eyes off her.

For as long as I could remember, I had loved Hawk. A time when I had not known the Dimension? That I could remember, yet a time when I had not known and loved Hawk with every atom of my body and soul—that I couldn't recall: she had become a part of me.

How many times had I chided myself—scolded myself for losing my head around her? For breaking out in chills every time our hands brushed. For failing to steady my voice when I spoke to her. For being unable to keep my mind focused when we were close—those days before she left, when we'd fought about the Dimension's fate, yelling into each other's faces.

How badly I had wanted to cup her face in my hands and kiss her.

To kiss her as I had never kissed anyone... because I *had* never kissed anyone before. To kiss her as I had kissed Delta.

No matter how much I swallowed it back, the sensation of lead weight in my stomach did not subside. I closed the file in front of me.

I pressed my forehead to my knuckles, taking a slow breath and becoming aware of the snatches of birdsong that came on the wind as it lapped past the canvas flap. Faintly, I could hear what sounded like the notes of a violin.

The wind had not sung in a long time. The sun was shining; the birds were awakening...

Has she found Icarus?

I should have been filled with joy at the prospect. Instead I felt my heart playing arsonist in my chest—threatening to set fire to what was left of me.

I lifted one of the sleek, dust-coated feathers from the vial on the desk's corner. Delicate stripes of burnt sienna and cream white, like velvet beneath my fingertips as I smoothed them with the grain.

Sensei's words resounded in my mind:

"The battle she faces in her world beneath the ravine, that you must leave her to fight on her own."

The only help I could offer the one I loved most was to lead the world she had left behind. That, according to the words of our teacher, was my task. And already I had failed.

I placed the feather back in the vial and dropped my face into the palms of my hands.

How greatly I had let her down.

I was pulled abruptly out of my thoughts as the canvas flap whipped suddenly aside. Glancing up, I met Areos's gaze through his wire-rimmed spectacles. He spoke before I could.

"Where were you?" he asked bluntly. "It's not like you to miss morning sessions. Gaia was ticked."

"Look, I'm sorry," I told him. "I just... I didn't feel like it."

Areos stared at me. "You didn't *feel* like it?"

It sounded pathetic and I knew it.

"I had a lot on my mind," I clarified. "I have... a lot on my mind. I..."

Areos waited for me to finish, still looking at me from across the room like I'd sprouted an additional head.

"We need to catch up," I confessed finally, focusing my chair around to face him. "I have... updates." I hesitated to say her name. "No doubt Delta mentioned something—"

"Something about an emergency gathering, yes," Areos interjected. "That's why I came to see you. Why?"

I heaved a sigh. *Where to start...*

"Areos, Sensei is gone."

His eyes widened. "Gone?"

I nodded gravely.

"What do you mean, gone?"

I lifted the folded parchment, revealing our teacher's handwriting scrawled across the front. "I went into his office the other day to ask him about... well, everything. Everything we've discovered the past few days—about Raiden, Hawk, Icarus. All of it. He wasn't there, but I found this."

"What does it say?"

I pulled in a deep breath, glancing down at the pages in my hand and then back to Areos. "That we're no longer fledglings. That the time has come for us to spread our wings and assume our true roles of leadership. And apparently this is something he feels must occur in his absence."

"You're joking with me."

"If only I were."

He pulled a chair away from the wall with his hands and threw himself down. "Because things weren't bad enough, right?"

Though I agreed, I said nothing. My gaze dropped down to the letter again.

"So what are we going to do now?" Areos spoke up again after a moment. "Duke it out at this meeting about how we should move forward?"

"I wouldn't have phrased it exactly like that," I replied slowly. "But yes. Basically."

He began bobbing his foot anxiously. "Sounds like a recipe for disaster."

I turned back to my desk, opening one of the drawers to place the letter inside. "What would you suggest?"

"A game plan." He thumbed his glasses up the bridge of his nose thoughtfully. "At least some framework set in place before the gathering. If you guys go into this with nothing, the fate of the Dimension will ultimately be decided by the reaction of the mob—and God knows it won't be pretty."

I considered it, then gave a slow nod. "We've all worked too long and hard to let that happen."

"Sensei wrote you the letter, Fin. Out of anyone he could have chosen to leave with a set of instructions to guide us, he chose you. He must have given you some idea as to how he wants us to proceed from here."

I tilted my head, thinking back to the words I had all but memorized by this point. "Yes and no," I answered. "He made one thing very clear—we must do this on our own and have faith that he's given us the ability to do so. But as to our mission?" I shrugged. "It is what it has always been—just as clear, yet unclear as ever."

"To save Earth from a destruction we don't even understand."

"Exactly."

He grunted. "No pressure."

"He wants us to start preparing ourselves for what we'll find there," I continued, pondering it myself. "He said we should wait for Icarus and ready ourselves for our reemergence into the natural world."

Areos shot me a dubious look. "Do you think Icarus will actually return?"

"Sensei said so," I replied bluntly. "Of course I believe it."

He paused, analyzing. "So they're alive down there," he mused. "And Sensei knows it."

I pushed back my chair to stand. "What doesn't he know? That's the question."

"But if they're alive, why wouldn't he tell his own students?"

"The answer lies in the question," I responded. "We are students. Learning, searching for more—longing for it. If Sensei merely handed us all the answers, there would be no room for trust."

Areos didn't seem satisfied with this answer. He shifted in his seat. "Shouldn't the education of the masses be held in higher regard than the development of their trust?" he asked, sounding a bit strained. "If you ask me, ignorance and guesswork are what will derail this place and our mission. Why didn't Sensei address us himself? Why didn't he at least instruct us as to exactly what he wants us to do?" He paused. "And… if he wants us to believe that Hawk and Icarus are, in fact, the patriarchs… why wouldn't he have just announced it himself? To hell with trust—what about order and truth?"

I pursed my lips as I studied the mist congregating below the pods.

Areos's argument was eloquent and perfectly logical. I would be lying if I said it didn't cause me to wish the Dimension did operate on such terms. But then again, if it did, none of us would be here. For which of us had intellectually dissected and organized the workings of our home before we were allowed to be initiated?

No, it was only our trust that was required. Not our understanding.

"These things can't be forced, Areos," I said. "As much as we might wish it sometimes."

"At least tell me you're going to fill them in on the contents of Sensei's letter to give your speech some authoritative merit."

"Sensei addressed the letter to me and didn't grant permission to share it," I answered. "Our aim is merely to announce that he has left and that he has told us to prepare ourselves."

"How are we supposed to prepare ourselves when we don't know what we're up against?"

I cast him a look over my shoulder. "By sharpening every skill set we possess. That's what this gathering is about—training, and training hard."

"And waiting around for someone everyone thinks is dead."

My jaw set. "That will come on its own—we can't know exactly how everything will happen, so there's no reason for us to attempt to explain it."

Areos didn't speak for a moment. The wind gently swayed the dormitory pod.

I spoke up after a moment. "Sensei wrote about what it's like at the bottom of the ravine. It seems as though its existence has only ever been questioned because it was a mere void waiting for someone to create their own small dimensions—not unlike this one. Layers of realities they will have to escape on their own, each of them. I only pray that Icarus finds her before Raiden does. Especially if he's in an alternate identity," I finished quietly.

Areos contemplated this for a moment and then cleared his throat. "Let's say that's the case—that Hawk and Icarus cross paths, reunite."

He stopped talking and I turned to look at him.

"Then what?" he questioned dryly. "How are they going to get back?"

I reached up to rub my forehead. "No idea."

"Sensei gave you no inkling in the letter?"

"None, except that a sacrifice must be made," I said. "And heaven knows what that could mean. A sacrifice on his part, or one that all of us will have to make... I have no idea. But right now what we need to focus on is assembling the student body tonight and getting everyone on the same game plan." I put emphasis on the last words. "The game plan we don't have yet. Any suggestions?"

Areos pushed back his glasses. "Well, since you ask..." He grinned a little, switching himself over to my desk chair. "I have a few ideas."

"Good." I exhaled the word while he whipped out a fresh sheet of paper. "Because we're going to need all the help we can get."

The canvas flap folded aside. "Who needs help?"

The new voice entered only seconds before the speaker did. A familiar, slender frame. A mane of red hair. Eyes that bored into mine from across the room as she passed the threshold.

Instantly, I felt my throat tighten. A sick feeling twisted at the bottom of my stomach.

She came to a halt as soon as she saw Areos seated at my desk. He turned to peer at her over the rims of his glasses and then shot me a knowing look.

"Wow, Fin," he jested dryly. "I would hate to be you when someone catches wind that you've invited a girl to your dorm."

Delta shot him a look and I felt my face turn crimson.

"Fin didn't invite me," she clarified before I could. "I'm intruding. We *are* in a state of emergency, you know—I think a few allowances are called for."

Areos grunted, sweeping a pen over the page in front of him. Delta turned her attention back to me.

"In all seriousness, I came to give you an update," she said matter-of-factly. "I clued almost everyone in at sessions this morning. They'll be assembling at sunset on the gathering platform."

"And you were sure to tell them—"

"That it was an emergency meeting, yes," she assured me. "No details."

I gave a single nod.

"In my opinion," Areos continued, as though our conversation had never been interrupted, "we need to abandon this ridiculous council system from here on out. We need a real leader—a captain we can trust enough to follow into battle, not assemblages of different sliders every time someone errs."

One of Delta's eyebrows shot up. She turned and looked at me inquisitively.

"Our system of organization may have worked under Sensei's supervision," Areos went on. "But no longer. It will only drag us in deeper. We need a leader until Hawk and Icarus return—the most experienced slider, who will be able to help us train and hone our abilities to the extent that I'm sure we will need them when we remerge."

Delta crossed her arms over her chest. "And how do you propose this leader be selected?"

"By vote."

"And what if the student body votes for someone we don't believe in?"

Areos shrugged. "That's democracy."

"But this isn't a country," I countered. "Or a college campus.

Sensei said to *wait*, not try to form some new system to govern ourselves with."

Delta's eyes shifted to me. "Then what do you suggest?"

"Surely we can't keep doing what we've always done," Areos cut in before I could respond. "We're living in *dire* times. We need something more dependable than this—this code that exists merely to punish those who cannot live up to its standard of perfectionism. It's the reason Icarus was executed, for God's sake! And Hawk along with him."

I couldn't deny that he had a point.

"I mean, did Sensei even issue these rules?" he asked, his gaze darting back and forth between the two of us. "Or was it the doing of the students he initiated? It's human nature to try to control the uncontrollable. We all, in some way, secretly crave power, but some things can't be controlled." He shot me a glance. "They have to be trusted."

Delta bit her lip, seeming anxious to object but finding no ammunition to fortify her argument.

"So enough with the code and all its meticulous standards." Areos resumed his furious scribbling. "We all wonder why Sensei never even goes to these stupid hearings, trials, and punishment ceremonies—has it ever crossed our minds that maybe he doesn't believe in them? Maybe it's never been about how perfect we are and how hard we try, but about *who* we are, intrinsically." He adjusted his glasses with his thumb. "Who he's already made us to be."

"Are you saying the code is worthless?" Delta questioned.

"Did I say it was?" He tossed her a look. "It's pure and true—all that we aspire to be. But who among us has kept it? Whose hands are spotless? I don't think even one of us has succeeded in that."

I lowered my gaze to the floor, my conscience running for cover. My mind couldn't seem to escape those resounding words I had so easily caved for: *Let go, Fin...*

And now her eyes pierced my own, trying, as usual, to unbutton my façade. I wanted to turn away again, but I forced myself to remain where I was.

"It's true that Sensei never intended for us to live by a set of rules," I agreed carefully. "He gave us power—that is what he wishes us to live by. Instead we chose to exercise that power by creating our own standards of governance."

Areos tapped the pen thoughtfully against his chin. "If ever there was a time to change the system..."

"It would be now," Delta finished, passing me to walk to the window. Areos followed her with his eyes.

"You yourself said that we need to stop depending on Sensei for the fulfillment of our every need, Fin," she went on. "That he expects us to use the power he's invested in us—that this is our time."

I was too lost in thought to respond.

"Maybe he's been warning us all along that this was to come," she reflected, almost to herself. "What better time for a new order to enter than after the old one has put to death our patriarchs?" She gave a wry grunt. "Or are we to wait until it has slowly but surely consumed us all?"

I glanced at Areos, who agreed with a nod. "We're both new initiates," he commented, jerking his head in Delta's direction. "Maybe we see the errors of the system with greater clarity than those who have lived under it for years."

I drew a breath. "While this is true, and I understand exactly where you two are coming from, I have reservations about bringing this up at tonight's gathering."

Areos cast me a look over his shoulder. "Why?"

"You yourself warned me of 'unruly mobs,' Areos," I reminded him. "In this state of unrest, are we sure that now is the time to tear down what remnants of order we have left?"

"So you're afraid of them?" Delta asked.

"I'm afraid *for* them," I corrected her. "Not *of* them. I agree that we're slowly choking ourselves out, but informing hundreds of people that their teacher is gone, and then ordering them to abandon the guidelines they've long adhered to..."

My words faded before I could finish them. I glanced finally at Delta. "In your efforts to liberate us, you may find only that you have tightened the chains," I concluded grimly. "People don't change that quickly—their desire to be ruled over won't die overnight."

The green eyes scrutinized me.

"Are you saying we do nothing?" she asked sharply. "We change nothing? We keep them in the dark and hope by some miracle we all make it out of this alive?"

"No," I shot back. "I just think we should trust Sensei enough to obey his orders."

"Which are?"

"To wait," I replied firmly. "To wait for Icarus."

Delta quirked an eyebrow. "And until then?"

I wanted to retort, but I couldn't. It was hard enough to talk to her, but with Areos here it was even harder. I was too tired to argue down their case—which wasn't even bad. Just dangerous.

Instead of speaking, I began to pace.

"You and I both know they won't wait, Fin," Delta continued. "They won't wait because they're afraid—and they'll be more terrified than ever when they learn that Sensei has left the Dimension."

"And they will cling to what they know," I argued, my voice rising a little. "Don't you see?"

"I don't," she countered stubbornly. "I think you are as Sensei says you are—hesitating at the edge when he is pushing you to jump."

Halting in my tracks, I flipped around to face her.

"He means for us to change something, Fin," she persisted.

I stared at her for a long moment before slowly shaking my head. "Not like this."

I brushed past her, pausing at the window again.

When Delta finally spoke again, her voice was more yielding. "What about Icarus, Fin?" she asked steadily. "Is the punishment he was dealt to be for nothing? Is his execution to be in vain?"

I gave no answer. My eyes leveled on the mist below, the fog that was beginning to scatter from the touch of the sun's long fingers.

"Is Hawk's?"

My heart trembled beneath the weight of her name. My eyes closed involuntarily, but only to find her dark, vivid ones staring back at me as they had from the photograph. As they had in the candlelight that I'd kept burning until dawn.

I swallowed, pulling back out of my thoughts. Gradually I turned to face her and Areos, who was waiting intently.

"No," I said, my jaw set. "It's not to be in vain."

CHAPTER TWENTY-SEVEN

Hawk

I awoke before Icarus did. The sun was barely up when I opened my eyes to find the soft features of his face only a few feet away—his dark eyelashes, tousled hair sweeping down across his forehead, and a scruffy beard shadowing his jawline. His lips were slightly parted by his soft inhales and exhales.

I felt my lips curve a little as I reached over to gently brush a lock of hair from his closed eyes.

"Icarus."

I said his name not to wake him and not so that he would hear, but so that I would. Because something about the sound of it—the taste, the feeling of it across my lips—awakened within me something reminiscent of spring, the melting away of ice. The giving way of death to life. White to fresh green. A stirring.

I rolled back into the grass, sighing. The sky was a patchwork quilt of dusty robin's egg blue and lavender bleeding through the canopy above. Mourning doves crooned from their hiding places, and the air around me was filled with the scent of dirt, rain, and softened leaves. I drank it in as I closed my eyes. Listening to the passive rhythm of Icarus's breathing.

I thought of the night before. Of how I had kissed him.

Why I had, I wasn't sure. What had possessed me, I couldn't identify. Icarus had been like fire in my hands, and something within me had enjoyed the light—the heat. But something deeper still feared the burns.

My fingertips wandered up over my arms to brush the markings, tracing the black ringlet around my finger.

I thought of how Icarus had told me that Sensei was not far from me. I recalled each detail of our conversation. All that I had told him about Maicoh when he'd asked, and how apprehensive he had been in return.

I knew he wouldn't want me to go back, and I was already planning how I would tell him that I had to.

I pressed myself up into a seated position, pausing to glance at my other half. His chest rose and fell against the sunlight. I looked down at my finger. At the black ring that wrapped it below the knuckle.

"A Sunrise marred by the fruits of this world." The words slipped out below my breath. "A Sunset marked by all that it could become."

The words that had once so ignited my half-soul with so much passion were now like lead weights. For when I spoke those words, I heard not my own voice, but my savior's. My father's. My teacher's. In those words I felt a gravity that was like the stillness that precedes a storm.

I was afraid. Afraid of what I felt, of what would happen when I returned and found Maicoh again.

I had to find out who he really was. There was no way I wasn't going back.

I rose to my feet and crept softly away from camp, stepping quietly around the sleeping wolves.

How did there come to be so many?

Up until I had found Icarus, there had only ever been the one white wolf. It was almost as though the event of my and Icarus's reunion had spawned the pack, which ebbed and flowed in number like the sunlight phasing in and out of the cloud cover. Here one minute, gone the next.

I reached a hand back through my tangled hair, brushing away the mild perspiration that sheathed my forehead.

This place was like Icarus. I noticed it everywhere I looked. The light shone through in certain places, while in others it faded to a dismal gray. The clearing before me brimmed with lush irises, while the forest to my left and right wound off in a confusion of overgrowth and vines. Filled with light, yet splashed with darkness.

Clear, yet chaotic. Open, yet buried beneath overgrowth.

It was as if we were living in physical manifestations of who we really were on the inside. Finally I understood why my world was made of so much ice.

I halted at the edge of the irises. With no trees to interfere now, the warmth of dawn flowed down over me. I knelt to pluck one of the blossoms, examining the petals in the palm of my hand. Another immediately grew up to replace it.

I lifted the purple blossom to my face and breathed in a scent like spring. Its petals were like silk between my fingers.

Weary of my wild torrents of long dark hair, I picked several more flowers and wove the stems together. I gathered my hair over my shoulders and gingerly tied it back with the fragrant strand I'd woven.

For a moment my thoughts drifted, and I felt myself swept back a hundred years. The afternoons I'd escaped the orphanage to dodge my way through the dismal streets and pick the flowers that grew beneath the trees in the park.

Never were these rebellious excursions carried out solo. It seemed as though he was always trailing just behind me—following like a shadow. Creeping up behind me when I wasn't looking to slip a flower into my hair.

Shivers clutched my spine as I shook free of my thoughts. I blinked back into reality, lifting my eyes back to what was before me. The circle centered in the bed of irises. The flakes that swam listlessly in the portal that led back to the snow-covered forest—the black wolf that stood silently among the irises at the side opposite. So statue-like was its stance that I wouldn't have noticed it had it not stood out so starkly.

I started, my mouth running dry as I stared across the expanse in front of me and into its unflinching golden eyes. I would recognize them anywhere at this point—Maicoh's wolf. The one that hardly left his side.

It didn't move a muscle, and neither did I. It was thinner than ever—starving.

Did it follow me? Did Maicoh already return to camp and find me gone?

A moment that felt like an eternity passed between us before a squall of snow erupted at the center of the circle, obscuring the wolf from my view.

My heart pounding in my chest, I strained to see past the turbulence as I rose to my feet.

A twig snapped behind me. Bracing, I whirled around.

Icarus was making his way toward me through the irises. He smiled, reaching back to run a hand through his messy hair. He was still shirtless; the sunlight cast shadows over his muscular build.

"Good morning."

I glanced back over my shoulder. The snow had fallen away again as the wind had died down. The black wolf was nowhere to be seen. I turned back to Icarus, who was now closer, and pushed on a smile.

"You wake up early and head off to explore without me?" he questioned, feigning disappointment. "But then I know how much I slow you down—since I can't fly or anything."

I grinned. "You finally figured it out."

Icarus laughed, stopping in front of me. His blue eyes brimmed with mischief. "Maybe you'll let me borrow some of that shifter blood of yours."

I pushed him backwards playfully. He let himself stumble and fall back into the sea of blossoms. I had to bite my lip to keep from laughing myself.

"Not a chance," I answered, throwing myself down alongside him. He laughed breathlessly and turned his head to look at me, sprawled on his back. I rolled to my side, resting my head on my elbow. "I'll just teach you to do it yourself—you have it in you already."

He looked at me for a moment, then sighed and shook his head. "I can hardly believe that, Hawk."

"Believe what?"

Icarus's eyes softened. "That I could ever deserve you," he answered, his voice like the breaking seas. "That I could ever be worthy of you."

He closed his eyes. His brow furrowed as if he were contemplating something painful. For a long moment he fell silent.

"I'm so far below you, Hawk," he went on finally. "I'm fallen."

I gave this no answer and instead waited for his eyes to open once again.

"I know, Icarus," I said. "And I came down to take you back."

"Hawk, the Dimension will not forgive what I've done."

"The Dimension will perish without you," I said, filling the space between his cold fingers with my own. "And so will I."

Icarus looked at me like I was something he couldn't touch, and I stared at him like he was the only thing I'd ever wanted to.

"Hawk?"

"Yes?"

His fingers tightened around my own. "Can I kiss you?"

The answer was yes, but I didn't speak it. I answered by taking his hands and pinning them to the ground above his head. I moved my lips softly over his, and I felt his heartbeat raging against my chest.

I pulled away slightly, though our foreheads remained touching.

"Icarus, I'm going to get you out of here," I told him in a whisper. "I'm going to get you home—back to them. They need you."

He pulled in a steady breath. "What about you?"

"I can't return to the Dimension yet," I said softly. "I have to go back."

A silence.

"Back?" he repeated. "Back to Maicoh?"

"I have to figure out who he is, Icarus."

"Why?"

"Because I couldn't have met him merely by chance," I explained. "Maicoh, the wolves, the seemingly different world I found him in—I must have found it all for a reason."

He sat up, heaving a sigh. "I don't like it, Hawk."

"Icarus—"

"You have no idea who Maicoh really is." He shot me a serious look, his eyebrows set. "He could be dangerous."

My lips pursed into a tiny grin. "So could I."

His eyes narrowed irritably, though his lips longed to smile.

"Hawk, I can't come with you into your world," he explained, sounding desperate. "I've tried—and I can't. It's like it's locked to me."

"Yet I can get to yours."

"Story of our lives."

I placed a finger against his lips. "Icarus, I promise I will come back to you," I vowed softly. "But I have to go back—I don't know why, but I know that I have to."

My voice stumbled over the words. I bit my lip.

"Have you wondered why neither of us has encountered Raiden down here?" I said, changing the subject. "Doesn't it seem strange that neither one of us found him, all this time?"

"Maybe he didn't survive." Icarus shrugged. "Maybe we only survived because we're the ones the prophecy speaks of."

I wanted to believe it, but something inside me rejected the idea. "Icarus, I need to know."

"Wait—you're saying this Maicoh person is..." I could see him trying to puzzle it out behind his eyes. "You think it's possible that he's actually..."

Honestly, I wasn't yet sure what I was saying. Since I'd fallen into the worlds beneath the Dimension, I'd been in a constant state of fight-or-flight survival. This crucible of sunshine and flowers and Icarus was the first moment I'd really had to consider it all.

"Raiden captured my blood," I recalled out loud. "Before you rescued me that day on the platform... he stole my ability to shift," I confessed. "That's why I couldn't turn human again until you saved me."

"So what are you saying?"

"That Raiden experienced shifter blood," I explained. "That day he attacked me, he partook of my powers, same as you. And he's a fast learner."

Icarus's eyes searched the air for a moment. "So you're saying you think Raiden can shift now?" he murmured. "But into what?"

I swallowed, feeling sick as the realization trickled in. "Raiden has killed many times before. And as a possessor of those many identities—most of which I wouldn't recognize, I'm sure—who's to say he doesn't still use them?" I paused. "Besides that, it would explain why Maicoh can easily shift into wolf form."

Icarus's blue eyes widened slowly. He turned to look down at me. The playful look in his eyes had vanished completely. "You think he's shifted into an alternate identity?" he asked apprehensively. "Why would he do that now?"

"To keep from being discovered?" I offered. "To keep me from recognizing him?"

Icarus sat in silence for a moment. I followed his gaze to the portal, where snow still phased in and out of our current dimension.

"Why wouldn't he want you to recognize him?" He spoke slowly. "If this mysterious guy is actually Raiden... why wouldn't he have attacked you like he did before?"

It was a valid question. To which I had no answer.

"That's what I have to find out," I answered. "That's why I'm going back."

"Hawk."

"And," I continued, ignoring him, "while I'm gone, you can start pondering how exactly we're going to get out of here. Because at this point your guess is as good as mine."

Icarus's jaw set irritably.

"I'll return to Maicoh's camp and assess the situation," I went on. "Time passage seems pretty inconsistent between the worlds down here—who's to say dawn has even broken there yet? He may not have even noticed that I left. He may not have even returned from the hunt yet."

"And what if that hunt is for you, Hawk?" he asked, stone-voiced. "You might be playing directly into his hands—and I won't be there to save you this time. You'll be on your own."

I glowered at him, though a tiny smile bled through my anger. "You don't think I can handle it?"

His eyes stayed fixed along with his expression for a moment before he melted. "Can you be serious for two seconds?"

I smirked. "I once asked you the same thing. But we're not very good at listening to each other."

"No." He bobbed his head in a nod of agreement. "No, we're both far too stubborn for that."

The wind brushed through the trees, and for a moment the conversation paused. Icarus seemed to listen for a moment.

"What is it?" I inquired softly.

"I just have a bad feeling about this, Hawk."

"I'll be fine, Icarus. I promise."

When he turned and looked at me again, I could see wars behind his iridescent eyes. "I wish I could come with you."

My gaze remained on his for a moment, then leveled to the ground. I lifted his hand in my own. "You are coming with me," I confessed quietly. "You're always with me."

With the other hand I gently lifted his chin. "Since the moment Raiden entered the Dimension, there was something about him… something familiar. Something strange," I said, thinking aloud. "I got the same feeling with Maicoh, and it's something I have to resolve."

I hesitated, considering the implications.

"If his identity is false," I said, "if he really is Raiden in sheep's clothing, this could explain why he wouldn't tell me where he came from or how he got here."

"It wouldn't explain why he hasn't killed you yet," Icarus countered. "It wouldn't explain why he's befriended you, given you shelter, and offered to help you find me."

I paused, thinking about it. I felt my throat suddenly tighten. "Wouldn't it?" I asked softly, my voice strained. "Wouldn't that be the very reason he would want me to survive?"

Icarus's dark eyebrows met in the middle of his forehead. "That reason being?"

"You, Icarus," I replied plainly. "He wants both of us."

September 2016

Mel was as predictable as clockwork. The more I tried to protect her, the further away she pushed me. She was like Charlotte in that sense. Little did she know that if I really wanted to stop her from going to him, I would have.

No, I wanted her to run to Ion. Because he was next on my list.

So when I found her alone in the study lounge that night, with tears streaking her face, I played the game.

"What happened?"

"You wouldn't understand," she sniffled. "Who's ever hurt you? You have everything."

"Oh, you'd be surprised."

She looked up, caught off guard. She thought I was talking about her. "Riley, he hurt me."

"Who?"

She rolled her eyes, dabbing back the black streaks dripping from them. "I think you know."

"Ion has issues, Mel. I told you."

"I know, but..." She shook her head. "I guess I just never expected him to break it off—not like this. Not just because of some stupid rule."

"Rule?" I asked. "What rule? What do you mean?"

Mel laughed miserably. "He told me not to breathe a word to anyone about it. He told me it's a secret."

My heart stammered over a beat. "What's a secret?"

She hesitated for a moment, looking down at her hands.

"Mel." I spoke again, leaning a little closer. "Do you think he would throw you away like that if he really cared about you?"

She swallowed hard, hurt in her eyes.

"I tried to warn you, Mel," I told her softly. "I tried to warn you because I didn't want you to get hurt."

"Well, you were right."

I gently placed a hand over hers.

"You don't have to protect his secrets, Mel," I whispered. "If he told you something that's making you uncomfortable, you don't have to keep it bottled up inside. It's okay to let it out."

She was silent for a long moment. I began to wonder if she would answer at all.

"It's not so much something that he told me." Mel lifted her gaze slowly. "It's... it's something he showed me. A place you wouldn't believe in if I told you, Riley."

Chills broke out over my arms. A smile twitched at the corners of my mouth.

"Then don't tell me," I replied. "Show me."

CHAPTER TWENTY-EIGHT

Fin

W e were back at the edge again. The drop yawned before us in all its yellow sunrise glory. It filled the void below us, and it sparkled in her eyes. The executioners readied the gathering platform below. I'd been back there so many times, something in me almost knew it was just a dream at this point.

The Dimension around us slept. We were awake. And sometimes it felt like we were the only ones who ever had been.

"So this is goodbye?" I asked, as I always did.

"I'm afraid so."

The response startled me, deviating from what it had been in reality.

"You'll take care of them for me." She gave me an inquiring look. "Won't you?"

"It's not as though you aren't coming back, Hawk," I told her, not sure who I was trying to convince. "You'll be back."

"Just answer me, Fin," she pleaded. "Please."

Something inside me trembled. "You know I would do anything for you."

"Because you love me."

I glanced at her, somehow unsurprised. "Because I love you, Hawk."

Hawk turned to look at me, something serious in her eyes. "Yet sometimes we have to let go," she whispered. "Don't shut out the light when you feel it coming in through the cracks. Let it in. Let yourself go to her, Fin."

"I would if I thought for a moment that I could love anyone but you, Hawk. I have let go of many things." I spoke softly. "But you... I cannot let go of you, Hawk."

Her eyes didn't move from my own. We were closer now, somehow.

"You've been by my side since the moment you came here, Fin. You've trained with me, you've fought with me—you've never let me down."

"I did nothing for you that you haven't done for me tenfold."

"Then *promise* me you will look after them in my absence." Her plea was a quiet one, but a storm brewed behind it. "Promise me you'll look after Icarus—that you'll help him."

She faltered, seeming to lose herself in thought.

"He can't lead alone, Fin," she added. "He won't force himself on others. Help him as you have always helped me."

I looked earnestly into her face, tension gripping my throat. "Hawk, why do you talk as if you're never coming back?"

For a moment, she made no response. Then—then she smiled, taking my hands in hers and glancing down at them as if each were something sacred.

"Though we have fallen together, we will surely rise together." She paraphrased Sensei's words. "As the sun does each morning." Hawk's dark eyes shifted up to mine. "Though not without a cost."

Cost?

"Hawk, I don't understand—"

My fingers wound around hers, but her body seemed to melt through my skin.

"*Fin!*"

I bolted awake, nearly toppling the chair I was seated in, hunched at my desk.

For a split second, nothing made sense. Then, like a photo developing, everything cleared into focus. The woven walls splashed in the rust of the sunset. The dwindling flicker of the candle at my desk, illuminating the inky pages cluttering the space in front of me. Hawk's feathers.

A hand shook my shoulder, then retracted again as it ceased its efforts to wake me. A hand that belonged to Areos. I straightened, rubbing the sleep from my eyes.

"What is it?"

His brow was creased in the shadows, his face scruffy with a five-o'clock shadow. "Fin, the gathering," he said urgently. "It begins at *sunset*—most of the student body is already there."

The letter from Sensei, my meeting with Areos and Delta, the gathering—it all came rushing back.

"Right," I murmured, scooping the papers in front of me into a coherent stack. "I... must have dozed off."

He grunted. "Since when do you ever sleep?"

I barely heard the question. My hands were trembling slightly; I couldn't decide if it was from the exhaustion that was beginning to take hold, or the dream.

"Where's Delta?" I asked, getting up to search for a shirt that wasn't soaked in sweat.

"Already there." Areos helped himself to the chair at my desk. "She sent me to come get you."

I nodded slowly, trying to shake the sick feeling in the pit of my stomach. I focused open the dresser drawer.

"So..." He trailed off, seeming cautious. "What's going on with you guys?"

I sucked in an unsteady breath, peeling off my shirt. "What do you mean?"

He grunted. "Come on, Fin. I'm not blind. You guys are together all the time. And when you're not, you're all she seems to talk about."

I felt my cheeks burning. I crumpled the sweat-soaked shirt and tossed it into the laundry basket.

"I can't imagine why," I said mirthlessly. "She has more important things to contemplate."

"So you're saying you don't like her at all?"

I stopped for a moment, turning to look at him. "I'm saying I'm an idiot, Areos," I replied, my voice hoarse. "A complete and utter fool."

"What do you mean?"

"I mean"—I pulled on the new shirt and slammed the drawer shut—"that I seem to unconsciously destroy everything that I hold dear. Why is that?"

Areos looked puzzled.

I heaved a sigh. "Don't answer that."

"Why would you think such a thing?" he questioned. "Because your feelings for Delta break the code?"

I walked over to the desk to reach past him and snatch my notes. "Because I have no feelings for Delta whatsoever."

The puzzled expression hadn't faded. "I don't understand."

"That makes two of us, Areos," I replied flatly.

He squinted at me. "So what are you going to do?"

I scanned the pages hollowly before crumpling them in my fist. "For now, I'm going to concentrate on this gathering—and hope to God we're doing the right thing."

***

The gathering platform was ablaze, not unlike the night of the emergency meeting that Sensei had called so long ago to inform us that we were leaving our natural worlds behind to seek sanctuary in the Dimension. A fire burned brightly at the platform's center, and flames danced over the fragrant oil that trimmed the edge. Though the frost and rain had taken their leave, everyone was still bundled in coats.

The farther the sun sank, the more I could make out the faint apparitions of my breath as it lapped the air in front of me. I buried my hands in the pockets of my overcoat.

I couldn't help but notice the stark difference in the atmosphere. We'd been like anxious children when Sensei had called the meeting to discuss our withdrawal. That night, although we had been afraid, we had been vibrant. We had been eager and bright-eyed. But now, we were simply cold. We were confused. We were crossing our arms and rolling our eyes and doubting in our hearts. My own heart was heavy: it wasn't Sensei and his power that I doubted. It was myself.

I watched Gaia recite the prophecy, her warm brown skin reflecting the firelight. When she finished, a hush fell over the audience.

Silently, I rose from my seat in the front row beside Delta, Areos, and Runner. I forced myself to walk across the platform, halting in front of the fire. I turned and faced the sea of students and colleagues.

I nodded to Gaia and thanked her quietly. My eyes locked briefly with Delta's.

"Thank you for making the time to be here tonight," I began, raising my voice. "I know this gathering is on very short notice, but, as I am sure you have been informed, it is urgent."

A soft murmuring arose from the crowd, then died out almost just as quickly.

I felt frozen, tossed like a ship in a storm.

What was I going to tell them? Flowery words to the effect that everything would be fine? Was I so above them that I needed to mask my fears for their sake? *I couldn't.*

I took a deep breath and squeezed my eyes shut.

"For some time, Sensei had withdrawn from our meetings and gatherings," I began steadily. "Since Icarus's trial and execution, we have known him to be a more silent figure among us." I paused, scanning the faces around me. "He offered little explanation for his actions except to those who sought answers. I was one of these few."

Mitsue, a few rows in, spoke up. "How do you mean?"

I pulled in a breath. "I mean that I wanted to know why things are the way they are. I wanted to know why we had plunged headlong into a winter, when the Dimension has never experienced one before. Why death had come to dwell among us—because of Raiden's entrance into our world. Why we were forced to withdraw from our natural worlds. And why there is such division among us, even now, when we should be pulling together more than ever."

"That's hardly fair." A new voice, Azalea's, rose above the murmur of the crowd. "Don't confuse your opinion with fact, Fin. We've all been pulling our weight as best we can."

"I'm not accusing anyone of being neglectful," I responded. "I'm merely stating a fact—if you haven't noticed, we are in a state of utter chaos, and I think everyone here would agree."

The tumult of hushed voices slowly died away. I closed my eyes to clear my head.

"And I'm afraid what I have to tell you won't aid in repairing this disarray," I said. "There is no way I can say it that will spare you alarm." I opened my eyes again and glimpsed what I knew would be the last split second of peace I'd experience for some time.

"Sensei has left the Dimension," I announced, my voice raw. "He's gone."

There was a pause, like the silence as a fuse burns its way through to the bomb.

In an instant, confused shouts lifted into the still evening air. I raised a hand for silence, and the shouting ceased.

"What are you talking about?" I recognized the voice as Mala's. "What do you mean Sensei's left? He's abandoned us?"

I shook my head. "Not abandoned—entrusted."

Azalea rose from her seat. "Entrusted us to what?" she barked. "H-how can you expect us to even believe this? What proof do you have?"

"I have a letter written by Sensei and addressed to me," I replied. "In this letter he disclosed that his reason for leaving was to avail us of the time and space we need to advance into the positions of power for which we have been destined." I looked around the platform. "So that we may begin to prepare for our reemergence into the natural world."

"And do you have this letter?" she returned, folding her arms firmly over her chest.

"I do."

"On your person?"

"In my room," I replied. "Selections of its contents are personal, and I am not at liberty to share it in its entirety at this gathering."

"So..." Her voice dripped with cynicism. "We're expected to take your word for it, then?"

Glancing away from her, I met Delta's eyes for a brief moment. Her lips were pressed into a frustrated line, and her brow was fraught with worry.

"As a fellow student who has pledged to abide by our code of conduct, yes," I answered her. "I expect you to believe that what I say is true."

Several voices attempted to speak at once, but Mitsue's rose above them.

"I cannot *believe* that Sensei would leave us with so little instruction," he said, glowering. "And that what he did decide to inform us of would be left exclusively with *you*—as if somehow you're better than the rest of us."

I stared him down for a moment. His dark eyes burned into mine from within the crowd. "That has nothing to do with it."

"What, then?"

"Maybe he would have told you if you had asked him." I spoke firmly, though my voice threatened to crack beneath the pressure. "I am nothing special—but I am curious. I have been placed in this world not to keep my mouth shut and my nose to the grindstone, but to ask questions. To learn. Is that not why Sensei initiated each one of us?"

Mitsue didn't respond. He stared back at me through narrowed eyes and slowly shook his head. Whispers swarmed in the air.

"Unless I'm mistaken," I went on, "we were brought here as students—not slaves. We weren't led to a place so beyond our wildest dreams simply to work ourselves into the ground, or bind ourselves so tightly to standards of our own making that we actually end up destroying ourselves in the process. Do you actually think this is what Sensei had in mind?"

"Are you saying our code of conduct is worthless, then, Fin?" another voice asked.

"Not worthless, no. But never something that was meant to measure our worth."

For a moment, the platform was an eruption of voices, a storm of confusion and fury.

Gaia looked at me from the front row, her large eyes beseeching. "Fin, when is this reemergence to occur?" she asked when the crowd had quieted enough for her voice to be heard. "Did Sensei tell you?"

It was a small consolation—a question from someone who actually believed what I was saying.

"He has instructed us to wait for Icarus," I answered her above the noise. "He said nothing else. I expect we will know what to do next after Icarus has returned."

"Icarus is *dead*," Azalea piped up again. "How on earth can you expect us to believe that this is what Sensei told you? It's a lie!"

Seemingly everyone agreed; the voices rose to a roar again. I raised my hands, trying to get a word in edgewise, but it was useless.

Several students rose and left, presumably to go check Sensei's room and see for themselves whether the news of his departure was true. Others simply seemed eager to escape the baying of the mob. I couldn't say that I blamed them.

"He was *executed*, Fin." Mitsue stood to join Azalea in her argument. "He was tried, he was found guilty, and he was put to death! How can you expect us to believe what you are telling us?"

Suddenly I felt a hand on my arm. Delta was now at my side.

"He's telling the truth!" she said staunchly, defending me. "I saw the letter!"

Slowly everyone quieted again.

"I, too, was cynical at first," she admitted. "For some time, I believed it was impossible that Icarus or Hawk were our patriarchs, or that they had survived." She gave me a sidelong glance, taking a deep breath. "But now I see the evidence all around me. Not evidence that can be provided, but the kind that the heart produces when it finally hears the quiet notes of the truth—even above the roar of the lies."

I said nothing. My eyes remained on her as she stepped in front of me, illuminated by the fire, to face the students spread out around us. A hush fell.

"We have to believe that Sensei left—and for a reason," she went on. "Yes, so that Icarus may return, but also, as Fin has said, so that we may use our power. So we may finally do what we have trained so long for—and this is just the beginning." She began to pace, slowly, steadily, and every eye seemed to follow her. "We were made for such a time as this!" Delta shouted, and her voice echoed down the ravine. "This is what we have trained for, studied for— fought for! Whether you believe Icarus is alive or not, whether you believe that he will return or not... what does it matter?"

She paused as though waiting for an answer, but none came. I felt my jaw tense as I swallowed, a sick feeling settling in my gut.

"We *have* to survive," she emphasized fiercely. "We *have* to make it out of this alive—and if we're going to do that? We need to stop executing ourselves. We need a new kind of order."

To my surprise, her declaration was met with less opposition than anything I had said thus far.

"What are you talking about, 'a new kind of order'?" Mitsue asked her over the murmurings, stroking his scruffy beard thoughtfully. "Do you mean we should disregard the code of conduct?"

Delta shook her head briskly. "Not disregard it—respect it. But also give it less priority during this *particular* time. We're in a state of emergency—we have been since the evacuation into the Dimension and my initiation. We can't continue to blindly go on as before."

"What would we have in place of the code, then, if we were to do this your way?" Mitsue questioned. "Without the code, we would quickly go from a state of emergency to a state of utter chaos!"

Shouts of agreement rose from the crowd, but Mitsue didn't take his eyes off his student.

"If we are to prepare ourselves for a reentrance into our natural worlds, that is no small task," he added. "That is a *huge* undertaking—one that cannot be taken lightly. Sensei has left us— my God, if we were taking things seriously before, we will have to be ten times more so as we move forward!"

Delta nodded solemnly. "Which is why we must do something differently. You cannot sow the same seeds and expect them to yield a new crop."

"Sensei told us to wait for Icarus," I said, following up Delta's remark. "But in the meantime, we must stop with the trials—and the executions. Our numbers are limited enough as it is."

Areos spoke up finally. "They're right. We have to prepare for what we're going to find on future Earth. We can't be wasting our time, and our numbers, like this."

Another silence crept in. I turned to exchange a glance with Delta.

"So what are we supposed to do in the meantime?" someone asked. "While we're waiting?"

"For someone who won't ever return," Azalea hissed under her breath.

"Nothing," I stated firmly. "We follow Sensei's orders. Can't that be enough?"

Mitsue snorted, standing once more. "It can be, if you don't mind ushering in Armageddon."

"Hardly." Areos gave a disgusted sigh. "Do you believe Sensei would leave us in this situation if it would amount to that?"

"How am I supposed to know *who* to believe anymore?" Mitsue said. "The Dimension is crumbling around us and Sensei is gone." His voice echoed off the cliff side. "Sensei wants us to use our powers? Fine." He gave a flippant shrug, but looked straight at me. "We'll use them."

Delta resumed pacing slowly across the platform. I could feel her tension rising. "What do you mean?"

"I mean that we need a leader," Mitsue said. "Someone more

advanced among us who is able to step into the void Sensei has left in his absence."

Delta spoke up. "But Sensei said—"

"Sensei isn't here!" Mitsue cut her off mercilessly. "Don't you see? We're on our own, Delta! You're the one who just said he meant for us to step up to the plate and lead this movement ourselves."

"I never said that!" Delta objected loudly, though few in the audience heard.

"Mitsue is right," someone agreed. "We can't go into this blind— we've never known anything beyond following Sensei. How are we supposed to go on without him?"

"By putting our trust in someone whom Sensei has personally trained." Mitsue's voice rose and his eyes shifted once again to mine. "Someone who has spent much time in the Dimension, learning the ancient ways of their teacher."

He stepped out from the crowd and began walking steadily toward the center of the platform.

"Someone who has proven that they have the desire, loyalty, and passion to fight in our corner." He spoke loudly, glancing around as he did. "Someone who has not only greatly honed their own powers, but also helped others do likewise—dedicating their time and effort toward furthering our purpose."

His footsteps slowed to a stop. I watched him carefully.

"This gathering was called to announce that Sensei has left us so that we may become the sliders we were always destined to be," Mitsue continued. "Could there be a more appropriate time for someone more advanced among us—a protégé, if you will—to step into their role of leadership?"

I glanced at Areos and found the same expression of worry that I wore.

"What better time for us to truly be honest with ourselves," Mitsue went on, "and appoint someone we truly trust to be our leader."

He turned and looked at me. A hush fell over the auditorium as he approached. The fire crackled in the sudden absence of sound.

"Now is not the time to fall apart." His voice was quieter now. "Now is not the time to wait… however much you might want to. It's high time we used our powers. It's time to appoint someone who has followed the code to a fault." He emphasized the last word, his gaze still locked with my own. "Someone who has followed in the footsteps of their teacher… Don't you agree?"

The rage quivering through my body instantly evaporated, and guilt took its place. I had to swallow back my heart as my eyes lowered to the floorboards below me.

My eyelids closed, heavy all of a sudden. And beneath them was my mother's face. My sister's laugh. My father's weathered hands. Hawk's face. That kiss. That kiss I had saved all those years for Hawk, knowing full well it could never be bestowed. The kiss I had given away. My chest ached. I wished silently that I could melt away in the firelight. *I wish…*

Who am I to stand before these people? Who am I to speak of following Sensei's command? I didn't know how to answer him. But I didn't have to.

Delta strode to the place where Mitsue stood, then halted. "Mitsue, you suggest we appoint someone we trust to lead us?" she asked, loud enough for everyone to hear. "The most experienced— the most dedicated? Loyal?"

She stepped closer. I glanced up—she was right in his face. He backed off slightly, but held her eyes. "Yes," he replied. "Yes, exactly."

Out of the corner of my eye, I saw Delta's wild red hair waver in the light from the flames. I didn't lift my head. I couldn't. She turned and faced the audience. "The most dedicated among us," she repeated, raising her voice. "The most loyal, brave, learned… The one we trust." She paused, and echoes of her voice clattered away down the ravine. "Who would that be?"

Everything around me seemed to fade away for a moment. I couldn't decide if it was exhaustion or if I was taking leave of my senses. I heard nothing until I heard my name spoken by a voice I couldn't identify. I looked up. My head felt heavy.

"Fin!" someone shouted. "Fin should be the one—did Sensei not entrust him with his instructions?"

I felt my heart stumble over a beat in my chest.

Yet another voice shouted their agreement and then another. Slowly my name surrounded me until it was like a chant around the fire. I could do nothing for a moment. I stood there frozen—stunned.

The voices gradually formed an uproar in the shape of my name, a roar that filled the ravine like a rushing river.

I stared at the hundreds before me, all shouting my name. I felt the fire at my back; my heart was in my mouth. Finally, I snapped out of it. I shook my head, backing away—catching Delta's gaze as I did. I could almost feel Mitsue's searing glare.

"Fin?" he reiterated, seething. "How on earth—"

I never heard the rest. I turned and ran.

"Fin, wait!" A hand snatched my wrist in a vise grip. "Where are you going? You can't just leave—"

"You don't understand, Delta." I jerked away. "I can't lead these people! I-I'm not the one."

"Sensei warned us, Fin," she shot back, stepping closer, though I could barely hear her over the crowd. "He told us this day would come—the day we would have to lead. This is your *chance*."

I hesitated a moment, staring back into her wide eyes, then leaned in close to her face. "No, Delta," I whispered, almost choking on my own voice. "Not like this."

Her eyes scanned my face. "Fin, we need you." Her voice was like a distress signal. "*Please*."

For a split second there was a war inside me; then I took a step back.

"That's where you're wrong, Delta." My voice was cracking, breathless. I could barely hear it above the crowd. "I'm the last thing they need."

CHAPTER TWENTY-NINE

Hawk

I held Icarus's hand until our dimensions separated us. I stepped back into my own icy little world, and the warmth of his fingers slipped from my own.

Why was it impossible for Icarus to enter my world, when I could so easily step into his? I didn't understand it. Part of me wished he could have come with me, but at the same time another part knew this was something I needed to face on my own.

Something about Maicoh made me very uneasy. He was young, but his eyes seemed somehow ancient. I had so many unanswered questions about him. I knew he was hiding something—and if that was a secret identity, I needed to know.

It was the same feeling I'd had when I'd first met Raiden. I had detected something unusual about him. Something I had never been able to put my finger on. How had he found out about Icarus and me in the first place? How had he known I was the Sunrise? How had he tracked us down? These were the questions that plagued me—the questions the council had neglected to ask, concentrating only on the crimes and not the person behind them. Was he just the power-hungry, ruthless slider he had painted himself to be? Or was there something more to his true identity than that, something I had overlooked?

I lifted from the ground, shifting into raptor form. I felt the cold less beneath my feathers. Scanning the ground below as I flew, I

244

watched for signs of the wolves. It was only when I dropped in altitude that I noticed anything out of the ordinary. By now I was close to the opening to the tunnel that acted as my portal to Maicoh's world.

Across the ground I could now make out the shapes of prints— wolf prints, I naturally assumed. But when I flew in for closer examination, I discovered I was mistaken.

The tracks spread out before me were not in the shapes of wolves' paws, but of a human's feet. Maicoh immediately sprang to mind, but as I studied them more closely, that seemed less likely. The tracks were small—the footprints no bigger than my own. In fact, they seemed almost to match my feet in size, though they were too fresh to be my own. I was also fairly certain I'd not crossed this particular part of the forest.

Dropping back into human form, I landed in a crouch alongside the tracks. The prints carried on for a hundred feet or so, leading me to the base of a large pine, where they abruptly ended.

How the…?

I searched the ground around the tree, but found nothing. Then I heard the sound of a twig snapping behind me. My blood ran instantly cold as I whipped around.

A black blur. It was gone so fast, I could scarcely perceive it.

I stood for a moment, frozen, as my eyes swept the forest around me. I saw no tracks, heard no telltale howls. A subtle stirring whipped through the brush to my left, but when I turned again, I saw nothing.

Chill bumps broke out on my arms and legs, though I was fairly certain it wasn't from the cold. I began to wonder if my mind was playing games with me. But then there was… what was it, exactly?

Not the same sound, not a rustling in the brush, not a wolf's howl. A voice. A whisper from just past my shoulder; a wisp of warm breath at my neck.

"Charlotte…"

Every muscle in my body seemed to grip my bones. I whipped back around, this time leading with a strong back-fist, but I never landed the strike: the air behind me was empty.

The word vanished on the wind, then came again in fragments.

"C-c-charlotte…"

And then the silence.

"Who's there?" My voice raced out into the emptiness. "S-show yourself!"

No reply came.

I looked down at the footprints again, tracing them to the trunk of the tree, then finally glanced up into the evergreen branches extending from the treetop.

My stomach bottomed out as my eyes locked there.

One branch was larger than the rest—extending longer, reaching farther. On it was seated a thin, ghostly white figure. A girl in a black, dirt-streaked dress torn at the sleeves. A long veil of black silk draped from her hand, wavering in the breeze.

My instincts told me to run, but I couldn't seem to move. The wind whipped mercilessly through her dark, tangled hair as she turned her head to look at me. I could make out her bloodied lips and bruised cheek even from where I stood. The blood that stained her hand. The black ring that marked her finger.

I felt dizzy, sick. A distant howl sounded through the quavering trees. I backed cautiously away from the base of the tree, my eyes still locked on the girl—the ghost. The figure didn't move, but her faded eyes followed me.

For a moment she attempted to move her lips; then, seeming to lose strength, she fell back against the trunk of the tree, listing to one side before slipping from the branch and tumbling violently down through the branches. My stomach lurched as I watched.

Dull, sickening thuds of flesh and bone crashing against wood rang through the air with each impact. Her body seemed to melt away before she hit the frozen ground below. All that remained was the length of black silk, which fluttered to the snow like an angel of death.

My eyes feverishly swept the forest around me as another far-off howl pierced the air.

The black fabric swayed in the wind for a moment then, gradually, its shape seemed to solidify. I squinted into the wind for a moment, dazed. The dark fabric rippled in midair, then compacted into a strange oblong shape. A shape that seemed to grow legs and paws, a tail and teeth. Before my eyes, the silk morphed into a thick, mangy black coat. As dark and matted as her hair had been.

A black wolf. It crouched on its thin legs, its shoulder blades pressing up through its sagging skin.

There was a split second of thunderstruck hesitation. Then I bolted.

There was an outbreak of sharp barks behind me. I didn't think about it. My feet flew beneath me.

My skin burned with the urgency to shift, but I couldn't focus. I couldn't get off the ground.

A dark blur darted towards me out of my peripheral vision. Instinctively, I dodged to my left, leaping up onto a large rock that lay in the path.

A throaty howl sounded close at my heels. I leapt off the rock and tore through the brush, ducking below tree branches. The snow thinned, and I picked up my pace.

A blur of mangy black fur lunged from my left.

Summoning every ounce of energy that remained within me, I leapt up to grab hold of the branch above me. Letting the momentum aid me, I swung forward and then back again—kicking out my legs and cracking the wolf squarely in the jaw. It yelped in pain and surprise.

Still grasping the branch, I finished the motion by hurling myself up and over it full circle, twisting around in the air and landing hard on my feet again.

I forced my focus ahead, at the grove of birch trees. It was familiar. I'd run with the pack through these trees—but of course now I was now running *from* them, with that name still echoing in my ears.

Charlotte, Charlotte, Charlotte...

Each breath, each pulse, each thunderous footfall behind me seemed to echo the word.

I ran, and I ran, and I ran until at last everything was a blur. Until I felt fangs graze my ankle. Until I stumbled, caught myself against a boulder—jumped over it. Until my head was spinning and everywhere I looked there seemed to be streaks of jet black chasing me down, chasing me deeper and deeper into the forest.

You need me... You need me, Charlotte...

I crashed through the brush, then stumbled out onto the banks of a narrow frigid stream. Heedless, I splashed through the icy water;

my boots filled. I heard the wolves plunge into the stream behind me, though I didn't dare turn my head to check—not until the tunnel was in sight. I could see the dead tree covering the entrance.

I was so close.

My lungs were fire and my skin was ice. I shot one glance over my shoulder—just as the pack leader leapt. Just as the snow deepened and my feet went out from beneath me. Gasping for air, I fell.

Headfirst, I impacted a boulder. For a split second I felt the wolf upon me, and then I felt nothing at all.

There was a great stillness, an eerie sensation of disembodiment—I felt nothing. I was nothing. I drifted in and out of weightless auras of color. Like the way sunlight looks through closed eyelids. It was a listless kind of feeling: floating, falling.

The colors churned, swirling together—blending until there was nothing left but pitch black; a length of silk tumbling downwards to cascade over my face, swallowing my body. I felt my lungs expand as they filled with the scent of roses.

I felt my fingers contract as I tried to breathe. Sweat pricked at the back of my neck.

Charlotte…

An echo. A voice like a specter.

No… I could scarcely tell if I'd thought or spoken the word. *No… just leave me, please…*

"Hawk…"

I rolled to my side, digging my nails into the soft ground. Everything was rushing around me; I felt like I was… longing for those familiar arms to catch me.

Sensei… Sensei, save me… please save me…

Everything around me came to a crashing halt. The world ceased its dizzying spin. I dropped back into my skin and stayed there. The scent of roses grew more powerful, and I felt the warmth of weathered skin on my forehead. Fingertips.

"Hawk…"

Slowly, I opened my heavy eyelids. Slowly, the world around me came into clear focus—burgundy rivers of rosebuds glittering in the golden folds of sunlight. A hand on my forehead. An arm etched with strength, though never used for harm. A face like the sun.

For a moment I lay motionless as his fingertips gently stroked my forehead. I stared up into the face of my teacher as one gazes awestruck at the night sky, and suddenly I was blinded by tears.

He smiled, his thumb moving to my cheek. "You're awake."

My lips quivered as my eyes squeezed shut. I felt a sob tighten my throat.

I needed only to reach out my hand for Sensei to lean forward and gather me into his arms. Sitting up, I buried my face in his chest and wept.

"Shhh, my love." He spoke softly, his hand running the length of my hair. "I'm here. I'm here, my dear little one."

And he repeated the words again and again and again. And each time he spoke them, they became more like a song. An anthem, a battle cry...

I'm never leaving, I'm never leaving, I'm never leaving.

I wept until his shirt was soaked and I had exhausted my strength.

"Sensei, you came back," I whispered finally.

He hummed a soothing laugh. I felt the vibration in his chest.

"Came back?" he repeated softly, a question. "But I never left you, Hawk."

I pulled back, sniffling. Looking him in the eyes, where I found my tears reflected. He smiled faintly, brushing away the streaks of saltwater from my cheek. "I never left you."

My eyes closed again, and I felt something inside me tremble beneath the weight of his words.

"Sensei, I'm so sorry."

"What are you sorry for, Hawk?" He stopped stroking my face and took my hand in his. "For how much you have grown?" he asked, his voice tender. "For how much you have risked to rescue the one you love? For how brave you have become?"

I shook my head, blinking back the tears. "I know nothing of love, Sensei."

"But I think perhaps love knows something of you, young one."

I glanced down at my ankle, where the wolf's teeth had grazed it, but there was no wound to be found.

"How did you find me? How did you save me from the wolves?"

"I did not save you from the wolves, Hawk," he replied. "The moment you fell unconscious, you lost your capacity to fear, and the wolves ceased to be."

I stared at him. "I don't understand."

"You stopped feeding them."

Anything I was about to say froze in my throat.

"Maicoh was not wrong when he told you that the wolves belonged to him—and he to them," Sensei went on. "For who of us is not at war behind the eyes—not with someone or something else, but with ourselves, with our own thoughts? In your world, thoughts of your past merely haunted you." He paused pointedly, gazing into my eyes. "Here they will hunt you."

I swallowed back a familiar tightness. "The wolves…" I paused. "The wolves are my fears… manifested?"

"Your fears, your thoughts, your greatest desires," Sensei clarified. "Darkness taking shape in darkness. The glorious, the good, the divine, on the other hand—"

"—are the *white* wolves," I blurted, struck by the revelation. "The white wolf led me to Icarus."

"Because your thoughts were with him."

I pressed the heels of my hands to my eyelids, trying to take it all in. My mind flashed back to the woods outside Maicoh's camp, to the dazzling white creature who had led me back into the snow and, finally, within reach of my other half.

"Maicoh is afraid of the white wolves," I thought aloud. "It attacked him, and he told me never to—" my breath escaped me "—never to follow the white wolf."

"For it would lead you to light, Hawk," Sensei replied. "And it is that light, not the white wolf, that frightens him."

"Only those who have something to hide are afraid of the light, Sensei."

"And you think Maicoh is such a one?"

My eyebrows pressed together as I thought about it. A gentle breeze swished through the roses.

"Sensei, I believe Maicoh may be one of the identities of Raiden," I explained, my words tripping over one another. "I found Icarus—he didn't die, and neither did I. So why would the fall have killed Raiden? I don't believe it did. I think he may simply be guised in one of the identities he stole from another slider."

Sensei didn't reply. He waited for me to go on.

"Sensei, why is this place so different from the one I entered when I fell? Maicoh spoke as if we *actually were* in our own separate worlds... How can that be?"

Sensei rose to his feet now, taking me gently by the hand and helping me up. "Do we not all create our own worlds inside—and then project that image before us, whether we realize it or not?"

"Are you saying I made that hellish tundra?"

He smiled. "You tell me."

I grunted. "A perfect reflection of my soul if there ever was one."

"Or of the decoy you wish us to mistake for the authentic."

I sighed, defeated.

"That is how I created the Dimension, Hawk. What makes you think that you are any different?" He walked a few steps away and leaned down to pluck a rose. "What makes you think that you could not do the same thing?"

"So... we've made our own dimensions? These worlds beneath the ravine?"

Sensei examined the flower in his hand. "Why not?"

I couldn't help but smile. I was asking him whether Icarus and I had essentially created our own universes, and he had answered as casually as if I had asked him what time it was.

"Sensei, I'm afraid," I said finally, refocusing. "I have no idea what I'm walking into with Maicoh—or whether I'm even right in my suspicions about him. It's just a gut instinct."

"Gut instinct?" he questioned. "You've spent too much time with Fin."

My lips curved into a tiny grin. "How is he?"

"I could not say," Sensei replied. "I have not been there in some time."

"What do you mean?"

My teacher stood where he was for a moment, taking in the blue sky overhead, and reminding me that I'd yet to even question where we were exactly. He walked back over to me again.

"I've left the Dimension, Hawk."

My mouth ran dry; my thoughts seemed to freeze.

Sensei went on. "When I breathed the Dimension into existence,

I intended it as a place of training for the anomalies of Earth. A refuge for you and Icarus. A place where you would grow to believe in who you truly are, and learn to trust that this power within you is yours. Where you would learn to lead, not be led." He sat down beside me once again. "But things do not always turn out as we intend, Hawk."

"What are you saying?"

"That your people are hungry for food that will not fill them," Sensei replied gravely. "They cling to that which they know and see with their eyes. I was becoming to them no longer a savior, but an impediment."

I shook my head, hardly able to believe what I was hearing. "Sensei, what are you talking about?" My voice came out louder than I expected. "You're our teacher! You're—you're everything to us! Our savior, yes—and our leader. Everyone looks to you, Sensei. Myself included—"

"Then you must stop, dear one," he interrupted firmly. "Have I not raised you? Or are you still a child that must be kept under constant supervision and given endless instruction?" He answered before I could. "You are no longer fledglings," he said resolutely. "You say they look to me—but what I wish is for them to look inside to what I have already given them."

"But, Sensei—"

"You may not understand now, but you will understand later," Sensei cut in. "It is to your advantage that I am going away. For it is only when I am gone that you can begin to understand that I have never left."

A lump was forming in my throat again.

"Hawk, you have come here to save Icarus." His voice softened. "To redeem him back into the Dimension—have you not?"

I swallowed hard, nodding.

"Then do not fear," he said. "This is the last advice I can give you: trust yourself. Trust the warrior beneath your skin, for she will not forsake you." He gently lifted my chin with his weathered fingertips. "To defeat the darkness around you, you must first defeat the darkness within you."

Our eyes remained connected for a moment; then I embraced him—as tightly as though I would never see him again.

"Sensei, I don't know how to bring Icarus back," I whispered, a tear spilling down my cheek. "The council condemned him to death. Why would they accept him back now? I don't even know how we're going to get home."

"Cross that bridge when you come to it, Hawk," he said. "All will be made clear. But there is one thing you must remember…"

He held me out at arm's length.

"They have chosen to live by the dictates of their code, Hawk," he said. "Not by the prophecy alone, but by *their interpretation* of it. And because that is so, you will be at the mercy of their system of justice…" He trailed off, looking deep into my eyes. "And fulfilling the demands of the law will not come without sacrifice."

Before I could speak, he gently pressed the rose into my hand, folding my fingers shut over its satiny petals. My eyes fixed on the hues of deep red peeking out between my fingers, the black band that wrapped my finger like a ring.

"Do not be afraid, Hawk," Sensei reassured me quietly. "I will be with you."

I stared down a moment longer before slowly shifting my gaze up to meet my teacher's. A feeling of iron resolve settled in my veins.

"I'm not sure how to find my way back to the cave in the woods from here." I lowered my voice, as though someone would overhear. "I don't even know where we are. Do you think you can help me?"

He smiled. Reaching out, he gently passed his fingertips over my eyelids, closing them.

"Clear your mind," he said quietly. "Let go of this place, and see yourself where you need to be."

Slowing my breathing, I began to focus, bringing to the forefront of my mind images of the birch grove and the swelling embankments of earth. The fallen tree and its faded branches.

"Sensei," I murmured, beginning to feel myself slipping away, "will I see you again?"

There was a pause. I could hardly feel him anymore.

"You will be with me soon, dear one." His words began to fade even as he spoke them. "Very soon."

"But when…?"

All at once, everything around me faded. The scent of pines replaced that of the velveteen blossoms. My eyes softly blinked open.

For a moment I stood still, scanning my surroundings as though I would still find him just a few yards away, among the trees or just behind me. But I was alone in the forest. The wind rattled through the branches of the dead tree laid across the embankment before me.

The gaps revealed swatches of fur, white as the moon. A pair of blue eyes stared out at me from behind the branches. I watched them closely before taking a steady step forward. The wolf lowered its head slightly, its ears perking to attention. It turned and vanished into the tunnel. Without hesitation, I followed.

Day 1: At the bottom of the ravine

I'd been defeated—slain by Icarus; that's what they would all say.

Yes, Icarus had pushed me—killed me. He was a murderer now, and according to their code, he would be put to death. Charlotte would die too. She couldn't live without him. My one consolation was in the fact that at least Icarus wouldn't have her either.

I could still feel Charlotte's blood coursing in my veins as I fell through the air and into the void. I could still remember the way she had looked at me when we finally met again: like she didn't know me.

My mind had raced back to that day in the safe room, when she had asked Mitsue to leave and told me to take a seat. The burning tree had crackled as I watched her pace.

She'd grabbed me by the hand and looked into my eyes as if she could see through me. She couldn't.

"You're not one student; you're many." Her authoritative tone had rung in my ears. "You're an assemblage of powers that others have spent lifetimes developing."

Oh, Charlotte... you always thought you could figure me out so easily. You think yourself so superior, yet you would know nothing about me if I didn't want you to. There is no secret you could decipher unless I let you.

"You think I've admitted everything, don't you?" I'd said aloud. "You think you know the whole story, but you don't, Hawk. Believe me when I tell you that..."

Telling Charlotte that Icarus was her Sunset had been the hardest thing I had ever done. I had lost my battle with the one I hated most— Icarus—and fallen into what they called the endless void.

But it wasn't, in fact. When I hit the ground, I awoke in a new world. A world where my thoughts, my desires, my feelings, my fears—they all leapt from my mind and became reality. A world where my identity was whatever I wanted it to be. And I had tasted Charlotte's blood: I could shift now.

Perhaps, once again, Charlotte had slipped through my fingers. Perhaps I had fallen to hell... but I had survived. Now I would simply wait for Charlotte to fall to me.

CHAPTER THIRTY

Fin

I locked myself in the safe room at the end of the hallway. There was no way I could go back to my dorm—not after what had happened at the gathering. Not when everyone was looking for me.

Squeezing my eyes shut, I slid down to the floor. I pressed the heels of my hands to my eye sockets, breathing for what felt like the first time.

In the quiet, the chants of the crowd still rang in my ears. Delta's voice: *We need you, Fin...*

I could see the fire's fading glow through the glass wall at the far end of the room. My head felt heavy as I tipped it back. I wasn't certain how long I sat there on the floor, listening. It could have been twenty minutes; it could have been two hours. Eventually the commotion diminished, and the sun's rays extinguished the firelight. A mist swelled in the ravine.

On the opposite side of the door, a faint set of footsteps grew louder and finally came to a stop in front of the safe room I'd barricaded myself into. A hesitation, then a few deliberate knocks.

"Fin?"

The voice was Areos's. I didn't respond.

He cleared his throat after a moment. "Fin, I know you're in there."

A pause.

"Look, you don't have to talk to me if you don't want to," he persisted. "But there's something you should know, and I want you to hear me out."

I withheld a sigh, closing my eyes.

"The gathering just let out. It, uh… it didn't go as I expected…" He trailed off, his voice slightly muffled. "I guess this is where I should say you were right, huh?"

I swallowed, opening my tired eyes again. "Why? What happened?"

"Exactly what you said would happen." He sounded frustrated. "They don't want to wait—and some don't trust that Sensei left you with that instruction. They're divided, Fin… They just want someone to tell them what to do—they don't want to have to figure this out themselves. All they know is that they're alone now, and they're afraid."

"And they want someone to fill Sensei's place."

"They want *you* to fill his place," Areos corrected me emphatically.

"That would be impossible," I answered flatly.

"And why is that?"

"Because it would go directly against Sensei's word."

Areos growled in frustration. "Fin, would you just *think* for a minute?"

I rolled my eyes up to the ceiling and waited.

"Mitsue is no friend of yours, Fin. You heard what he said back there." His tone was grave. "Who do you think will gladly jump in to pick up the slack for you?"

I opened my mouth to reply, but then hesitated. Mitsue's words replayed in my mind—his power-hungry speech, which had only backfired on him.

"Of course *he* would," I muttered despondently. "He would like nothing better."

"So you're going to just let him win?"

I said nothing.

"There's a time and place to be an idealist, Fin." Areos dropped to the floor on the other side of the mahogany door. "Sometimes things cannot be as perfect as we want them to be. The situation we're in is already compromised. Icarus fought with Raiden, and it screwed the system, so we had to pull out—though that *might not* have been Sensei's original intention." Areos paused for a breath.

When he spoke again, his voice was even firmer. "Sometimes you have to compromise, Fin. Even if you may not want to."

"I understand what you're telling me, Areos," I answered finally, "but I'm the wrong man for the job."

"*The wrong man for the job?*" he repeated. "The wrong man for the job? Fin... Fin, are you out of your *mind?*"

Sighing heavily, I slowly rose to my feet.

"It's *because* you think that way. It's *because* you don't want it," he countered, his tone urgent. "That's the *exact* reason why you *should* lead us! Don't you get that?"

"Sensei said to wait," I replied, my voice heavy in my throat.

"Sensei isn't here! He has no idea what's going on."

Doesn't he, though? Didn't he tell me that he was most present when I could not see him?

"Fin, listen to me. Listen." Areos tried the handle of the door, though it didn't budge. "Delta wasn't kidding when she said we need you—we do need you. You're one of the last sane, capable, and experienced sliders left."

"I can't do this for you and Delta, Areos."

The tumblers jingled again as he strained to pry open the door. "Then do it for her."

Something in my chest faltered. I turned and looked back at the door. "For wh... who are you talking about?"

"Hawk."

The name sent my heart spinning.

"Areos, she... I..." I pressed the heel of my hand to my forehead. "You don't understand."

"But don't you think she would want you to at least *try* to keep the world she left behind in one piece?"

Anything I'd been about to say, I swallowed. Turning, I walked the length of the room, coming to a halt at the glass that overlooked the ravine.

"She trusts you, Fin," he continued. "She doesn't trust Mitsue or Azalea or—or the council or anyone else. It's always been *you*. Can't you see that? You've been here for, what, years? I've been here only since the evacuation, and even I can see that Hawk loves you, Fin."

"No!" I pushed the thought away. "No, she... she doesn't, Areos."

He kicked the door and cursed. "You think Delta and I want you to do this for us? Fin, if you don't accept this leadership role, we will all suffer for it. *All of us.*"

What would Hawk want me to do? Would she really want me to accept the position—even when Sensei instructed me otherwise?

Am I really meant to do this? Is it possible that I trained so long for such a time as this?

"Fin, please." Areos's voice seemed far off. "Don't tell me you're going to let us fall apart again—with things as bad as they are."

Each time I blinked, I saw the gathering platform—filled with students. Familiar faces, most of which I had helped train. I saw the despair in their eyes, confusion, and fear. I couldn't help but wonder now if I was meant to take that away.

Am I really going to let Mitsue get the upper hand? Even when his desire was to separate me from Hawk—to see her executed?

I tried desperately to clear my head. I could still hear remnants of Areos's speech, but I could no longer make out the words. Everything around me was muted.

Just do it... Just tell him you'll do it...

I thought of Hawk—of what I had read in her file, of what she could be facing even now at the bottom of the ravine. Then of the grief in Sensei's eyes. Each word he had written in the letter.

Do not lose faith, Fin. Even when it seems that all has been lost— for all is never lost.

I could almost hear it, so close did his voice seem as his words pounded against my heart. Suddenly it was as though the veil was pulled from my eyes. Suddenly there was no doubt in my mind.

Tuning back into Areos's voice, I walked briskly back across the room, unlocking the door with my focus and throwing it open. Areos stumbled inside, his glasses nearly spilling off his narrow face. I halted in front of him, looking him square in the eyes.

"I appreciate your trust, Areos," I said solemnly. "I hope you know that."

He looked back at me for a second before quickly shaking his head. "Don't say b—"

"But," I interrupted, clapping a hand on his shoulder as I continued past him, "I cannot accept the position."

He stood there and watched me go, not saying a word until I was halfway down the hall.

"Fine," he called after me. "I just hope you don't live to regret your decision." Then he added, "I hope we *all* don't live to regret it."

———✦———

Though the rest of the Dimension slept, I did not. I sat on the edge of the training platform, overlooking the sheer drop into the ravine, and I lost myself. Normally, morning sessions would have been starting about then, but the dawn after a gathering was always an exception.

Since before I could remember, I'd been an insomniac. It was how I'd found the portal in my closet when I was younger. It was how Hawk and I had become friends; she slept at odd hours, and I was up all night—what better way to get channeling practice in?

Usually my melatonin deficiency drove me to train more, but that morning it was working in the opposite direction. The gathering had drained my energy. After what felt like a long time, I forced myself to stand and take position nonetheless. My thoughts were eating me alive, and this was the only way I knew to combat them.

I coached myself into deep, relaxed breathing as I closed my eyes and cleared my thoughts. I floated my hands up in front of me and instantly channeled a ball of invisible energy into the space between my palms.

I tossed the humming orb from one hand to the other, my eyes still shut. I zoned out of the sounds around me—the wind, the rustling in the thatch overhead, the patter of rain as it began to gently drizzle. I focused on what I saw in my mind's eye: the ravine beyond the rail, the tired sky as it came down in pieces. I saw the emptiness, the distance, the dead leaves in the wind, the traces of her face. Her eyes, her hair, her lips as they parted in the shape of my name.

I could contain it no longer. I threw.

I opened my eyes as the orb ripped through the air, burning bright red, vacuuming away the oxygen as it bulleted beyond the platform and exploded in midair.

For a moment I was frozen, then, as though released from the grip of some unseen force, I sucked in a breath. My joints ached, and my fingers trembled as my hands went up to my face.

"Someone's fired up."

Somehow, I wasn't surprised by the familiar voice, the familiar accent. I turned and found her standing several yards behind me, arms crossed, hair pulled back into a loose bun. She was wrapped in a crimson cloak. Her face was pale in the dull morning light, emphasizing her spattering of freckles.

When I said nothing, she came closer.

"Areos told me, Fin."

"Then I'm assuming we have nothing to talk about."

Ignoring her now, I attempted to form another orb, but found that I couldn't.

"I didn't come to convince you that you should lead, Fin," Delta told me quietly.

My hands fell to my sides.

She studied me for a moment before continuing. "What's going on with us, Fin?" She paused, pressing her fingertips to her forehead. "I know these are uncertain times—chaotic, actually. But I think you know that I…"

I forced myself to hold her gaze. "I'm sorry, Delta." My voice came out quiet. "I just…"

She shook her head, pinching her eyes shut like she was in pain. "Don't say that. That's what you usually say when you're about to say 'I can't.'" She opened her eyes again and blinked away tears. "I get it."

I fought to get my voice out in one piece. "Delta, it's not that I… I didn't mean for you to think that I—"

"That you loved me?" she cut in, her voice barely audible above the patter of the rain. "You didn't mean for me to mistake your confidence, your attention, your flirtations for anything more than friendship?"

"There were no flirtations, Delta," I came back, my voice quiet. "I came to you because you were one of the only people I felt I could trust—you still are."

Delta's eyes hardened. "Oh? Are you sure about that, Fin?"

I began to respond, but my voice faded in my throat.

"I'm the only other person who read that letter, Fin." Her jaw set as she spoke. "I'm the only other person who knows that something happened to her."

My stomach twisted. I swallowed back a sick feeling. "*Nothing* happened to her."

She stepped closer now, her eyes blazing. "Oh, but I think you know that something did, Fin. Sensei may have left that part out of his letter, yes, but I think you know full well that a man wouldn't hunt her down through time for no reason."

"The killer hunted *both* of them," I corrected her firmly. I felt sweat beginning to prickle at the back of my neck. "He tried to kill Icarus and Hawk because they are the patriarchs."

She observed my expression for a moment. "Yet there's something about Hawk... isn't there? Something Sensei had to rescue her from."

I shook my head firmly. "Delta, I... I let you read that letter in confidence." I was quickly becoming aware that this had been the worst decision I'd ever made.

"As I recall, it was more than that," she said, her voice bitter now. "You *kissed me*, Fin. Are you telling me that meant nothing?"

I quickly shook my head. "Not that it meant nothing, Delta, I..." I faltered, fumbling for words. "I was... torn apart. I shouldn't have kissed you—"

"But I was there, so why not vent your emotions, right?"

"No," I replied. My voice sounded strained. "Those are *your words*, not mine. I care about you, Delta, but I... I cannot be the man you want me to be for you."

Hurt lingered in her eyes for a moment, but then it iced over. "Because you don't love me?"

"Because my heart has long been promised elsewhere," I replied quietly.

She stared at me for a moment. The cold rain pelted the thatch above us.

"Hawk?" The name was a question, but she spoke it like a curse.

I bowed my head in the affirmative.

She gave a cold laugh. "Fin, you think the Sunrise of the Dimension is going to fall for you?" she asked bitterly. "You think she's going to—to save Icarus, bring him back, and then leave him to be with you? Are you out of your mind, Fin? You desire someone who can never, and *will never*, desire *you*."

Delta was quiet for the first time as she caught her breath.

It was nothing I didn't already know. Nothing that didn't plague my thoughts as I lay awake each night and stared at the ceiling. Yet hearing it spoken aloud still stung like the slash of a blade.

"I know that, Delta," I said quietly. "I... I know."

"Yet you're still in love with her?"

I was silent for a moment. "I will love her as long as I draw breath, Delta."

Finally, it was as if she'd received the response she had been prodding for. She took a step back. "I see."

Without a word, she turned to walk back in the direction of the platform steps. When she reached the middle of the platform, she stopped and turned back to me.

"You know, before I met you, I was loyal to Mitsue," she stated carefully. "He's an intelligent, capable slider, Fin, regardless of your biases."

I felt my jaw tighten.

"Those who stand with him will undoubtedly rise with him. It will be inevitable," she went on coolly. "Since you've turned down the position of leader, I hope you realize I have no choice but to support whoever is elected to lead us in Sensei's absence."

I held her gaze. "And *I* hope I can expect your discretion, if no longer your confidence, Delta."

I didn't mention the letter. She already knew to what I referred.

Delta tipped her head back, an indignant look in her eyes, masking what I knew was really hurt. "Expect nothing from me, Fin," she intoned coldly. "Nothing without a cost."

I stood in silence, and for a moment she did the same. Then she turned once more and walked the rest of the way to the stairs. Descending them, she disappeared.

I was alone on the platform once again, adrenaline coursing through my veins.

How could I have been so naive? How could I have let things come to this?

I had hurt Delta—and, in doing so, left a carefully kept secret of Hawk's exposed. Delta didn't know the full truth, but I knew she was confident in her suspicions... which happened to be accurate.

Will she tell Mitsue? Will she tell everyone?

Why had I trusted her—why had I let her read the letter? Had I needed her that much? Was I... was I still so *human*?

My thoughts were interrupted by a loud crack of thunder.

Startled, I looked up.

A thunderstorm? In the Dimension? It was unheard of.

Crossing the platform, I stopped abruptly at the edge, gripping the rail as I peered down into the ravine.

What had only hours ago been a peaceful, listless fog was now angry billows of ashy black clouds broken only by the blanket of rain covering the Dimension and bolts of lightning flashing overhead.

For a moment I squinted, unsure of what I was seeing, but then I caught the scent of it on the breeze, and it was unmistakable.

Smoke.

CHAPTER THIRTY-ONE

Icarus

I was so tired of standing outside looking in. I'd lost Hawk before. I wasn't going to lose her again.

I stood staring into her world, standing in the center of the stone circle, gazing up at the frost-covered trees, at the snow as it swirled furiously in the wind. I could see her tracks in the snow.

She was out there.

Walking to the edge of the circle, I stretched out a hand, only to watch it disappear. "And I'm trapped here."

Something inside me was ticking like a time bomb as I stepped off the circle and through what felt like an invisible wall of energy that welcomed me back into my world, into the forest full of wolves and swaying purple flowers with birds chortling overhead.

In spite of the frigid climate I'd just emerged from, sweat was beading at my hairline. I followed the sound of gurgling water to the stream that ran through the thicker part of the forest, a glinting emerald vein.

Dropping to my knees, I submerged my head. For a moment everything was muffled by the pulsing sound of water as it rushed past. The world came back when I needed to breathe. I flipped my head back, sending out a spray.

For the first time I noticed my reflection as the water's surface once again grew still.

My hair was beginning to look feral, and my jaw was covered with a scruffy beard.

I'm surprised she recognized me.

Leaning down again, I cupped my hands to splash water up against my chest and over my back.

Why could she stroll freely into my world, while I was barred from hers?

I growled into my dripping wet palms, unable to contain my frustration any longer. I felt one of the wolves brush gently up against my back.

"Why can't I get to her?"

At first there was silence. Then the sound of footsteps as soft as wind through the tall grass.

"You can only enter a world into which you have been admitted, Icarus."

A movement in the reflection grabbed my attention. I caught a glimpse of a figure standing just behind me—a familiar, aged face. Peaceful yet iridescent blue eyes.

My breath caught in my throat as I whirled around, anticipating a face-to-face encounter with my teacher, but I was met only with a deeper sense of delirium.

Aside from the wolf still seated behind me, lapping its large front paws, the forest around me was still and empty.

My breathing quickened as I craned my neck, peering around the large trees. I heard a familiar chuckle in response.

"Oh, you of little faith." Sensei's voice was as close as if he stood just behind me. "Did I not teach you to trust the heart above the deceiving eyes?"

I turned back to the stream and peered down into the reflection again. Sensei smiled as he gazed up at me from the water's surface.

"You're in the stream?"

He laughed. "I'm in *you*, Icarus."

I couldn't help but grin.

"Why is Hawk like vapor slipping through my fingers, Sensei?" I pounded a fist into the water's surface. "Do you have any idea how frustrating this is?"

He only smiled, as though expecting me to question him further.

"So these are separate dimensions, then…" I puzzled. "This place and the snowy forest I can see from the stone circle."

He dipped his chin affirmatively.

"What do you mean, I can only be admitted into her world if she wants it?" I asked, my eyes narrowing. "She seems to come and go from my world as she pleases."

"But have you not yearned for it since you fell?" he asked. "For Hawk to become part of your world?"

"Of course."

"There."

"So does that mean..." My voice weakened. "Does that mean that she doesn't want..."

"Have you asked her that question?" Sensei asked, his face wavering slightly in the gentle current.

I shook my head. "I—no. I was..."

"You have given her your heart, Icarus, and thus she can access it freely," he said. "For it is you who have let her inside. You are at liberty to give yourself to another, for your heart is free."

My heartbeat seemed to stutter slightly at this. "And hers isn't?" I asked, a tight feeling gripping me inside. "Didn't she kiss me?"

"Have you given your heart to everyone you have kissed?"

Touché. I reached up to rub the back of my neck.

"Is love but a kiss, Icarus? A word, a look, a sigh?" He shook his head, answering himself. "Oh, but it is far more, my son. A force unseen, yet nearer than your breath. Stronger than the desire for life—it is the willingness to lay down your life for the redemption of another."

"But, Sensei," I protested, "if not to me, then... who has she given her heart to?"

Sensei's expression became stern. "Why do you ask such a question, Icarus?"

My face still burned. "Because I... I love her, Sensei. More than anything."

"Then it shouldn't matter whether she's ready to love you likewise."

The dull ache in my chest only increased. "Of course." I clenched my teeth. "Of course. I just..." My eyelids pinched shut. "God, Sensei, I'm scared."

I felt a hand on my shoulder, but when I turned, there was still no one there.

"What is fear's enemy, Icarus?"

"Bravery?" I asked.

"Love," he answered.

I fought back the lump that was forming in my throat.

"Sensei, if Maicoh is who she suspects, I can't just stand by while he kills her—or forces her to lead him back here to kill us both," I choked out. "I don't care if I have to *break in* to her world: I have to get over there. I was born to fight for her—it's killing me to be trapped here."

"When the student is ready—"

"Please give me something better than that line."

My interruption was followed by a silence. I cursed myself inwardly.

"Sensei, I'm sorry," I groaned. "I'm a disrespectful ass."

The only reflection I found in the blue green water was my own.

"Sensei?" I glanced around, though I could already sense that his presence had gone. "Sensei, are you still there?"

I turned and found the white wolf still seated behind me, a look of expectation in its large blue eyes.

You blew it, Ion, a voice in my head told me, reverting back to my human name because that was what I felt like. A stupid, confused, aching human. *When are you going to learn to just shut up?*

"I put my foot in it," I mumbled, getting to my feet. "Come on. Time to go check on her."

Like Hawk needed me to—she was rocket fuel and I was water. It seemed like I was always waiting for Hawk. I was sick of pacing through the irises and waiting for things to happen. I knew myself enough by now to know I had more inside me than that.

Because, of course, water doesn't burn bright like rocket fuel does. But sometimes it breaks rocks.

The spiders scurried away as I led several of the wolves into the circle. I felt the sting of frozen marble beneath my feet.

"There has to be a way out."

Or should I say, in...

I was muttering to myself now, but the pack seemed to take notice. The white wolves circled around me, heads low to the ground as if they had caught on to some particularly interesting scent.

I walked the perimeter of the circle, scanning the ground and the sides of the pillars, searching for something—anything.

I had no idea what I was doing. I just knew that if I stayed still, I would combust.

Suddenly one of the wolves threw back its head, and a howl split the air. The others started to attention—as did I. Chills coursed up and down my spine as I looked to the wolf that had given the call, the one that had first found me in the forest that night. Its breath was like a pillar of steam rising into the air. Several of the wolves darted away from the circle and into the snow.

"What is it?" I dashed to the edge of the marble circle, staring after my bestial counterparts. Something was amiss.

I looked back at the wolf that was still standing in the circle's center. Though the rest of the pack was frantic, it remained strangely calm.

I started towards it, but came to a quick halt. I suddenly caught the scent of something the wolves had apparently already noticed.

"*Smoke?*"

Rapidly, I scanned my surroundings. The wolves were scattered among the trees now, racing towards what looked like a mere gray smudge tangled with the evergreens in the distance. It took a moment of squinting before it all clicked. I watched in growing horror as flickers of yellow began to feed angrily up into the trees, rising from the ground with a hungry roar. Fragments of ash drifted on the breeze and soon began to rain down where I stood.

My mouth ran dry.

Fire.

The reverberating crack of distant explosions rang through the air; following each one, a new burst of fire would surge upwards in a different section of the forest.

Hawk.

I lunged towards the circle's limits, but the wall of energy only permitted me entrance back into my own world, sending almost translucent rings rippling through the air from the impact. I drew back. Whipping around, I tipped my face towards the sky.

"What do you expect me to do?" I yelled, my breath painting the air. "Sensei—I know you can hear me!"

But no response came. Only the howling of the wind and the thundering of my heart.

Okay, okay, okay, Ion. Think...

I pressed my eyes shut, attempting to clear my thoughts.

No... Icarus.

I wasn't the lost boy at the bottom of hell anymore. I wasn't still fighting to remember who I was—I *knew* now. And that person was not Ion. No, I'd left Ion in the riverbed, and it was time to inform my mind of that fact.

My thoughts raced back to Sensei's reflection in the stream, the look in his eyes, his unfinished words.

When the student is ready—

When I opened my eyes, I found the wolf still standing there before me, head back, ears perked to attention. A strange feeling washed over me. Then I stepped closer and knelt before it.

I stretched out a hand cautiously; it lifted its paw likewise and placed it in my palm, which still bore a scar from the last cut I'd inflicted to give the wolf my scent. The same hand Hawk had cut to allow our powers to entangle.

I stared at the paw in my hand before my gaze shifted up to its eyes.

"—the teacher will appear."

Scrambling to my feet, I snatched one of the fallen fragments of crumbled marble, a sharp rock that lay at the base of a pillar. I returned and found the wolf still poised, one paw lifted.

Okay, Sensei... I can take a hint...

I concentrated first on cutting my own hand; then I turned the wolf's massive paw in my free hand and held the knife in levitation as I replicated the damage. A vein of what looked like melted gold rose to the surface of its skin.

What the...?

The wolf didn't so much as wince. The almost iridescent liquid pooled and spilled from its paw, melting to the ground below, where, instead of accumulating, it simply vanished away.

I leaned in a little farther to examine the gash, the shimmering substance that oozed from it like blood.

Was I seeing things? Because last time I checked, real, living creatures needed blood in their veins in order to survive...

I reached out and slowly, cautiously, touched the gash, my fingers grazing the liquid. It disintegrated against my fingertips as though it were only imaginary.

My thoughts faded away as I stared into the wolf's eyes. The dreams I'd had of being in a wolf's body flooded my mind now: the confrontation with Maicoh—the boy who could turn into a black wolf. The boy I'd fought against to get to Hawk, only to awaken without victory. I'd felt the world around me through its skin, inhaled the scents it picked up, and seen Hawk's tracks through its razor-sharp vision.

I stole a glance over my shoulder at the forest behind me. Tongues of flame feathered up from the treetops close to us now. My heart beat faster.

I lifted my hand to meet the wolf's paw. I felt a quick sting, and then warmth flooded my veins as our blood fused.

Real, living creatures bleed crimson. But maybe you're about as real as my shadow, I thought as I watched our blood slowly mix. *Real only because I am...*

I could still hear the fire crackling behind me, but now it was suddenly in front of me, too. And then, just as its blood had vanished, the wolf now faded from my sight, leaving behind tiny flecks that cascaded over my arms and burned like sparks. I watched in astonishment as they danced against my skin, and then started in terror as they ignited.

Heat overtook my body as violent billows of gold swallowed me. I was thrown back and then lifted bodily off the ground. For a moment I writhed in midair, held in suspension above the platform. A melting sensation overcame me, as if my skin were peeling off. A strange feeling of déjà vu twisted my stomach.

I felt my voice roar from my body uncontrollably as I screamed. At first I could hear only that agonized wail ripping through the flames and the smoke, but then, all of a sudden, it was something else. Something deep and throaty and terrifyingly familiar.

A howl.

CHAPTER THIRTY-TWO

Fin

I was out of breath by the time I burst into my dorm, looking for Mitsue. My heart beat wildly as I scanned the empty room. Shielding my eyes from the rain, I reemerged outside. Squinting at the rope bridges around me, I began to realize that I wasn't the only one who had noticed something was amiss.

Alarmed students were emerging from their dorms and filling the pathways to peer downward into the clouds of ash as the smoke billowed higher. Thunder rolled through the thick air.

I searched the crowd for my missing roommate, but he was nowhere in sight. Knowing I wouldn't be able to make it through the crowd without being stopped, I turned and began walking briskly in the direction of the gathering platform, reminding myself of the possibility that some of the council members might still be there, discussing the outcome of the emergency gathering we'd called. I hadn't taken five steps when a voice stopped me.

"Yo—hey."

I turned and noticed a familiar swath of navy blue hair bobbing after me. The rope bridge rattled with his sprinting pace. I kept walking, and a moment later a hand slammed down on my shoulder.

"What's up with this thunderstorm, man? And all the smoke?" he asked, leaning on me heavily as he caught his breath. "Like, when—where did it all come from?"

"Logic would suggest it's coming from below." I kept my stride.

Runner tossed me a pointed glance. "You know what I mean."

"Yes, Runner, I know what you mean—but I have no answers for you. In fact, I'm looking for Mitsue now—or any other member of the council I happen to encounter first."

Runner straightened up. "Oh—oh, well, you won't find them. They're in a meeting."

I halted in the middle of the path and turned around to face my student. "In a meeting?" I repeated. "Since when?"

"Since you left us all hanging last night."

"Meetings are supposed to be announced," I reasoned aloud, though more to myself. "Not held behind closed doors. The code of conduct—"

"Was shot down, in case you're forgetting," he interrupted, pulling his T-shirt up over his nose. "They want a new leader, Fin. And you refused to be that person, so…"

"So now the council takes matters into their own hands behind the rest of the student body's back?" I shook my head in disbelief. "Who did they appoint in my stead?"

"No one yet." Runner kept pace with me as I resumed my quick stride. "It was undecided, last I heard."

"Left up to the decision of the council, no doubt?"

He nodded, squinting to see through the smoke as we proceeded. I picked up my pace. "I can't believe this."

Runner sighed and tossed his arms for lack of a better gesture. "I don't know what to tell you, man. You should have grabbed the opportunity while it was in front of you."

"Do you know where they are convening?"

Again, Runner nodded. "Yeah, Gaia mentioned they're meeting in one of the safe rooms."

"Gaia?" My eyebrows lifted in surprise. "I can't believe she's involved in this. She's always been so—"

"Don't blame her. It sounded like she was kinda pushed into it," he interjected. "She said she was going to 'make sure things stayed sane.'"

I blew out a frustrated sigh and gestured towards the drop. "Is *anything sane* anymore?"

With his shirt still masking his face like a bandit, Runner stepped in front of me to lead the way up onto the training platform. Smoke was already beginning to accumulate under the thatched roof, choking us as we crossed the open expanse to the south-facing hallway. Runner came to a stop in front of the second-to-last sliding pocket door. Tilting his head slightly, he listened for a moment.

"Sounds like they're in there." He jerked a thumb at the door. "Best of luck."

I stepped up to try the door. It was locked, naturally. I heard the voices inside waver at the sudden jingle of the tumblers. Someone cleared their throat—someone I could immediately identify as Mitsue, without him even uttering a word.

"Who's there?"

I gave Runner a glance over my shoulder. He folded his arms over his chest.

I turned back to the sliding door and reluctantly let my focus zero in on the handle. An instant later, the tumblers burst and the door flew open with a crash.

A long, low table had been drawn to the center of the room, around which the council, made up of several students, including Azalea, Gaia, Mitsue, and to my surprise, Delta, had gathered. All eyes in the room turned to the source of this sudden outburst. I stepped forward.

"Fin." Azalea was the first to speak up, her blue eyes flickering away from the intensity of mine. "Th-this is a private meeting. What are you doing here?"

"A *private meeting*?" I repeated, walking farther into the room. The glass wall had been dimmed to exclude any prying eyes from beyond the boundaries of the platform. "A private meeting? Since when was this something we ever condoned?"

Mitsue's eyes narrowed.

Azalea wrestled with her words. "I just—Fin, you must see that—"

"See what?" I interrupted tersely. "That we're falling apart?"

"That things are different now that Sensei is gone," she corrected me bitterly. "There's an old human saying: desperate times call for desperate measures."

"So this secret meeting is justified by an adage?"

Mitsue threw back his chair and sprang to his feet. "You have no right to be here, Fin." His voice rose as he spoke right in my face. "You had your chance—you lost it. Get out."

I stared at him, searching for something, anything, in his eyes that I could potentially reason with. Something that bitterness, like a corrupted Midas touch, hadn't yet turned to stone.

"I don't want power, Mitsue," I answered steadily. "Yes, I believe we are living in desperate times—but we cannot betray one another's trust like this. Not if we want to make it out alive."

Mitsue's lips twitched angrily. "We don't require, or request, your advice, Fin."

"Mitsue, Fin has sat on this council many times." Gaia straightened in her seat at the table. "He has every right to be here—this shouldn't be something that's discussed behind closed doors."

No one said a word. Delta leaned back in her chair and folded her arms over her chest, casting me a narrow gaze. I tried my best to ignore her.

"You can't just go against the expressed wish of the student body." I lowered my voice urgently. "You can't just deny them—"

"Why not?" Mitsue cut in smoothly. "You did."

I opened my mouth to reply, but Delta spoke first. "Fin believes in having everything out in the open, Mitsue," she commented carefully, though her eyes remained fixed on my own. "He doesn't like secrets."

Translated: *Watch your step, Fin.*

I felt my throat tighten. I forced my focus back to Mitsue.

"Fine," I said, stepping incrementally closer. "In Sensei's absence, the code has been abandoned and a new leader will be chosen—has been chosen already, I'm sure. Who is it?"

It was a decoy question; I knew full well the appointed was none other than the man standing before me. But nevertheless, I gave him the courtesy of a response.

Mitsue tipped his head back slightly, suppressing a smile. "They wanted a leader, Fin. It was our duty to appoint the most qualified—"

"Right, right," I said gruffly, cutting him off. "And that being the case, I'm assuming we can count on you to explain the fire in the ravine to the 'mob' outside?"

Mitsue's expression barely changed, but I could detect a twinge of confusion as it passed through his eyes. A bewildered murmur arose from the table. Delta was the first to jump up from her seat, walking quickly past us to lighten the tint veiling the window. As it turned out, it barely made a difference—the smoke did the job just as efficiently.

A confusion of gasps and a few choice words instantly filled the air, leaving Mitsue staring wide-eyed in disbelief as everyone else scrambled to the glass wall.

"It's burning!" someone shouted. "The ravine—the Dimension—it will be destroyed!"

I shook my head calmly. "The fire hasn't touched us. It's from something below."

Gaia slowly tore her eyes away from the window, leaving one hand pressed against the glass. "But… there is no bottom to the ravine," she mused, her voice full of doubt. "It… it doesn't…"

"It doesn't exist?" I questioned, finishing for her. "It's just a myth? No… It's not." I pushed past the small cluster of students to a clear space in front of the glass. "And nor is the fact that we have fallen on our own sword—attempting to slaughter our own patriarchs."

Mitsue gave an irritated grunt. "You're seriously going to start this nonsense again?"

"Mitsue." Gaia spoke up before I could answer. "Fin is entitled to his own opinion—"

"Not if it jeopardizes our mission." He fixed his eyes on me as he answered her. "Not if it divides us more than we already are."

I said nothing. I watched his expression as he stepped away from the window.

"Hawk and Icarus are not the patriarchs, and I don't think a single person in this room, other than Fin, believes this to be true." He scanned the faces around him, waiting for a response. No one offered one. He smiled bloodlessly, satisfied. "Would Sensei remain silent on the matter if, indeed, they were our founders?" He gave a short, cynical laugh. "I think not. Nor would he have left us at such a time." He turned slowly to me now. "But perhaps Fin has an explanation for this too."

The remark was spoken in jest—meant to be cutting. I chose to answer it seriously. "I don't know why Sensei left us, and I won't pretend to," I said quietly. "I only know that I…"

Mitsue waited. Everyone did. In the momentary silence I could hear the faint sounds of the students' shouts outside.

"I trust him," I finished quietly. "I trust him with my life, with all that I am. I trust that he knows me better than I know myself—and that if he says our time has come... then it has."

Mitsue, still standing in front of me, drilled me with his stare for a moment. No one else spoke.

"Oh, yes," he responded slowly, pointing his finger thoughtfully at me. "The letter... that Sensei allegedly left in your hands—"

"He did."

"Then why didn't you show it to us at the gathering? Why didn't you let everyone read it?"

I could feel droplets of sweat beginning to bead at my hairline. My gazed lowered from his.

Only two people in the room knew the answer to that question.

"Ah, yes." Mitsue answered his own question. "Because it wasn't in his handwriting. It was in yours—if it even exists at all."

"It *does* exist." My jaw tightened. "Do you really think I would lie?"

The eyes of the council were on me now as Mitsue gave me a long, scrutinizing once-over.

"I honestly don't know what to think anymore, Fin," he said, stepping away from the group now. "I'm going out there now to calm the rest of the students and reassure them that this is but another unaccounted-for abnormality in the weather—yet another prompting for us to train to leave this place." He paused and shot a glance towards the smoky glass. "No doubt an omen of Sensei's displeasure at our performance," he muttered.

"Our performance?" I reiterated, stunned. "Our performance— Mitsue, do you really think that's what this is about? You've been with him all this time and you really believe that's what he's like?"

He said nothing. His eyes didn't shift from the glass. I stepped forward before he could move.

"Mitsue, *please* just listen to me for once," I pleaded, dropping my voice. "Hawk and Icarus are down there—they *need* us. The rain, the cold, and now the fire—do you really not see the connection? We have to do *something*."

The white, sterile room, now tinged with the scent of smoke, fell completely silent. For a moment Mitsue's expression remained frozen. Taking one more step, I gently extended a hand and placed it on his shoulder.

"Mitsue, *please.*" I lowered my voice almost to a whisper. "Please don't do this."

For a moment longer he didn't move, didn't speak, didn't even turn to look at me. I could sense the gears were turning as he stared out at the smoke. Then, softly I added something only loud enough for him to hear. "It won't bring them back."

I felt Mitsue tense. Abruptly, he shoved my hand aside. When he turned to face me, any sign of hope had dissolved from his eyes, replaced by a steel resolve.

"One more word," he intoned with seething emphasis, "and I will make you regret having questioned my leadership."

I could tell he had more to say to me, but just behind me stood the rest of the council, watching to see how their new leader would respond. Without another word he turned and left the room.

Slowly, everyone else followed suit. Delta's eyes lingered on me as she passed; then a moment later I felt Gaia's hand gently brush my shoulder. She said nothing when I turned to look at her, but her large brown eyes seemed to speak volumes. She hated this as much as I did.

Then she too departed, leaving me alone in the large room overlooking the ravine. My eyes stung as I walked to the glass to stare out at the Dimension. The smoke was already beginning to die away now, recoiling incrementally back into the ravine's belly.

Mitsue would tell them it was Sensei's doing. Mitsue would tell them it was time for us to train harder than we ever had—to stop relying on the code to simply beat us into shape. And in a way, that was true. But what he didn't realize was that the code was but a reflection of something Sensei insisted already lived inside us, like gold buried in the darkness of a mine. What he didn't realize—what none of us did—was that the code was as engraved into our hearts as the prophecy was. What he didn't realize, and what I wouldn't allow myself to admit aloud, was that things would never be the same again.

What he didn't realize was that Icarus was coming back.

I pressed my forehead against the glass. A tear streamed down my cheek. There was a sound of tentative footsteps in the hallway and then in the safe room.

"You tried, Fin." Runner's voice echoed slightly in the emptiness of the room.

I didn't respond.

A moment passed before he said anything else. "What happens now?" he asked. "We wait for Hawk and Icarus? That's what Sensei told you?"

I took a deep breath, my forehead still pressed against the glass. "No," I said quietly. "He told us to wait for Icarus."

Beyond the blur of my tears were plumes of smoke. Beyond the smoke were the depths of the ravine. And somewhere at the bottom was someone my heart was beginning to tell me to let go of. Someone who I knew, deep down, I would never see again.

I swallowed, closing my eyes. "Just Icarus."

CHAPTER THIRTY-THREE

Hawk

The sun was beginning to rise as I trekked back through Maicoh's world, trailing the white wolf at a distance. Each of my footsteps seemed loud in the still air as I followed it through the trees.

My heart pounded hard as I remembered Sensei's words—his command to not fear. His reminder of a sacrifice.

What sacrifice? What was he talking about?

I felt a pang of anxiety at the thought of leaving Icarus alone in his dimension. I wanted to be there. But I knew this was something I had to do. I had to know how Maicoh had gotten to the bottom of the ravine, although I was fairly certain I already knew. I felt as though I'd finally placed the familiar look in his eyes—the same haunting glint I'd noticed long ago in Raiden's that day in the safe room when he had burned the tree and told me that Icarus was the Sunset.

I still wondered how on earth he had known I was the Sunrise. *How did he know?*

If Raiden was Maicoh's true identity, it would explain how he'd come here and why he could shift. It would explain why Maicoh seemed strangely familiar... though not why Raiden had.

A snap of a twig pulled me out of my thoughts.

A hand clapped over my mouth from behind, and I was pulled swiftly behind one of the large trees. The forest blurred around me.

My heart roared in my rib cage as I felt a warm body tense behind me.

"Not a sound until it's gone." A hot whisper in my ear. "Not a sound."

I struggled to nod, and slowly the hand retracted. I breathed softly, closing my eyes for a moment to steady my pulse.

I felt him lean forward to peer carefully around the trunk. My mind raced as a moment passed like an eternity.

"I told you to stay at camp," Maicoh hissed as he drew back. "I told you the wolf was about."

I turned to look at him. His face was only inches away, and his eyes still frantically scanned our surroundings.

"What wolf?" I bluffed.

Maicoh's dark eyes were distant. Perspiration beaded on his upper lip. "It was up ahead." He was breathless as he spoke. "Among the trees. Did you not see?"

"No—no, I didn't."

He checked around the trunk again, then let out a breath and grabbed hold of my wrist. "Quickly, this way."

I twisted in his grip, but he held tight. Maicoh wove deftly through the trees and brush and then released my hand so that we could run. He waved for me to follow.

The quiet woods streaked past us. I shot desperate glances over my shoulders, searching for the white wolf, but it had vanished as quickly as it had appeared. We were back at camp before my mind had even fully comprehended the journey there.

The black wolves were waiting. The fire was almost out.

My heart, as if it were made of stone, sank in my chest with a feeling of dread. It was me against the pack—and I wasn't a fan of the odds.

"How many times have I warned you?" Maicoh shot me a fiery glance. "The white wolf is dangerous."

"So you say."

"Do you not believe me?"

I walked around to the opposite side of the fire, kneeling down to place the last log on the hot coals. "It's not that."

"What, then?"

"I think there are things you aren't telling me, Maicoh. Things about the wolf, things about you..."

Maicoh swiped the sweat from his broad forehead, the expression on his face morphing into one of confusion. "I don't understand."

I remained silent, pursing my lips.

"The fire is going out," I said at last. My eyes slid up to his from where I was still crouched. "We're out of wood."

A black wolf crouched at his feet now. Maicoh reached down to muss its fur with his knuckles. "It will soon be warmer as the sun rises higher."

I began chewing my lip, my mind groping for another excuse to get him away from camp, but it wasn't needed.

"But if it pleases you, I'll go," Maicoh said, stretching his muscular arms overhead. "It is just that I am tired from the hunt."

The hunt. The hunts he left camp for each night—the hunts he always went on yet returned empty-handed.

"What is it you're hunting for, anyway?" I asked before he could turn away. "It seems as if you are always out hunting, yet you never have anything to show for it upon your return."

"Because I have not found what I am looking for yet," he said quietly. "I am still searching. I am still..." For a long moment Maicoh said nothing. He stared at me. "I am still hungry."

There was something in the way he said it, something that unsettled me.

"And you?" he asked. "Did you find what you left camp last night to look for?"

"What makes you think that I was looking for anything?"

I glanced away. There was a silence. After a moment I heard him shift his weight, taking a step backwards.

"Are you not still searching for Icarus?"

"Of course I'm searching for Icarus," I said carefully. "But I... I didn't find him."

He said nothing in reply. When I looked up, he was heading for the tree line.

"Stay at camp," he said. "I'll be back."

I nodded once.

"Promise me."

"Fine," I said, feigning compliance. "I promise."

A few more steps backwards, watching me, and then he turned around and threw himself forward into the trees, landing on all four paws, a black wolf once again. Two of the other wolves took after him at a run, leaving the third hunched motionlessly at the side of the fire opposite me; its eyes remained fixed on my own.

I waited with bated breath until the sounds of their footsteps had faded out of earshot. Then I slowly shifted my gaze to the fire, checking on the wolf out of my peripheral vision.

Incrementally I rose from the ground, pressing up from the soft earth, which was still laced with dew. The wolf mirrored my actions without delay. Clenching my jaw, I fought to keep my cool, ignoring it as best I could. Slowly and cautiously, I back-stepped to the entrance of Maicoh's shelter.

The wolf didn't move a muscle, but it didn't blink either.

I reached a hand back and parted the curtain of grass to let myself inside. The early morning streaks of sunlight shone down through the cracks like vapor. My eyes scanned the same objects I had examined previously. The stone knives, the arrows, the paper—all artful instruments of Maicoh's making. But now something new caught my eye.

Beside the bound stack of sketches I had earlier rifled through, there was a small sketchbook. A familiar black sketchbook.

The wolf watched carefully from the other side of the threshold, its eyes visible between the slivers of grass. It made no move to come inside, but I monitored it nonetheless as I knelt, separating the delicate covers between my hands. It opened to the center crease.

The page was faded and finger worn at the edges, and in the center there was a sketch. A charcoal drawing, with delicate strokes and detailed lines. Thin streaks for intricate details, and thick, almost violent strokes for the outlines.

It was precise—uncanny, in fact. Startlingly realistic, ugly and beautiful all at the same time.

It was a picture of me.

Imagined from the chest up, my shoulders were bare and my neck was swanlike, curved and deeply shadowed to match the penetrating darkness in my eyes and the wild tangle of hair that crowned my head.

I turned the page. There was another.

In this sketch I was seated at the fire, and a black wolf hunched beside me. The page beside it portrayed a version of me play-fighting with the pack, feathers in my hair. Hawk feathers.

The following page portrayed me in one of the safe rooms back in the Dimension. Light came in through the window in shafts, and the side of the ravine was visible beyond the pane of glass. A tree burned in the background behind me. Beside the picture was what looked like a journal entry.

It was so hard that day. The hardest day I've ever lived, actually. Harder than the day I left her—the day that I fell. The day that I had to tell her he was the one she had been searching for.

For so long had I ached to be such a one. For so long had I wished to extinguish Icarus and take his place, but I knew she couldn't live without him. I would lose both the wine and the wineskin. I needed him alive. I needed both of them.

A simultaneous death would be the only way to capture them. The only way to control the future, to have, at long last, the power I'd searched a century to find. The power I'd longed for all my life. Yet the thought of losing her cut like a knife.

Still cuts. Still hurts.

Because I still remember what she used to be like.

My hand shook slightly as I reached up to brush my hair from my face. By this point I was scarcely aware of whether the wolf still stood at the door or not. My vision had tunneled to focus solely on the pages in front of me.

The author was Raiden. There was no doubt in my mind now.

But what did he mean that he'd "searched a century" to find power? How was that possible? How had he known I was the Sunrise, and why did he talk about me as if he had known me for years? How had he known I was searching for Icarus?

I flipped to the next page, angling the book into the shaft of light.

She was made of satin, and I was made of stone. We sat on the ledge of the window on the third floor and smoked cigarettes as we watched the dirty streets swarm with dirty people. She would frown—she would say, "One day I'm going to escape this corner of hell." Her hands were callused, her fingers blistered as they poised the stub at her faded ruby lips.

"Where will you go?" I'd ask, as I always asked. I always wished she would correct it: "Where will we go?" But it wasn't about us; it was about her, wasn't it? Wasn't it always about her? Wasn't she always leaving me behind, leaving me behind like everyone always did—even my mother, who had brought me into this world?

Why did she leave? Why did everyone always leave?

"Somewhere warm," she'd reply, swinging her feet over the muddle far below. "Somewhere where the sky comes up blue with the dawn."

I almost dropped the sketchbook. My fingers trembled as I hung on to it, leaving traces of sweat as I now feverishly began flipping through the pages.

A sketch. Charcoal. A girl in a black dress. A girl with cheekbones showing through and her sleeves rolled up enough to reveal the marks wrapping her upper arms like mourning bands. A girl with tired eyes and wild hair.

Me. Charlotte.

I turned the page and found another similar drawing and another and another. I was always in black, my lips always slightly parted, my eyes always glinting, my hands always moving, reaching, touching someone else's hand. Someone who was never drawn into the picture, but seemed always to be just at the edge of it.

I could feel sweat trickling down my lower back, my mouth running dry as I rapidly leafed through the numerous entries and drawings.

No, it can't be… it can't…

All at once now, I brushed aside the rest of the pages, spreading the book open at the back cover. My heart leapt to my throat.

The last page was streaked with dirty fingerprints and crinkled with humidity. It contained no drawing; it bore no trembling scrawl, no words that reiterated phrases I'd spoken a hundred years prior—

no. Two words were written in the bottom left-hand corner. A faded glimpse of a name. The ghost to whom this book of Charlotte's eulogies belonged.

Edwin Wraith.

The book slipped from my hands and tumbled to the earth below. My hands shook uncontrollably as I stumbled backwards, crashing against the wall of the shelter. The commotion set off the wolf, who still stood by the door. A howl pierced the air.

Feverishly, I snatched the book from the ground again.

Maicoh was Raiden, and Raiden was really...? No—no, no, no, no, it couldn't be. It...

I staggered numbly backwards, tearing past the curtain and reemerging outside. Smoke billowed up from the fire that was beginning to catch. Several black wolves had stepped forward out of the trees surrounding the clearing.

The world seemed to spin around me as I clutched the book tightly. The sound of footsteps caught my attention.

Two black wolves skidded to a stop at the edge of the clearing just as Maicoh emerged from the forest. He stopped dead when he saw me.

"Hawk, what is it?" he asked. "What's wrong?"

I strained for a response, only for it to catch in my throat as I stood there, my eyes locked into his dark, familiar ones. Familiar ones like Raiden's. Familiar like the shadow that had haunted my dreams since the night I'd left Earth, the night Sensei had rescued me. Old, experienced eyes in a young, inexperienced body.

The Edwin to my Charlotte. My nightmare, standing before me in the flesh.

He stepped closer, still breathing heavily from the exertion. "I came back because I—"

I already knew he had heard the beckoning of the wolf—the warning call. I lifted the book to his eye level nonetheless, trembling but holding my ground.

"Because you forgot this?" My words sliced into his sentence.

His eyes glinting, Maicoh attempted to snatch it from my grip, but I jerked it just beyond his reach. His upper lip firmed.

"Hawk, I can expl—"

I backed away before he could finish, but he countered my actions immediately, lurching for a fistful of my hair.

I sprang backward instinctively, my muscles recoiling like springs. A fiery orb exploded into my hands as they retracted up over my head. Maicoh didn't react—he didn't have time to. I hurled it into his chest with every ounce of strength I possessed.

His long black hair caught fire instantaneously as the impact sent him hurtling backwards. He slammed against the trunk of a tree with a sickening thud. Letting out a panicked cry, he morphed involuntarily back into what I knew now to be his original form: not Raiden, not some other identity of a slain anomaly. Not merely one more of the masks he had grown used to hiding behind.

The crackle of the flames faded away, and there he was. The boy I'd grown up in hell with. Edwin Wraith. Moon-white skin wrapped in a tattered trench coat. His hair was how I remembered it: black like the curtain he'd dropped every night on the stage. Black like the cigarette smoke he'd blown from his lungs. Black like the bruises he'd given me.

My stomach lurched as century-old memories came flooding back into my mind. For a split second I thought I would be sick. Adrenaline pulsated hard through my skull.

This can't be real.

I forced myself to follow him, not allowing him to gain the distance I'd forcefully put between us. I stood over him, wielding another crackling orb in my hands.

"If this is another test, screw it!" I screamed, raising the flame over my head. "I am sick of constantly being reminded of who I was—I'm done with it!"

Who was I even talking to? Sensei?

No. No, I was talking to me.

"I am not a figment of your imagination, Charlotte." His voice rose hoarsely from his throat as he eased cautiously up to sit, crumpled, against the tree trunk. "I'm... I..."

"Finish," I ordered, winding back my arms threateningly. "Or I'll finish you."

He looked steadily up at me. A grin spread slowly over his lips. "Oh, but she wishes she could," he said, a glimmer of saliva glossing his lips. "Oh, did she not wish to, every day, every hour, for so long, to be rid of me? Did she not run wild through space and time to escape me?"

He paused, blinking back a dampness in his eyes. His fingertips clawed into the soil.

"Charlotte ran," he said, his voice a soft growl. "But I raced Charlotte… and Charlotte lost."

The fire in my hands wavered slightly as Edwin began to slowly climb to his feet.

"Go on," he said, his voice a gravel monotone. "Throw your fire like I taught you to—the way I learned when I inherited Maicoh's identity."

"Inherited?" I croaked. "*Stole!*"

"It was all to find you, Charlotte." He stepped closer. "It was all for you. For you, for you."

The wolves were gathering around us now.

"Y-y-you killed to keep yourself alive," I breathed, the revelation sending it all clicking into place. "It wasn't… *Raiden* who killed. It was—it was *you*! He was but one of your many victims—your many sources of lifeblood!"

"I had to stay young somehow. I wasn't immortal like you," he replied, continuing towards me like a tiger from the grass. "I did what I had to because I knew I had to find you."

"Why?" I shouted sharply, maintaining the distance between us. "Didn't you hurt me enough? Didn't you—didn't you get what you wanted?"

He cracked the slightest of delusional grins. There was a slight gap between his two front teeth, just as there always had been.

"You think it was your body I sought, Charlotte?" The question rose from his lips then dropped like a dead weight. "You are mistaken. It was never your flesh that I desired. It was your soul. It was always, always your soul."

A fight-or-flight instinct was surging through my veins, and my intellect was screaming for the latter. The last thing I wanted to do was fight—I was alone in the forest with my nightmare made manifest.

But as the fire dwindled over my head, as I stared into his eyes, as I shook at the knees, and as the wolves circled warily around me— I remembered why he was here. That there was truth hidden in the dark folds of his jealous words.

It was indeed my soul he desired. But not just mine.

I took a few more steps back, though Edwin only countered them with his own quiet footfalls. More wolves were falling behind him in formation, coming out from among the trees as the red sun rose to stain the fog lifting from the forest floor.

"Run, Charlotte." He clenched his dirty hands into fists. "Run like you always have, my love."

I felt the fire growing stronger between my palms, lapping furiously at my skin. Something inside me still hesitated, teetering at the edge.

To defeat the darkness around you, you must first defeat the darkness within you.

Abruptly, I halted between the trees. Soft wisps of steam swelled from the earth's lips to wrap my legs and veil the wolves as they stalked forward.

I waited—then, taking aim, I threw.

The orb exploded into Edwin's chest. His coat instantaneously caught fire, and it took but a split second for the fire to spread. He laughed as the flames surged over his body, feeding rapidly up his torso.

A sickening feeling twisted in my gut as I stood there, bathed in the radiant heat as the macabre scene unfolded in front of me.

The flames licked higher, caressing him like fingers, and suddenly his laughter turned to screams, and the screams, finally, into throaty howls. His body levitated, writhing, and his skin began to evolve into a thick coat of black, wiry fur.

He dropped to the ground again, landing on all fours to crouch before me. Around him the pack gathered, muscles tensed and eyes blazing, as they waited to see what he would do.

Then he sprang.

My mind comprehended nothing but the fear thundering through my veins as I turned and sprinted. The black wolves surged forward, multiplying around me. I jumped for the trees, reaching for a low branch to lift myself from the ground, but instead I fell.

Triumphant howls erupted around me as I hit the ground, gasping. Instinctively my hands extended out in front of me, shooting a stream of flame like a blast from a furnace. This kept the wolves at bay just long enough for me to scramble to my feet again, splotches of blood stinging my knees.

The fire fed on the thick blanket of tinder-dry pine needles, dirtying the air with smoke. I held my ground as Edwin howled, commanding the pack.

My arms trembled at full extension in front of me. All my focus channeled into the space between my hands. The wolves surged forward like a river, and I doused them in flame just as fast. Edwin hung back, merely watching. Waiting for my energy to drain.

I slung my fist out as a wolf leapt for me, having dodged the fire. My burning knuckles impacted against warm flesh. The wolf shrieked as the angry shades of orange and red blistered through its fur. It staggered backwards only to stumble straight into the flames. Instantly consumed, its body seemed to burst, sending what looked like gold liquid splattering.

I jumped back, but I couldn't avoid the spray. Breathing heavily, I stole a glance down at my torso. Flecks of gold danced against the faded black fabric of my shirt before melting away to nothing.

For a moment my focus wavered as my mind tried to understand this strange phenomenon. I felt a sharp impact as a set of teeth lunged for my leg and another hurled itself at my eyes.

With a roar of outrage, I bulleted the last of my energy into their faces, running backwards as fast as I could while keeping my hands poised in front of me. The fire was climbing the trees now, cracking the sky with pillars of ash gray.

Edwin threw his head back and filled the air with a quick succession of throaty barks—a command to the black wolves to persist, to continue their attack.

More wolves emerged now from the choking blanket of smoke billowing behind Edwin. In compliance with his sadistic order, they stepped willingly into the fire, their coats bursting into flame. Like kamikazes, they rocketed toward me as fast as their paws would carry them, only to be bathed, one after the other after yet another, in consuming flames.

I threw everything I had and ran. The heat swelled behind me. *Faster, faster...*

The tree line burst open to the meadow. Stumbling into the tall grass, I threw myself backwards into the air. For a moment I spun in a momentary levitation, just a few feet up. For an instant I could feel fire on my skin—but then the sensation began to dwindle.

Come on—shift, shift, shift!

My thoughts were like frantic blinking lights as I strained to focus into hawk form; sweat trickled down my spine. For a moment my focus began to take its hold, but then I saw a blur of black beneath me. Black being feasted upon by red. Terror seizing my heart in its claws, I tumbled to the ground below, landing just a few feet from the frantic wolves and the trails of wildfire that ripped around them.

A sound like thunder cracked the air as one of the trees at the edge of the forest came crashing to the ground, violently ablaze. The silent meadow caught like gasoline.

Edwin emerged from the forest, back in human form, just as it all went up in flame. His face was bloodied and burned.

His eyes met mine from halfway across the field just as the burning wolves began to dissipate, exploding in bursts of liquid gold. He stared at me for a moment over the chaos we had together created. Then he lifted one stone-white hand and signaled the pack forward.

They raced past him in a swarm, streaming through the flames and charting a course directly for me.

Scrambling to my feet, I raced the wolves and the sea of fire across the meadow to the deeper forest on the other side. The portal came into view. I threw myself to my knees and scrambled into the darkness. Dirt flung into my eyes as I clawed my way furiously through the tunnel. Echoes of seething snarls thudded in the small space.

As I pushed myself forward, I started to formulate my plan of attack.

It's time to wake up from this nightmare.

In a moment I would reemerge into the icy world of my making, and the wolves would follow. I would lead them into the trees, into the thickets, and into the deepest snow—as far from Icarus as I could. I couldn't let Edwin find the portal that connected my world to his.

The barks behind me turned fiercer, but my brain was locked on the end of the tunnel.

Hurry, hurry, hurry—they're getting closer.

I reached the opposite end of the tunnel, leapt out, and somersaulted into the welcoming, frigid air, shifting into my feathered form.

I gazed down as the wolves spilled from the mouth of the tunnel, still burning.

Why weren't they exploding yet? Why was it that the faster and farther I ran, the stronger and more numerous they seemed to become?

Letting out a sharp, attention-grabbing trill, I hovered in midair, fighting the blasts of snow-freckled wind as I waited for the wolves to look up. When they did, I tumbled down through the air and cut a rapid course through the trees, staying close enough to the ground to entice them to chase harder than they had before.

I couldn't help but steal a quick glance in the direction of the portal, the deeper part of the forest where I knew it was safely tucked away.

Icarus.

His name turned restlessly in the background of my frantic thoughts as I flew. I could hear the commotion of the wolves just a few feet behind and below me.

There was no way I would be able to outrun them. I needed to trap them in deeper snow. The only catch was, I had to stay in hawk form. And with my energy dwindling fast, I could already feel myself fighting to keep the human trapped below my feathers.

Focus, Hawk. Focus.

Shutting the door on every other thought, I locked my eyes on what lay in front of me: the darker part of the forest—for it was sunset in my world, not sunrise as it had been in Maicoh's.

Or should I say Edwin's?

I would be lying if I said I wasn't afraid, and as I slipped in among the towering pines shrouded in the twilight, I became even more so. I stole another glance down at the wolves below me, at the streaks of fire that had spread now to the trees. The world below was now a long, glittering brushstroke of forest fire.

I whipped my head back to center—and impacted a thick branch at bullet speed.

My vision splintered into a thousand flecks of convulsing light, and I reeled in the air, numb with shock. It was hard to process anything beyond the searing pain as it swelled through my body, but I knew I was losing altitude—fast.

Before I could correct my course, another hard impact rattled through my bones as I hit the ground where the snow was apparently thin. My body burst back into human form. Stunned, I lay on my back, gasping for air. The glowing sky whirled sickeningly above me, and over the roar in my ears I heard a fresh volley of hysterical yelps and howls as the pack, led by the burning wolves, came in for the kill.

Rolling to my side, I flung my arms in the direction of the howls, gathering my strength to blitz the wolves with orbs of energy. Fire was useless at this point—the wolves were already ablaze. I felt a circle of energy gather between my hands, but my body was too weak to sustain it. Sweat trickled down my neck as it wavered and then extinguished altogether. I struggled to my knees and groped for the trunk of the tree I'd crashed into, trying to steady myself. I shook my head, trying to clear my swimming vision, and suddenly I was knocked face-first to the ground by a heavy blow to my back. I smelled hot wolf breath and felt a set of burning claws rake my skin.

I heard my own agonized scream as though from a distance as I slammed into the snow. My eyes blinked open to find splotches of my own blood staining the soft powder. Tears blurred my vision, and blood trickled from my nose. The wolf was still on me, its jaws snapping at my neck and shoulder. I flung my arms over my head, rolled to my side, and staggered to my feet. The lead wolf retreated a step and then lunged at me with renewed fury. Its massive paws slammed into my chest, knocking the breath from me, and I went down onto my back this time. I kicked out furiously, trying to free myself, and then felt another ragged scream tear from my lungs as a wolf rushed in and clamped its jaws onto my ankle. I writhed and twisted to release myself, but the weight of the first wolf pinned me where I lay. Its jaws widened inches from my face, spraying me with hot saliva.

"Stop!" I screamed. "Stop! Please, Edwin!"

Immediately, a forceful bark split the air. The teeth withdrew from my throat, and the vise grip around my ankle melted away. They backed down.

For a moment I lay panting in the snow; the trees overhead were a fiery blur. I slowly pushed myself up into a seated position. Blood and burn marks spattered the ground.

In front of me stood a large black wolf with a rail-thin frame and deep-set golden eyes, a familiar, haunting figure that studied me for a long moment as I sat gasping for breath. After a moment, the black wolf shifted into his original form. Edwin Wraith stood before me. Burned in places, but far better off than I was.

"Are you proud?" he asked, breathing heavily. "It was from you that I learned to shift, Charlotte—to wear someone else's skin as if it were my own."

My chin trembled as I stared up at him, a silhouette against the smoky sky.

"My name isn't Charlotte," I whispered fiercely. "And I wear my own skin."

"Oh, but you wish you did." He stepped closer to tower over me. "Haven't you been trying to escape its prison since I tainted it?"

My gaze lowered to the bloodied ground, a lump forming in my throat as hot tears welled in my eyes.

"You can run as fast as you can, for as many hundreds of years as you want." His voice leveled out into a growl. "You can try as hard as you can to be Hawk instead, but you will never be more than Charlotte to me. Charlotte, whom I saved—"

"Saved?" My gaze shot up to meet his. "*Saved?* You never saved me, Edwin—as I recall, I saved you! I saved you when I should have let you die! I should have let you die."

My eyes pinched shut, and I fought to control my breathing, sniffing back the blood.

"No," I said. "You may wish to be my savior, but that role belongs to someone far greater—and it is by him that I am defined, not you! Not by anything you have done or could ever do!"

I stared up at him once more, defiant, and clutched my chest.

"This," I shouted. "This you may 'taint.' This you may hurt, maim—yes, even kill. But, Edwin, even though you have lived a hundred years, as I have, even though you have hunted me and fought to claim the position of the patriarchs—you can never and *will* never take from me what Sensei gave back to me that day he saved me from you!"

My eyes met his, and I angrily brushed away a tear.

"You will never, ever take away my faith." My voice cracked, but I shook the weakness away. "Faith, Edwin! Faith in the fact that, even though I may fall, ache, hurt, and bleed, there is something far greater ebbing in the undertones of this war we wage—this life we have been given. There's a purpose that reaches beyond this place, beyond this world, beyond you and me—and it will not be stopped by *anything*." I clenched my teeth. "Not by *anyone*. It will not be stopped by *you*."

I saw Edwin's jaw tighten, saw his Adam's apple bob as he swallowed, backlit by the ferocious red flames. In two strides he was in front of me. Slowly, he knelt to my level. His gray eyes locked with my own, impenetrable. His hand clamped beneath my jaw, and he jerked my face closer to his.

"Where is he?" I felt flecks of spittle as he hissed into my face. "Where's Icarus?"

I held his gaze, said nothing.

"Charlotte," he said, feigning patience, "we can sit here together until this forest burns to the ground and takes both of us—and the other half of your soul—with it." His voice trembled with rage as he slowly pronounced each word. "Tell me where he is."

His other hand rose now to my arm and gripped my bicep. His fingers closed painfully around the black marking. His fingernails dug in.

Everything inside me twisted. I could feel chill bumps rising on my skin as the landscape seemed to alter around me, flickering between the inferno and the dark, familiar room that swallowed me in my dreams each night.

"I'll *die* before I tell you where Icarus is," I said, fighting to keep my voice from trembling.

He stared at me for a moment, the fire reflecting in his dark eyes, before he rose to his feet and stepped backward. Raising his hands overhead, he began to channel an orb of white energy, white that faded to yellow, then orange, and finally, a deep crimson. He turned it in the palms of his hands until it had grown to twice its size.

I tried to push myself backwards, out of reach, but my injuries were too severe. I fell back on my elbows, breathless with terror.

"Yes, Charlotte," he said, smiling slightly as he took aim at my chest. "Die you will."

My muscles tightened as I braced for impact, my fingernails digging into the frozen ground.

Edwin wound back his arms, took a deep breath, and released a chilling battle cry as he began to throw. Then, as quickly as it had begun, the cry morphed to a helpless scream. The orb rocketed up into the trees and exploded among the already roaring flames as something blurred past at rocket speed, tackling Edwin to the ground.

A blur as white as the snow around us.

CHAPTER THIRTY-FOUR

Icarus

The forest was on fire, yet all my senses could seem to comprehend were the scent of her footprints and the faint flickers of her voice I could hear in snatches on the wind.

I ran, and the pack of white wolves were like a river flowing behind me. The ground thundered under my paws, threatening to explode.

Hawk's reality, her world of flawless white, was swiftly fading away to ashes. Limbs came crashing to the ground as we darted beneath the blazing trees, weaving through the tongues of flame. Everything was ten times more vivid than it was when viewed through my human eyes. But this time it wasn't a dream.

I skidded to a stop in front of a burning tree leaned up against an embankment. Beyond its branches I could make out a charred black hole—what looked like a tunnel.

The portal to Maicoh's world. This has to be what Hawk was telling me about.

Ashy paw prints surrounded the entrance, along with a jumbled set of boot prints that spilled from the opening and then vanished altogether.

She'd shifted. Thank God.

Throwing back my head, I howled, then turned and, with my pack at my heels, began to follow the disarray of charred wolf tracks.

She was leading them away from the portal to my world—away

from me. That screamed volumes: Maicoh was Raiden's mask. I could come to no other conclusion.

The farther we went, the more numerous the prints became. My own pack, behind me, seemed to gather strength as my mind locked on Hawk.

My ears twitched forward, listening carefully for the sound of her voice tumbling in the bellows of the wildfire. My eyes scanned the forest as I sprinted, blinking, through the smoke. Then I slammed to a halt as something large and black stepped out from among the trees, blocking my path.

The pack skidded to a stop behind me.

Another wolf, dark and supple as a shadow, slipped out from the trees; smoke rose from its tattered fur. Beside it, a second one emerged and noiselessly joined it, followed by a third.

Where are they coming from?

Without warning, the first and largest lunged for my neck, snarling as it bared its teeth. The second followed at its heels, jaws snapping. They came so fast, I was almost out of the game before I was in. I jumped back at the last second, losing only a large chunk of fur.

I growled, sinking into a low, defensive stance. My white wolves stood silently, watching, seeming to wait for something, though I didn't know what.

The black wolf, its mouth frothing with particles of white fur now, whipped around and went for my jugular. This time I was ready: I swiped it hard across the face, leaving a trail of gashes. It yelped as it fell away to the side only to clamber back to its paws just as fast, streaks of gold staining its muzzle now. Snarling murderously, it gave three hoarse barks, and suddenly the other two wolves were on me.

I spun around, mauling the air frantically, though barely landing a single blow. Pain seared through my body as teeth sank into the scruff of my neck. I thrashed my head furiously—though the effort only brought about the sickening prickle of claws as they sank into my hind leg. I twisted away and felt my flesh separating from my leg. Tears blurred my vision.

Furious now, I snapped my jaws in attempts to bite back, but the black wolves moved too fast.

Out of my peripheral vision I could still see the white wolves standing among the trees. Their numbers had dwindled; some of them had either faded away into the trees or succumbed to the fire. I watched, stupefied, as one, trapped beneath the burning limb of a tree, exploded. A shower of searing hot gold showered down to sizzle against the snow.

Suddenly I remembered the act of entanglement I had carried out with the white wolf on the stone circle in the deep woods, the portal between my world and Hawk's. In my mind's eye I saw the golden liquid that had risen from the wolf's cut flesh instead of blood.

The wolves aren't real. They are mine to command.

Gasping for air, I gave an anguished cry for help. One of the black wolves countered by taking a heavy swipe at my face.

It was punished tenfold.

The pack, as if breathed to life again, surged forward to my aid, snarling as they lunged at my attackers. Fur flew in every direction as the packs collided. Taking advantage of the distraction, I thrashed to free myself and, as the first wolf's fangs released my neck, I streaked off into the woods. I heard panting behind me and turned to see it following me at a gallop, its eyes blazing.

I swallowed back curses.

Picking up speed, I swung a sharp left, then looped back around to my charted course, praying that would throw my pursuer off my trail, but a quick glance behind me told me my efforts had been fruitless. I veered right and leapt over a fallen, burning limb, then continued parallel with the footprints I was still trying desperately to follow.

To my dismay, the black wolf, not having bought my fake-out, had simply continued on the trail and now glanced over its shoulder at me, its tongue lolling, almost as if it were taunting me. Its golden eyes glowed like embers among the flames that crackled on both sides of us.

The wolves aren't real, Icarus. You create the wolves—you create the wolves in your head.

The white wolves came when I called. The white wolves were at my command, yes. But what if the black wolves were too? If the white wolves responded to my courage, then... what if the black wolves responded to my *fear*?

Stop thinking about it.

I turned my attention back to the path in front of me. I heard howls occasionally, sharp barks surging into the air, but I kept my gaze resolutely ahead. *Focus, Icarus.*

My mind searched desperately for something more stable, more constant than the firestorm around me to focus on. *Think, think. You can do this...* An image of a window over a kitchen sink, a sun-sprayed landscape beyond the glass. A yard across a driveway. A girl dressed in black with her thumb pressed over the mouth of a garden hose.

Hawk.

The longer my mind lingered on the image, the more vivid it became, until, finally, it was as if it absorbed me—swallowing me whole until *it* was reality, and the fire around me the fantasy.

My mind's eye focused on her face until she was no longer a vision or a memory—she was right in front of me. There—she was sprawled on the ground and marred with claw marks. And there *he* was, a silhouette cut out from the fiery backdrop, armed with a blazing orb.

A fresh flood of energy surged through my veins as I streaked forward across the snow. I shoved the ground away from under me, leapt over a flaming log and crushed Hawk's attacker to the ground just as he let go of the flame. It soared up into the trees.

Snarling, I sank my claws into his chest and pushed my muzzle into his face, my fangs bared. He thrashed away from my jaws, and for a moment he was simply a blur of black hair, but then with an almost superhuman effort, he whipped his head around to face me once more, so that his empty eyes were staring up into mine. The human pinned beneath my paws was not Raiden, nor was he anything like how I remembered Maicoh from the dream. He was bone thin, pale as stone, and scarred with burns.

Before my eyes, his face began to change, decaying rapidly to fragments of ash, black particles that first dispersed beneath me and then hovered in midair for a moment before gathering themselves into a distinct, familiar shape: the black wolf.

It landed heavily on its massive paws and then leapt for me, snarling. I jumped to the side and it missed me, but only narrowly. I scrambled over to Hawk, who had inched away from the fight and was sitting, pale with shock, holding her leg. Her ankle was badly wounded, blood spilled between her fingers, and I could tell she didn't have enough energy to heal herself.

The black wolf emitted a low, throaty growl as it spun to face me yet again, with eyes that reflected the forest around us. It was Raiden—it had to be. He could shift shape—he'd taken that ability from Hawk. I wasn't about to allow him to take anything else. I sank into a defensive crouch as he shot forward, letting out a seething roar as his front legs extended. I felt Hawk brace herself behind me. Launching myself forward and slamming into my attacker in midair, I caught him off guard and he was knocked, limbs flailing, to the ground. He let out a pained yelp as I landed next to him, which only seemed to spur him to claw all the harder. He attempted to throw me aside, but I only lunged in to wrap my paws around him, struggling to get my jaws around his throat.

I could hear the faint sounds of howls erupting around us. We rolled furiously and I hung on until I felt his hind claws sink into my underbelly. Pain shot through my spine as he pushed out hard with his hind legs, and I was catapulted through the air. I landed hard against the trunk of a tree.

With a split second to recover, he jumped back to his feet and came in for my throat. I coiled back and let my hind feet fly into his face, my claws blazing a crimson trail across his left eye.

An anguished howl escaped him as he reeled backwards. I leapt to my feet, frantically sucking in oxygen, my front paws trembling beneath my weight.

I howled, beckoning the white wolves just as the pack of their darker counterparts surged forward like an incognito army through the trees.

Then I attacked.

He was still stumbling from his injury, and I was able to pin him against the thawing ground. I swung a paw for his face, faking him out long enough to get my head around to his jugular. He let out an unearthly shriek as my fangs sank into his flesh.

But the pain, instead of stifling his movements, seemed only to pump renewed energy into them. He threw himself to the side hard enough to send me flying; my teeth came away with fragments of his skin. The sky blurred overhead as I somersaulted through the air;

then everything came to a crashing halt as I hit a boulder—headfirst.

Stars shot like fireworks through my vision as my body tumbled back into its original form. It couldn't have happened at a worse moment.

"Icarus!"

Hawk's scream split the air only seconds before I felt hot breath on my face. My eyes shot open at the same moment my fist instinctively flew forward to nail the black wolf in the eye. My vision wavered for a second and then cleared, giving me just enough time to scramble to my feet. The wolf was staggering backwards only a few feet in front of me, one eye squinting and the other swollen and bloodied.

"Icarus, run!" Hawk shouted hoarsely from behind me. "Get out of here!"

Oh, Hawk, if you think I'm going to run now, you don't know me. I'm done running—I'm never leaving you.

I could barely breathe. I didn't answer. My mind zeroed in on my target.

Sprinting forward, I flung myself on top of the black wolf as he wavered, and I landed a punch to his snout—his most sensitive area. Wailing, he fell to the ground. I followed up my punch with a hard kick to his gut—as his shape shifted back into the stranger I'd seen before me only moments ago.

In a heartbeat I was on top of him, my hands wrapped tightly around his throat in a choke hold.

"Who are you?" I shouted down into his face, breathless. "Tell me now, or so help me God, I will kill you!"

For a moment he said nothing, and then his jaws widened into a macabre, bloody grin. I felt his throat move under my fingers as he swallowed painfully.

"Ask…" he began, a thwarted whisper. "H…her…"

Then he nailed me in the guts with his knee.

I crumpled, the wind knocked out of me. He rose to his feet, still wearing that sickening grin, and slammed me back against something hard. In two strides he was right in my face. He clutched my shirt and pulled me in close. I felt his hot breath on my face. Through the tide of adrenaline surging through my veins, I felt the whirlwind of déjà vu.

The nightmares… the ones Hawk and I shared. The hands that always found me in that familiar, sickening darkness. The deadly phantom from whom I could never seem to escape. Those hands…

No… Impossible. This couldn't…

The revelation hit me like a physical blow. His eyes seared into mine, wide—wild. His hands slid up to clench my throat.

"Ask her." His voice was a trembling rasp as he stared into my eyes. "Or don't you already know?"

My eyes turned to connect with Hawk's across the expanse that lay between us. Blood trickled down her face, and her dark brown eyes were wide, wild, as they stared into mine, relieving me of any doubt.

I felt hot blood rising to the places where his nails pressed against my throat. It was getting harder to breathe. The fire was building—overtaking the forest. White wolves darted through the trees and into the clearing to circle the black wolves, baring their teeth.

I turned my attention back to him now, relaxing in his grip for a split second. Then I threw myself forward so that our heads collided. He flew backward, clutching his nose and spewing curses.

At the same time the two packs crashed into one.

Quickly bringing my hands overhead, I channeled a bright blue orb and threw. He rolled to the side, dodging it. I channeled another and threw it, and another, and another—but every time, the orbs only impacted the ground, sending up a spray of slush and mud.

His movements slowed, and for a moment I thought he was running low on energy. But then he gathered himself and launched backwards into the air, turned 180 degrees to face me again, and landed on four paws in his alternate form.

With my pack preoccupied, I did the only thing I could do: I threw orb after orb, blitzing him, planting myself firmly in front of Hawk. He leapt behind a massive pine to avoid the barrage, but I didn't let that stop me—I aimed straight for it, blowing out a large portion of the trunk.

"Icarus, you have to get out of here," Hawk yelled over the roar of the fire and the wolves. "Don't you get it? You're what he wants! We have to stay separated or he'll kill us!"

I channeled another iridescent blue orb into my palms, squinting to see past the falling branches and tumults of thrashing fur.

"If you think I'm leaving you, you have another thing coming, Hawk." I shot her a quick glance. "Can you heal yourself?"

I locked eyes with my target as he ducked out from behind the damaged tree and wove among the battling wolves, attempting to camouflage himself.

"I'm trying, but it's n-n-not working." Hawk stammered.

I narrowed my eyes, taking aim at my target once more. "I've got your back," I said to her, keeping my voice as low as I could. "Just be ready to jump."

"Jump?"

The orb rocketed out of my hands and towards my target. I ground my teeth in frustration as, anticipating my move, he stepped aside. The ball of deadly force instead impacted one of the white wolves. I winced as it shrieked and fell to the ground. A split second later it imploded in a spray of fluid gold.

I set my jaw and squared my shoulders. He was on the offensive now, weaving rapidly through the smoke and flames and the battling wolves to get closer to me. Each time I fired an orb, he seemed to sense it coming and ducked nimbly behind a burning tree.

In a moment, I knew it wouldn't matter if I hit him or if he attacked me. The forest was an inferno now, and I could tell the trees wouldn't hold out for much longer.

Taking as deep a breath as I could in the smoky air, I threw myself upward and shifted back into wolf form. Hawk watched, wide-eyed and stunned as I landed and shook my fur. I gave a sharp bark in her direction, shaking her out of her daze, and then rushed to her side, butting her gently but insistently with my head. She threw her arms around my neck and pulled herself up onto my back, and I bolted. Panting, my eyes watering in the smoke, I sprinted through the trees. She buried her face in my fur, keeping her head low.

My sense of sound was heightened in this form, and my ears caught the unmistakable sound of paws just behind us, of throaty, outraged snarls. Behind him, I could hear the muted roar of the packs as they fought on.

Focus, Icarus, focus...

Fixing my eyes on the path in front of us, I ran harder.

We dodged falling branches and wound around collapsing trees that crashed to the earth in showers of sparks. I propelled myself over steep embankments and sprinted across snow-coated clearings, until at last, at last, the tree line opened up before me to what looked like a large meadow. But as soon as I took a few strides out onto the surface, my paws began to skid out from under me.

What the…?

I felt Hawk tense on my back as I scrabbled on the slick ice, attempting to maintain my pace. Hawk lifted her mouth to my ear.

"This place…" Her voice was frantic. "We-we have to get off this lake, Icarus!"

I lowered my head and plunged on. There was no way we were heading back into the wildfire—head-on into Raiden. Or whatever his real name was. Only Hawk knew.

"*Icarus!*" Hawk's voice was frantic. "You have to stop! We're going to get killed if we go any farther!"

I had no idea what she was talking about, but I trusted her more than my own logic.

Fine, we'll stop, I wanted to tell her. *But we're not going back into the forest.*

Reluctantly, I slowed to a halt and turned to face the shoreline. The sun was sinking on the horizon; billows of smoke poured up from the engulfing flames to blot out the first stars. The black wolf, one eye marred beyond recognition, stood at the tree line and stared at us as we stood in the center of the ice. The rest of his pack surged around him like a black tide and thundered out onto the ice. In moments they were upon us. With Hawk still on my back, I braced my front legs and stood my ground. To my astonishment, instead of lunging for us, they stopped as though at an invisible barrier and began to circle us. Prowling, eyeing us, panting, waiting…

Then, slowly and deliberately, Raiden stepped away from the tree line and out onto the ice. Never taking his eyes from mine, he came forward, one black paw after the other, steadily closing the distance between us.

I lowered my head and motioned for Hawk to dismount. Eyeing the circling wolves uneasily, she slid to the ground. I felt her hand on my shoulder blades as she stood beside me.

My eyes stayed locked on Raiden's as he moved across the snow-covered ice, backlit by the orange glow from the burning forest behind him.

The white wolves were nowhere to be seen. Hawk and I were on our own and fully surrounded. But something inside me seemed to know it didn't matter.

This was Hawk's battle. And I would be her white wolf.

Raiden reached the circle of wolves, and they parted to allow him to stand facing us. Wiping her face in the crook of her arm, limping, Hawk began to step forward until she and Raiden were just a few yards apart. Every muscle in my body was screaming to move forward—to defend her, to tear him to shreds. With an almost physical effort, I stilled myself and held my ground.

Raiden's golden eyes shone brightly in the darkness as he stared up at her, his lips retracted to reveal his ivory teeth.

Hawk stayed still as a stone, though I noticed her fingers trembled.

"Edwin, stop this!" she commanded. "What is it that you want? Me? Him?" She threw a hand in my direction. "The position of the patriarchs? To control all that will never belong to you?"

Edwin?

The black wolf lunged for her—and somehow, incredibly, missed.

"You will never be a patriarch, Edwin," Hawk continued, steadying her voice now. "Though you have tried and failed to take it from me for the past century—no. You will never have that within you. You will never take that from me."

She stood straighter, and as if in response, the black wolves moved in closer, still circling. Their footfalls were like drumbeats against the thin ice.

"I know who I am." Hawk's voice rose and echoed in the night air around us. "And I don't care if you chase me for the rest of eternity—I will *never* be afraid of you again."

The black wolf lunged at her again, jaws wide, but each time he attempted to land a blow, his teeth merely passed through her as though she were a ghost. With a growl of frustration, he threw himself into the air and became human once more.

"Charlotte," he seethed. He stepped closer, fists clenched. "Charlotte, you can't. I won't give up. I—" He broke off, puzzled, as the black wolves began to gather around him. He turned his attention back to Hawk. "Charlotte, listen to me—"

His voice died in his throat as a black wolf leapt and took him to the ice.

Hawk stayed where she was, never taking her eyes from his.

"Charlotte, I hate you!" His voice rose to an anguished scream as the wolf sank its teeth into his flesh—the rest of the pack lunging in. "I hate you! I hate you! I hate—"

A frenzy of snarls and yelps rose into the night sky, drowning his words.

I looked away and felt Hawk's face in my thick mane as she shielded her eyes. I tried not to listen to the howls, to Edwin's dying screams. I tried to concentrate on the sound of her breathing.

Then a cracking sound caught my attention.

"Icarus."

The ice shifted beneath us. Hawk reflexively clutched my fur, and I staggered, trying to keep my paws under me as the world tilted beneath us.

I heard her scream, "Icarus!" and then there was a rushing sound as my head went below the surface. We plunged together into the icy black water, and everything—the roar of the fire, the chortle of the pack, the moaning of the wind, Hawk's voice—deadened to the muffled whoosh of water around me.

I quickly focused myself back into human form and reached for Hawk, but my hands closed on icy water. Where was she? I started kicking, digging frantically at the water with my arms.

My mind flashed back to the day I'd awoken in the riverbed. In my world at the bottom of the ravine, where I'd lived and suffered alone and lost until Hawk had found me.

Now I had to find her.

I flailed around in the water, squinting and coughing in the blackness, but she was gone. My chest burning, I burst to the surface once more, gasping for air. I shook my hair out of my eyes and felt a jolt of disbelief. The ice was gone—all of it. So were the wolves. And so was Edwin.

Shivering, I treaded water, scanning the lake's surface as it flickered eerily in the light from the fires on shore. *There.* A short distance away the surface of the water rippled and churned. I swam furiously towards it.

At first it was bubbles, and then, in a burst, Hawk splashed to the surface, gasping for air.

"Icarus?" She coughed. "Where are you?"

"I'm here." I reached out a hand, and a second later I was close enough for our fingertips to brush. She seized my hand and we pulled each other closer.

"I'm here, Hawk," I repeated, breathing hard as I looped my arm around her. "I'm here." We treaded water together, our breath steaming in the cold night air.

As our movements calmed, the water quieted around us. I supported Hawk with my arm, and together we treaded water at the center of the lake, watching the forest around us burn to the ground.

CHAPTER THIRTY-FIVE

Icarus

The fire burned all night. Dawn was just beginning to make its first appearance as we swam for shore, exhausted, though no longer shivering. Almost as quickly as the ice had melted, the deep lake had warmed incrementally until it was hard to imagine that it had been ice only hours before.

Where towering pines had once trimmed the shoreline like lace, skeletal forms stood guard at the water's edge. Songbirds flitted overhead, seeming to search for their nests, and crickets chirped from the marshy brush that the fire hadn't found to its taste.

My body ached with every stroke, but when the water grew shallow enough to stand, I scooped Hawk into my arms regardless. Sloshing out of the water, I carried her up onto the shore, dropping to my knees after only a few steps.

"Thank you," Hawk murmured as I gently set her down. "Are you hurt?"

I shook my head, panting. "No... just scratches."

"Let me see."

I planted my hands on my knees as I caught my breath, shaking my head. "No, you first. You bore the real brunt of it." Settling alongside her, I reached out to examine her ankle. I hesitated as my fingertips made light contact with her skin, turning to look at her. "May I?"

Her lips formed the slightest of smiles and she nodded.

I gently folded my hands over the wounds.

Hawk sucked in a sharp breath. "They have sharp teeth." She forced a small laugh. "I've learned that much."

I smiled a little, but I didn't answer. I focused all my energy into her wound, slowly moving my fingertips—watching as a clean trail of flesh followed.

"I… I should have told you, Icarus." Hawk's voice trembled slightly as it dropped to a whisper. "About… about Edwin."

I shook my head, moving on to the scratch marks on her arms.

"It was your battle, Hawk," I responded quietly. "I don't need explanations. I just helped you because I…" I trailed off, my heart pounding hard in my chest in that moment of quiet. I took her hand in mine.

She lifted her other hand to my face, placing her palm against my cheek. "Don't say it, Icarus." Her voice was a tired whisper. "Please."

I felt something in my chest twinge. I wanted to ask her why—why she didn't want me to tell her something that was truer to me than anything else in the world. But something inside me swallowed it back, and I turned my attention to healing the deep scratches on her face.

"A hundred years is a long time to run," Hawk said softly after a moment. "A long time to wrestle with the nightmares and hide from the shadows." She let out a weary laugh. "I guess that makes me a coward."

My fingers hesitated against her cheek. "*You* stood up to the wolves, Hawk, not me," I answered, my voice gentle but unrelenting. "Most people spend their entire lives trying to outrun the pack, but you *fought* them. And in my eyes, that doesn't make you a coward. That makes you brave."

Hawk's eyes searched mine for a moment before they finally flicked shut, a tear narrowly escaping to roll down her face.

There were a thousand things I could have said. I wanted to tell her what I would have done to Edwin if I'd been there that day so long ago. I wanted to tell her I was sorry I hadn't pieced it all together, that I hadn't protected her and defended her in the ways that I should have—the ways I longed to.

Beyond that, I wanted to tell her that she was my Sunrise—not just because the prophecy declared her to be so, but because I had fallen in love with her. I wanted to tell her that she was the first thought to cross my mind each morning and the last one to fade from my consciousness each night. That she was beautiful, pure, whole, and brave. That I looked up to her in more ways than I knew how to describe. That she was my teacher, my friend, and my better half. That even if we had just been normal kids, living in an ordinary dimension, doing ordinary things, I would have been just as tempted to drop down on one knee as I was in that moment.

But I remembered what Sensei had told me about Hawk's world and why I hadn't been able to enter.

You have given her your heart, Icarus... It is you who have let her inside.

Hawk wasn't ready. But it didn't matter—I knew that I loved her. I didn't need to hear myself say it; I didn't need to put it on display with elegant words. No, I wanted to *show* her. Sensei was right: even if she didn't love me now—or ever—that didn't alter my love for her. It didn't change it.

"Can you stand?" I asked softly, pulling back my hand from her face. Color was returning to her skin. She nodded, taking my hand and allowing me to help her to her feet.

Rolling her ankle, she gave me an approving smile. "Your turn."

I sat patiently while Hawk tended my wounds; her fingertips felt like fire against my skin. When she finished, we ventured cautiously into what was left of the forest as the sun crept higher to illuminate it. For hundreds of yards in every direction, the woods had been leveled to ash. But as we trekked farther, we began to notice subtle signs of life. Grass began to spring up in our path. The charred trees collapsed gently into the ground to reemerge as lively young saplings, their branches heavy with buds. Our footsteps slowed and I turned to Hawk in awe.

Gone was the snow, the ice, the bitter wind. The sky above was blue, and bees hummed in the air to accentuate the songbirds' chorus. Fiddlehead ferns and purple irises pushed their way up through the dirt, and streams gently trickled over lush beds of moss.

"But...it..." Hawk fumbled for words as she took in her surroundings. "It was winter... it was always winter."

I could hardly hold back my smile. "It's a projection of your subconscious, Hawk. You make it."

She parted her lips to speak again, but no words came. She walked forward a few paces, reaching up to touch a low-hanging tree branch now covered in white blossoms.

I slowly followed in her footsteps, the imprints of her boots where tiny violets were beginning to bud. I drew up beside her, squinting up through the chaos of cherry blossoms blown out by the golden streams of light.

"Just like I made the black wolves," she said, so quietly I almost missed it. "All that time… and I didn't even realize it."

I was silent for a few moments, my eyes scanning this new dimension as it unfolded around us.

Hawk's expression was one I couldn't easily read. It was as strange and new as the spring that had seized her cold world by force. Slowly her hand found its way into mine.

"You know what humans say about hitting bottom," she said. "You can only go up from here."

"Up?" I whispered, uncertain. "Up as in—"

"Home," Hawk finished, and the word was like breathing for the first time. "Yes, Icarus. Home."

"But…" I started, then trailed off. "But how?"

Hawk placed a finger to her lips and tugged me forward. "Ask nothing, Icarus—just follow me."

I followed her as she stepped out from under the tree's fragrant boughs and led me deeper into the forest, deeper still until everything around us was bursting—overflowing with life and growth.

Hand in hand, we wove our way through pines, birches, and flowering trees. Then the forest opened to a clearing I almost didn't recognize at first, so different was the landscape. But then it clicked: the crumbling marble pillars, though buried beneath tumbling waterfalls of vines, were unmistakable.

"The portal." I exhaled the word, stumbling forward over the soft earth. "I never would have remembered how to find this place."

"I seared it into my memory," Hawk said softly. "When I left to confront Maicoh… Edwin…" She looked over at me. "I knew I would have to find my way back to you."

She let go of my hand and walked to the stone circle just as a rustling arose from the brush at the opposite edge. I turned toward it and saw Hawk tense. Holding our breaths, we stood, watching silently. All was still except for the warble of the songbirds. But then it came again: a rustling that grew louder and more vigorous until at last the source slowly emerged.

Gracefully making its way to the edge of the circle, the white wolf shook its thick mane. Its eyes were bluer than the sky as it looked at us, first Hawk, then me.

Hawk stepped closer, not entering the circle, and in response the wolf lowered its head, almost in a gesture of respect. It raised its head once more, and its gaze remained on her for a moment before it turned to me. I stood rooted to the spot as it lifted its head and let out a long, low howl.

Hawk turned to look at me. "I think... I think it wants us to step in."

"But the portal only leads back to my world."

Hawk's eyes narrowed thoughtfully as she looked again at the wolf; it pawed the earth as if it were anxious. She drew a tentative breath. "Or does it?" Suddenly a light seemed to come on in her eyes. Carefully Hawk turned to the circle's perimeter and placed one foot onto the smooth ivory surface. Then the other.

Then she was gone.

My pulse racing, I quickly stepped into the circle after her. My fingertips brushed the ivy as I slipped from Hawk's world into another. Hawk stood in the center of the circle now, staring. I blinked in astonishment as my eyes adjusted—then my heart skipped a beat.

"How...?" I whispered, lost for words.

Hawk smiled. "Nothing you can imagine is ever impossible, Icarus."

Surrounding us were the familiar, geo-studded walls of the cavern. The cavern that acted as the Dimension's portal. My mind reeling, I stole a glance over my shoulder.

Behind me, rather than another solid wall of stone, was the world from which we had just emerged. Hawk's reality, bursting with life and sunshine, encompassed half of the platform before fading gradually to the more familiar foreground—a world that was neither mine nor Hawk's, but Sensei's. The familiar mahogany exit door was centered in front of us, a splinter of light visible under the crack at the bottom.

"Hawk." I was almost afraid to ask. "Does this mean..." I didn't finish my sentence. Taking a deep breath, I walked to the door and stood staring at it, taking in the grain of the wood, the light that beckoned beneath it. I looked back at Hawk; she was a silhouette contrasted against the humming backdrop of her world. She didn't make a motion to open the door herself, but she waited with expectancy in her eyes.

My strength renewed, I turned back and reached out a hand to clasp the doorknob. It was solid in my grip—real—as I turned it. The dark cavern was doused suddenly in shafts of golden light as the door yawned open before us, exposing the long, familiar hallway lined with glass windows.

For a moment I was numb as I stood there, a strange energy surging through me. Then I felt Hawk's hand on my arm.

"Yes, Icarus," she answered finally. "It means you can go home."

It took a moment for her words to sink in.

Home. You can go home…

Sliding my hand over Hawk's, I turned to face her.

"*We* can," I corrected her.

Clasping both her hands in mine, I walked backwards, gently pulling her with me, until I was at the threshold, and then stepped over it. For the first time in what felt like an eternity, I felt the warmth of the Dimension on my back. I could detect the far-off voices of my peers as they practiced on the training platform.

For a moment I was filled with something I could only describe as pure joy. The happiest I had ever been. But when I looked down at my hands, they were empty. Hawk's hands were no longer in my own.

A tidal wave of anxiety spilled over me as I stood for a moment, frozen in place. Then everything rushed forward at once.

"Hawk!" My voice was frantic as I crossed the threshold once more. The warm sounds of the Dimension faded away as I stepped again into the circle's boundary and through what felt like a wavering curtain of invisible energy. "Hawk, what happened?"

Hawk stood several feet from the threshold, her eyes focused on the ground. She said nothing.

"Hawk, come on. This is it," I pleaded. "We have to go—now."

Hawk looked up into my eyes, much like she had only moments ago beneath the blossoming tree. But now, there was something heavy, resigned, in her gaze. Forcing her lips into a tiny smile, she shook her head and closed her eyes.

"No, Icarus." Her voice came out a broken whisper. "Just… just you."

Part of me felt like I was dreaming, like this was some sort of cruel, vivid hallucination, playing with my head to torment me. Something I needed to awaken myself out of.

"Hawk, what are you talking about?" I closed the space between us. "We're here! We're finally, finally here—and because of you!"

"Icarus, I can't." She choked back a sob.

I opened my mouth, but nothing intelligible came out. Hawk opened her eyes and slowly shook her head.

"Hawk, what are you saying?" My voice cracked in anguish and disbelief. "No. No—"

"Icarus—"

"No!" I yelled, cutting her off. I seized her by the wrist, pulling her forward. "Don't you—don't you dare say it!"

She tried to object, but I wouldn't let her—I pushed her in front of me, extending our arms together over the threshold and watching as they breached the wall of warm energy. I felt my blood go cold as I stared past the doorway and into our homeland. Once again, Hawk's hand had disappeared, leaving only my own extended in midair—empty.

Swallowing hard, I withdrew and turned to look at her. She stared me squarely in the face, her arm still outstretched. Her arm had vanished at the elbow, as if her body was somehow forbidden to cross into this world—just as I had been barred from hers. She pulled back, and her arm restored itself to our vision.

A tightness gripping my throat, I slowly backed away, shaking my head. Her eyes still hadn't left mine.

"No," I choked out. "No… no, no, no—Hawk, no."

"Icarus, please listen."

"No," I insisted, pressing the heels of my hands to my forehead. "No, Hawk… I can't—I'm *not* leaving without you. This—there has to be something wrong. This has… There must be some mistake—"

Hawk lifted a hand gently for silence, stepping closer now. When she spoke, her voice was unsteady but retained some of its Everest strength. "It's not a mistake, Icarus. It's… it's the only way you can go back."

I was still shaking my head. "I don't understand."

"Sensei told me, Icarus," she said gently. "We've written our story—our code, our destiny; we, as a collective of renegade anomalies." She paused, a sad smile on her lips. "Sensei always told us to forgive, to love, to hope—not to judge. But justice was too great a temptation, wasn't it? Somehow its charms beguiled us beyond that beautiful thing we call 'forgiveness.'" She closed her eyes, reaching up to touch her forehead as though she were suddenly profoundly weary. "They won't welcome you back, Icarus—you cannot even *enter* their world unless... your crime has been paid for, your guilty blood replaced with that of the innocent," she said. "Because although they condemned me too, I did nothing to deserve their punishment. I accepted it for this purpose—to bring you back."

She fell silent for a moment and then gently opened her eyes again.

"My life for yours," she finished quietly. "So that the code of our own making might be fulfilled—the penalty of death paid."

A cold feeling dropped through my body as I stood there, staring at her. Unable to believe a word of what she was saying.

"Hawk, you're not listening." My voice rose only slightly. "I'm *not* leaving here without you."

"You have to."

"I don't *have to*, and I won't," I said stubbornly. I took her by the hands again, staring down into her eyes, blinded now by tears. "I won't leave you, Hawk. I need you—they need you! I can't go back to them without you—I'm only *half* the leader they need... the leader that they deserve. They need *you*."

"And I'll be with them." Hawk placed a hand on my chest. "Though I will not be there physically, my soul will be joined with yours. You will lack nothing in leadership, Icarus. I will be there with you always—"

"No!" I backed away from her touch. "No, no, no—I tried that already, Hawk. I tried to give you my life and you refused it! I cannot—I will not—"

"That was different."

"How was it different?"

"Because this isn't about just us anymore!" The tension in her voice rose. "This is about *them*—everyone back home, everyone who will ever live on planet Earth, Icarus. This is about *them*!"

Hawk stopped, pressing her hand to her lips as she withheld a sob. A sick feeling clutched the pit of my stomach.

"This isn't about me." Her words were ragged. She drew in a breath. "You were born for this, Icarus… You were trained for this." Her voice cracked, fading in her throat as a tear rolled down her cheek. "I *chose you* for this."

I wanted to stop her—I didn't want her to say another word, but I was empty. Nothing I felt could be put into words. I closed my eyes as they stung with bitter tears.

"Don't let me down now, okay?" she whispered. I felt the palm of her hand against my chest. "Don't let them down. They need us… both of us."

The tightness settled in my throat.

"Can you do this, Icarus?" she asked. "For me?"

Unable to speak, I forced myself to nod, trying and failing to keep the tears back as I opened my eyes again.

"I can do anything for you, Hawk."

For a moment she just looked at me, holding me at arm's length. Then gently her arms wove around me, and she buried her face in my chest.

My body was still numb, trembling, terrified. But now I brushed all of this aside. My arms went around her and I pulled her close. For a moment I felt her shaky inhales and exhales against my skin. Her hot tears mixed with my own. I summoned my courage and did something I had wanted to do for the longest time. Stooping slightly, I let my arms slide a little farther down, and I gently lifted her off her feet. Hawk's hand slipped to the back of my head, and her face rested in the curve of my neck, and mine in hers.

With her long soft hair in my face, I closed my eyes and drank her in. Her scent swept into my lungs; the sound of her sobs filled my ears. I felt the warmth of her hands against my skin, her heartbeat raging against my own.

For a moment we stood on the threshold of two worlds, holding each other—knowing this would be the last time.

Hawk, the girl next door. Hawk, the student who had dragged me into the closet. Hawk, the one who had opened my eyes to a world I otherwise would never have found. Hawk, the teacher who had told me to jump, to trust, to believe. Hawk, the spirit who had poured herself out to me on the top of a skyscraper, and who had listened to the story I'd never before been brave enough to tell. Hawk, the other half of my soul, who had refused to take my life to save her own, so long ago. Hawk, the savior who was giving me back my life and my world while she faced oblivion alone.

"I can't let you do this," I whispered. "I can't live without you, Hawk."

She pulled away a little as I set her down again. She searched my eyes through her tears. "You will never be without me, Icarus."

Our fingers interlocked, just as they had the day we'd entangled. But this time there was no need for blood. We knew now that what flowed through our veins was one and the same.

The energy began to surge through my arms like electricity. My hands began to heat up.

"When you don't see me," she whispered, though her voice was becoming muffled, "I am there most, Icarus."

Refusing to let my body succumb to the burning sensation that was beginning to take over, I kept my eyes focused on hers until her forehead came to rest against mine. She breathed out sharply, as though in pain, and slowly I began to feel the skin around my upper arms heat up. My ring finger throbbed, as if electrified.

Hawk pulled back suddenly, breathing heavily now as she looked up at me. I watched helplessly, shaking, as fresh tears blurred my vision and as the color slowly drained from Hawk's skin.

No, no—I tried desperately to jerk away, but it was too late. Our hands were bound in what seemed an invisible vise, a force from which I couldn't break free, no matter how hard I tried. A black band had wrapped around my finger, leaving Hawk's stone-white; the markings on her arms began to fade.

Frantic, my heart thundering now, I glanced down at myself and found two dark bands now wrapping my upper arms. I shook my head in disbelief and then turned wildly back to Hawk. My eyes locked with her tired ones for a moment before, with what energy she had left, she took a breath and pulled me closer.

For a split second, the world froze as her cold lips met mine in a kiss. Then she exhaled, her breath forcing its way down into my lungs and ricocheting through my body as though I'd been struck by lightning. In a bursting wave of deafening, clear energy, our bodies were forced apart. I was thrown to the ground, and Hawk was hurled upward, where she hung motionless in midair.

I scrambled up off the ground. "Hawk!" I reached for her as her body was consumed in a burst of fire and feathers, flames that quickly burned from gold to pure white, staining each of her plumes as she writhed helplessly in the air.

No... I was powerless to help her.

Then, as quickly as it had appeared, the fire roared to a crescendo and then ceased altogether. Released, Hawk returned slowly to the ground, in the form of a hawk as white as snow.

For a moment there was stillness. Her light blue eyes beheld me, seemingly without recognition. My heart stumbled over its next beat as I rose slowly to my feet. My eyes, sore and swollen with tears, remained steadily fixed on hers.

"Hawk." Her name fell from my lips, a broken whisper. I stepped forward, my hand outstretched. But before I could get any closer, she leapt from the ground, spread her wings, and climbed toward the sky.

"Hawk, no!" I shouted hoarsely. "No—stop!"

I sprinted after her, my feet pounding against the marble as I raced her back to the boundary line of her world. She was a fray of feathers against the bright blue sky.

"Hawk, wait!" My blood pounded in my ears as I ran, shouting, pleading. Hawk bulleted past the ivy-crested pillars and soared up into the cloudless sky. "Please!"

Racing to the edge, I stepped off the marble surface—and hit a stone wall.

I winced, my hands clasping cold, damp stone. My fingertips caught against the sharp edges of geodes. All that I found before me was the wall of the cavern, trickling with condensation. Gems sparkled in the light.

Like a heavy door slamming shut, Hawk's world was gone. Everything that had been before me only an instant before was swallowed by a cold, damp darkness.

I sucked in a frantic breath, pulling back as my hands slid down the surface in front of me.

"Please." The word died in my throat as my fingers contracted against the stone.

The silence rang in my ears along with my own heartbeat. Although I knew it was useless, I threw my fists against the wall now.

"*Please!*"

The only reply was my own aching voice echoing in the void around me. I stood there, my battered hands at my sides, breathing heavily as my eyes ached to see through the stone to what had been there only a second before. With an anguished cry, I clenched my fists and pounded them again against the unrelenting stone, a sob roaring from my throat. Finally, spent, I collapsed against the wall and slid to my knees, pressing my forehead against the cold surface.

"Please."

I don't know how long I stayed there, alone in the cavern as I wept. It could have been minutes; it could have been hours. I didn't care anymore—time meant nothing.

In the Dimension it was always day and never night. But for me, time would rewind and replay for the rest of eternity to that last moment I had with her. I would relive it. I would turn it over in my mind and hold it in my heart—it would be with me forever. Just as she would—her human half. Her soul had rescued me from death and joined itself to my own.

I unclenched my fists, my hands easing up over my arms, my fingers clutching the places where the markings now lay. I closed my eyes.

For a moment there was a silence. A numbness. A void that could be filled by nothing.

Then slowly, I became aware of sounds nearby. Voices. I opened my eyes and turned to look at the door. A fragment of light dared to slip underneath it, along with the echo of distant chatter.

My peers, my students, my friends. The anomalies of Earth in all their fragments and messiness. With all of their rules and anger and hurt and judgment. The chosen ones. The ones born to save us.

My body numb, I forced myself to stand and stagger forward a few paces. My footsteps echoed.

Can you do this, Icarus? Her voice was nearer than my thoughts as a tear trickled down my cheek. *For me?*

Reaching out, I turned the knob in my hand. The door swung slowly open, and there was that long, familiar hallway, echoing with far-off voices and filled with light as it fell in golden shafts.

For a moment I stood there silently. Then, swallowing back the tears, I stepped out into the hallway.

I closed the door behind me.

Did you enjoy Worlds Beneath? Let me know by leaving a review on the novel's Amazon page! Reviews are critical for indie authors, such as myself, (we're not backed by large publishing or marketing companies) and I would be extremely grateful for a review if you enjoyed the book. It really makes a difference.

- Kate

Don't want to miss the release of the final book in The Blood Race trilogy?

Join the email circle, and receive personal updates from the author – sign up here: http://kaemmons.com/

Or message the author on Facebook Messenger: @kaemmonsauthor

Also follow Kate on:
Facebook: https://www.facebook.com/kaemmonsauthor/
Twitter: https://twitter.com/emmonswrites
Instagram: https://www.instagram.com/thebloodrace/